Say YOU WILL

EVANGELINE WILLIAMS

Copyright © 2024 by Evangeline Williams

Published by Evangeline Williams

All rights reserved.

This book or any portion thereof may not reproduced or used in any manner whatsoever without the express written permission of the publisher except for the use of brief quotations in a book review. No portion of this book may be reproduced in any form without written permission from the publisher or author, except as permitted by U.S. copyright law. This is a work of fiction and any resemblance to actual persons, living or dead, is solely coincidental. Names, businesses, characters, places, locales, and events are either used in a fictitious manner or the sole product of the author's imagination. They are intended solely for the purpose of entertainment and are in no way based on real events.

Edited by Kaitlin Slowik

Cover by Quirky Bird Covers

Content Notes

Contains Spoilers

Your mental health is important. Please be aware this work of fiction contains adult themes and language that may be disturbing to some readers. Content Notes may be found on the author's website at evangelinewilliams.com.

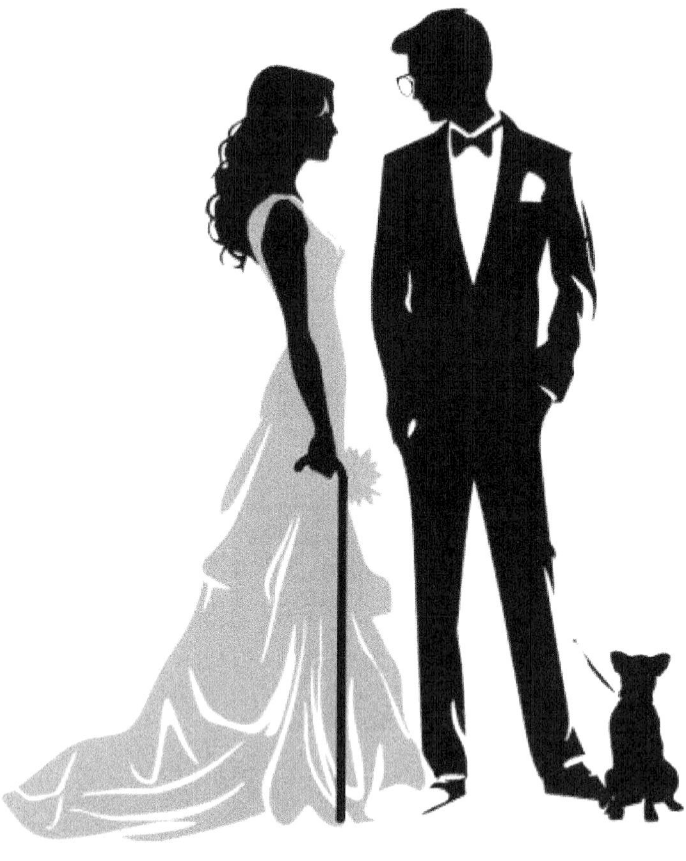

A Note to Readers

Dear Reader,

Henry and Franki's story is, first and foremost, a romance. It's not intended to be a story "about" RA or autism. However, this book does contain a female main character with rheumatoid arthritis (and one leg slightly shorter than the other) and a neurodivergent main male character.

Autoimmune disorders/physical challenges and autism occur on a wide spectrum. Henry and Franki's experiences may mirror yours or those of someone you know, or they may not. In addition to characters being based on my own lived experience, I made every effort to be sure the portrayals were done with sensitivity and respect, including research, and utilizing autistic beta readers, as well as a professional sensitivity reader.

Please know how much I appreciate each and every one of you who have taken the time to read this labor of love.

Happy Reading!

Evie Williams

Playlist

Music has always helped me connect to characters and emotion, and I'm really excited about the songs I've included in this playlist. They provided the soundtrack to Henry and Franki's story as I wrote it.

Listening to the playlist is not a requirement to enjoy the novel. However, if you're like me and enjoy music as an additional emotional connection, you can access a playlist directly using the QR code below or by logging into your Spotify account and using the search feature. You can also enter each song title/artist as it appears at the beginning of each chapter into whatever music streaming service you prefer. You can listen to the playlist songs at any time: before, during, or after reading.

Hope you love it!

For Kurt

Who not only accepted my weirdness, but loved it.

Contents

Epigraph		1
Prologue		2
1.	Henry	8
2.	Franki	20
3.	Henry	28
4.	Franki	35
5.	Henry	44
6.	Franki	53
7.	Henry	66
8.	Henry	72
9.	Franki	79
10.	Franki	87
11.	Henry	96
12.	Franki	100
13.	Franki	108
14.	Henry	112

15.	Franki	116
16.	Franki	126
17.	Henry	133
18.	Franki	141
19.	Henry	148
20.	Franki	156
21.	Henry	164
22.	Henry	169
23.	Franki	178
24.	Henry	188
25.	Henry	197
26.	Franki	208
27.	Franki	216
28.	Henry	223
29.	Franki	231
30.	Henry	238
31.	Franki	247
32.	Franki	251
33.	Franki	260
34.	Henry	266
35.	Henry	273
36.	Henry	281
37.	Franki	292
38.	Henry	303
39.	Henry	310

40. Franki	317
Epilogue	325
Thank You	331
Also by	332
Acknowledgements	333

"Silently, one by one, in the infinite meadows of heaven,

Blossomed the lovely stars, the Forget-Me-Nots of the angels."

—Henry Wadsworth Longfellow "Evangeline of the Acadie"

Prologue

Fifteen Years Ago

Henry

Chasing Cars | Tommee Profitt, Fleurie

"What are you doing in here?" I scowl at the skinny little girl who has no business being in my bedroom, let alone lying on my constellation carpet.

She's obscuring just enough of Orion's Belt to make it impossible to make out the entire thing, but not enough to completely cover it. It sets my teeth on edge. It should be one or the other. All the way or not at all.

I dragged myself up here ready to collapse in my bed and try to sleep without closing my eyes. I'm getting good at it. The trick is to read something distracting or study the stars until I don't remember the falling asleep part. Awake with my eyes open. Then asleep. None of that in between with my eyes closed.

I'm starting to think the place where I was shot is always going to hurt because the doctors said I was "recovering nicely." But it still pulls and burns, and when I close my eyes blood is all I see.

The little girl in my bedroom is one of my sister's friends, so she can't be more than eight years old. She sighs gustily, and blows her wispy light brown bangs out of her eyes. She's wearing glasses and doesn't seem to care that they've slid halfway down her nose. Her hands rest on her abdomen, and she's laid out exactly like a painting I once saw of a dead lady, except the lady was holding flowers and wearing a filmy white dress while this girl is in pink rubber ducky pajamas.

That painting didn't look at all like the real dead people I've seen.

I shudder, then square my shoulders. "You need to leave."

"Is this your bedroom?" she asks.

"Yes, and you shouldn't sneak around into strange men's bedrooms. It's violating my privacy."

At that, she rolls onto her stomach, props her chin on her palms, and says, "You're not a man."

"I'm twelve." I sniff. "Compared to you, I am."

I expect her to continue to argue, but she sends a nervous glance toward the door, then back at me. "I have to leave?"

For the first time, I notice that her eyes are rimmed in red. Her face is splotchy, and her nose is tipped pink. Her eyelashes are all spiky, too, framing deep brown eyes.

I move closer and crouch down next to her, frowning. "Did someone hurt you? If they did, I'll do something about it."

She shrugs her bony shoulders and rolls onto her back, assuming her former dead lady pose. "Just my heart, and that doesn't count."

"Do you need to go to a hospital?"

The girl vaults into a sitting position. "I don't want to go anywhere. I want to stay here for the sleepover."

At the muffled shriek of laughter from the room full of little girls across the hall, I shoot a glance at my door once more.

"I'll go back to Bronwyn's room when the movie is over," she says.

At this, I stand. "You don't like the movie?"

"It's scary."

"Bronwyn isn't allowed to show you scary movies. Does my mother know about this?"

"No one else thinks it's a scary movie. They think it's funny. There's a doll with button eyes." She lies back down and shudders.

Ugh. Button eyes are horrifying. "You're supposed to be watching *Coraline*?"

She shakes her head. "They don't care. When something scares me at home, Mom says it means I have to do that thing more, so I'm not a stupid baby about it. But I don't have to do it here. Bronwyn said it was quiet in your room. She said you have the best carpet, and you wouldn't be home for hours. So I'm lying on your floor, imagining my heart doesn't hurt."

"Why does your heart hurt?" Mine does too. More than my heart. My entire chest and throat and pit of my stomach ache all the time, but I know it's nowhere close to the same reason as hers.

"My mom is sending me to live at a school in Vermont because I love Nanny who changed my diapers when I was a baby, and she loves me, so she got fired because I'm not supposed to love employees, only my mom. And my father liked Nanny too much too, so my parents are getting a divorce because my mom is a narstick bitch, and my father is a filannering asshole."

"Philandering."

She blinks at me, and I explain, "Your mom is narcissistic, and your father is philandering."

She heaves another gusty sigh. "That's what I said."

She looks back at the ceiling. "I wanted to be away from noise and pretend my heart doesn't hurt."

"You should talk to a therapist. They can help you feel better."

"Does a therapist teach you not to care when it hurts?"

I frown. "No." Mine teaches me to understand what people mean when they say things that don't make sense and how to avoid overstimulation. "Lately, he tries to convince me not to blame myself for making mistakes."

"Everybody makes mistakes. Nanny says, '*mistakes are for learning.*'" She lapses into a sad silence.

"Not all mistakes are about math problems." *Some mistakes cause people to die.*

She shrugs and makes no move to get up to leave.

"Slide over a little," I say.

She frowns but doesn't move, so I indicate the partially covered design. "You're on Orion's Belt."

Her smile is sweet as she slides over. Then it falls away as she resumes looking at the white ceiling.

"Want something to look at while you forget it hurts?"

"Maybe."

I stride to the light switch and flip it off. When darkness descends, she laughs, the sound a twinkle. Like Christmas jingle bells. "Funny joke. Now it's black and there's *nothing* to look at."

"Give it a minute. Let your eyes adjust. It won't be quite so stygian in a moment." I fumble to find the basketball-sized dome on my bedside table.

"You're smart. You talk like a grown-up."

Warmth blooms inside my chest at her praise, but I have to admit the truth. "I like vocabulary words. I memorize them and learn new ones every day, but sometimes I forget which words are normal ones and which ones aren't. I'm good at math and spatial relations too. I've already taken a couple college classes."

"That means your brain is so big and full of smart things you don't have room to be small anymore."

For safety reasons, I don't usually talk to anyone outside of our family's inner circle about being neurodivergent. I don't understand why I want to tell this girl. Maybe it's because she radiates uncomplicated acceptance.

"Some people think autism makes you stupid. It doesn't. Then there are people who think being autistic automatically makes someone a savant...a special kind of genius. That's equally as annoying. There are things I'm good at and things that are hard. Everyone is different, like having blue eyes and brown hair."

"Or being short or tall," she says. "I have a short leg."

I glance down at her feet. The difference is slight. I'd never have noticed if she hadn't mentioned it, but her heels don't line up. "Yes. I like studying the stars. That's what I want to do for a job when I'm an adult. I'll work for NASA. Or teach people about space. I love everything about it. The real, scientific things, not science fiction like *Star Wars.*"

"That's cool. I like stars. You can't see them in real life here in New York. But I saw them on TV."

"That's because of light pollution. But there are a couple of places like the High Line and Brooklyn Bridge Park where they're visible on a clear night."

"Jonny won't take me to Brooklyn Bridge Park."

"Who's Jonny? Your driver?"

"My dad."

"You call your father by his first name?"

"That's how it is. Sometimes dads don't like to be 'Dad.'"

She shifts slightly. "What was that word? About the dark?"

"Stygian?"

"I like that word. *Stygian.*" She stretches the syllables out. "It sounds like a warrior in the dark. A good one. A place for secret battles where the warrior fights his enemies. Like one of my mom's movies. She played a lady named Helen, and whole countries fought for her."

I smile. "You're brave enough to be a warrior. You're going on an adventure to Vermont."

She smiles. "Really? *The Stygian Warrior,*" she intones like she's voicing a movie trailer.

Now that I can make out her shape in the darkness, I carry the projector over to where she remains prone on the carpet. After I place the object on the floor, I lie next to her with about two feet between us. "Are you still watching the ceiling?"

"Yes."

When I flick a switch, the girl gasps as my bedroom becomes a planetarium. Fake, of course. Just a light show. But Dad's research and development company designed it for me. I know Dad was trying to give me something else to think about other than the screaming and blood. It's a relatively sophisticated piece of equipment that I can program with latitude, longitude, and a date, and the computer inside configures the constellations.

I'm about to explain, but she points and says, "There's a W."

"That's Cassiopeia."

"Pretty."

"I guess it is."

"My name's Francesca, by the way," she says. "But everybody calls me Franki."

"My name is Henry. Everyone calls me Henry."

We lie there for a long time. In my head, I silently name all the constellations. Then I picture star charts for different times of the year for the Northern Hemisphere. I don't tell her about them, though, because I think she might need the quiet as she struggles with the pain in her heart.

Finally, I peer at her through the gloom. The deep darkness is lit by a wash of violet and blue with stunning diamond-bright points of light that play across her round little face. Like this, I can't see the red of her nose or the tears still hovering at the edge of her lashes.

Much later, when she's left, I close my eyes and try to sleep. For the first time since that night, it isn't blood I see when I do. In my mind's eye, I only see stars. Reflected off Franki's glasses and sparkling in her pretty brown eyes.

ONE

Henry

Present Day

Fire | Barns Courtney

I don't give a shit that a yacht is on fire behind me. People, mostly men, but some women, scream pointlessly in desperation, begging us to bring our smaller crafts closer. To do something to save them.

There are no lifeboats or life jackets for the guests onboard *Felicity's Folly*. I know because I'm the one who made certain of it.

My brother Gabriel, dressed in black, approaches with a teenage girl wrapped in a thin blanket. "Tell him what you told me," he says, voice altered by his obsidian helmet to a mechanical tone.

The girl, maybe fourteen years old, thin, with dark brown skin ashen from stress, swallows hard. "You missed one of us. She was really little and climbed inside a duffel bag because she thought no one would look there. I didn't know you were saving us." The longer she speaks, the higher her voice gets.

My gut tightens, but my voice, disguised by my own helmet, is matter-of-fact. "Same place I found you?"

"Yes. I'm sorry. I was afraid."

"Not your fault. It's going to be okay." Gabriel soothes as he motions for Brooke, one of the women on our team, to come over and take the girl back to the others.

Punching something would be a waste of time. Instead, I radio our pilot. We have three boats on the water and a helicopter above. "I've got a kid left behind. Can you drop me back on deck?"

"Roger that. But if the fire spreads or approaches the fuselage, you'll need to find another way home."

"Let me do it," Gabriel insists.

"No, you coordinate with Dante to get me clear of the scene once I find her. We may need someone in the water to retrieve us."

"Don't get yourself killed, Henry," Gabriel grinds out.

"Not planning on it."

A mid-October bluster cuts through the sturdy fabric of my clothing. If possible, I'll avoid the frigid water. The tactical gear weighs me down, but leaving it behind isn't an option. An audience watches my every move, so reboarding with stealth is out. The ocean isn't rough, but the waves lift and fall, and my stomach drops with them.

We'd expected our quarry to head for the tropics, but at nearly the last hour, they'd changed their plans, I assume in an attempt to avoid detection. Above us, the helicopter moves into position, churning the steely gray sea under overcast skies. My chief of security, Dante, in full gear, as all of us are, drops a ladder and crouches in the opening, hanging onto the chopper with one hand.

Launching onto the ladder, I secure myself with SPIE rigging. *I fucking hate heights.* It took me nearly as long to learn how to force myself to ignore my fear as it did to stop gagging at the sight of blood. I overcame those visceral reactions long before I left my teens. Now, I spare them a thought and move forward with what I need to do.

When I'm in position, the chopper flies me above the soon-to-be-sinking ship. Cockroaches swarm as I approach. Anyone who sells or buys children doesn't qualify as human in my mind.

Grasping, desperate hands claw toward me. A famous movie producer, Caucasian, balding, and probably in his fifties, lifts his Glock. I don't give him time to make a demand or shoot me off the ladder. Opening fire on him and everyone else standing beneath me, I neutralize those obstacles before I reach my destination.

I drop to teak decking that's turned slippery with blood, my knees bending deep, before I straighten and step over the bodies.

By my estimation, fewer than a dozen people remain alive on this cesspit of depravity. An eighty-million-dollar yacht has become nothing more than a funeral pyre in progress. Our team has already removed everyone even *possibly* innocent. All but one little girl who, apparently, hid in a damn duffel. *How small do you have to be to hide in a bag? Mistake. Mistake. Mistake. If the kid dies, it's my fault. Don't think about it. Don't feel anything.* That way lies madness.

Flames gnaw their way across the ship, though I can't see the fire as I descend below deck. Black smoke filters through the corridor, hazy, not as thick as it will be. When heat meets fuel, this floating tomb will become an inferno. I have to be out of here before that happens.

The breather on this helmet is state-of-the-art and straight out of my family's research and development lab, the only part of our business empire my father has any interest in, whatsoever.

Dad has left my grandfather's businesses in my hands, too obsessed with his quest to rid New York of organized crime to waste time on boring things like finances, but vigilante shit costs money. Lots and lots of money.

Besides, my great-grandfather built those companies. He passed them to his son, Arden McRae II. Over time, the business expanded from real estate, property development, and railways, to include shipping and tech industries.

Now, most of those businesses have skipped a generation and fallen to me. As long as they exist, some part of my grandfather's legacy remains.

The helmet cam projects a 360-degree view inside the visor. No one gets in my way as I follow a direct path to the berth where the traffickers kept their victims, but any moment, a new threat could emerge.

"If I don't make it out of here, you better be at my office first thing Monday morning, ready to step in." My mic sends my words directly to my brother's earpiece. It's not the first time I've delivered that line.

Gabriel's laugh cracks as he delivers his own, right on cue. "You're the golden boy. I'm the fuck up. Remember your place, and I'll remember mine. Stay alive, asshole."

"Roger that." The berth I'm seeking comes into view. If the kid isn't here, chances of survival are much lower. I don't have time to search for her.

Through the open doorway, I can see most of the small cabin, but as I enter, I do a sweep anyway. The duffel bag sits on the mattress, lumpy and lifting and falling with the kid's ragged breathing. The fact that I missed it the first time is inexcusable.

"I'm here to help you. Don't be scared."

When I draw the zipper down, a vicious, growling screech sounds. I wrest the wooden hanger out of her hand, just as a little, red-haired demon swings at me, attacking like a feral animal.

"Good job, but we don't have time for this right now. The boat is on fire. Did you learn about firemen in school?"

She trembles and frowns. "You're not a fireman," she whispers.

"I don't look like any of those bad people, right? That's because I'm here to help you get home, but I need you to cooperate."

The kid coughs and struggles, staring at my black headgear in horror when I lift her into my arms. "No! Monster!" Her words cut off with a hacking cough.

The visor raises when I click the button, so she can see my normal, human, blue eyes. "Not a monster. Look."

The girl, I'd estimate her age somewhere between three and four, shakes her head. If she doesn't cooperate in the next fifteen seconds, I'll have to terrify her into submission. Fighting her and any obstacles in our path at the same time will be a challenge.

I take off my helmet. "Look. I have freckles like you do. My sister says my hair is goofy. Is it sticking up all crazy?" I'm due for a haircut. When I let it get like this, the cowlicks in my brown hair are out of control.

She blinks. "Yes."

"Did you just take your fucking helmet off?" Dante barks in my earpiece.

The kid coughs again.

"Put this on. It's going to make it easier for you to breathe. No bad people can hurt you when you have this on your head. It's special."

"Like Iron Man?"

Not even close. "Yes. Just like that."

When I fit the helmet over her head, it wobbles, far too large, but the air is cleaner for her than it is for me.

"Shit for brains, Henry. I have no idea why people think you're a genius. Get the fuck out of there." I don't need to see my chief of security to know he's clutching his own headgear in agitation as he hovers nearby in the waiting chopper.

I'll be gone before my breathing becomes a problem, and I already killed everyone on this part of the ship. The greater concern is an explosion, and no breather will save me from that.

"I'm going to run with you really fast. It will be loud. Hold on as tightly as you can and don't let go of me until I say so. Do you understand?"

"Yes." Small arms squeeze around my neck, her child's voice distorted through the helmet.

"Close your eyes. Don't look."

She nods, then crams her helmet-covered head against my shoulder. I wrap a makeshift harness around the two of us. She's too small. Too easy to slip out of it. Something to consider for the future. My mind hadn't let me go to a place where I imagined needing a baby carrier.

Emerging on the upper deck brings the relief of moderately fresher air, but only because the smoke is blowing in the other direction.

"You're getting me off this boat or I shoot." The voice comes from my left, and I stop, turning toward the US senator who was lying in wait.

His eyes flare wide in recognition, despite the contacts I wear, rather than my usual glasses. "Hen—"

My roundhouse kick knocks the gun from his hand, followed immediately by a slice across his throat with my bowie knife.

The girl screams, and I waste precious moments preventing her from clawing at my face and escaping my hold. The distraction is dangerous, so I clamp down, trapping her arms against her body. My shoulder and thigh take a beating from her head butts and kicking feet, but at least I can see now.

"Be still," I grate out.

Sheathing my bloody blade, I run and jump for the ladder as the chopper lowers toward us. Her added weight is negligible, but considering I can only use one hand to grab the ladder and blood makes my grip slippery, I nearly drop us both into the ocean.

"I'm letting you use your arms. You have to hold onto me. If you let go, you're going to fall all the way down and die." A harsh yell. A monstrous thing to say to a child. But true.

Her squeal barely cuts through the *chop chop chop* of the machine above us. I loosen my hold. When she grabs onto my neck, I release her for two heart-stopping seconds to get a better grip on the ladder and secure the rigging. She clings to me, then I anchor her against me once more, holding her tightly in case she panics or tries to squirm away. We fly out over open water, wind and sea spray thrashing us as the team pulls us up.

When I reach the top, Dante tries to take the girl from me, but she refuses to let go, so I climb in and settle onto a seat with her on my lap.

As soon as the door closes, I remove the harness, and the girl scrambles away to shiver on the floor, turning her head from me to the pilot and the other men around her, then back to me. I reach for her, prepared to check for injuries, but draw back when she screams. "No! You're bad too. You're bad."

Crimson splatters mar her pink T-shirt. I've left a bloody handprint on her side. She'll be in the care of medical and mental health professionals soon.

Will my face fill her nightmares? Will she ever understand what she saw? Pointless to wish she'd closed her eyes. "I'm sorry."

She rocks in place. She may not even hear me over the sound of the propeller.

"You're safe now. No one else is going to hurt you," I say.

Two little arms wrap over her head.

Blood coats the black fabric of my sleeve, and my glove-covered fingers glisten. *Revolting*. Fishing a wet wipe from a go-bag Dante passes my way, I clean my gloves and the worst of my sleeve.

When Dante passes me a brown teddy bear and one of the soft blankets we keep for situations like this, I set them both down near the girl without touching her or getting closer. "What's your name?" I try to be loud enough for her to hear me.

The kid wraps herself in fabric, ignores the stuffed animal, and doesn't answer. I don't press her. She's terrified, and I don't know how to make her not feel that way. The blood from someone I killed in front of her is all over her shirt.

Dante gives me a new helmet. When I fit the thing on my head, the noise of the blades becomes tolerable. From my wrist unit, I power off the voice amplifier on the new helmet, so when I speak it doesn't transmit to anyone who isn't locked into our shared channel. Little Miss won't hear our conversation from where she sits near my feet, but I can still hear her.

In the distance, *Felicity's Folly* explodes. I check my watch. "I'm certain this detour cost us valuable time. No way I'm making it to that wedding tomorrow. Better luck next time, I guess."

My brother snorts in my earpiece. "Nice try. We've got more than enough time to return to New York."

"You can handle this alone. Do you really need me?"

"Dude. Suck it up. Live a little. I thought that was your new mantra." Gabriel's voice sounds in my earpiece. He's on board our own yacht below, heading away from the scene of the crime before the authorities manage to clock us.

"I don't have a mantra. I have a grandmother with control issues," I snipe.

According to her, I have an unhealthy obsession with work. When I requested she sell me her McRae Property Development shares, she came back with what she called "incentive," and I call "an unreasonable ultimatum." I've been trying to find my way around it ever since.

With my grandfather's death, Dad's rejection of his own father's companies took on new and deeper significance. I'm the only McRae left with both the willingness and the ability to take on the mantle of the empire my family built. MPD is only one of a long line of family businesses I've needed to swoop in and rescue from mismanagement.

"*It's only a company. When you understand that, I'll know you can handle it.*" What a nonsensical thing for Grandmother Rose to say. Obviously, it's a company. What else would it be?

"I'm not saying I agree with her, but she's doing it because she wants you to be happy," Gabriel says.

"MPD will make me happy." I deliver the word "happy" like a pat of butter melting on a stack of pancakes. Happiness is an absurd goal. Does Grandmother Rose expect me to float around with a ridiculous grin on my face?

My siblings and I were raised into this world. When we were kids, Dad was the lead prosecutor in a case against a mob boss. They made the mistake of threatening his family. Dad built a private army and annihilated the threat, but as long as organized crime keeps trying to gain a foothold, it will never be over. Our methods are unconventional at best. Barbaric, at worst, but we do what's necessary. Sometimes we have months, even years, of peace, but it never lasts. My life doesn't have room for happiness.

Dante cracks open a plastic food storage container and passes it over to me.

I flip up my visor and place the container on the floor within the child's reach. She doesn't trust me, but the others indicated they hadn't eaten in hours. The physical need for food may be enough to overcome fear, at least in the short term. "Hungry?"

After a brief hesitation, little fingers reach out and curl around a treat, then she slides her entire hand up under the mask.

She can keep the helmet. I'll have to scrub my DNA and wipe the systems first, until it's nothing more than something to cover her head, but I'm not taking it back permanently. She appears to have developed an attachment.

She reaches for a second puff.

"The cooking class? Best idea, yet," Dante says.

Gabriel groans. "Are you guys eating without me? You suck. What did you make this time?"

"Cranberry brie puffs." I tap my pointer finger on my thigh, a subtle form of stimming that, to most other people, looks like an impatient man ready to get on with things.

"They're delicious, aren't they? You're rubbing pastry deliciousness that I can't have in my face," Gabriel says.

"Mmm. So good." I'm not eating, but I enjoy harassing him. Who says I don't know how to have fun?

Cracking open a water bottle, I waggle it in front of the kid until she snatches it away, only lifting the helmet far enough to expose her mouth to gulp at the water. I'd like to hold her and comfort her, but she doesn't know any of us. I'd only make things worse if I try.

"The wine-making wasn't bad, and I eat my cereal from the bowl you made me in ceramics class every day, but cooking wins. Hands down," Dante says.

"The bowl you stole." I press the button to close my visor once more.

"Semantics," Dante argues.

In the past eleven months, in an attempt to provide my grandmother proof of my rich and meaningful life, I've participated in no less than seven new and varied hobbies. They range from fly fishing, which I enjoy, to knitting, which, shockingly, I also enjoy.

"Maybe you'll find your future wife at the wedding. You're running out of time. What have you got left? Two months?" Dante asks.

My eye twitches. "One." If I don't meet Grandmother's deadline, she's planning to give her shares to her sister's grandson, Lawrence. She chose him for the simple fact that she knows I will go to extreme lengths to prevent him from getting his hands on that company. She knows if she gives them to Gabriel, he'll hand the reins over to me as soon as the ink is dry on the contract.

"If you care about those shares so much, then you have to pick a woman and just do it," Gabriel says.

"There has to be another way," I mutter.

I can't marry someone else. That's not an option I can even consider. I flinch internally at the idea of chasing Franki down before she's ready. She's working toward her PhD and has years left before she comes home, but the clock is ticking.

"I've decided to approach the situation as a business merger." One thing all this time that I've spent fishing and knitting and thinking has done is give me the grudging realization that my grandmother is partially right. I'm numb as hell, but what she doesn't understand is that I like it that way.

Grandmother's mistake is assuming that's something I need, or want, to change. Anyone who's seen and felt the things I have would be a masochist to volunteer for that kind of pain again. "My situation is too complicated for anything else right now."

"Find some temporary company, then. Go out once in a while. Find a woman to take home and let the word spread. Maybe it'll be enough if Grandmother thinks you're looking." Gabriel's voice sounds in my ear.

"That won't solve my problem." If it were only the issue of navigating the security risks that sleeping with random women carried, I might consider his suggestion, but touching another woman would be a betrayal. Gabriel would call me insane if I told him that. In order for there to be "another" woman, I'd need to have a woman in the first place, and I don't. She was never mine.

I once saw the definition of a Welsh word: *hiraeth*. It's homesickness for someplace or someone you can never return to. Sometimes, it's a yearning to return to something that never even existed at all. Understanding resonated inside me immediately upon learning the word. I've never found a better way to explain the hole inside me that's only grown deeper over the last five years.

"Your grandmother isn't going to accept some fake marriage," Dante argues.

"It won't be fake. It will be practical," I say.

"Unless you ease up on your requirements, you're not finding anyone at all. You'll need someone financially motivated, which immediately calls her trustworthiness into question," Gabriel says.

"I'm someone financially motivated, and I'm trustworthy," I say sourly. "I'm not changing my requirements. I'll explain to Grandmother that I'm searching but haven't found the right person and request an extension."

"She'll ask what you're looking for in a wife and realize you've made an impossible list as an excuse," my brother disagrees.

"It's not impossible," I scoff.

Gabriel snorts. "She has to be fluent in German *and* French, even though you don't speak those languages. You won't accept anyone who isn't within an inch either way of five-foot-seven, for no reason whatsoever, except that you held your hand out to a certain height one day, and said, 'Spencer, find a tape measure, that's how tall she is.' And she should be a dog person, even though you don't have a dog."

"I like dogs, and it makes perfect sense that I would want my wife to be fluent in languages that I'm not. It's a practical consideration that reduces the need to hire a translator in any number of circumstances."

"Yeah, okay," Gabriel says in patent disbelief.

"Why does she have to be interested in both astronomy and world history? Those interests are too different from each other. If you find someone into astronomy, she's not going to be into history. We're not stupid. You did it on purpose," Dante says.

"At least the one about being loyal and trustworthy makes sense. You can't have a wife you're worried will stab you in your sleep. That's the real impossibility. No one could live with Henry and not want to kill him," I can hear the grin in Gabriel's voice.

I roll my eyes.

Dante snorts. "And if he did manage to find someone who meets every one of his other criteria, he won't accept her if she doesn't have brown eyes. To be honest, the last two sound like a golden retriever, not a wife."

"How incredibly offensive." I maintain a bored tone, despite the irritation that floods through me. The list is nothing more than a description of Franki. If she's changed, my list will have to change.

"What is she supposed to get out of this?" Gabriel asks.

"The obvious answer is money. I'll consider making adjustments to my requirements on an as-needed basis. I'm not budging on the height, eye color, languages, or education. Trustworthiness has to stay. As does her liking dogs."

"You're actually going to do it." Gabriel's shock is clear in his voice.

Dante shifts back, sprawling in his seat. "You're not going to be satisfied if you acquire your wife as a business merger."

"I won't care how I acquired her once I have her." I keep my voice deliberately bland. If I say it enough, I'll convince myself it's true. The only way I can have Franki Lennox as my wife is by offering her a practical arrangement, so that's what I'll do.

From her place near my bloody feet, the kid rocks in place. "Monster. Monster. Monster."

Two

Franki

Mind Over Matter | Young the Giant

Do other people get a jolt of dread every time they get a phone call? Because phones are now the bane of my existence.

Hair still dripping and towel wrapped around my chest, I eye mine like it's a snake. The phone, in its pretty black and silver star-covered case, vibrates on the tiny desk in my hotel room. I turned the ringer off three days ago, but it still buzzes, and that's enough to make me jump with a jolt of adrenaline.

Oliver, my little brown dachshund, lifts his head from where he's been napping in the corner, then dismisses my mother's call the way I wish I could.

It's time to deal with her, get today's meltdown under control, and move on with my life. This is better, really. I'll get it over with before I meet up with the other bridesmaids for the wedding, rather than having it hanging over my head.

I answer the call and leave it on speakerphone as I move to my suitcase. "Hey, Mom. How are you?"

"I thought you were dead. You didn't answer your phone."

Her last call came less than twenty minutes ago. *"Dead"* is a pretty radical leap of logic. I drag on my clothing as we speak. "I was in the shower."

"I need you back in California. My schedule is falling apart without you. The personal assistant you hired for me is a joke."

"Give your PA time. He's still learning your habits," I soothe.

"A PA isn't my *child*. A PA doesn't care about me. I don't trust him the way I trust you."

I squeeze my temples with one hand. "You made it without me all those years when I was a kid. You can do it. This is just a transition." I keep my tone upbeat and encouraging. All *"Atta girl"* with none of the frustration I feel bleeding through.

"My life was hell without you. I made sacrifices for your sake; the least you owe me is some gratitude and appreciation now." She's ramping up to anger. Zero to sixty in the space of six sentences.

"I am grateful. I know it was hard for you to be away from me when I was a child. I'm sorry you went through that." The words are rote. Something she's expected me to say my entire life.

"You're still trying to punish me for something that isn't my fault."

This is an old conversation, recycled and rehashed. I'm tired of it. I have things to do today, and catering to my mother's fragile ego isn't on my list. "I'm not punishing you. I'm doing what normal people do when they grow up. I'm trying to build my own life."

"You're not normal. You can't expect to do what other people do."

I clutch the air in a silent expression of fury, then speak calmly. If I escalate her, it only gets worse. "I'm not abnormal."

"Don't put words in my mouth and act like I'm attacking you when I'm trying to help you."

I need to steer this conversation back on course. "Why don't you ask David for help? You don't have to be alone. You have support. He loves you." She's been in a quiet relationship with David Vance for years.

"I can't do that, and you know it. I don't get to be sentimental about these things. It's about public perception. The people like to imagine I'm in love with my co-star, not banging a stunt actor they've never heard of."

Ugh. Gross.

"Just come back, Franki. You only have so long before the money you stole runs out," she says.

I roll my eyes. "I didn't steal anything. I saved the money you insisted on giving me because you didn't want me to get a job while I was a student. I'll find one now."

I tried to find employment before I left and applied for all sorts of positions in New York. None of them responded…until one did with a kindly worded email telling me best of luck since I'd withdrawn my application. When I wrote back, they'd already filled the position.

My mother had sabotaged all of my applications. When I confronted her, she said those jobs would have been "too hard" on me. There's no reasoning with her. The only thing I know how to do is work around her "good intentions."

"That money was for your daily expenses, so you could pay for lunch and put gas in your car. It wasn't meant for you to hoard so you could sneak off."

"I didn't sn—"

"I'll pay you to be my PA and let you go back to grad school. Then you can say you have the independence you want so badly." She uses her coaxing, reasonable voice, as though autonomy is a silly, selfish goal for a twenty-three-year-old woman.

This is her backing down from her latest ultimatum, then. "No amount of financial assistance with school is worth my self-respect."

"I can't understand why you chose this hill to die on. I wasn't criticizing you." Anxiety leaks through her words.

I scrub my forehead with my fingers. "I don't want surgery for the sake of meeting some beauty standard I don't even care about. It doesn't matter to me what size my breasts are, and I have more important things to worry about than weighing a few pounds more than what you think is my 'ideal weight.'"

"Seventeen is not a few, and it's not what I *think*. It's what our trainer agrees is the healthiest weight for you. What's the difference between this and when I paid for your surgery for that terrible overbite? I'm helping you to be the best version of yourself."

Insurance paid most of my orthognathic surgery costs, and for the braces before and after to correct the problems caused by my upper and lower jaws growing at different rates, but if I say that, she'll point out that she paid for the insurance. "My overbite caused jaw pain and headaches. It was a medical issue. I care about how I'm functioning. I exercise to stay healthy, and I stop when I'm causing more harm than good. This body is the only one I've got. I'm giving myself grace."

She scoffs in disgust.

I don't expect her to understand. My mother's obsession with maintaining her own physical perfection is hard to watch without feeling pity. My best friend's mother Charlotte was my true role model. Not that I was stupid enough to admit something like that in front of my mother. I'd have never been allowed to stay with the McRaes again.

Five years ago, Mom's obsession with her own appearance expanded to include mine. I never figured out exactly what made her decide it was time for me to move to England with her. She simply showed up one Christmas break from school, and at the end of it, decided she was going to keep me with her for the last half of my senior year of high school.

I had chronic headaches at the time, and she took me to a doctor who recommended I see a surgeon for my jaw. She'd seemed to relish the process. She transitioned from love bombing to someone obsessed with what she felt she "created" when my new jawline emerged as a result of the surgery and braces. It was a power trip for her, and she set about transforming me from the awkward, bullied girl I'd been, into a clone of herself.

According to her, I owe her for my very existence. Guinevere Jones doesn't quite see me as a real person, no matter what she says. I'm an accessory. Like a pretty pair of shoes. I exist to boost her ego and be available for her needs.

When my best friend nearly died in a stalker attack and Mom didn't even want me to see her, I knew I had to come back to the East Coast and get away from my mother for good. Bronwyn's recent brush with death put things into perspective for me. I'm done living as my mother's possession.

One thing after another kept me at her home in California, but I'm here now, and that's what matters. "I'm looking for work. I explained—"

"The McRaes are not your family. They kept you during holidays and summer breaks from school as a child out of pity. I'm your mother. I don't mind keeping you, but you can't go there and expect to stay with them indefinitely while you look for a job. You're taking advantage of them. I have secondhand embarrassment just thinking about it."

I grit my teeth. How she manages to zero in on my every fear and insecurity, I'll never know. "When Jonny gets back from Paris, I'm sure he'll let me crash at his place."

I'm sure of no such thing. To say my father is inconsistent in his affection or availability would be generous, but Charlotte swore she wanted me here. If she hadn't, I'd have found another way to leave my mother.

"Do you think I don't know you're there because of Henry McRae?"

I heave a silent sigh. "I was eighteen when I told you I had a crush on Henry. It's ancient history. I haven't even spoken with him in almost five years. I got over the puppy love, Mom."

"You tried to go back there within six months to return to people who didn't want you. Every time you decide to leave, it's with some insane plan to return to New York."

When I initially left with Mom, I didn't have insecurities about the McRaes or my friendship with Henry. As time passed, however, her words wore a groove in my memories until I got to a place where I didn't know if I'd been oblivious to the fact that they simply tolerated me or if they really did care about me. I distanced myself emotionally, unwilling to be an unwanted fifth wheel or an object of pity.

Regret sits like an unmoving ball of lead in my gut. If Bronwyn hadn't been the kind of person who would track me down, and Clarissa and Janessa hadn't been the kind of friends who insisted on including me in group texts even after I'd withdrawn, I'd have become completely isolated.

I've been trying to find a way to extricate myself from living with my mother since nearly the beginning. My surgery, then later my rheumatoid arthritis diagnosis, my education, the constant need for bodyguards, even Oliver's vet bills, have kept me wrapped in silk cords that look like she's providing care and protection from the outside, but from the inside feel like a cage.

Mom also isn't wrong that I still have feelings for Henry, but she doesn't have any way of knowing that. Most people don't hang on to teenage crushes the way I have.

"You were assaulted less than six weeks ago. There's no reason to rush this," she says.

"I was shaken up. I wasn't hurt."

"Someone tried to *kidnap* you. Don't dismiss this as if it's nothing. This is the third time someone has gone after you in the last two years," she says in horrified tones.

Gee, thanks for reminding me, Mom. "Obviously, they thought I was you. That isn't going to happen when we aren't even on the same side of the country. I changed my hair color, and I've gained weight. If I'm not coming and going from your house, no one will make the connection between us."

To my way of thinking, it's one more reason to want to put distance between us.

"Distance won't make a difference. The only reason you weren't hurt was because David was there to save you. You don't have anyone to help you like that in New York. I spend every moment visualizing you murdered or worse," she says.

"The McRaes have security out the wazoo, and I'm headed back there tomorrow."

"What if Oliver gets sick again? Or you do?"

"We'll be fine."

When Charlotte called to tell me about Bronwyn, I'd tried to leave immediately to go to her. Before that could happen, someone tried to drag me into his car.

Then Oliver got into something, and I had to turn to my mother for help with the vet bills. Then some jerk stole my car. Between stress and the immunosuppressants I take, *I* got sick. Finally, when Oliver and I were well enough, I managed to get on that plane.

It was a mess for me. For my mother? It was proof that I wasn't ready to live away from her, let alone on the other side of the country.

She takes a steadying breath. "You can't take advantage of the McRaes forever, and you can't live like a normal person. Every single time you try, sooner or later, some sick asshole thinks you're me and comes after you. The only reason nothing terrible happened in the past was because I provided you with protection. I know it's not fun, believe me. And I know it's my fault that people target you, but you can't live on your own. For so many reasons. You can't."

"Can't you understand that living with you and covering for you all the time only makes that situation worse for me?" It was convenient for her to have a live-in double. It allowed her privacy, as I distracted the paparazzi for her. I stuffed my bra, wore her clothing and sunglasses, and kept my head down as I hustled with a bodyguard from our house or car to another location. Photographers rarely caught on that it was the daughter they were following.

Mom takes a shuddering breath. "When you can't find a job because you got a useless degree and realize you need to finish grad school, you let me know. I'm removing you from my health insurance until you come to your senses. If you're the 'adult' you like to say you are, then you'll find a way to deal with it. I won't punish you when you come back. We'll forget this ever happened."

I knew she was going to do this. Hoping she wouldn't use every tool she has to control me would have been an exercise in futility. "Jonny will put me on his insurance if I need it, I'm sure."

With any luck, I'll find a job with benefits soon and won't need his help at all. I've been hoarding my meds by taking less than prescribed in case she did this. It's a bad idea, but I will chew my own leg off like an animal in a trap before I move back in with her. "I'm not coming back to California."

"I'll be here when you need to come home."

Beep. Beep. Beep. My shoulders relax, and I let out a slow breath when she hangs up.

When I sit on the edge of the bed, Oliver rises from his corner, stretches, then trots over to me. I smile and lean down to pet him. In response, he stands on his back legs to lean against me.

I give him a rub behind his ear. "Don't let her get to you. I'll find a job. Then I'll find a place to live. It's going to be great. It's exciting."

His tail swishes in response, his long, skinny body raised up like a prairie dog and his chin held high. I call it his "majestic wiener dog" pose.

My cousin Finn is providing this hotel room after I accepted the last-minute position as his fiancee's bridesmaid when one of them dropped out. I'm the right size for the dress. The shoes are half a size too small, but I'll make it work. After that, I'll go back to Bronwyn's parents' place for a couple weeks while I look for a job and apartment.

I click on the banking app on my phone to check my balance. I'm extremely lucky that my parents paid for my education to this point. So I don't have that anvil looming over my head, at least. I don't take it for granted, for a moment, but I have zero credit. In an absolute emergency, I could ask Clarissa or Bronwyn for help, but the thought makes me shrivel inside.

According to the bank app, my account currently holds $548.72. Not desperation-level, but not enough for even one month's rent, let alone first and last.

It's been less than a week since I loaded up my luggage with everything I could manage to fit and booked a one-way flight for me and Oliver. I saved for six months, and it's nearly gone already.

"I'm a strong and capable woman. My education isn't useless, and needing physical accommodations doesn't make me unemployable." I lift him, carefully supporting his back. "This is another one of our adventures, Oliver."

He lays his head on my shoulder and sighs loudly. If I didn't know better, I'd say my wiener dog is telling me I'm full of bologna.

Three

Henry

Seven Nation Army | The White Stripes

"Does anyone actually like this shit?" I mutter.

My personal assistant, Spencer, a curly-haired ginger with milk-pale skin and chronically florid cheeks, dogs my heels as I stride through the Hunter-Lund wedding reception.

"I do. It's understated elegance," he says in his crisp British accent.

"There's nothing understated about it."

Looming above us, silk-swathed rafters feature massive chandeliers dripping with Austrian crystal. Elaborate gold candelabras lord over every table, and if I never see another red rose in my life, it'll be too soon.

Perfume, flowers, food, cologne, music, talking, laughing, the scrape and clink of flatware against plates. People getting too close to me. All that smiling, most of which can't possibly be real.

I instinctively scan for threats. The sheer size of the assembled crowd makes the back of my neck itch. "How do you not feel suffocated?"

As I search the Park Avenue hotel ballroom for *her*, Spencer trips along behind me. "I don't think most people would. Now, regarding your search for a bride, I've taken a few moments to . . ."

I stop short and lose the thread of Spencer's words because there she is.

Franki Lennox is *here*. Until I'd laid eyes on her earlier in the church, I'd thought she was still in California.

Before the wedding ceremony, I hadn't seen her in four years, nine months, and twelve days. And then there she was, standing at the front of a cathedral in a black bridesmaid dress with a bouquet of flowers in her hands.

Following the ceremony, I lost her briefly when she disappeared with the bridal party for whatever it is that happens in the time between the wedding and reception. I've found her now, and I'm not losing her again.

I drink in the sight of her. The shape of Franki's face has changed, and her body looks subtly softer. Her light brown hair now has streaks the color of caramel popcorn that shimmer under the ballroom chandeliers. Her eyes have the same sparkle.

Spencer pushes his tablet into my line of vision. "As you can see, I've—"

"What are you doing?" Interrupted from my musings, I turn my head toward Spencer and lift an eyebrow. "Your workday is over. Come to think of it, do you even have an invitation to this wedding?"

He yanks his collar away from his neck. "I'm not here as a guest. You don't attend social gatherings, as a rule, and it will likely be some time before an opportunity to meet so many women at once is available to you—"

"Stop. Go"—I wave a hand and shake my head in exasperation—"enjoy the party. Have a drink. Do whatever it is people do at these things."

"I understand that, typically, this would be a non-working event. However, given your recent decision to find an appropriate bride, I've assembled a list from the guests in attendance here tonight. This is the perfect time to meet some of these women in an organic setting and establish—"

"I don't want to see it."

"I've already spoken with several potential brides. Brittney Belgoise is first on the list. She's five-foot-eight and has brown eyes. She's agreed to dance with you."

When Spencer attempts to show me his tablet once more, I lift my upper lip in disgust. "Brittney Belgoise?"

"Yes."

"No."

"She's perfect," Spencer protests.

"She's hideous."

"She's extremely symmetrical and has an Instagram page with over a million followers lauding her attractiveness."

"I said I wanted a woman who didn't like social media. You're not finding her on *social media*. Give me that list." I snatch the iPad from his hands.

His face falls as, one by one, I delete the names as I read them.

"Absolutely not. . . . No. . . . Never. . . . Are you joking? I said 'gentle.' That woman would castrate a man with a spoon in his sleep if he pissed her off."

Finally, after deleting all fifteen names from his list, I type my own choice into his tablet.

Francesca Louise Lennox

He looks over my shoulder at the screen. "Who is that?"

Nodding in her direction, I say, "The bridesmaid on the end. Right there."

"I didn't notice her."

"That makes no sense. She's the most interesting girl in the room."

"Oh, wait. She's in the extended security circle. Standard monitoring for friends of the family. One of your sister's friends?"

"Yes. She's the one." *She's the one. Sunny without being irritating. Not too talkative, but never mopey or silent.*

Lacey Montgomery, wearing a black cocktail dress that clings to her like Saran Wrap, sashays toward me.

Pretending not to recognize the look of welcome in her eyes, I turn my back on the woman and face Spencer directly. "Did you tell all the women on your list that I would be dancing with them?"

"Yes. Of course."

"I'm not. Fix it. Now."

Eyes wide, he sputters.

Lacey claws her fingers into my bicep and purrs into my ear. "A little birdie told me you were looking for me."

Nothing for it now but to brazen it out, I turn to Lacey with a manufactured look of mild surprise.

Her pale skin shimmers, as though she's been dusted in an ultra-fine glitter, and her teeth are straight and white. They remind me that Franki once had braces. Lacey's dark blonde hair flows all over her head in a curling lion's mane.

I have only a passing acquaintance with this woman and no interest in her, whatsoever. Frankly, I'm surprised she approached me, even with Spencer's prompting. I'm a dick and everyone knows it. I am, however, a dick with a massive bank account.

I move my lips into a smile. "I believe there's been a misunderstanding."

At my words, she drops her own smile, and her brow furrows. She smooths long, wavy hair back behind her shoulder. I can acknowledge that she is, indeed, quantifiably beautiful, intelligent, and by all evidence, socially adept. She's also the correct height and has brown eyes. But she's not Franki.

Lacey looks toward Spencer, who has buried his nose in his iPad. Then she lasers her focus on me. "I thought you were interested in getting to know me better."

She walks her fingers up my lapel. "I'm very interested in getting to know you."

I brush them away. "Why?"

She blinks, her mouth dropping open before she says, "You're very attractive."

I lift an eyebrow. "Am I?"

"Yes."

"Anything else?"

"I've, er, heard nice things about you."

Beside me, Spencer chokes, then clears his throat.

"It sounds as though you have me confused with my brother, Gabriel. He is," I search the ballroom. When I find Gabriel, I place one hand on each of Lacey's shoulders and steer her in his direction. "Right over there. He's chatting with someone right now, but don't let that stop you. The more the merrier."

I give her a nod. "Go get him, tiger."

She stumbles away, then pauses to look back in confusion. I mime walking fingers, and she turns back, straightens her shoulders and saunters forth to flirt with my brother.

As soon as I'm confident she's really gone, I turn my attention to Spencer. "Remind me again why I haven't fired you."

"Because you appreciate my enthusiasm and attention to detail." He reaches into his suit jacket, extracts a sealed antibacterial wipe packet and hands it over. "Also, I'm the only assistant who hasn't cried."

I rip open the packet, deposit the torn packaging onto his waiting palm and wipe off the gold shimmer I picked up from Lacey's shoulders. When my hands are clean, I give him the crumpled wipe, lift my glasses, and rub the bridge of my nose. "Go deal with these women *without* causing some society catastrophe that my grandmother will need to *discuss* with me."

"Right away."

"And Spencer?"

"Yes?"

"No other names. I'm done with my search."

His face glows with excitement. "Really? Do I get to plan the wedding?"

"Leave."

"Leaving."

A shot of tequila is in order. Not because I'm nervous. I'm not the kind of person who gets nervous. I deal with life and death situations as a matter of course. I'm a successful businessman. I'm not afraid to talk to a woman. I'm thirsty.

Shoving one hand in my pocket, I twist the fidget spinner I keep there and head for the open bar. One shot. Then I'll say, *"Hello, Franki. It's been a long time."*

She'll smile and say, *"It sure has. How are you, Henry?"*

After that, I'll ask her to slow dance.

Sweat prickles at my temples, and I dab it with a logo-emblazoned bar napkin. Why is it always so damn hot and loud in these places? At least three different perfumes clash in the air around me. I sniff my own arm where Lacey touched me. *Shit*. She pressed her entire front against my side when she approached me. Glitter sparkles on my jacket sleeve, and I smell like a woman. Fuck me sideways.

Where was I?

Dancing. At which time I'll talk with her and discover her current situation. If financial recompense isn't enough incentive, Franki may be willing to help an old friend out as a favor.

After we dance, I'll secure a meeting with her tomorrow. I can easily imagine the reactions of my friends and family if I tell them I secured her agreement to be my wife in twenty-four hours, but the clock on those shares is ticking.

Besides, it's not really twenty-four hours, is it? Franki and I have ten years of friendship and nearly five years of at-a-distance monthly reports on her welfare. Not that Franki knows I've been monitoring her. I did my best to give her as much privacy as I could while maintaining our family's standard security protocols. That doesn't mean I didn't perseverate over each and every report when it came in.

At any rate, when there are whispers that a lucrative property is about to come on the market, do I wait around for a bidding war, or do I get in there and make it mine before anyone else even realizes what they're missing? The answer is *"I make it mine."*

The blonde bartender smiles. "What can I get you?"

"A shot of mezcal." A deep breath through my nose. "Make that two shots."

I turn back toward the dance floor to keep an eye on Franki. When I scan the area near the head table, I realize she's moved from her original location. I can't lose track of her.

There. She's turned slightly away, standing in a corner near the edge of the dance floor. Her silky-looking gown fits her like a second skin.

I have the strong urge to take off my jacket and cover her with it. Not because she isn't gorgeous, but because, if I still know her at all, she despises the cut of that dress.

Flicking the fidget spinner in my hand, I give myself a silent pep talk. I can do this. It's just talking to her. She won't *not like me anymore* because five years have passed.

Her tinkling laugh rings out as she speaks with someone out of my view, her companion hidden from me behind a towering display of roses.

The man moves in closer, and I catch a glimpse of a tuxedo-clad arm. Then, wide shoulders. Pretty-boy features that belong on a male model come into view. A flirtatious smile plays on his lips as he stares at Franki's mouth. With a casual hand, he brushes back wind-swept brown hair that he's styled that way on purpose. His eyes are the exact same shape as mine, but green, rather than blue.

Then my brother's hand is on my future wife's lower back.

"Here you go." Two shots land on the bar, but I'm already gone.

Four

Franki

Can't Pretend | Tom Odell

THE CANDELABRAS TWINKLE, AND the music provides a romantic soundtrack as the crowds swarm through this ballroom, a bunch of little worker bees relentlessly networking under the guise of having a fantastic time. Or maybe everyone really is having fun, and I'm jaded after spending the last five years of my life on the periphery of the film industry. I'm not what anyone would call a social butterfly. Mostly I do my best to blend into the background.

The crowds press closer, and I search the venue for somewhere a little quieter. When I spot a large floral arrangement that will provide partial cover in a corner, I head straight for it. Ten minutes. That's all I need. The corner beckons, the lighting even dimmer than the rest of the room and promising a moment where I can, at least, kick off these shoes and wiggle my toes.

The gorgeous Jimmy Choo's are not only too small, but the design doesn't accommodate the lift I wear to compensate for my left leg being a couple inches shorter than the right. An entire day of balancing on the toes on my left foot has become tiring. My joints aren't happy with me either. I could stop the balancing act and lean into it. It's slight enough that no one would notice if I did, but I don't want to end up with my sacroiliac joint popping out of place as a result.

When I get to my rose bower of potential bliss, I reach down to slide off the icepick heels, transferring them into my left hand, and nearly groan in pleasure as the cool marble floor soothes my abused feet. Straightening, I take as deep of a breath as I can manage and press my palm flat to my stomach.

When I told my aunt I could fit into this dress without trying it on, I'd taken my size change into account, but not that the shape of my body is different. The steroids I'm currently on for my RA go straight to my middle. The corset worked to suck me in and give me an hourglass figure so the dress would zip, but it's a cage I'd like to claw my way out of.

Straightening my shoulders, I start my mental list designed to recenter myself into a positive mindset: *1) The bride and groom appear to be wildly in love, which is, ultimately, the only thing that actually matters on any wedding day. 2) Dinner will probably be delicious.*

I shift my weight and wiggle my toes as I think. I can conjure up at least three positives for any situation I find myself in. This should be a cakewalk. *Ha! Cake.*

3) I will be eating a delectable dessert.

"Who are we hiding from?" A masculine voice stage-whispers to my left.

Wincing at the realization that some random guy found me in a dark corner, I turn in his direction, determined to make a polite excuse and rejoin the crowd. As soon as I take in the sight of the man who's snuck up on me, however, warm recognition floods through me, and I beam in welcome instead. Gabriel McRae stands beside me with a hand in his pocket and another holding a tumbler of amber alcohol.

I heard he showed up in Paris two summers ago when Bronwyn, Janessa, Clarissa, and I were on vacation, but I was already on my way back to Los Angeles when he arrived.

"Hey, you," I say.

His gaze runs from the top of my head all the way down to my toes and back up again as a small smile plays at the corners of his lips and eyes. "Tell me what brings a stunning woman like yourself to a corner like this."

I groan at his cheesiness, but end on a smile. "Family obligations. The groom is my cousin. Why are you here?"

"Same. Bride's side. Did you bring anyone special with you tonight?"

"Definitely not. You?"

His eyebrows lift, and he chuckles. When he lifts his tumbler to his mouth, he lists slightly to the left before correcting his posture and swallowing a surprisingly large mouthful of what I assume is bourbon. "Definitely not."

I peer at the throng. "I don't really know anyone here beyond my aunt and cousin. My father is in Paris at the moment. It makes for a long day."

"I'd be happy to provide some entertainment. I'd love a little company."

I laugh. A ballroom full of people teems around us, and we're talking about needing company. I know what he means, though. It's nice to see a friendly face that isn't *work* to talk to.

Seeing Gabriel is like running headlong into nostalgia.

Gabriel's smile widens at my laughter. "Can I give you a lift anywhere when this little party is over? I'm happy to share a ride."

"That's so sweet of you. I have a room here for the night, though. So, no traveling necessary."

His expression alters subtly, his gaze moving to my mouth. I blink, then tense when he places his hand on my lower back. This dress is the *devil*.

"I'm Gabriel McRae, by the way. What's your name?"

I stop breathing.

Gabriel doesn't know who I am. He was flirting. He thinks I was flirting back. *Oh my God, he thinks I was inviting him up to my room.*

If I keep holding my breath, can I pass the heck out and sleep for the next five years?

I suck in a pathetically shallow breath of rose-scented air and press my palm against my heart. I spent most of my holiday breaks in the McRae mansion from the age of eight to eighteen. How could he forget me?

My mother wasn't wrong, then. I was the weird little girl they let hang around out of pity.

"Uh-oh. What's that face for?" He cringes and takes his hand off my back. "I misread your cues? I apologize."

I shake my head and laugh at the absurdity of it. "Gabriel. It's *me*."

He wiggles his eyebrows. "*And you are . . . ?*"

Henry, mouth set in a firm line, strides into my line of sight, then straight for us, his attention zeroed in on his brother.

My heart catches in my throat. *He's here.*

Henry isn't even looking at me. The fact that Gabriel doesn't recognize me is embarrassing, but if Henry doesn't know me, I'll do my absolute best to sink straight into the floor.

On the other hand, when I last saw Henry, I was an awkward girl with a chronically unflattering haircut, jaw issues too significant for braces to correct on their own, acne, and glasses that slipped down my nose. Gabriel's lack of recognition is painful, but maybe I'm expecting too muc—

Henry physically shoulders his brother out of the way and leans in to kiss my cheek.

His lips are cool against my skin, and he smells delicious, like warm bergamot and cedar and black tea and . . . *jasmine*?

Henry straightens to look into my eyes, and my knees go weak.

"Hello, Franki."

My heart pounds out a staccato rhythm in my ears as I stare back into Henry's twilight blue eyes. My hand creeps up to cup my cheek. *I'm holding his kiss against me like a weirdo.*

Flustered, I drop my fingers. "Henry."

Gabriel laughs. "You're kidding me. *Little Franki?*"

"She's barely two years younger than you are. Can you not behave as though her adulthood is some shocking discovery?" Henry places a protective arm around my shoulders.

Gabriel lifts his eyebrows. "Okay."

"Would you like to dance, Franki?" Henry asks.

"Not really. Thanks, though." The fact that I'm turning down a dance with Henry when this would have once been a Cinderella dream-come-true moment for me is almost tragic in its irony, but I can't. I'd fall flat on my face at this point. My knees and feet have had it. Maybe he'll stay and talk, though. We could find somewhere to sit quietly. The Henry I knew would have preferred that over dancing any day.

Henry runs a hand through his light brown hair. He's always despised sitting for haircuts and procrastinates, stretching out the time between them as long as he's practically able to. He gets thousand-dollar haircuts so it looks good at every stage, even its current mop-like iteration. He adjusts his glasses over his lightly freckled nose, then loosens his bow tie as he appears to contemplate the mysteries of the universe. "Hmm."

Gabriel looks at Henry, then he skims a clinical gaze over me, as though he's cataloging my features. He snaps his attention back to his brother, an open-mouthed look of, apparently, astonishment written on his features. "Is this what I think it is?"

Henry glances at his brother. "How would I know what you're thinking?" he drawls.

Gabriel grins at me. "You don't happen to speak German and French, do you?"

Henry heaves a long-suffering sigh.

I frown, looking from one to the other in confusion. "Yes."

Gabriel's smile grows. "What did you go to college for? I'm not sure I ever heard."

I shake my head. "I studied history."

Gabriel claps his brother on the shoulder with a laugh. "You sneaky devil."

"Go away," Henry says.

Unfamiliar anticipation builds inside me with a physical wash of electric sensation. I'm hyperaware of every place Henry's body touches mine. The weight of his arm across my shoulders. The strong, masculine hand as it rests near, but not touching my breast. Henry's side is pressed against mine for nearly the entire length of my body.

After all this time, his scent is still warm and familiar. Henry has never worn cologne. Instead, he smells like the cedar hangers in his closet and the Earl Grey tea he drinks. That is, aside from one new, and jarring, feminine note. Henry has clearly been close to a woman other than me recently. Very close.

Gabriel runs a hand through his hair. "I'm headed for the bar. I need another drink." He gives Henry an encouraging nod. "Good luck."

Henry stiffens next to me.

Gabriel inserts himself close enough to put his arms around me in a hug that reeks of alcohol, though Henry never relinquishes his hold. "It was great to see you, Franki. We'll have to catch up soon. I apologize for the misunderstanding."

"It's good to see you too."

Gabriel steps back and his expression gentles. "I hope the last five years were kind to you."

None of the McRaes liked or trusted my mother. Somehow, after years in her presence, I'd almost forgotten that.

"They were educational," I say with a rueful smile.

Henry frowns at his brother. "I believe you were going somewhere."

Gabriel's smile returns, and he lifts what remains of his drink, finishing it in one go. Then he turns and strides away, and I'm left standing, speechless, in the circle of Henry's arm.

I wait in silence for him to move or say something. After several fraught moments where neither of us seems to know what to do next, Henry removes his arm, steps back, and shoves his hands in his pockets.

"You don't like dancing, or you find the idea of dancing with me, specifically, unappealing?" Henry looks almost bored as he asks the question, eyelids heavy, expression flat.

I lift the shoes in my hand and stick my left leg out through the thigh-high slit in the dress. "It's the heels. I can't wear a lift with them. Nothing to do with you."

His hot gaze lingers first on my foot, then slowly works his way up my leg farther and farther until his attention lands squarely on my eyes. I stare back, breathless with wonder. Henry has never looked at me like that in my life.

He leans in subtly closer. "How long are you staying this visit? A week? A month?"

I've spent my life "visiting," so it's a reasonable assumption. "I'm hoping it's not a visit at all. Where I land on the East Coast permanently is going to depend on what job I can find and cost of living. I don't suppose you know of anyone hiring someone with almost a master's degree in history?"

Those blue eyes of his sharpen with interest. "I may, indeed, know of a job opportunity for someone with your qualifications, but I thought you wanted to complete your PhD."

I smile in confusion. "Did Bronwyn mention that? A PhD was the plan. I suppose it's tacky to talk finances, but the truth is that I can't afford to finish school right now. I need to build my credit first."

Expression intrigued, he says, "So, practical considerations have gotten in the way of your dreams?"

"That's life. It's time to shift gears and figure out a new plan."

His smile is slow, and, if I'm honest, devastating to my hormones. I can barely believe the thought that keeps bouncing down to tap me on the heart, but I'm almost certain that Henry is into me. I can feel it.

A passing waiter offers us champagne. Henry shakes his head, but I give the man a smile and accept. Having something to sip is a good way to give myself a few extra seconds when I don't know what to say next.

"Where are you staying?" he asks.

"With your parents in the Hamptons until I find my own place. I'm heading back there tomorrow."

He straightens with a satisfied expression. "No one mentioned that to me. It's been a long time since you were at the house."

"If it were up to my mother, I'd still be in LA. But it was time for me to take the leap, if you know what I mean."

He nods. "I absolutely know what you mean."

"What have you been up to for the last five years?"

"Work," he says.

I nod and wait for him to expound. When he says nothing, I nod again, take a sip of champagne, and glance around the ballroom as I try to think of another question that's slightly more specific.

When I look back at his face, dawning awareness lights his features, and Henry tips his chin down and says, almost triumphantly, "I've also taken violin lessons and a cooking class."

My face breaks into a wide smile. "Cool."

He adjusts his glasses and shakes his head. "The violin isn't going particularly well. I like cooking when I have the time, though."

When I laugh, he frowns in apparent confusion.

"Sorry. It's just that you're good at everything you do. It makes you seem more human to imagine you struggling with the violin."

His frown only deepens. "You see me as inhuman?"

"Not at all. But you've always seemed bigger than life to me. Above things like struggle or failure."

His eyebrows lift. "That's an inaccurate perception."

"It's the nature of hero worship, I guess. It lacks nuance."

"I'm not a hero."

I dip my chin in acknowledgment of his words, but I refuse to agree with him.

When we were kids, I'd told Henry everything that made me smile and made me cry. I imagined myself carrying a shield into my "adventures," and that shield, more often than not, was the sound of Henry's voice in my head saying, *"You're a warrior, remember?"* When I became a teenager, Henry's voice in my head also became the occasional *"Fuck 'em, Franki."* He was my hero.

For Henry's part, he told me things about himself that I wasn't supposed to know. Never details of specific missions, but enough for me to come to a general understanding. That, alone, would have been enough for me to admire him, but, of course, there was more. His kindness. His resilience. Even the unique way his mind works.

I shift my weight and wiggle my toes.

He glances down at my feet, then back up to my face. "You're in pain. The wedding photos are complete. What would you say to ditching this place and finding somewhere a little quieter to talk? We could go to my place. You've never seen my penthouse. I think you'd like it."

I hesitate, not because I'm going to say no, but because I'm trying to work out logistics in my head.

"I'll cook for you," he coaxes.

"It might be easier to stay here at the hotel and order room service. Oliver is upstairs with a sitter, and I can't leave him alone for very long."

Henry smiles. "You brought him with you."

Charlotte and Arden have done enough by allowing me to stay with them. I wasn't about to ask them to babysit my dog when I wasn't there. "I take him pretty much everywhere. My mother nearly had a stroke when she realized you gave me a dog, but he was the best thing that could have happened to me."

"Good."

"I should warn you, he might be a little territorial. He's well-trained, and his behavior is perfect in every other way, but he gets really protective when men come near me."

Henry's lips twitch and something that looks bizarrely like satisfaction lights his eyes, but all he says is, "Lead the way."

Five

Henry

Eight | Sleeping at Last

F RANKI SHAKES HER HEAD as she shifts in her chair and looks down at Oliver where he sits near her feet. "I can't believe how well he's behaving with you. He doesn't normally let men get near me."

I slide my foot slightly closer to Franki under the small room-service table in her hotel room, lean down, and give him a scratch behind his ear. Oliver thumps his tail. "He probably remembers me from when I trained him as a puppy."

She was in a boarding school surrounded by haters, and I wanted to give her an animal that would double as a guard dog. But, she found Oliver at a shelter and fell in love. I'd been fully prepared to bully or bribe the school administrators to allow Franki to keep him with her. Instead, her mother showed up for her winter break and took her away at the end of it.

I straighten, move my place setting aside, and take a sip of water. Clear my throat. Tap my finger against my water glass. "We've known each other a long time."

She props her elbow on the table and puts her chin in her hand. "We have."

Franki smiles like she knows all my secrets. Her eyelashes flutter over warm, dark amber eyes, and my heart rate picks up for no reason, whatsoever. I take another sip of water. I can't think when she's looking at me like this. "You and I each have something the other needs."

Her eyebrows lift. "Interesting way to put it."

"You've placed your education on hold for financial reasons. You have nowhere to live, and no job. I can take care of your financial issues, in exchange for . . . a favor."

Her brows lower slowly, her body shifting with apparent discomfort or embarrassment.

I lift my glasses and rub my eyes. "That's not what I....Not sexual favors. Unless you wanted...."

She glares, and I snap my mouth shut.

"Allow me to start over. My grandmother is in possession of a company that I would like to acquire. In exchange for the company, she has asked me to find a suitable wife by no later than November 14th."

"That's insane."

"Nonetheless. I want that company, and you want to complete your education. I believe the two of us could come to an amicable agreement mutually beneficial for both parties. I can offer you a home, and, in addition to generous financial compensation, I'm more than happy to pay for you to complete your education."

Oliver lifts his head to huff at me in annoyance.

At Franki's silence, I straighten my cuffs, then hold eye contact with her. I've been fidgeting like a rank amateur. I know better.

"Let me see if I understand this. You're asking me to *marry* you?" Franki's palms flatten on the table. Her voice is sweet and soft, as always, but she sounds...unimpressed.

"Yes."

"We haven't seen each other in five years."

"Four years, nine months." *And twelve days.* "You're the same person. Time is irrelevant. I know the core of your character; I don't need to have *spoken* with you."

She shakes her head.

"You disagree?"

"You're not the same person, and neither am I. The last time I spoke with you, you wanted to teach astrophysics, not be some business tycoon. You didn't want anything to do with your grandfather's companies."

"And then I grew up. I have responsibilities. There are things only I can do for this family. They need me."

"I see." She looks down at my hand where it rests on the table. Runs her thumb over the silvery scar above my ring finger, then releases me and leans back. "You'd have been a wonderful teacher. You were the only person who could make calculus make sense for me."

I remember. Hours spent at my parents' kitchen island while she gamely worked on equations that she claimed were utterly incomprehensible. She never gave up until she understood. Franki is brilliant, intuitive, and far smarter than I am in many respects, including emotional intelligence, but math and science never came easily to her.

"My PhD was an indulgence. My parents didn't want to burst my bubble. I was never doing anything else with my life than what I'm doing now. Teaching is a goal for someone who believes in humanity. I no longer do."

At that, my future wife's brows furrow with obvious sympathy. "That's sad."

I don't need or want anyone's pity, especially Franki's. "It's not *sad* that I'm realistic about what is worth the investment of my time and effort."

She makes a *"pfft"* sound and shakes her head. "Why has your grandmother given you such a short timeline? That's not long enough for you to meet someone and fall in love."

"She gave me a year. I was seeking an alternate solution until it became obvious that a wedding was my only option."

"Then you'll have to start dating if you need a wife to get your hands on those shares," she says.

"Absolutely not. Have you tried it? Talking to people you don't know about things you aren't interested in but are supposed to pretend you are. I'm not doing that. It's annoying."

She taps her fingers on the table. "It isn't worth the investment of your time and effort."

I'd grown impatient and abandoned my plan to wait until tomorrow, but jumping to the proposal too soon was clearly a tactical error. I clear my throat and attempt to salvage these negotiations. "A stranger doesn't meet my requirements for loyalty and permanence. While you don't know details, you're already aware that, in addition to my companies, I have other *unconventional responsibilities.* You're a minimal security risk since you've already proven your loyalty to me."

I shared things with her in the past that, according to my father, I shouldn't have. But I'd known, even then, that she'd never betray us.

"How romantic."

I frown.

She frowns back.

"I'm not talking about romance. I'm discussing marriage."

"No thank you."

"You like me," I say slowly.

Her eye twitches. "Usually."

"I would provide you with a comfortable life."

"I'll make my own comfortable life. It'll just take me a little longer."

"You wanted a job. You could consider it employment if you prefer. You can have your own bedroom. You'd essentially be paid to live in my home, wear my ring, and occasionally be available when I need you."

She covers her eyes with her hand briefly before dropping it and saying, "I'm sure you wouldn't be deliberately cruel, but you're asking me to live my life for another person. I already did that with my mother."

"It's not living for another person." I gesture with two hands to make my next point. "It's you living your life. Me living mine." I bring my palms together, nearly touching. "Next to each other."

She shakes her head.

"I like you. I know that I'm not an emotional or romantic man, but I do know how to make money. I can provide things that will make you content."

"In exchange for me providing a service."

"Yes." Spencer would never have found anyone else I deemed acceptable. And when he finally worked his way through my list of acquaintances, he'd have found Franki. I'd have had a legitimate excuse to explain why I'd tracked her down before she was ready to come home.

She's here now. It didn't come to that.

Come to think of it. I pull my phone from my pocket and add **Franki Lennox** to my list of requirements, then put the phone back in my pocket. *She* is the primary requirement.

"What was that?" she asks.

"Hmm?" I assume an innocent expression.

"You just typed my name on something that looked like a list."

I recall Gabriel and Dante's less-than-positive reactions to my criteria. The way they compared my future wife to a golden retriever. This list is going to get me in trouble. I can feel it all the way down to the soles of my shoes. And yet, I can't bring myself to lie to her. "I created a list of requirements for my future wife. You meet every criteria. Additionally, I like you, I trust you, and I could sleep with you."

I can't imagine any woman I'd permit to be near me when I was vulnerable like that. Except for her.

I've never seen Franki's face go hard before this moment. I've fucked up these negotiations. Took a wrong turn.

Dammit, I should have stayed focused on what was in it for her. That was a rookie error. My only excuse is that I'm clearly coming down with something. My heart is racing and sweat prickles under my arms.

Franki's reactions aren't what I thought they'd be. There are years of her life I only know about peripherally. She's not the same girl, after all, who stood on the library balcony with stars in her eyes and told me someday she'd be back. She'd said, *"You could wait for me."*

I rub my aching sternum. The reports on her indicated she hasn't had a single boyfriend. I thought when she responded to me so enthusiastically downstairs and told me she was back to stay . . . she'd come back for me.

My family reminds me often that I have an over-developed ego. Clearly, that was the case here, but I'm not ready to let this go. "You should know I'd have no expectation of sex unless it was something you were interested in pursuing."

I can only interpret the look on her face as *"You have to be joking."*

A strange burn lodges in my throat, so I reach for my water glass. Ice clinks as I sip and give her time to formulate her response.

Finished with her meal, Franki lifts Oliver onto her lap. As she rubs his back, he cuddles into her, resting his chin on her shoulder like a baby. His tail goes *thwack, thwack, thwack* against the edge of the white tablecloth.

"Thank you for a lovely dinner and your proposal. I'm afraid, unfortunately, that I have to decline," she says gently.

"What would it take for you to say you *will* marry me?"

Though her voice is soft, I detect some underlying emotion that I don't recognize. "I'm not interested in a business arrangement or being the person you chose because I was the easiest option."

She scratches Oliver behind his ears. "I've never been anyone's priority in my life. That's fine, but I won't sign up for a marriage custom-designed to remind me of that fact. It's better to be alone."

Marriage will demand a great deal more of my time than I initially planned for. The thought is strangely satisfying. I'll strike **doesn't like too much attention** from the list. Later. When I'm not here for her to see it. "I can add you to my itinerary and make you one of my priorities. It's a fair compromise. I have certain responsibilities that will always come first, but I'm willing to make reasonable adjustments. You're my first choice of a wife. Does it follow that I value you less simply because you're also the most convenient option?"

"Here's a hint: the next woman you ask this question to, leave off the 'convenient option.' It makes me want to stab you with a fork," she says, gentle exasperation in her tone.

Since she has, in no way, moved toward her cutlery, it's clear her threat is an empty one. I lean back in my chair. "You need romance and emotional investment."

"To accept a marriage proposal? Yes, I do. From both parties," she says, voice sweet, but firm.

Tapping my finger on the table, I look away from her and around the hotel room as I formulate my thoughts and consider my next steps. By all common sense and reason, I should cross her name off the list and look for someone else, but the thought of walking away from her creates a sensation I can only describe as claustrophobia rising in my chest. Franki is the only person I find remotely suitable for the position. She *will* be my wife. If she needs a romantic relationship, then I have to learn how to give her that.

I rise. "I understand."

Franki joins me.

Methodically, I unroll and button my cuffs. Then I walk across the room and reach for my tuxedo jacket where I'd draped it over the end of her bed. Shrugging it on, I turn back to her. "I'll be visiting my sister tomorrow. I'll give you a ride back to the house. There's no need to take two vehicles or inconvenience one of my parents' drivers."

"Oh. I wouldn't want to inconvenience your parents. I can take a taxi." Her lips press together, and she looks away in clear distress.

I attempt reassurance. "It's no problem at all for me to do it. I'm already heading in that direction. We may as well carpool. I'll pick you up at nine sharp. I also have an employment opportunity to discuss with you on the drive if you're interested. Specifically, I'm in need of a translator. It's a full-time, salaried position with benefits. Your hours would be flexible. There may be some travel involved."

I'm literally making this up as I go, but if I have to buy a company in Germany or France to give Franki a job and keep her close to me, then that's what I'll do.

Her dark eyes flare with a glint of excitement and maybe a hint of distrust. "Really?"

"Yes. Nice little coincidence there for both of us. Serendipitous, I think you'd call it." I don't like how financially vulnerable she seems to be at the moment. I would never coerce her or manipulate her, but someone could. She'd refuse a handout or offer of financial assistance. A job, on the other hand, will go a long way to shoring up her resources. She's always been a great student. No doubt she'll be just as dedicated in a professional capacity.

"It would make me breathe a little easier, I'll admit. I was concerned about losing my health insurance," she says.

What the fuck have her parents been doing that she doesn't have health insurance? I've never liked Guinevere Jones or Jonny Lennox, but for two overtly wealthy people to refuse to help their own child with her education or healthcare is despicable. Particularly when that daughter has multiple serious health issues. My last report on her was three weeks ago, so whatever happened with Franki and her parents is recent.

With Oliver close at her heels, Franki walks to the heavy, black-painted hotel door, and I follow, accepting her cue for what it is: a request for me to leave.

I don't want to cross that threshold, but strategy is everything. Ignoring the suspicious glint in Oliver's doggy eyes, I bend close to press my lips to her cheek. Smooth warmth. The faintest sweet scent. I have the strange desire to nuzzle against her and breathe her in. To simply live in this moment for the rest of my life. When she doesn't pull away, I linger, absorbing her closeness.

This is an echo, or maybe a mirror, of that last night before she left.

"Will you come back?"

"Yes. I promise. This is just while I finish school." Franki looks down at her new puppy where he gnaws noisily on a stuffed toy. She takes a deep breath before looking into my eyes and stretching up to kiss my mouth.

I turn my head to give her my cheek. She stays, pressing against my skin for a long moment, as I stand with my hands raised in surrender so I don't touch her. After long, too- tempting moments with her sweet lips pressed to my skin, I step back.

"I can't, Franki." It's not appropriate. She's eighteen to my twenty-two, but hasn't graduated from high school, yet.

"You could wait for me."

I'll wait for eternity. "I'm not going anywhere. I'll be right here."

Now, I'm the one with my lips on her, and I wait for her to step away. She's twenty-three now. Older than I was that night. Eighteen-year-old Franki would have jumped at my proposal and accepted anything I gave her. It was part of why it would have been so wrong. This Franki wants to stab me with a fork for my audacity.

She wraps her arms around me beneath my jacket and leans into me. I reach my own around her, tugging her close, my right hand splayed flat against the silky warmth of her lower back. I slide the fingertips of my left hand up, then down, over the exposed skin at the nape of her neck, and her flesh erupts with goose bumps. The sheer intimacy of it has me forgetting to breathe.

I refuse to be the one to pull away this time. Instead, I move my lips up to speak against her temple. "I missed you, Franki."

"I miss you too," she whispers. *"Miss you,"* not *"missed."* The difference feels significant.

She backs away, and the loss of her arms around me leaves me cold and hollow once more.

She smiles, but her eyebrows are furrowed in a way that indicates sadness. "Still friends?"

"Of course." Determination made of pure steel settles inside me. I have time to fix this and secure my wife before Grandmother's ultimatum comes to fruition. "Until tomorrow, Franki."

Six

Franki

Achilles Come Down | Gang of Youths

I juggle my key card, purse, leash, and rolling luggage as I escort Oliver from my hotel room with a half hour to spare for Henry's nine a.m. pickup time. Backing up, I nearly run into a housekeeper's cart and turn with an apologetic smile. "Sorry."

The housekeeper, a woman with dark hair highlighted with natural silver and scraped back into a tight bun, looks my way. "No problem."

"I—Oh my gosh. *Nanny*?" I stare in joy and confusion when I finally look into her eyes.

Her own brown eyes widen as she takes me in. After a moment, her shoulders lower, and she asks tentatively, "Franki?"

"Yes!" I reach to hug her, and she folds me into her arms, hugging me back fiercely. "Oh, my girl. How have you been?"

"How have you been?"

We ask the question at the same time, then both laugh.

I don't want to come right out and ask her why she's working in housekeeping rather than in childcare. Maybe it's a side gig or she became burned out. It's not my place to intrude.

She smiles. "I'm hanging in there. Look at you, all grown up."

"It's nuts how that happens, huh?" I grin. "Things are good for me. I tried to find you on social media when I got older, but I couldn't remember your last name and 'Nanny Lisa' didn't help." I laugh.

She puts her hand on my cheek. "It's Bedford. Lisa Bedford, honey, but . . . I don't use social media. You don't need to bother looking me up."

She pulls her hand back and glances behind me, looking for something. "Are you here alone?"

"I have Oliver."

She leans down to pat him. "He's a cutie."

Oliver yips, and I crouch beside him, looking up at Nanny Lisa. "Would you let me take you to lunch sometime? I'd love to catch up."

She hesitates. "It won't cause problems with you and your mother?"

I shake my head. "Whatever went on with you and my father is ancient history and none of my business. She's on the West Coast, anyway."

Lisa grimaces and huffs. "Nothing went on with me and your father."

We both straighten, and I try to make sense of her words. "Mom said you and Jonny—"

At Lisa's look of distaste, I stop short. "Mom fired you because she was jealous about something that didn't even happen? That's horrible."

"Your father had nothing to do with it."

The look she gives me is weighted, as though she wants me to connect the dots. When I can only shake my head in confusion, she gives me a sad smile. "Honey, she was jealous of my relationship with you. She was gone for six months at a time on location. The last time she came home, she accused me of trying to steal you from her. She told anyone who would listen I told you to call me 'Mommy,' and I was pretending to be your mother."

I stare at her in open-mouthed shock. "How could she do that?"

"I suppose she felt insecure because you appeared to be more attached to me than to her. Guinevere never seemed able to stand other people's happiness." She cringes. "I shouldn't have said that. The truth is, I don't know why she did it."

The original shock of her statement fades quickly. The only thing truly surprising about what she said is that she managed to stay employed as my nanny for eight years. Mom cycles through employees faster than the recommended time between dental cleanings. *"Difficult to get along with"* is an understatement. She's very good at convincing herself that she's been wronged, like the way she accused me of stealing from her. "I'm so sorry she took out her insecurities on you."

"I'm not worried about me. That phase of my life is over. How've you been? That's the important part."

"I'm"—I shake my head—"great. I'm great. Just moved back and excited to find a new job and a place to stay."

Lisa smiles. "You look good."

I glance down at myself ruefully. She's being kind. When Henry left last night after his horrible marriage proposal, I moped around for half an hour. Then I went downstairs to the gift shop, bought twenty dollars worth of chocolate, which was, sadly, hardly any chocolate at all, took it up to my room, and ate every last bit of it while watching a documentary on the Tudors. After which, I tossed and turned and rehashed every word Henry said in my head all night long.

He's changed, and it breaks my heart. All his enthusiasm, his idealism, his softness....It's all gone, buried under the weight of living for other people. Does his family recognize what's happened to him? He's given up every one of his dreams *for them*. Do they even appreciate the sacrifices he's made? Did it occur so gradually they didn't notice? Bronwyn never said a word.

Henry's grandmother demanded a marriage, and he disliked the idea so much that he put it off for eleven months, as he attempted to find a way out of it. He's as trapped by his family's expectations as I was with my mother. Marrying me....Marrying *anyone* isn't the answer.

I understand his thought process. He's attempting to control his situation with logic. But the old Henry wanted so much more for his life, and he wanted more for me.

I woke with dark circles under my eyes this morning, and, too exhausted to bother with makeup, I didn't put a single swipe of mascara on, let alone concealer. I covered my head in a Yankees ball cap and put tortoiseshell frame glasses on my nose. My clothing today is baggy and comfortable: Black drawstring pants and a soft long-sleeved white T-shirt with an oatmeal-colored cardigan thrown on top. A pair of sneakers with my two-inch lift tucked inside are on my feet. A simple compression brace hugs my left knee, out of sight but providing support.

I glance at my phone. "I'm so sorry, but my ride is going to bring his car around any minute. I need to check out, but I would love to keep in touch. If you'd rather put everything behind you and forget about me, I totally under—"

"Don't be silly. Franki, I grieved over you. Worried over you. Give me your phone. I'll put my number in, and you call me."

"I'm taking running into you like this as a sign of all the good things that are in store. If I were still in California, this wouldn't have happened. If I hadn't said yes to being a bridesmaid, I wouldn't have been in this hotel this morning."

She smiles. "Always my sunshine girl. I'm glad to see you've held onto your optimism."

I pass her my phone. Oliver twists in a circle, and the leash tangles with his legs, so I bend to help him while Lisa adds her information to my contacts. When I straighten, she passes it back with a smile. "Call me or text me anytime. We could have dinner? I'll cook your favorite."

The corners of my mouth lift. "Mac and cheese with dino nuggets?"

She laughs. "I was thinking spaghetti and meatballs, but I could pick up a bag of frozen nuggets."

"I'll be in touch soon. It was great to see you."

"You too." She looks behind me down the corridor. "You better go now while there's not much of a wait for the elevators."

She's right that I'm going to be late if I don't hurry. Traffic on Park Avenue is always a nightmare. It would be beyond rude to keep anyone who took the time to pick me up waiting, but I hug her one more time anyway.

By the time Oliver and I make it to the lobby and complete checkout, I have less than ten minutes until Henry's scheduled arrival. Oliver and I move to stand near the far wall with a clear view of the revolving doors as I wait. The usual Sunday morning crowd mills around the lobby, perfumed air clogging my nose. I'm anxious to head back toward Long Island, but butterflies dance in my belly too.

This first meeting with Henry is going to be awkward, without a doubt. Last night, I finally managed to drift off to sleep around three in the morning, then woke to our photos plastered all over the internet. Someone took pictures of us at the wedding. In one of them, Henry is looking at me in exactly the way that had me convinced he wanted me. Seeing it and the comments about "Henry McRae in love" was vindicating, at least. I'm not the only person who thought he was giving me heart eyes. But nope. He was giving me "I want a company, and you're just the woman who'll help me get it" eyes.

There were other photos as well. One with his arm around me. Several of him escorting me with a hand on my hip to the elevators to go up to my room. I wasn't the big news. It was Henry, the so-called "Prince of New York," who has never been seen in a relationship. It took no time at all for people to figure out who I was, though.

Oliver, on a leash and wearing a black bow tie, sits patiently between my feet and our luggage, and I bend to give him a treat from my pocket for behaving so nicely in public.

If Bronwyn, Janessa, Sydney, or Clarissa see any of those photos before I text them about it, they'll start a group chat with questions, but I wasn't ready to talk last night, and I haven't had time to give them a heads up this morning. When my phone vibrates, I straighten to take it from my pocket. I may have no choice in the matter.

On the other hand, it's a far better option than if it's my mother calling. She's the last person I want to talk to right now. If it's her and I don't answer before Henry gets here, she'll call me over and over, until I pick up. I won't mention seeing Lisa to her. The last thing I need is to give her one more thing to rant about.

When the contact shows my father's name, rather than my mother's, I blow out a breath in relief. *Finally*.

I lift the phone to my ear and move further against the wall, turning to give my back to the lobby. "Jonny, how are you?"

He chuckles. "I'm fine, sweetheart. I've been really busy. You know how it is. I'm sure you've heard that I've added a home decor line to my brand."

"Someone from your office told me you were in Paris?"

"I arrived back in New York three days ago, but I'm swamped."

I'd called again yesterday and was told he wasn't even in the country. "I'm in New York too. I thought we could meet. For lunch. Or, if you don't have time for that, maybe coffee. If you can't leave work, I could stop by your office for a few minutes to say hi sometime this week or next week. It's been a while." Fourteen months since I spoke with him last.

"I don't have time this week or next, but if you'll still be in the city in six weeks, I'm having a party. I'll have my assistant send you the information."

"That sounds nice."

"It'll be good to see you, kid. I'll send you a dress to wear from my new collection."

No matter how many times I tell myself it doesn't matter that he isn't interested in me and tries to fob me off with trips, haute couture, and cash, every interaction with him turns me into an eight-year-old. "Thanks."

"I have a little favor to ask of you." He laughs. "Actually, it's more of a favor for yourself."

"Really?"

"I have a business associate named Leo Kingston. You've heard of Kingston Hotels. He's interested in commissioning my decor line for his luxury hotels. Worldwide. It'll be a spectacular launch of my brand."

"That sounds amazing."

"You know what else is amazing? He saw your photo online and asked for your phone number. Your mother is a bitch, but there's no denying she's beautiful. You've got her bone structure, and you've grown out of your awkward teenage years. You're Guinevere Jones if she were twenty-four years younger, had a natural body, and a decent personality."

Ick. "I don't want to be rude, but I'm really uncomfortable with this."

"How can you be uncomfortable? You haven't even spoken with him to know if you'll hit it off or not. He's good looking. Just meet the man. For me."

"If Leo Kingston wants your new home decor stuff, that's great. Going out with me shouldn't have anything to do with it. Leave me out of it."

Jonny heaves an impatient breath. "Why are you making such a big deal about giving the man a little attention?"

Oh, the irony. "Because I have zero interest in going out with some random guy whose only interest is based on seeing my photo online."

"What can it hurt? It's not healthy the way you insulate yourself. Always with your nose in a book. You need to get out more. You'll have fun," he cajoles.

A huff of laughter leaves me. "No I won't." There's not a question in my mind. "I don't even believe Leo Kingston is his real name. It sounds fake. He's basically calling himself 'Lion King.' I'm not interested."

"A lot of people use pseudonyms to create their brands. Everything works together to create an impression. An image. Don't judge the man for making a smart business move," Jonny soothes. "You should be salivating at this opportunity. He'll be in New York in a few weeks, and I *told* him you'd entertain him."

My lips tighten. "You can't speak for me and expect me to go along with it." I'm trying to keep my voice down. The last thing I need is for someone to hear any of this conversation and spread it around.

"You've grown into a beautiful young woman. Now a man who owns some of the most spectacular hotels in the world wants to take you out. I'm not asking you to sleep with him. Just give the guy a chance." He's speaking to me as if I'm a child who won't eat her broccoli, his voice equal parts exasperation and coaxing. As if the man were ever around to try to get me to eat anything.

Jonny is a shitty father. He always has been, but some part of me has always wanted to please him. When he smiles and gives me a hint of approval or remembers my birthday, it's this unreasonable high. It makes no sense. I've always felt as though, if I make him proud enough, he'll love me. But I'm not a child any longer. "I'm not doing it."

"If you do and he signs those contracts, I'll pay for you to finish school and put you on my health insurance."

What is wrong with people? He's the third person in twenty-four hours to attempt to buy me. The fact that he hadn't mentioned a thing about school or me needing insurance before now, either, irks the crap out of me. He obviously got my messages. He ignored them until now when he thinks he can leverage the information against me. "That bribe didn't work with Mom either. I said, '*no*.'"

"He's calling. You're going." He bites out the words as he loses control of his temper.

"You're a terrible person." I've reached my limit. My reaction is cumulative frustration after speaking with Lisa. Jonny could have defended her. He could have stepped in, but he didn't because it wasn't something he cared about. Both of my parents are blending in a toxic miasma of assholery in my mind right now.

He scoffs. "I'm a terrible person because I want my daughter to do something other than talk about dead people? I've provided financial support for you for years. I'm asking for one thing, which you will enjoy once you've done it. And you think *I'm* unreasonable? When you've gone out with the man and the contracts are signed, I'll pay for your graduate school." *Beep beep beep.*

I pull the phone away from my ear and stare at the glossy screen after he hangs up. Is there a point when being emotionally blindsided becomes so commonplace that I'll become numb to it?

I swivel to face the lobby and pocket my phone. I shouldn't have turned my back to people in the first place. I'd only done it because Jonny's call distracted me so much that I forgot to practice situational awareness. It's not safe to be oblivious to what's going on around me in a place like this.

I'll let Leo Kingston's call go to voicemail. Maybe he'll text, and I can text back **"New phone. Who dis?"** My father's calls, if he even makes them, can go to voicemail too. It's what he's done to me all my life.

Hands shaking, I tighten my ponytail under my cap and adjust my glasses. I can't help but draw an uncomfortable parallel between Jonny's request for me to date his colleague in exchange for his financial assistance and Henry presenting marriage as a job.

Logically, I understand that no one is perfect, but in my mind, Henry *was*. I hero-worshipped him, and maybe he's right that I hadn't seen him accurately, but even the fact that he didn't let me kiss him that night was something to admire and celebrate. Henry was *noble*.

I barely recognized the man who sat across the table from me in my hotel room. When he hugged me at the door, for me, it wasn't "good night." It was "goodbye" to the person I lost.

My attention catches on Henry as he pushes through the revolving door. He always walks as though he has somewhere important to be. It doesn't matter if he's headed to the kitchen or the beach or a meeting. The only time I've seen him not do that is when he matches his pace to walk beside me.

Dressed more casually today, he wears black trousers and a tan sweater-vest over a white button-down. Today's glasses frames are black. He heads directly for me, his long stride ground-eating, his expression intent.

Somehow, Henry and I coordinate with each other today, as if we stood side-by-side in front of our shared closet and said, *"Let's dress like we belong together."* Stuff like that used to happen with us all the time, and neither of us could explain it. We were both "in the mood" for a certain color on that day.

He stops approximately three feet away and dips his head. "Hello, Franki. Hello, Oliver."

My lips twitch without my consent. He doesn't talk to Oliver like he's a dog. Nope. It's a dip of his head and a "hello." That hasn't changed, at least.

"Are you ready?" he asks.

I give him a thumbs up. "Ready Freddy—"

"—Steady," he finishes with me.

A couple of men, probably in their mid-twenties, stand nearby, dressed casually and checking their phones. One nudges the other, and they both zero in on me, then look back at each other.

Shit. Shit. Shit. No one was supposed to notice me. Why do people do this? I don't even have the same color eyes she does.

One of them, trailed closely by the other, approaches and says, "Are you . . .?"

I shake my head. The two men continue to move in my direction, and I take a step back. Oliver snarls.

"From a distance, you look just like her," the blond says.

The other guy laughs. "Dollar Store Guinevere Jones."

Oliver bares his teeth aggressively, but they ignore him. When they get within five feet, I take another step backward, even as I paste on my smile and prepare to tell them I have somewhere I need to be. Before I get the chance, the men's faces grow pale and they scramble away.

Henry stalks toward them even more aggressively than they'd moved in on me, and they scurry backward across the lobby. Their eyes widen as they shake their heads and put their hands up in a show of surrender. With his back toward me, I can't hear a word Henry says or see his face, but the men look terrified. Sure, Henry has an umpteenbillion degree black belt in at least three different martial arts disciplines. The whole McRae family does, but these guys don't know that.

They look like they're running away from a sweater-vest-wearing astronomy professor.

"We're sorry, ma'am. We're leaving you alone now. We respect your privacy," the one with the patchy beard calls.

"Sorry!" the blond shouts. "You're not the dollar store version of someone else. You're . . . er . . . Gucci . . . of . . . yourself."

This time I hear Henry's voice. "Now, run away."

They virtually run for the lobby doors.

Henry turns toward me, and his familiar disgruntled expression settles something inside me. Last night at dinner, his eyes were cold enough to make me shiver. Anger may not be the most comfortable emotion, but it's real. Under the circumstances, it's reasonable. This is the expression of the same kid who once asked if someone hurt me, because if they did, he'd do something about it.

Tension leeches from his shoulders when he returns to me.

"What did you say to them?" I ask curiously.

"I told them to apologize to you or I would . . ." he runs a hand through his hair, then admits, " . . . surgically remove their tongues without anesthesia."

I can't keep the disbelief out of my voice. "They looked like they *believed* you."

He huffs a laugh, his eyes crinkling at the corners, and picks up my luggage. With a palm on my lower back, he guides me to the revolving front door. "Let's get out of here."

Oliver gives Henry side-eye and one incongruously deep bark before he patters beside me, nose in the air, head bopping side to side.

Henry's SUV waits directly in front of the hotel, blinkers on, and a man stands beside it. I recognize the posture and the black suit of a McRae bodyguard from my years spent with them. Henry opens the door for me, himself. No chauffeur in sight.

"Oliver's car seat is in my suitcase."

He stops and eyes Oliver. Then he glances back at me. "Of course. The main compartment?"

"Yes, but I'll—"

Henry has already unzipped my bag and reached inside for Oliver's fleecy, blue car bed. As he drags it out, I cringe as stretchy lace in a variety of colors clings to the fleece.

The two fabrics together create a staticky combination.

Henry's face is utterly blank as he takes in the sight of Oliver's lingerie-covered bed.

Heat starts somewhere around my belly button and shoots all the way up and out the top of my head.

I make a grab for the bed. Before I manage to get ahold of it, Henry pulls a scrap of lace off the fleece. A zap of visible electricity sparks, and the lace clings as he lifts it between two fingers and his thumb.

I see the exact second Henry realizes what he's holding in his hand. His face goes so red that between his white shirt and blue eyes, he looks positively patriotic.

Henry blinks. "Panties."

I hiss, "Don't say 'panties.' I don't like that word."

His eyebrows lift. "What word do you prefer?"

I snatch the other two pairs off the dog bed. "Just call them underwear," I mutter under my breath.

Face still red, his fist clenched around the fabric in his hand, he says, "These are not underwear. If you want to see underwear, I'll show you underwear. They're made out of cotton. And they are white. Sometimes, they are black or navy. They are not . . . not . . ."

He waves the scrap of red lace in the damn street, and I shoot a concerned glance around to be sure no one has a camera out.

"These are panties, Franki," he whispers.

"Call them what you want, then. But stop waving them around. Put them away and let's go."

He nods brusquely. "Put them away," he repeats. *Then he shoves my underwear in his pocket.*

"Henry?"

He runs a hand through his mop of hair. "Yes?"

I planned to tell him to take my underwear out of his pocket and put them in the suitcase where they belong. But he's so embarrassed, and so am I.

If I tell him what he did, it'll just prolong it.

And he's my Henry. We've both been through things, and he's clearly struggling. But this flustered man in the sweater-vest *is* my friend. I saw it in the way he spoke to Oliver. In the way he smiled with his eyes, not just his mouth. The way he defended me so ferociously, and, yes, in his flustered reaction to my underwear. He's still in there. He may be buried, but he's not dead. Not gone. He needs someone in his corner who *sees* him. No matter how frustrated and angry his proposal made me.

So, I don't tell him he put my underwear in his pocket. He'll figure it out sooner or later.

Instead, I say, "Let me strap Oliver's car bed in, and we can get on our way."

Seven

Henry

In the Beginning | Fahrenhaidt, Alice Merton

I zip up the suitcase and stow it in the back while Franki stuffs the panties from the dog bed into her purse and pulls out Oliver's harness.

Stop thinking about her panties.

As I move around to stand behind her, Franki straps the car bed into the backseat and lifts Oliver into it. He wiggles his butt, sighs dolefully, then rests his head on the edge of the collapsible box-like structure, watching me the entire time with what I can only describe as an "I've got my eye on you" glare. I dip my head in acknowledgment. Oliver's hackles aren't up, but he's clearly disgruntled, viewing me as competition for Franki's attention. Smart dog.

"Good boy. Play with your toys," she says.

He huffs, then obeys, snuggling a stuffed toy hot dog like it's his own child.

When we're all settled into our seats, I check my mirrors and pull out into traffic. Beside me, Franki sighs and kicks off her shoes. We have more than an hour's drive before we get to the Hamptons, which gives us time to talk.

"Can you turn my seat warmer on?" she asks.

Reaching for the button, I click it and glance at her in concern. "Are you cold?"

The weather is mild today. No jackets necessary.

She shakes her head. "No. Just a little achey."

"Heat helps?"

"Sometimes." Franki sinks back into her seat.

As I navigate the congested streets, I take the time to simply enjoy sitting beside her. I've always found Franki an unusually peaceful person to be around, and today is no different.

Her panties didn't have me feeling peace.

Tightening my hands on the steering wheel, I try to think of something else. The last thing I need right now is to start obsessing over those tiny lace—*Stop*. I swear to God, if I get an erection right now, I will . . . do literally nothing except hope I don't embarrass her.

I want to know every single thing that's happened to her in the years she's been gone. I don't ask, though. I know better. She always preferred quiet when she closed her eyes with that look on her face.

Fifteen minutes of quiet introspection later, and Oliver's snoring becomes soothing background noise that offsets the muffled cacophony of traffic.

Franki turns her head in my direction and says, "You recognized me yesterday."

I shoot a quick glance her way. "You think I wouldn't know you because you took your glasses off?"

She watches me like she's trying to figure me out. "It's a little more than that. Even Gabriel didn't recognize me."

"My brother was on at least his third drink, and you took him by surprise. If he'd seen you somewhere with Bronwyn, he would have recognized you sooner, but you were out of context for him."

"But not you?"

"I can't imagine you ever being out of context for me. You don't look like a different person. Your eyes are the same. So is your smile."

Her brows draw together. "My smile is completely different."

"You mean your teeth? I suppose so. I meant"—I make a vague gesture to her face—"the way you light up. The way your face holds happiness."

I indicate her left arm. "May I?"

She holds her hand out to me, and I rub my thumb over the familiar, small, raised freckle on her pinkie finger.

She blinks rapidly, her brows lifted in the center.

"Franki, I would know you in absolute darkness by the touch of your hand."

Twenty minutes of quiet conversation later, I flip on my windshield wipers as the occasional raindrop gives way to a blustery October drizzle. "Bronwyn's husband ended up building the thing a house made of sticks."

"I can't believe Dean let his toddler keep an earthworm for a pet."

"Keep is an overly generous description. He told her she could visit the worm's stick house outside, but Mr. Worm might be out with his friends when she stopped by."

Franki shakes her head with a smile.

Eye contact is normally a deeply uncomfortable thing for me. I do it because it's a necessary social interaction, but Franki's dark amber eyes hold mine and I *like* it. I only look away at all because I'm driving. I clear my throat. "I think I may owe you an apology. It occurs to me that my proposal last night may have been insensitive."

Her humor subsides. "What makes you say that?"

"Your reaction. I could see that you were disappointed in me. Later, I wondered if I hurt your feelings. If I did, I'm sorry for it."

I don't understand social cues the way most people do, but I've learned to adapt. The truth is I don't know why she would perceive my proposal as insensitive or unkind. I certainly didn't mean it that way, but I've learned to recognize certain body language, facial expressions, and tone to draw conclusions about how other people perceive things. It's an analytical approach, rather than instinctual.

She takes a deep breath. "Would you like me to explain why my feelings were hurt?"

"Yes."

"It felt as though you were telling me I wasn't worth time or attention. That I should accept something so much less than what I want for my life because I wasn't worth your love or the love of any man. You wanted to buy me like I was a product on a shelf instead of a person."

How she can explain the way I hurt her with so much patience, I'll never understand. "I didn't mean it that way. No one deserves happiness or to be loved more than you do. I know you're a person." I rub my chest. I may have to make an appointment to see my doctor and get an EKG. Something is wrong with me.

I look her way. "You weren't just hurt. You were pissed."

Her lips twist. "You're the only person who ever catches on when I'm angry."

Other people hear her sweet voice and make assumptions. I look at a number of data points, including body language, facial expressions, and the pacing and emphasis of people's words.

"If I promise not to propose another business marriage, could we start over?" I ask.

"What would that look like?"

I ponder the question. "I think it would look like us getting to know each other again."

"As long as you understand I'm not marrying you so you can get your hands on a company. It's not happening."

"You made that clear last night. I understand." She'll never marry anyone for mercenary reasons, only emotional ones.

I tap my fingers on the steering wheel. "What's your favorite song?"

She considers for a moment. "I guess right now it's 'Twin Size Mattress' by The Front Bottoms."

"Is that a real song or a joke I'm not understanding?"

"Jokes are only funny when we're both laughing. It's real."

I nod and relax. "My current favorite is 'The Night We Met' by Lord Huron."

"I love that song."

"Good." I smile.

"What's your favorite movie?" she asks.

"I don't watch movies. I watch documentaries. That sort of thing, but I still prefer to read. Mostly nonfiction, but sometimes science fiction."

Her mouth tips up at the corner. "You don't like movies?"

I shake my head. "I haven't watched a movie in"—I grimace—"I can't remember. A lot of years and only then because my mother asked me to."

Her smile grows until it seems to encompass her entire body.

I lift an eyebrow. "Why does that amuse you?"

"It doesn't amuse me. It makes me happy. This sounds terrible, but my mother is so famous for her movies that whenever I meet anyone new, it pretty much ends up the only thing anyone wants to talk about. That's especially true with guys. I couldn't begin to tally up the number of men who have called me my mother's name."

Like those assholes in the lobby. She was afraid of them. That much was clear. I don't make threats in anger, but something hot had roared to life inside me. They were moving too close to her, telegraphing aggression in every word and step. In that moment, kerosene poured onto embers of emotions I'd thought were nothing but cold ash and lit me with fury. Then I'd turned back to Franki and seen *kindness*.

"Women see me, and they see status and money. I'd like to believe it's the least interesting thing about me. Your parentage is certainly the least interesting thing about you."

Her lips twist. "I can't tell if that's an insult or a compliment."

"Always assume I'm complimenting you."

She shakes her head with a little smile.

I smile back. Not the kind where I move my lips because I know I'm in a situation where it's expected, but because there's some light thing inside me that's insisting on exiting my body. Through my face.

"What's your favorite dinner?" she asks.

"Croque Madame and tomato bisque."

She leans toward me. "That's still your favorite?"

"I'm a creature of habit. My favorites don't change. Once I love something, I always do."

"Have you tried pumpkin bisque?"

"I have not."

"It's really good. We should do that. Have pumpkin soup. Us. At the same time." She straightens her spine and nods as if in resolution. "Together."

"We will," I promise, even though the idea of eating soup that reminds me of pie isn't something I'd normally do.

I'm making headway with her, and I haven't even begun my campaign.

Franki reclines back, her shoulders relaxing. "Thank you."

"For pumpkin bisque soup?"

Her next words are so quiet, I almost miss them. "For still being my Henry."

I keep my eyes on the road, unsure how to respond. I'm not the nice kid she used to know. When I finally glance over, Franki's eyes are closed, her features relaxed in slumber. Her oversized cardigan bunches around her; the thin material of her black pants creasing around the outline of her knee brace.

As she shifts in her sleep, a lock of hair slides out of her cap and drops to cover her face on the right side. Reaching out, I smooth it back, unsurprised to find Franki's hair is as soft as her skin. She's turned toward me, weight resting on one hip, long lashes fanning beneath her glasses.

When Franki was eight, she tried to trim them with scissors because she hated the way they bump against her lenses.

She says we don't know each other after all this time.

I can't imagine any woman, let alone someone as sweet as Franki, would want any part of me if she really knew me. *I enjoy long days at my desk and longer nights in Interceptor Body Armor. Oh, by the way, I know hundreds of ways to kill someone. If you need an assassin, I'm your man.*

She has only the vaguest idea of the things I've done. If she ever truly understands, she'll call me a monster too.

Eight

Henry

Wake Me Up | Avicii

A MUG OF EARL Grey tea grows cold at my elbow as I type "How to give a woman an orgasm" in the search bar on my laptop.

If I ever convince Franki to give me a chance, the last thing I need is to turn out to be the worst sex she's ever had. Being a bad lay is the opposite of romantic.

When the patio doors open behind me, I close my laptop with a snap and turn to see who's joined me. Dad, striding out with an unpeeled orange in one hand, lifts the other in surrender. "I didn't see anything."

I'd classify his words as a blatant lie.

I slouch, leaning back in my cushioned wrought iron chair and tip my head back to look at the overcast sky. It's not chilly, and it's no longer raining. The flagstones glisten with a damp sheen, and the brightly colored fall foliage pops dramatically against the dreary gray backdrop. My father is the only person I'd ever speak to about this. And I will. When I'm done procrastinating by staring at the sky.

Once I've admitted to myself that I'm avoiding the subject, I can no longer continue to do so. With a sigh, I sit up straight and take the bull by the horns. "I'd like to speak to you about something in confidence. I need this to stay between the two of us. Personal, not business."

Dad nods, pulls out another of the chairs, takes note of the fact that a staff member put out dry cushions after the rain, and makes himself comfortable. Only after he's settled, does he look my way and say, "Go for it."

"I've never had sex."

Dad, visibly struggling to regulate his expression of surprise, contemplates my words as they hang in the air between us like a leaf caught on the wind. Finally, voice devoid of judgment, he asks, "Why?"

"I didn't want to."

Dad lifts dark eyebrows and drops his chin briefly. "That sounds like a perfectly good reason to me. Do you consider yourself asexual? Demisexual?"

I lift my mug to my lips and finish off the last of it before I admit, "I'm attracted to women sexually, but I refused to allow myself that level of physical vulnerability."

Dad peels his orange. "Do you think it's because it was a woman who nearly killed you when you were a child?"

"Some of it. Trust isn't something I give lightly, and I believed it an unnecessary hurdle to overcome simply for the sake of sexual gratification."

I collect my thoughts, then say, "That was true of my teens into my early twenties, anyway. After that, I was waiting."

"You were waiting for someone you could trust?" Dad asks.

"Yes." When I realize I'm tapping the patio table, I still my hand and repeat, "Yes."

Dad offers me half his orange, and I shake my head.

"Have you found her, or have you decided you no longer want to wait?" he asks.

"It's Franki. I asked her to marry me."

Dad's slice of orange hits the table when he fumbles it on the way to his mouth. He recovers and clears his throat. "You were waiting for *Franki*? That's why you never had relationships?"

"You think that was foolish. To wait almost five years for a specific person."

"Not even a little. I hadn't been with anyone in at least that long when Charlotte and I got together." Dad huffs. "I can't believe it's Franki. I've never seen two people so different from each other as the two of you. That's saying something, considering your sister married Dean."

I frown. "Franki and I are incredibly alike." I could make a list as long as my arm of similarities we share. But maybe Dad is referring to her gentleness. Her optimism. The way she values feelings over practicality.

Dad's mouth quirks, and he leans back in his chair. "In love with Franki Lennox. I never saw that one coming."

I shake my head. "I'm not in love with Franki. I like her and I trust her."

"You waited your entire adult life for her. I don't believe you."

The niggling suspicion that this is going to be even more complicated than I'd imagined when I'd spouted off my list of criteria tickles my conscience, and I actively shove it out of my mind. "She meets all of my requirements for a wife."

"I heard about that list from your brother." Dad leans back in his chair. "None of that is a good enough reason to get married. You marry when you find the right person, not to check a box. Franki is too sweet for what you have planned. If you offer her a business arrangement, she'll be miserable with you."

I'll take it as a compliment it hasn't occurred to Dad that she could . . . did . . . refuse my proposal. "I know she requires romance and emotional investment. I've decided to amend my approach to accommodate her needs."

"Hmmm. But you're not in love?" A breeze ruffles his steel gray hair as Dad watches me intently.

I shake my head.

"It would be best to tell her you changed your mind and avoid any hint of the two of you being near each other. Stay away from the house while she's here. Go out with a few other women in the next couple of weeks."

"I'm not going out with someone else." *Has he paid no attention to a word I'm saying?* "It's Franki or no one." I rise, energy crackling through me.

If I can't win her over, I lose those shares, but I refuse to look for another prospect. Failure isn't an option. I recognize the illogical nature of the choice, even as instinct compels me to make it.

I'll keep my cake and eat it too. The thought immediately segues into a sexually charged picture in my mind. Panties. Or more accurately, what those panties would look like on Franki's body if I pulled them to the side and— *What the hell is wrong with me?!*

I move to the edge of the patio and reach for the fidget spinner in my pocket. When I don't encounter plastic, I pull up short in surprise. Beneath my fingertips, something unfamiliar, silky smooth, yet textured, teases the corner of my mind. *What the f—?*

I draw the item out and stare. Franki's panties. As if I conjured them from my thoughts alone.

"Are congratulations in order, then?"

I hastily return my ill-gotten booty to my pocket and turn back to my father. "She rejected my proposal."

Dad's eyebrows lift. "Did she now? Good for her."

I scowl.

"Don't be offended. She made the right choice for both of you. The last thing either of you needs is an arrangement lacking love. I've had the type of marriage you're talking about, and it's hell."

"Your marriage now is happy?" There's that word Grandmother used.

Dad smiles. "Yes. I love Charlotte and she loves me."

"I need Franki to be happy."

Dad smooths a hand over his hair. "You really want this woman? Her, specifically?"

"She's not *a woman*," I say. "She's Franki."

Dad grins. "First word of advice: don't tell her that."

"It's a compliment."

"I know what you mean by it, but you can find a better way to make her feel special that isn't also an insult."

Dad gets up and wanders to the short wall. He lowers himself to pluck a stray red maple leaf from the stone, then straightens. "I'm worried about her. You picked an innocent ball of sunshine. Franki is delicate."

"You think she's weak." Disbelief laces my words.

"She's fragile."

"Franki Lennox is the most resilient person I've ever met. She lives with pain every day of her life and still manages to care about other people's problems. She has a shitty family, and despite that, has goals, the capacity for humor, and, most remarkable of all, gentleness. She doesn't break under pressure because she knows when and how to bend. Just because she isn't hard doesn't mean she isn't strong."

Dad nods, and I see the gleam in his eyes. He baited me deliberately to see if I'd come to her defense. His lips quirk, and he delivers his next words as if they're a closing argument in a trial. "You waited for Franki your whole life. Your list of requirements for a wife were nothing more than her description, you want to make her happy, and you just professed your admiration of her character."

Dad shakes his head. "You love her. Otherwise, what's the point of any of it?"

I try to explain. "I used to feel things. It was torment. The faces of the victims from our missions haunted me. My brain buzzed with a constant onslaught of suffering. When it was over, I continued to hear the screams. I experienced guilt for not getting there fast enough. Not finding everyone. Not being enough.

"And it *should* disturb me. That's part of being human, to flinch at the pain of other humans. But I closed that part of myself off. I robbed it of oxygen until it died. Now, I feel nothing when I'm in the middle of it and nothing when it's over. I do what's necessary. That's it."

Dad watches me for a moment before he speaks. "You were a sensitive child."

"That was a long time ago. I don't *feel things* the way other people do now."

"Sometimes, we grow that hard shell to protect ourselves. If it's prevented you from suffering, then I'm grateful for it." Dad's expression turns fierce. "It doesn't make you a bad person. It makes you someone with coping strategies. You still care about your family. You're capable of patience and gentleness and kindness. You can love. And you are lovable."

He's reminding me that love is more than a feeling. It's a set of behaviors. I can't do the whole "in love" thing, but I can provide care and attention.

I scowl. "I plan to love her. If she marries me, I'll do it."

Dad swipes a hand down his face.

The lace in my pocket is between my thumb and fingers now, a convenient outlet for the tension inside me. *Flick. Flick. Flick.* "I don't know where to start."

With narrowed eyes, Dad's expression transitions slowly into a sly smile, and suspicion floods through me in response.

"I'm trusting you not to sabotage me," I say.

He laughs at my frown. "I wouldn't do that. Okay. I'll be honest, it's been a very long time for me, and I wasn't exactly conventional. But first, I'd say you need to chill out some. Don't say anything about sex at all for a while yet. Say something about her eyes or her hair. Let her know you admire her mind and personality."

"All right."

"Stop talking about relationships or any feelings for now. I know I said to love her, but you need to go slowly. You have the seeds already in you, but real love takes time to grow."

I frown. I'm on a schedule here. I can't afford some long, drawn out thing.

"Spend time with her. Find out what her favorite flowers are."

"Peonies."

"Ah. Good. So, listen to her when she speaks. Take her out to her favorite restaurant."

"She doesn't like eating in restaurants. She prefers to eat at home."

Dad shakes his head. "Okay, then cook her favorite dinner. Laugh at her jokes. Express concern if she's upset. Ask about her day and listen to her when she answers. Touch her arm or her hand when you speak to her. Watch her body language for signs of interest or discomfort. After a couple of months, you can talk about feelings. A few months after that, you can think about commitments."

"I see." His timeline isn't going to work. I need a ring on her finger in less than four weeks. But the rest of his suggestions, I can manage. He's telling me things I'm already doing naturally. That's a good thing because it means I'm on the right track. It's also disappointing that he isn't offering some secret advice that would convince her to want me instantly.

I don't understand Dad's caution to wait months and months to move forward.

"Don't smother her," Dad says.

I move my lips into a smile as I process his conflicting suggestions. Compliment her, but only certain parts of her and only in certain ways. Tell her I'm attracted to her, but don't profess to wanting a relationship. Seduce her, but be "chill."

"You might consider asking Gabriel to take over some of your responsibilities. He's bored and idle. He needs something to keep him on track, and it would give you time with Franki. Otherwise, you'll be too busy to cook her dinner or convince her to give you a chance."

It's true that when we're working seems to be the only time Gabriel isn't partying, but I'm not certain that increasing his responsibilities is the answer. I have no plans to risk our reputation or profits in an experiment to find out. That is, if he even agreed to more responsibility, which is highly unlikely. I'll make time for Franki, but I'll carve it from somewhere else in my schedule. It'll be easy if I give her a job that keeps her by my side.

Dad rises and picks up his orange peels, heading for the door.

I call after him. "I'm not planning to give Franki a miserable life." For some reason, it seems critical to me he understands that.

Dad looks back over his shoulder. "You have to plant the seeds for a happy one. Misery grows all on its own."

Nine

Franki

Anchor | Mindy Gledhill

B ronwyn rests on her bed, a folded washcloth over her eyes, pale blonde hair spread over her pillow like corn silk. The lights are off and the curtains drawn, but it's still bright enough to exacerbate her residual headache. Without changing position, she pats the empty spot on the bed beside her. "Bring it in, Lennox. Oliver too."

I kick off my shoes, lift Oliver, and climb on the bed beside her. Gingerly, Oliver and I scooch close. I lie on my side and he climbs up onto my hip, stretching out to lie on top of me. I wrap my arm around Bronwyn's middle.

"I'm sorry," she says quietly.

"You don't have to do this now. Apologize when you feel better. I won't love you any less, either way."

She pats my hand where it rests on her stomach, tosses the washcloth to her bedside table, and rolls onto her side to face me.

"I love you too, Franki." She shakes her head. "I never should have kept my marriage a secret from you guys. I broke Girl Code over and over. And for what? Because I was insecure? You never would've done to me what I did to you."

After a brief hesitation, I say, "No, I wouldn't have. It hurts that you didn't trust me."

Bronwyn plucks at a string of embroidery on her comforter, her brows furrowed. "It wasn't that I didn't trust you. It was that, in my heart, I knew my marriage was a mess, but I didn't want to face it because I was too afraid to lose him."

I open my mouth to protest, and Bronwyn's crystal blue gaze holds me captive. "You'd have told me I'd made a mistake and to find a way out of that prenup. Talking it all out with you would have helped me cope better. The ironic part is, Dean never would have left me. If I'd stood up and told him I wouldn't tolerate half a marriage any longer, he'd have found a way to fix it. I didn't have a clue how much he loved me."

Lifting her hand into mine, I admit, "We all tell each other what to do constantly. I can't speak for Janessa or Clarissa, but I'll do better. You can tell me anything, and I promise I'll listen without judgment or advice unless you ask for it."

Fifteen minutes and one new confession from Bronwyn later and I regret my promise. Just a smidge.

I peer out her window, down to the flagstone patio below and the matte blue of the pool cover. Despite the McRae's team of dedicated landscaping crew, a few colorful leaves take up temporary residence on random places like that pool cover or the short stone wall between the patio and lawn.

I almost regret that an industrious crew will sweep them clean. Real beauty requires the unexpected. Life needs some chaos. With a grimace, I turn back to where Bronwyn sits on the edge of her bed and mentally amend "a *little* chaos." What she's planning is not a good idea. "Would you . . . er . . . like my advice?"

Bronwyn gives me a mischievous smirk. "Nope."

At my pained expression, she snickers. "Does it hurt to hold the advice back?"

I clutch my stomach and confess with a laugh, "So much."

"You can tell me the bright side to my plan."

"Oh, ha! This is a test. Let me see." Tapping my chin with an over-dramatic finger, I pretend to think. "It could actually work, in which case you'll be blissfully happy, though wracked with guilt. So, we'll call it 'gappy.' But gappy is better than utter misery, so it's a win."

"You'll note the guilt only gets one letter while happy has four. Clearly, happy is the greater part of the equation."

"There you go. Positive thinking," I encourage.

Bronwyn smiles before her face scrunches into concern. "You could come with me. You remember the house I inherited in Blackwater. There's tons of space. Mom is taking care of finishing the renovations, so everything'll be updated, but it's still a crazy mishmash of Georgian mansion and Pennsylvania farmhouse. You'll love it."

"You want me to move in with you, your new husband, and stepdaughter? Why? I'd be in the way of your family bonding time."

At her hesitation, the reason for Bronwyn's offer becomes clear. "You pity me because I can't stay with my father, and I don't have an apartment yet."

Bronwyn's cheeks turn pink. "It's just . . . I know you don't like to be alone, and I'm worried you'll feel awkward staying here without me and try to leave before you can afford to."

I dart my gaze to the door then back to her. "Do they not want me here? Am I a nuisance or—"

"Think about my parents, especially my dad. Be for real. Arden McRae III isn't tolerating anyone he doesn't like in his home. He wouldn't feel an iota of guilt about it either. They *love* you. The invitation was Mom's idea in the first place."

Tension unfurls and I breathe out through my mouth. "I'll enjoy my visit and when I find a place, I'll be fine alone." I indicate my sleeping pooch. "Alone with Oliver, anyway. It'll be a million times better than living with my mother."

"But you're sad."

I laugh. "How in the world did you decide I'm sad? I'm always looking on the bright side."

"Because you always have to look on the bright side."

Silence falls between us.

"I challenge you to tell me something that stinks," she says.

"That's negative thinking."

"Acknowledging that some things suck sweaty monkey balls isn't negative. It's accepting reality so you can move past it."

I squinch my face up in disgust. "Unnecessarily graphic, but okay."

I hesitate, then say, "Something that sucks is your brother offered me a paycheck to be his wife so your grandmother will give him shares in a real estate development company."

It takes three solid beats of my heart before Bronwyn explodes. "That *bonehead*."

I shrug. "I turned him down, obviously."

"*Obviously*," she says dryly. "Did he think because you had a crush in high school that you'd fall at his feet now? How rude can he get?"

I smile ruefully. "I'm not sure he realized how big of a crush I had. It's fine. He apologized and accepted my refusal with good grace."

Bronwyn's brows come together. "Really? *Henry* accepted defeat gracefully?"

I nod. "He's a practical person." A hard ball of stress tightens in my stomach, and I clear my clogged throat. "He offered me a job, though. He's in the beginning stages of acquiring a small tech company in France, of all places. He needs a translator that can act as go-between. I'm excited about it."

She tilts her head slightly to the side. "Interesting timing."

"He calls it serendipitous. It is for me too. I can do this job. I'll be good at it. My French is flawless, and he says I can use voice to text when my body isn't cooperating with me."

Despite the squinted eyes from her headache, a smile breaks across her face. "You're right. It's perfect."

"You want to know something else unpleasant about my life? My father expects me to keep some old hotel magnate *entertained* until the man signs a contract with him."

Bronwyn's expression morphs to disgust. "Why do I get the impression you're not talking about an hour of conversation in your father's office?"

"The guy saw my photo and wants to 'get to know me.' Jonny made it sound like whether the deal goes through or not depends on how friendly I am."

"That's revolting."

I glower. "I know."

"When are you going no-contact with your parents? They are so toxic."

"I'm getting better at boundaries with them. I'd still be in California with my mother and I'd have agreed to date that guy for my father if I weren't."

Before Bronwyn can interject and tell me that's not enough, I go on. "Besides, what's the point of going no-contact with my father? I hear from the man once a year, if that. Everything goes through his PA."

She shakes her head.

"You," I accuse, pointing a finger, "are giving me unsolicited advice. We just agreed to stop doing that."

She grimaces. "Oops."

"You and Henry with your 'oopses' and your 'hmms.'"

Her eyes widen. "Did you just pull a *'you're just like your brother'* on me? Henry and I are nothing alike. At all."

"Don't tell me you haven't absorbed some of his techniques in handling people. I won't believe you."

"They're effective," she defends.

"No doubt."

A tap on Bronwyn's doorframe, and at Bronwyn's call to enter, Henry, himself, stands with one hand in his pocket. Nodding to me brusquely and adjusting his glasses, he says, "Your hair looks different. Nice. Good job."

My insides turn to pure, delighted mush, and I pat my fishtail braid self-consciously. "Thanks."

Bronwyn's voice drips with warning. "*Henry.*"

He looks back at her. "Yes?"

Glancing my way, Bronwyn shakes her head at my sunny expression, visibly shores herself up to keep her mouth shut, and mutters, "Never mind."

Henry turns his attention back to me. "I wondered if you'd like to have dinner with me this evening. We can discuss your new position and your requirements for an apartment. I can look into some possibilities based on your needs."

For a moment, when he asked me to dinner again, I lit up inside like I was full of the lightning bugs we once caught together on a summer trip to Blackwater. But this isn't an invitation to a date. It's about my new job and finding me a place to live. I rejected his marriage proposal. Now he's being friendly. Totally makes sense. It's what I asked for. What I want. Sheesh. *Get it together, Franki.*

"No—Yeah." I take a slow breath and try again. "*Yes.* I would love to have dinner with you and discuss plans to get started on my job."

When Oliver trots over to sniff him, Henry crouches and pets his back. Unimpressed, Oliver puts his nose in the air and pitter-patters his way back to me. When he reaches me, he stretches the entirety of his long body across both of my feet and gives Henry side-eye. The message is clear. *"Mine."*

Bronwyn, apparently unaware of the interchange between Oliver and Henry, huffs and twists her lips as she looks down at the sneakers lying on the floor near her feet. "Must be nice to leave the house. Except for traveling from the hospital to here, I haven't been outside in weeks."

"Are you up for it? I'll help you with the stairs if you want," Henry says.

She nods. "I need it. Just for ten minutes or so."

Henry must notice her hands shaking at the same time I do because we both find ourselves kneeling in front of her and reaching for her sneakers simultaneously.

When we go for the same shoe, my fingers brush his, and we still. Henry's gaze takes mine captive, the sparkling twilight depths hiding . . . something from me. His lashes fall briefly, then Henry dips his head, picks up the other sneaker, and holds it out to me. "Trade you."

I'm crouched directly in front of Bronwyn's right leg, but I have her left shoe. It's the silliest thing in the world that his eyes on me and the way he's offering to swap shoes has my heart racing and a giddy sort of happiness rising in my chest.

He's so close I imagine I can feel the heat of his body sinking into my skin.

There's no reason for us to touch when we make the swap, but Henry's fingers coast over the back of my hand when I pass him mine.

Henry is tall and lanky, and his hands suit the rest of him. They're lean, but strong, with long fingers and wide palms. Masculine. Capable. The hands of a surgeon or a pianist.

I noticed last night that several scars litter his knuckles, and my gaze falls on them now. The worst of them is a broad, silvery-white slash across the knuckle above his ring finger. Most of those scars happened after I left for Europe, but I knew some of what he'd been doing before I left.

I have the insane urge to tell him everything will be okay. It makes no sense. He's not in pain or in trouble, but my heart hurts at the sight of them.

He kneels in front of his sister, carefully fitting her foot into her shoe and tying the laces.

Henry's hands tell the story of two men. One capable of heartrending kindness and one of unspeakable brutality.

He saw that his sister needed care, and he's providing it.

Janessa would roll her eyes and say something about the bar being in hell for me being impressed by that, but anticipating another person's needs isn't something most people do.

Bronwyn squirms. "This feels a little weird guys."

She lightly shoves her brother away. "I appreciate the help, but I don't need the ladies' maid treatment, especially not from both of you at the same time."

Since we're done tying her shoes anyway, we both move back. Henry rises, then offers to help me to my feet.

I place my palm against his as I stand. Henry doesn't let go afterward. Instead, he holds on, twining his fingers through mine and staring at our hands with an intent expression on his face.

"Henry," Bronwyn says quietly.

We both glance her way. She looks down at our hands, then back at her brother, giving him a frown and the tiniest shake of her head.

It's a sort of ingrained shorthand in this family. One of those things hardly anyone ever notices. Bronwyn is younger than Henry, and in every overt and obvious way, he's been her protector. He's the older brother who takes care of her and tells her what to do.

That may be what it looks like on the outside, but on the inside, there's nuance most people will never understand. Right now, she's trying to protect him from me. Bronwyn wants Henry to mask his autism, as though I'm a stranger or someone who would use it against him. She's afraid I'll misinterpret his actions and hurt his feelings.

When Henry attempts to release my hand in response to his sister's signal, I refuse to allow it. He's not letting me go because someone else, someone *not me*, says he should.

Henry lifts his eyes to mine in surprise.

Holding his gaze, I try to impress on him how serious I am. Not for the first time, I wish I had a deeper voice or that I could make myself sound stern the way Janessa does. I settle for giving our clasped hands a shake. "We're friends, Henry. Please don't worry about trying to fit some socially acceptable mold with me."

I lift my shoulders and offer him a self-deprecating smile. "I'm still just Franki."

He shakes his head, his gaze flicking away. A lump lodges in my throat.

When he looks back, Henry's attention shifts to my eyes, then my mouth. Then back to my eyes. In response, my breaths grow shallow and too fast.

Never, outside of fear, have I experienced this kind of chemical reaction in my bloodstream. A hot mix of adrenaline and electricity courses through my body, controlling everything from the beat of my heart to the air in my lungs to the hyper-awareness of his calloused skin against mine. My veins sing with it, but I don't want to run away or hide. I want to know what his kiss tastes like.

His words, when they come, are quiet, fervent, and sound outright offended. "There has never been any such thing as '*Just* Franki.'"

Ten

Franki

One Day Later

The Archer | Taylor Swift

At six thirty in the morning, excited for my new job, I'm ready to start my day. Careful not to wake Oliver as he cuddles in his bed near the window, I open the guest bedroom door in Henry's penthouse to make my way to the kitchen. When I see what's on the other side, I jump and immediately shut the door again.

A quiet knock sounds and a British accent calls, "Ms. Lennox? Are you quite all right?"

I open the door slowly. The ginger-haired man in the three-piece suit is still *right there*. Smiling, he holds an iPad in one hand and a porcelain cup on a saucer in the other.

"Henry is on a conference call in his home office at the moment, but he said if you woke before he returned, to make certain you're comfortable. My name is Spencer, and I'm at your disposal."

He passes me the cup of tea.

"Thank you." I take a sip. One teaspoon of honey. Exactly the way I like it.

"I've arranged for your canine companion to be walked by a member of the security team this morning."

"I appreciate your thoughtfulness, but I'll do that myself. There's no need to pull someone else away."

He glances at his watch. "There's simply no time. Frankly, we should have started half an hour ago, but Henry insisted no one disturb you."

Henry suggested we start work this morning at his penthouse and to feel free to bring Oliver to work with me. He *also* asked me if I'd mind staying in the guest room here until I move into my own place.

According to Henry, daily transportation into the city would be a "waste of resources" and that, as a long-time friend of the family, it makes sense to stay with him.

As always, his arguments were logical and reasonable. What wasn't reasonable was his offer to buy me a place of my own because *"You said we're friends. Friends help each other."*

After that, staying in his guest room seemed almost as though I were the one helping him by not taking advantage of his generosity.

"How long has Henry been up?"

"He generally rises at four thirty, exercises for an hour, and is ready to begin his workday by six."

Oh my stars.

Spencer gives a shallow bow. "If you'll follow me to the kitchen."

Awkwardly, I trail behind. "Are you my boss?"

He stops abruptly, swiveling in my direction. "Certainly not, Ms. Lennox. I'm merely acclimating you to your new home and position."

I frown in confusion. I suppose he means because I agreed with Henry that staying here will make things more convenient for him until I find my own apartment. Under any other circumstance, the question I'm about to ask would sound absurd, but this is Henry we're talking about. He'd do it just to see people's faces when Spencer opened the door. "Are you the butler?"

Spencer's already perfect posture straightens further. "I'm Henry's personal assistant."

"I apologize. It's really early. My brain isn't quite online yet."

"I suppose it is early for some people." He spreads his arm. "Right this way, Ms. Lennox."

When we enter the kitchen, a tall black man with broad shoulders and a ready smile lifts his coffee cup in greeting. "Hey, Franki. I'm Dante, Henry's head of security."

I smile and lift my hand in an uncomfortable wave. So many new people, so early in the morning. I expected to see Henry, not strange men.

Spencer slides a phone and a 3-ring binder across the white quartz countertop toward me. "I'm Henry's personal assistant, but you may consider me yours, as well, until we find you candidates to interview yourself."

"I don't need a PA," I say, dumbfounded.

"When you no longer have to handle scheduling your appointments, shopping, or planning your outfits for the day, you'll wonder how you ever lived without one."

"I'd prefer to do those things myself."

Spencer smiles like I just made a joke, then indicates the phone. "Your old phone isn't secure. Corporate espionage is a concern, as is Henry's safety. Don't use your personal phone for any communication related to business or to take photos within or near any of his properties. This one has everything you need. As long as you don't disable the security features on it, there are no restrictions on how you use it."

That makes sense. It also means that I'm no longer beholden to my mother for her cell phone plan. This could not be more perfect. If I'd made a list of everything I needed, it would be exactly what Henry has provided for me. A place to stay where Henry sees my presence here as convenient, not a hindrance. A job I'm qualified for with benefits. Even the fact that the security here is so hardcore makes me feel loads more comfortable.

I'm usually cranky in the morning, but a shot of unadulterated triumph shoots through my veins. I'll keep the phone Mom gave me so she can reach me, but I don't *need* it, anymore. I won't give her my new number at all.

Spencer taps a pink binder. "I've color-coded everything for you here if you're a more tactile learner. This information is also accessible on your phone, work iPad, or new laptop. You'll find those on the desk I've set up for you next to Henry's in the home office. He felt that would be most convenient. I hope you like rose gold. Henry is coded navy.

"In the front of the binder," he continues, "you'll find a folder and envelope. These include all of your security access codes and keycard. Dante will perform the retinal scans this afternoon."

I nod. I take my anti-inflammatory in the morning, and I have to eat before I do. Otherwise, my stomach will feel like it's gnawing on itself. Besides, something smells *delicious* in this kitchen. "Not to be a pain, but do you mind if I grab some breakfast while we do this?"

Spencer opens the oven and, using black oven mitts, removes something I can't see from the rack. After plating a piping hot oversized blueberry muffin with crumble topping and three sliced strawberries cut into mini-fans displayed in a half-circle around it, he presents me with the white and gold china and a linen monogrammed napkin. "Henry made these this morning and put them on the warmer for you in case you indicated you were hungry. If you prefer something else, please inform me. Would you like a smoothie as well? Or something more hearty?"

Good heavens. "This is wonderful. Thank you." I nod at the binders. "You can explain while I eat. I don't mind."

As I dig in to the tart and sweet, buttery deliciousness of my breakfast, Dante lifts a strawberry from the cutting board and leans toward Spencer. Spencer backs away from him and shoots a glance my way. Smooth as you please, Dante switches direction and takes a bite of the strawberry, himself. I'm almost certain his intention was originally to feed Spencer.

Cheeks red, but with a small smile on his face, Spencer straightens his bow tie and opens the rose-gold binder, indicating two folders attached. "The security folder is coded red. You'll find a coordinating tab in the binder right . . . here." He indicates a section approximately an inch thick of single-spaced pages printed front and back. "These are the protocols you're expected to conform to at all times. In anything but an emergency, you'll need to request twenty-four-hour pre-authorization from Dante for any deviations from the list."

I blink at the pages and Spencer smiles. "A little light reading. I know. I had the same look on my face when I had to memorize these, but most of it ends up being common sense. Well . . . some of it. It certainly requires an adjustment. The most important thing is to memorize the codes and emergency procedures. Dante will run drills with you later."

I glance at Dante, then skim the first page. Most of the rules don't look unreasonable. No letting unauthorized people into the penthouse. If I meet someone I want to invite over, they have to pass an advance security check. That might bother some people, but to me, it means where I'm staying is a private oasis. No sharing private details of our home or posting photos of it online. Wait for the driver's go-ahead before stepping out of a car.

The approved itinerary with twenty-four-hour notice isn't happening. My personal time is my business. What if I get a spur of the moment craving for tacos? I'm not waiting, *taco-less,* until someone gets around to putting "visit food truck" on my schedule. I'm not giving anyone my personal schedule at all. It feels too much like my mother needing to control my every move. "What's the rest of the binder for?"

Spencer indicates a second folder at the front. "A credit card for your use and access to a checking account."

Company expenses. It makes sense, particularly if, as Henry said, travel will be part of my job.

Spencer gives me a tight smile. "It behooves me to point out that if you spend more than a million dollars at one time, Henry will be sent an alert for him to confirm the purchase. It's not that he's attempting to restrict you in any way. It's simply a place where security protocols and finance meet."

Spencer's dry humor is hilarious. *It behooves me....A million dollars.* I laugh, and his brows draw together before he presses on, flipping to different sections. "As I said, these are color-coded. This navy tab is everything you could need on a daily basis regarding Henry, himself. I've included a list of approved gifts, should you be inclined to get him something. His birthday is in May."

I snatch the folder toward me and look at the list. "I know when his birthday is. You can't be serious. If I want to buy him a present, he expects it to be approved?"

Spencer shrugs. "It's an exhaustive list and quite flexible. For example, if you wish to purchase a sweater, you would cross-reference that with this yellow tab to find the sizes, designers, materials, and brands he prefers. But you may purchase anything within those parameters. And that leaves a great many choices for you."

I grit my teeth. "What if someone wanted to get him something that isn't on the list?"

"Acceptable as long as it falls under the heading 'sentimental' or 'need-based.' Though if you give him something sentimental, please explicitly state its purpose and why he should appreciate it, so he doesn't needlessly reject it."

I swallow a sip of tea, my muffin suddenly dry and sticking in my throat..

"You'll find a list of Henry's preferences for entertainment, food, etc. here. You may find it useful to memorize these, so you don't need to refer to the folder constantly."

"Is this a prank?" I have a terrible feeling it isn't, but hope springs eternal.

Spencer purses his lips. "As long as you live in the same residence with Henry, I expect you to cooperate with the established protocols of this household. You're entering his sphere, not the other way around. The least you can do is be respectful of his preferences."

Dante mutters, "Whoa. Ease up."

Spencer tugs at his bow tie. "Back to your binder. Here we have . . ." On and on he drones.

"And that," he finally says, dusting his hands, "is that."

He pulls up his iPad. "Now, we need to go over your gift, entertainment, and food preferences."

I shake my head, my mind working on a plan to go back to Charlotte and Arden's house. I can't stay here. "Move on to my job, itself."

He steeples his fingers. "Certainly. Your primary function is to be available, as necessary. However, Henry is generous and would prefer to know what things he can offer for your comfort."

Available to translate? "Financial bonuses based on performance are more than enough," I say warily.

He scrunches his face like he smells something terrible. "I'm not certain exactly what you imagine you'll be *performing*, but that's not how Henry operates. I imagine he would find an exchange of that nature"—he rakes his eyes over me—"distasteful."

I frown as his implication sinks in. *"What is that supposed to mean?"*

Henry swoops into the kitchen from the hallway. One moment, he's nowhere to be seen. The next, he's snapping the rose-gold binder closed, swiping it off the counter, and smiling at me without showing his teeth. "Franki. You're up early. I expected you to sleep for at least another hour."

"Really? Inspector Javert over here said I was half an hour late for work already." I cross my arms and throw Spencer under the bus so fast it's not funny. *Fuck this dude.*

Henry lifts an eyebrow. "His name is Spencer."

"If I were starving and stole a loaf of bread, I don't have a doubt in my mind that he'd chase me for the rest of my life to remind me it was against the rules."

Dante snorts. Spencer sniffs.

Henry cringes and pushes the white ceramic cookie jar toward me. "Have some more sugar. Do you need caffeine?"

I reach into the jar, but resent it mightily. I want a cookie. But I don't *want* to want a cookie. This is nothing like what Henry sold me last night at dinner.

I select a chocolate chip cookie, but when I bite down, I taste raisin. I force myself to chew and swallow and not spit the mouthful into the trash.

"This is the list of approved jewelers from whom you may select your engagement ring." Spencer slides a laminated piece of paper toward me.

I drop the cookie on the counter. "What?!"

Henry slaps a hand down on top of the paper. "Don't look at that. How ridiculous. I hired you to be my *translator*. For my company." He laughs. "Spencer enjoys practical jokes."

Spencer turns his head in his employer's direction. "I must say—"

"I need you to leave," Henry says in a rush.

"I beg your pardon?" Spencer asks.

"I need you to go find me macadamia nuts. Coated in chocolate. Green-tea-flavored chocolate-coated macadamia nuts. I'd like them for my mid-afternoon snack. Please. Go find them, now. I'll speak to you later privately to discuss the macadamia nuts once you've located them. Franki, do you have any snack requests?"

I shake my head, the motion so small it's likely barely perceptible.

Spencer's mouth tightens, and he lifts his chin. "Very well. I'll return with your snack."

Spencer leaves and Dante lifts his eyebrows in some form of silent communication with Henry. "I'm headed for a team meeting. I'll go over the drills with you later, Franki."

Like heck, he will. I won't be here.

When Dante takes his coffee cup with him and heads for the front door, I turn to Henry. "Staying here isn't going to work for me. I'm going back to the Hamptons."

"Because of the binder? Spencer can be overly enthusiastic. I'll talk to him."

"It's too uncomfortable for me to be here. Spencer obviously believes I'm going to marry you." I shudder at the idea. Every image I had of what a business marriage with Henry would look like took a downgrade after speaking with Spencer. That's saying something, considering my initial impression was pretty darn bad to start.

"Spencer made incorrect assumptions. I'll clear those up when he returns. You live here. He works here. He takes direction from you, not the other way around," Henry says.

All the practical reasons for staying remain. Anything else means an unhealthy strain on my finances, but I have my doubts this is going to work, even in the short term. "We'll see how it goes. You and I in the same space may not be a good fit for either of us."

Henry puts an arm around my shoulders. "Let's give it a try. What do you say we take Oliver for his morning walk? Then we'll come back up here and get started. I have a proposal I'd like you to translate this morning, if possible, and a phone call scheduled with Mon-sewer Mercy-er at three where I'll need your services."

I lower my shoulders and blow out a breath. "I'm looking forward to it." I hesitate. "You haven't called him Mon-sewer Mercy-er to his face, have you?"

Henry's eyelids go heavy and his lips curl. "Why?"

"It's pronounced '*Monsieur Mercier.*'"

"Mercy-aye," he says, his attempt to match my accent cringeworthy.

"Closer. Mercier," I say.

"Thank goodness you're here. I'd be lost without you."

Eleven

Henry

One Week Later

Look After You | The Fray

Sun streams through the expansive windows of Bronwyn's home in Blackwater, Pennsylvania as I haul Grandma Miller's carved oak rocking chair into the family room. I sigh aloud at the disappointing, but not wholly unexpected, sight that greets me.

Bronwyn's husband Dean, dark hair in disarray, scruff covering his jaw, and wearing nothing but a pair of blue gym shorts, is asleep after a night curled up on a blue velvet sofa far too small for his bulk. At my deliberately noisy entrance, he opens bleary hazel eyes and glares.

I don't take offense. The man is constantly scowling unless he's looking at his kid or his wife.

"Henry. What are you doing here?" Dean's usually mild Virginia accent gets stronger when he's tired. His voice is the next thing to a disgruntled twang this morning when he sees me.

I place the heavy chair in the corner with care. It's an antique, after all. I'm not dinging it up out of irritation simply because my brother-in-law is sleeping on the sofa instead of growing a pair and talking things out with his wife. "I'm the one who drove Bronwyn here yesterday. I spent the night at my maternal grandparents' farm, and needed to check in this morning, because, as you know, I won't be leaving my sister until I'm certain she's properly cared for."

Dean refused to bring his wife home, telling her she needed to stay with our parents until she was healed to his specifications. She decided he could kick rocks and needed an ultimatum. I fully agree.

I wasn't happy to leave Franki in New York for this trip, but she has breakfast planned with an old friend from boarding school this morning. It hasn't even been twenty-four hours, and I already miss her.

"I'm here. You can leave," Dean says.

I absolutely cannot. Bronwyn's marriage isn't on track yet. My sister's formerly secret husband needs support, whether he likes it or not.

"Something wrong with your bed, Priester?" I ask, voice deliberately mild.

"None of your business."

"Bronwyn's well-being is my business, and since you are part of that equation, I disagree. However, I'm a man who knows my limitations. I suppose you need a woman's touch to encourage you to open up and better express your feelings. I happen to have brought the perfect person along with me for that job."

A thunderous scowl settles on his face. "What are you talking about?"

I lower my eyelids to half-mast and move my lips into a smile as I turn my head and call, "Grandma Miller, Bronwyn's husband is in the family room. He's excited to meet you."

Dean doesn't say another word. He's too busy scrambling to cover his junk with his pillow before Grandma makes it in here.

Grandma Miller, all five feet zero inches of pure energy, barrels in behind me and straight over to the sofa. The contrast of the two sides of my extended family often amuses me. My father's mother glides when she walks, even at eighty-four years old. Grandma Miller . . . *bops*.

Dean flinches when she plops down next to him and inspects his shoulder. He's a big guy. As a former Army Ranger, he also took some damage while he was active duty. Those scars are a testimony to a great deal of pain and several surgeries. That, and the fact that I had a private investigator dig into every aspect of the man's history are enough for me to figure out the PTSD and tragic family backstory he's hiding from my sister.

Part of me even understands his behavior. However, I can't admit that I know what I do without also admitting to what my mother would refer to as "a gross invasion of privacy." I call it common fucking sense when we're allowing someone to become a member of this family, and my father agrees.

"My goodness, you're a big one, aren't you? Call me Grandma . . ."

I'd like to give Dean hell right now, or, at the very least, irritate him. My sister, without a doubt, has hurt feelings that he slept down here, but Grandma has him blushing like a fourteen-year-old girl. So, I let her do her thing and make my way down the hallway, through the kitchen, and out to the back porch.

Breath fogging in the crisp morning air, I do a quick security scan, then lean against the white railing as I check my phone. As expected, there's no message from Franki, but since I'm here and not sitting across the breakfast table from her, reaching out is the reasonable next step.

According to my father, I should be easing into this, not declaring an end goal at the start, which, apparently, is too calculated and not "organic" enough. Therefore, I've spent the last week forcing myself to move at a snail's pace. Despite my frustration, I've never had more fun in my life. Even when we're working on different things and in my office versus home, it's been remarkable to have her nearby. I catch myself smiling multiple times a day.

I tap the side of my phone and consider what to type. It's surprisingly difficult to decide. Finally, with a shrug, I type: **Good morning**

I wait with my gut in knots for her to respond.

After a few moments, three dots dance across my screen, then her greeting appears.

Franki: Good morning

Her text includes a sun emoji and a smiley face surrounded by hearts.

Are those emojis a mystical feminine indication of romantic interest or is this the kind of text she sends to all her friends? I wait, hoping she'll start a conversation. When she doesn't, I blow out a breath and dive in. I figure I'll start with the same thing I would if she were in front of me.

Me: How did you sleep last night?

As I wait for her reply, I reach into my pocket to run my thumb across the irresistible lure of Franki's panties. That bit of lace has turned out to be far more effective than any fidget spinner I've carried in the past. I told myself I'd leave them in my suitcase, but I changed my mind. I like that little scrap of lace.

This morning, I was disappointed to realize they no longer smell like her laundry detergent or whatever soap or lotion or . . . whatever it is she uses that makes her smell the way she does. They had a lightly feminine fragrance when I'd inadvertently stolen them. Now, they smell like my laundry. Maybe when she gets here, I'll slip these ones back into her luggage and take a new pair in exchange.

When I'm done with our morning chat, I'll need to get to work making preparations. I may not be able to leave Blackwater right now, but it sure as hell doesn't mean I'll be spending another night without Franki.

Twelve

Franki

This Is Me | Kesha

I CHECK THE TIME on my phone before sliding it into my bag and taking a sip from my sweating water glass as Penelope Stanton breezes into our breakfast date thirty-two minutes late. At my finger wave, Pen flips her honey-blonde hair over her shoulder, sashays over, and leans down to give me an air kiss. "Mwah."

I smile. "How are you?"

My former boarding school roommate seats herself with a swish of expensive ivory fabric and strong perfume. "I'm very well." She holds out her left hand, and a flashy diamond sparkles on her finger.

I squeal, mostly because I know that anything less will disappoint her. "That's so exciting. You're getting married."

She nods. "The date is set for six months from now. *Brock Randall*."

Pen's green eyes flare wide when says her fiancé's name, as though it's someone I should recognize. Maybe he's a pro athlete or something. I smile and try to appear impressed. "Cool."

"Amazing, right?" With a shake of her head, Pen gives me a smile. "But look at you. I almost didn't believe it when I saw your photos online from that wedding. You're a whole different person."

With effort, I smile and manage not to squirm. "I guess."

"And to land one of the McRaes? Well-played. I always thought they saw you like a weird little cousin or something." She crosses her legs, lifts her chin, and snaps her fingers at a server before pointing at our table.

"I'm not trying to land anyone. Henry isn't—"

"Smart. Just keep doing what you're doing. Everyone saw the way he was looking at you at that wedding. He's completely gone for you. Just don't let it go so far he gets bored."

I shake my head, but our server, a young woman with a harried smile, stops by our table for our order. I mouth "Sorry."

She winks back. "What can I get you?"

"A yogurt parfait and a glass of lemon water, please. I only have half an hour before I have to leave." If I'd realized Pen would be so late, I'd have factored that into my plans. I need to get back to the penthouse, give Spencer, who's become far more pleasant since Henry spoke with him, instructions for petsitting Oliver, pick up my prescriptions at the pharmacy, and pack before Gabriel arrives to carpool with me to Blackwater.

Pen gasps. "You're leaving already?"

I flinch. "I'm sorry, but I'm heading out of state. I wouldn't have needed to rush, but"—I fidget with the napkin—"you're a little late."

She rolls her eyes. "Oh my God, these things are not set in stone. When someone says breakfast at nine, they mean nine*ish*."

"Yeah, sorry. I forgot about that."

She gives the waitress her order, and when the woman walks away, she flicks her fingers at me. "Reschedule."

I huff a laugh. "I can't throw off everyone else's plans for my own convenience."

She frowns in confusion, like I spoke a foreign language. Finally, she readjusts in her seat and leans forward, rampant curiosity in her eyes. "So. Is it true you're living with Henry?"

I freeze. *How would she know that?* "For the moment. We're working together."

Pen's eyebrows lift, and she smirks. "Cozy. There were paparazzi photos online of you walking a dog together. Very domestic."

"We're friends," I say.

She snorts. "Y'okay."

My yogurt arrives, and after thanking our server, I dig in. Pen's lack of consideration is the reason I have no time, and I need some kind of food to fuel me.

"What have you been up to?" I attempt to bring the conversation around to Pen.

She waves her hand. "I'm busy with wedding planning and redecorating. That sort of thing. How about you?"

"I'm working as a translator." If I sound proud when I say it, I can't help it. I love this job and the independence I'm building with it. Technically, I don't actually work *for* Henry. At his suggestion, a separate company hired me, then contracted my services as a consultant. At the moment, Henry is my client. He made a joke about public relations, but I definitely get where he's coming from. Our history, friendship, and living arrangement muddy the waters. It's not a perfect solution, but it helps, as does the paperwork we both signed acknowledging our personal relationship.

Pen wrinkles her nose. "I can't imagine doing something so boring, but you always were weird about that stuff." She waves a hand. "Whatever. Okay, never mind jobs. You. Look. Amazing."

I spent every one of the years since I left boarding school being groomed by my mother. The love bombing and the *My Fair Lady* makeover of the first three months were exhilarating. The remaining years were exhausting.

I smile. "Thanks."

"No really. You did the whole ugly duckling into a swan thing. All you need now is to have a little more work done."

There's no covering the small huff of disbelief that comes out of my mouth. My real friends would pull their own fingernails out with pliers before they said something judgmental about the way I look, then or now. My face and body are no one's business but my own. She sounds like my mother gave her a script.

"Freaky Franki," she muses. "Unbelievable." Pen laughs and waits for me to join her.

When she realizes I'm not, she gains a belligerent expression. "What?"

"You know I cried over that nickname. Why would you use it now?"

For a moment, Pen looks like a deer caught in headlights, unable to process the fact that I called her out. Then she collects herself and gives a one-shouldered shrug. "It was a long time ago. I didn't think it would still bother you. You don't look like that anymore, and I'm sure you grew out of lying on floors and doing that weird self-hypnosis." She says the last part in a reassuring voice.

A hard, soundless breath punches out of me. *Has she always been this rude?* Maybe she was. In comparison to the girls who bullied me, she seemed nice at the time. "I'm not a different person because I had surgery and learned how to do a smokey eye. The self-hypnosis is meditation I learned in therapy to manage stress. I haven't 'grown out of it.'"

"No need to get sensitive." She smiles brightly and indicates my outfit. "That's from your dad's new fall collection, isn't it?"

"Yep," I say, tone flat.

"So cool that he always sends you those pieces. Does he still make you give them back at the end of the season?"

"Yes." Technically, one of his people sends them. I'm certain it's nothing more than a standing order on the calendar for someone else to perform. Like an oil change.

My mother told me I was an idiot not to realize that an assistant was the one sending birthday and Christmas gifts from Henry in the same way. That turned out to be a lie. One among many.

When we were in school, I never explicitly gave Pen any of the clothing my father sent. She borrowed them, though, and never returned several items. I'd had to make up stories about damaging them accidentally. It's really too bad Jonny asks for them back. I could have sold one of his purses online, in season, and covered Oliver's vet bills.

She huffs. "Your father is so controlling. Good thing your mom is so nice."

Pen grabs her phone and signals for the server. "We need a photo."

I shake my head, but when the young woman hurries over, Pen hands her the phone, anyway. "Take a pic for us."

Pen immediately strikes a pose and leans into the table toward me. "Come on, Franki."

"I'd rather not."

"I need it for my IG," she wheedles. "Don't be a party pooper."

Determined to get it over with, I carefully drape my body the way my mother taught me to do and manufacture a small smile. The server snaps the pic, hands the phone back to Pen, who approves it, and slides the gold case into her bag.

Pen watches me with a knowing look. "How would *you* like to be one of *my* bridesmaids?"

I pause with my yogurt almost to my mouth. Lowering my spoon, I shake my head. "That's kind of you to include me, but I don't know what I'll be doing in six months." My job is keeping me busy at the moment, and travel is a real possibility. Mostly, though, I'd rather lick a New York City subway turnstile than be a bridesmaid in Pen's wedding.

Her expression turns sly. "Are you thinking you won't be available to be my bridesmaid because you're moving back to California with your mother?"

It's the hopeful tone more than anything else that clues me in. "What is my mother giving you to spy on me?"

She stills, her eyes wide before she recovers and glances to the left. "I'm not spying on anyone. I saw your photo, realized you were in New York, and decided to reach out. I don't remember you being so paranoid."

Stand up. Say the words. Then walk out with dignity. One more boundary. A bridge in flames behind me.

I set my spoon on the table, drag my bag over, take out my phone, and check the time. I could chat for at least fifteen more minutes.

I won't be doing that.

Removing forty dollars from my wallet, I drop it onto the table and stand. I pull out my mental shield. *"Fuck 'em, Franki."*

"Don't call me again. We're not friends." I manage to say the words without shaking. Her status as the least horrible roommate I had at boarding school doesn't qualify her to be in my life now.

Pen leans back, expression stunned, before she manages to sputter, "You're in no position to act like a bitch to me."

I place both hands on the table and lean over into her space. "I don't care what you think."

I turn and walk away. My knees and hips ache, but I control my expression and my limp as I leave the restaurant. When I "dressed the part" this morning, I chose fashionable shoes that look great with this outfit but do a horrible job of "shoe-ing." At least for me. They're pretty torture devices I willingly subjected myself to.

I keep walking, faster and faster. As the crowd mills and shoves around me, I come to a standstill to catch my breath, my heart pounding in my chest. I can't believe I cut her out of my life like a scratchy tag in a piece of clothing. My breaths grow easier as the stress surrounding our conversation subsides.

I snort. She was so shocked that I'd stood up for myself that she didn't even know how to respond. I don't have a doubt in my mind that her late arrival was a power play. It's something my mother does to make people feel at a disadvantage. I gave Pen the benefit of the doubt, but the longer she talked, the more obvious her attempts at manipulation became. I guess I am different than the girl she knew in boarding school, because I read her like a book.

"Francesca?" A male voice sounds behind me, deep and unfamiliar. Warily, I turn to look.

"I thought that was you." The thirty-something man, wearing a blue suit tailored to perfection, stands a couple of inches shorter than Henry, with dark blond hair and sharp green eyes.

"I didn't mean to startle you." Smiling, he puts out a hand to shake. "I'm Leo Kingston."

Yikes. He was supposed to text, and I was supposed to pretend he had the wrong number. I also thought he was going to be my dad's age.

I ignore his hand, pretending I have to fidget with the straps of my purse to avoid it. When he's dropped his own, but still retains his charming smile, I say, "Jonny mentioned you. It's nice to meet you. This is awkward, but my father didn't know when he spoke to you that I was seeing someone."

It's a lie, but I've found over the years that it's far safer to provide a "mystery partner" than outright look a stranger in the face and say, *"No thank you. I'm not interested."*

Some men respond to rejection with good grace, but there's no way of knowing for certain whether Leo will be one of those or one who gets angry and aggressive. It's why when the men calling me "Dollar Store Guinevere Jones" approached me at the hotel, I'd smiled while they insulted me.

Leo's expression turns rueful. "I saw photos of you with McRae, but you never know what's real when it comes to social media."

I wrinkle my nose and laughingly shake my head. I hadn't wanted to put a name to my fake boyfriend.

Leo's attention zeroes in on my ring finger. "He hasn't locked you down yet."

This guy gives me the creeps.

Leo's eyes crinkle at the corners, and he puts his hands in his pockets, leaning toward me. "You're not married, Francesca. Why not explore your options? I won't tell if you don't."

My mouth turns down in disgust.

He leans back, his expression charming, but, somehow, predatory. "Not much of a talker, are you? Dr. Henry McRae has you wrapped around his little finger, then?"

I snort. If I disagree, he'll claim I'm available. If I don't, he'll make a crack about breaking free from my "controlling" relationship. Leo Kingston has nothing on Guinevere Jones's skill at manipulation. He's a rank amateur in comparison.

He smirks. "Nice. I had it backward. Henry McRae is your puppy."

I tense in case he retaliates and stare him down. "You've clearly never met him. No one manipulates or controls Henry."

He runs his tongue across his bottom lip. "A loyal woman. I thought those were a myth. I imagine Henry would be a very sad boy if anyone took you away from him. I imagine he'd do almost anything for a woman like you."

"I have somewhere I need to be. Excuse me."

"Of course." He stretches out his hand and slides a thick black acrylic business card with a lion's head logo printed on it in gold into the front pocket of my purse. "This may seem a little off topic, but your father mentioned you have a history degree. I've recently purchased an older hotel in Chicago, and I'd like to restore it as faithfully as possible. I'd love for you to take a look at it."

I blink stupidly, frozen in fear, while I process how close he came to me and his change in tactics. Belatedly, I step out of his reach.

He nods toward my purse. "It's a paid position. If your boyfriend turns out to be more Beast than Prince Charming after all, or you need a great hotel room," he laughs at his own sales pitch. "Or anything at all," he dips his head to the card and winks. "The QR code will load my private number into your contacts. I'm not stingy."

Leo smiles and gives me a salute. "Until we meet again, sweet Francesca."

Thirteen

Franki

Someone to Stay | Vancouver Sleep Clinic

Henry greets me with a kiss on the cheek the moment Gabriel and I walk in the door of Bronwyn and Dean's house. "Hello, Franki."

I fight the urge to close my eyes, bask in the comfort of him, and breathe in his scent. Henry is my friend, and I'll be moving out of his place soon, anyway. Getting attached like this is a bad idea.

Leaning slightly on my cane for support after stiffening up on the drive here, I narrow my eyes in an attempt to look stern. "Who surprises someone with a party in their own house?"

Before Gabriel and I arrived, Janessa teased Bronwyn in our group chat about everyone unexpectedly walking in on Dean *dining out* on Bronwyn in the family room. Apparently, no one actually saw anything, but I still feel horrible for both of them.

"Don't worry, I made extra staff accommodations," Henry says.

"I wouldn't have come if I'd known their housewarming party was you ambushing them," I say.

"I'm glad you're here." Henry beams with a blinding smile so unlike his typical reserved expression that I blink and forget my train of thought entirely. Dazzled and barely able to string words together, I gaze back at him with stars in my eyes.

Henry leans toward me conspiratorially. "Be glad you and Gabriel are a couple of hours behind the rest of the crew."

Still befuddled by Henry's beautiful smile, I nod as if thirty seconds ago I wasn't giving him heck for setting up this party in the first place.

Henry's attention skips to Gabriel. "I'll show her where she's sleeping."

When Henry reaches for my luggage and attempts to tug it out of Gabriel's grip, his brother doesn't let go. The muscles in Henry's forearm flex beneath a light dusting of hair and his eyes narrow.

"I can guess which room she's staying in." Gabriel smirks.

"I'm headed in that direction, anyway," Henry says, voice impatient.

"Of course you are." Gabriel winks.

Henry sighs. "Could you act your age?"

"I could, but this role reversal is irresistible. Do you need any advice? Any words of wisdom? I'm here for you, Henry." Gabriel starts out sounding sincere, but he ruins the effect by snickering at the end.

I swivel my head back and forth like I'm watching a tennis match before I finally venture, "Henry?"

At the sound of his name on my lips, Henry doesn't just glance my way. He turns his entire body toward me, his heated gaze roving over me. Cataloging me. My eyes, my hair, my face, my neck, my shoulders. I'm afraid to put a name to that look for fear of giving myself unwarranted hope. It's what I'd done at the wedding reception, after all, and hours later he'd dashed my confidence against the rocks of his horrible proposal.

When I don't say anything, Henry asks gently, "Are you okay? Is there anything you need?"

I shake my head. "You're find. I mean . . . we're find—fine. *I am fine.*" Heat crawls up my neck.

Henry nods his own head repetitively, never breaking eye contact.

"Henry," Gabriel murmurs, "Get some rizz."

A ghost of a smile hides in the corners of Henry's eyes. "I'll show you to your room."

Gabriel releases my suitcase. "I'll see you in a bit, Frank."

As Gabriel walks away, Henry guides me up the stairs, then down the hall. "Why is he calling you Frank?"

I shrug. "It's left over from when we were kids. Who knows why it started, but I like it better than 'sweet Francesca.'"

"Who called you *'sweet Francesca'*?" Henry asks with a note in his voice that, if he were anyone else, I'd call jealousy.

"Nobody important."

Henry opens a door second from the left at the end of the corridor and ushers me inside the quaint, farmhouse-style bedroom with the brass bed frame and the pretty quilt and braided rug. I lean my cane against the bed and remove my jacket, taking in the homey feel. This house may be newly renovated, but Bronwyn kept a lot of its original character. The room boasts four doors, counting the entry. I assume one is an en suite bathroom and one a closet, but I don't know what the third could be.

After depositing my suitcase on top of an antique dresser, Henry strides across the room and opens the first door. "Bathroom."

He indicates the next with a sweep of his arm. "Closet."

Finally, he points to the last one. "My room. If you need anything at all, feel free to come find me. My door is always open."

Oh. Oh, this is . . . A jolt of excitement goes through me before I talk myself down from it. I'm sure he means if I need fresh towels or an extra blanket or something that I shouldn't bother Bronwyn about—

I don't even see him cross the floor back to me, but suddenly Henry is inches away, lifting my hand to his chest.

"Whatever you need, Franki. Come to me."

I blink up at him like an owl, my breath catching as his meaning becomes inescapable. Henry is flirting with me. Heart thundering wildly, I lift my free hand

and lightly touch my fingertips to his lower lip. "You're saying . . . if I need towels . . . ?"

He quirks a casual eyebrow, but his chest lifts as he sucks in air like fireplace bellows as he speaks against my fingers. "Come to me."

"I see. And, if my pillow is lumpy?"

He leans closer, his voice so much hoarser than usual. "Come to me."

"What if . . . I'm cold?"

"I'll be devastated," he says quietly, his breath warming my skin, "if you don't come to me."

His head dips closer. I close my eyes as the clean scent of him floods my senses. His lips are soft against my fingertips, and his heart pounds beneath the palm of my other hand, the crisp cotton of his shirt warm where we're touching.

If he were taking my pulse, he'd know my own heart is pounding, too, with a beat so loud that it thunders in my ears.

As if he senses the direction of my thoughts, he circles my throat, his thumb on one side and the calloused pads of fingertips on the other, gently skating over my carotid. He doesn't exert the slightest pressure, but the world halts its rotation in response, throwing me headlong into something I can't brace for. I was going seventy miles an hour on the highway, and someone slammed on the brakes. I'm in the passenger seat without so much as a seatbelt to halt my trajectory.

I open my eyes, and his blue gaze arrests mine, searching. Searching.

He reaches up a hand and removes his glasses, tossing them onto my suitcase. Then he runs his left hand through my hair until he's cradling my head. He's anchoring me. One hand collaring me, the other moving my head where he wants it.

He must feel me swallow beneath his palm because he frowns in response. "Am I making you nervous?"

"Yes. Am I making *you* nervous?"

"Fuck yes," he says fervently.

Then I kiss Henry McRae.

Fourteen

Henry

Wild Things | Alessia Cara

This wasn't on my schedule yet, but I'm in it now, and I'm not sorry.

The physicality. The instinctive reactions. The back and forth. The way I've lost conscious awareness of everything in the world, just the two of us and what we're doing right now, feels like fighting. But so much better. It's my body and hers. The two of us coming together. Pulling apart and coming back again. The way we anticipate each other feels like we're circling a target, but rather than colliding for maximum damage, we're all about feeling good.

So. Damn. Good.

Franki's lips are soft. Her skin beneath my palm, pure warm silk. Her tongue tangling with mine shoots electric arousal straight to my cock.

I hadn't expected kissing Franki to be like this. Sex, maybe.

I explore Franki's mouth with mine. Clutch her head and move it one way, then the other. The silky strands of her hair spill through my fingers and over my forearm, and I slide my other hand from her neck across her collarbone, her shoulder, and the long, elegant line of her arm, finally coming to rest at her waist and tugging her closer.

Adrenaline floods through me, my veins alight with it, but, unlike combat, I don't have the slightest desire to hurt or defend. I want to turn this heightened awareness into pure, decadent, pleasure for her, the way it is for me.

Dizzy with the sensation flooding me, I'm standing in one place, but feeling as though we're spooling out into space. She could slay me where I stand, and my last words would be, *"Was it good for you?"*

Be careful. Don't hold her too tightly. I need to stay aware of her reactions and signals so I don't accidentally hurt her.

She tastes like honey, some type of lip balm maybe. Her tongue is glassy and smooth as she tentatively tangles hers with mine.

The feel of it has my cock, already stirring behind my zipper from her closeness, hard as steel.

I told Gabriel once that kissing was disgusting. Mouths aren't sanitary. I've never kissed anyone before this moment.

Not only do I no longer care about *sanitary*, there isn't a part of Franki that I don't want to taste.

I'm attuned to her every reaction. Her indrawn breaths. Her elevated heart rate. The slight flush on her cheeks. When I slide my hand down to her hip, I feel the stiffness in her posture a split second before she pulls away.

I allow my hands drop to my sides, and Franki fusses with her skirt, chin down, almost as though she's embarrassed. Surely, she isn't afraid of me. I would never hurt her.

She kissed me first. It's the best thing that's ever happened to me.

Without lifting her chin, she raises her eyes to mine, peeking through those gorgeous long lashes.

"Was that okay?" I ask.

Cheeks pink, she smiles. "It was wonderful."

"I can work with wonderful."

She laughs, though I wasn't trying to be funny, and I find myself laughing too. "Do you need to rest?"

"No. I've been sitting in the car too long. I need to move. I'm stiffening up."

"Would you be interested in accompanying me to a pumpkin patch?"

"Pumpkins? Really?" Her eyes are huge, but I can't figure out if that's because she likes the idea or is shocked by the horrible thought of a rural autumnal adventure.

"Do you dislike pumpkin patches?"

"I've never been to one. I'm not sure I can keep up with everyone. It might be a drag for people to wait around on me."

"Anyone who has a problem with you moving slower than they do is garbage at being human, but, as it turns out, this trip is you and me only. And I'd never leave you behind."

She gnaws on her lip.

"Franki?"

She swallows hard. "Tell me this isn't you manipulating me. Tell me you meant it."

"I'm not manipulating you, and I absolutely meant that kiss."

She looks at the rug. At the window. At our hands.

"Trust me," I say.

She blows out a breath.

"Maybe that's too much to ask." Dad cautioned me against asking for too much too soon.

"I do trust you," she says.

I trace my fingers down her throat, coming to rest lightly at the divot between the wings of her collarbones. Her pulse flutters, and the space contracts and expands with her breath. This thing between us is fragile. Attraction almost staggering in its intensity, combined with what, for me, is soul-deep knowing, and a history that she almost certainly doesn't remember the same way I do.

This isn't a "done deal." If I don't approach her correctly, her attraction for me could melt away like cotton candy in a pop-up thunderstorm. How can I say, *"trust me"* when I don't understand exactly what she needs from me to feel happy and secure? Love. Romance. They're vague concepts that mean different things to different people.

Meanwhile, the ticking clock of Grandmother's ultimatum looms over us. I have just under three weeks left to make her mine.

New emotions are seeping unbidden into my psyche, like water settling into cracks in concrete. Two weeks ago, I believed nothing was worth the pain of allowing myself to feel, but if my own vulnerability is the price for her heart, I'll pay it. For Franki, I will.

Fifteen

Franki

Teenage Dream | Stephen Dawes

With a crooked smile, Henry draws his hand back and shoves it in his pocket. "You've never been to a pumpkin patch?"

"Never. It sounds... pumpkin-y." It sounds *romantic*, actually, but Henry says he doesn't do romance. So, I'm guessing maybe it has something to do with his niece or a favor for his sister.

Henry shakes his head and fake scolds me, "City girl."

"You're a city boy," I remind him with a smile.

He tilts his head to the side. "I'm a city boy out of necessity. My businesses are there, and it's where I was raised. If I could do anything I wanted to, I'd live somewhere like this. There's nothing in the world like being able to go for miles and never see another person. It's peaceful in the country, and there's minimal light pollution."

I've traveled some, and I've occasionally seen a beautiful night sky, but I spent most of my time surrounded by concrete and artificial lights. None came close to the places Henry and I discussed wanting to see. "Stars?"

"The porch roof is outside that window. On a clear night, I can lie out there and visibility with the naked eye is unlike anything you'd find in populated areas. It's better if I take a telescope out to one of the fields, but even without one, it's incredible."

His enthusiasm makes me smile. "I'd like to see that."

"Then I'll show you." He guides me out of the bedroom with a hand on my lower back.

True to his word, as we descend the stairs, he keeps pace beside me and gives no indication of being in a hurry. When we reach the front door, he holds my short, red trench coat for me, and I place one arm, then the other in the sleeves. I pull my hair from beneath my collar and reach for the first button. When the closure gives my stiff fingers trouble, I decide to leave it open. I'll wrap the belt around to stay warm, instead.

Henry lightly brushes my hands away but doesn't go further. "May I?"

Did he notice me struggling? "Why?"

He grins like a naughty schoolboy. "Because I want to touch you."

"Oh." I grin. "Okay."

He completes the buttons, ties the belt, then ushers me out the front door.

"Should we tell anyone where we're going?" I haven't seen Bronwyn yet. It feels rude to run off before saying hello to my hosts.

"Absolutely not. I don't want anyone to tag along or turn this into a group event."

The idea of seeing where things go with Henry has me the next thing to giddy, but I'm not going to make assumptions again. The night in my hotel room was brutal, and I can't even lay the blame entirely at his feet for him being insensitive. The reason it hurt so much was because I had expectations of something else. Kissing me back and admitting to wanting to touch me doesn't mean that he's changed his mind about relationships. I'm not going to allow myself to get excited over nothing. I need him to tell me what this is.

We walk to his car where it's parked in the drive. "You said you had no interest in dating, but this seems a little date-like, doesn't it?"

"I love the way you don't dance around things. This type of blunt communication is by far my preference." He opens the passenger door to his SUV. I take his hand as he assists me into my seat, then prop my cane against my legs and fidget with the belt on my jacket as I wait for him to say more. He may love the way I communicate, but he hasn't answered the question.

He leans in. "Dating would require significant amounts of both effort and attention from me."

I huff and lean back in my seat. So, he likes me but doesn't want to have to make an effort? I have news for him, he already has been. All last week. Just because we didn't leave the penthouse and go somewhere didn't mean that he wasn't paying attention to me.

"The idea of finding things to do together that we both enjoy and learning about you . . . listening to you? I can't remember the last time I looked forward to anything more. So, if you're amenable, one small-town, pumpkin patch, apple-cider-donut *date* coming up." He watches me with an assessing gleam in his eyes.

I scrunch my nose and smile, my cheeks warm. *He was teasing me.* "Okay. We're on a date."

He closes my door, walks around to the driver's side and folds himself into his seat. I spend the first few minutes enjoying the scenery as we drive. The sky is a blue so bright it almost doesn't look real, with fluffy white clouds floating overhead. The trees are a riot of color that look straight off some screensaver or calendar. Almost too perfect not to be photoshopped.

"What are we going to do with the pumpkins when we get them?" I ask.

"It depends on the kind of pumpkins we get. We could carve faces in them. Stick a candle in them and put them on the front stoop."

"I've never carved a pumpkin in my life. Is it fun?" It sounds idyllic.

"Some people think it's fun."

I give him a knowing smile. "You don't."

He shoots a glance my way. "Why do you say that?"

"I don't know. It's a feeling I have."

He sucks on his eye tooth briefly before he admits, "Pumpkins have guts."

"What do pumpkin guts look like?"

His lips turn down in an exaggerated grimace. "They're cold and slimy and stringy at the same time." He gives me a sly grin. "We could shoot the pumpkins."

"Shoot them?"

He mimes an explosion with his right hand. "We'd need a lot of pumpkins, or it would be over fast, but a hollow point bullet makes them explode."

I laugh. "What did the poor pumpkins ever do to you?"

"The pumpkins don't care, Franki. We're not hurting their feelings."

"Then it's wasteful."

"More wasteful than using them as candle holders?"

"Good point, but, yes, anyway," I tease.

"How do you feel about shooting at paper targets attached to hay bales?"

"Much less squeamish than shooting at poor, unsuspecting gourds."

His lips twitch in a suppressed smile. "Grandma Miller gets little pumpkins that she turns into pie."

My eyes flare wide. "Have you made pie before?"

He shakes his head. "No."

I twist my lips and laugh. "Me neither."

"Do you want to?"

"We don't know how."

"Not knowing how to do something has never stopped me from doing it," he says dryly.

I laugh, but I suspect he's not kidding. If he doesn't know how to do something, he figures it out. "Is that your motto?"

"My family already has a motto. I don't need another one."

I wrinkle my nose. "Love hard. Remain loyal. Fight dirty."

"That's the one."

"I like the first part, anyway. Not sure fighting dirty is something to aspire to."

"When it comes to survival, there's no such thing as fighting too dirty. If you're ever in a position where you need to protect yourself, I hope you use every dirty trick you can think of," he says.

He has a point.

"What's your motto?" he asks.

"There's always a silver lining."

Henry looks like he wants to argue with me, but all he says is, "The silver lining on not knowing how to make pie is that it'll be fun to learn."

"I really want to do that." Carving pumpkins and making pies with Henry sounds like a blast.

He taps the steering wheel and muses, "We could also make pumpkin bisque soup."

"Could we?"

"Why not?"

I laugh. "Right. Why not?"

He lifts a finger in a "just wait" gesture, and says, "Siri, call Grandma Miller."

Two Hours Later

"Put them on the table." Henry's grandma waves an arm.

We dutifully deposit our pumpkin offerings onto the long, scarred farm table that seems to be fulfilling the job of a traditional kitchen island.

"Thank you so much, Mrs. Miller. This is so kind of you." I smooth my hands down my thighs and smile nervously. I haven't seen Henry's grandparents since I was a teenager, and then almost always as part of a large crowd.

With a look of mild disappointment, Henry pokes through a ceramic cookie jar shaped like a pig on her counter. He settles for an oatmeal raisin cookie, huffs, then takes a begrudging bite.

Henry's grandma pats my arm. "It's no trouble at all. And don't call me Mrs. Miller. Call me Grandma."

I shoot a cautious look Henry's way. I've never called anyone Grandma. It feels presumptuous, as though I'm claiming a relationship I have no right to. "Er . . . um . . . I couldn't call—"

I stop talking to figure out what Henry is trying to communicate as he nods with exaggerated enthusiasm. He mouths "It's okay."

"I . . . er. Thank you . . . Grandma."

She beams. Warmth spreads through my chest, and I smile back.

Grandma waves her hands in a shooing motion. "Henry, show Franki where the bathroom is. The two of you go wash your hands and find some aprons in the pantry. We don't want to ruin your clothing. You're too beautiful to get messy, Franki."

My mother wouldn't think so. She'd find my messy bun sloppy, and she'd be horrified by my comfortable outfit.

A curly wild shock of faded brown and gray hair wreathes Grandma's head. The wrinkles creasing her face, especially around her eyes and mouth, are evidence of an awful lot of smiling and some pain. She has such kind eyes.

Impulsively, I take her hands in both of mine. "You're beautiful too." I hope she hears how much I mean it.

She smiles and lifts a hand to my cheek. "Such a sweet girl."

Turning to Henry, she says, "That's the kind of girl you need. Someone nice. They say opposites attract."

I shake my head, grinning at the way she teases him. "Henry's nice."

Henry puts an arm around my waist, guiding me from the room. Shouting over his shoulder toward the kitchen, he calls, "Did you hear that, Grandma? Franki thinks I'm nice."

She hoots with laughter. "I'm not deaf, Henry. But that poor girl might be blind."

Twenty minutes later, Henry wields a big-ass knife with expert skill, then scoops the guts into a bowl.

"I can't believe you keep surgical gloves in your car," I say.

"I keep a lot of things in my car," he drawls.

"It's convenient that you have them."

He uses his shoulder in an inefficient attempt to push his glasses back up his nose. "I can still feel the guts. They're cold and slippery."

I slide closer to him. "Do you want me to do it?"

He frowns. "No. Then your hands would get cold."

I reach up and push his glasses back into place for him. Sunshine streams through the window over the sink lighting Henry's blue eyes, but the sparkle in them looks more like mischief than sunlight to me. When I step back, he murmurs. "Oh, no you don't. You need to come back here so I can say 'thank you.'"

I glance toward the kitchen door where Grandma disappeared about two minutes ago when a neighbor stopped by to pick up a carton of eggs. She'd handed over the carton, then followed the woman out the door relaying how Grandad has had to beef up the fencing around the farm because the coyotes "won't stay away from them chickens." Their fencing is *robust* unless coyotes climb walls taller than I am.

Henry nods at the door. "Grandma will be talking for at least fifteen minutes. Will you come back, so I can I say thank you?"

Over the years, I've fallen for so many people pretending to befriend me for so many different reasons that I don't trust my own instincts. My own mother is at the top of that list. The more I think about his flirtation, the more suspicion creeps in about Henry's motives.

I feel like an umbrella where one minute the rain was pouring down on top of me, and I was doing my umbrella thing, fighting off the deluge. Then the wind came at me from another direction and whipped me inside out. Am I naive to believe this doesn't have anything to do with trying to get me to marry him? I don't know. There's nothing in his behavior that hints at deception. Nothing inconsistent or manipulative. *Except for the timing.*

"I can hear your 'thank you' from here." I need to think.

Henry heaves a sigh, then relents. "Thank you for fixing my glasses."

Women were all over him at that wedding reception. He could easily find someone more mercenary and significantly less demanding than I am if he's still looking for a wife to meet his deadline. Does he plan on marrying someone else for business purposes and dating me on the side? It sounds so unlike him that I dismiss the thought immediately.

I turn back to the open cookbook to read through the list of ingredients, double-checking that I've got everything laid out. Flour dusted on the counter? Check. Rolling pin? Check. Egg wash? Ready to go.

"*Dammit.*"

At the sound of Henry's swearing, I turn and choke on a laugh when I see what he's done.

"Is this funny to you?" he asks with great dignity, one arrogant eyebrow lifted.

Henry must have forgotten he had pumpkin guts on his hands and attempted to push his glasses up again out of habit.

"Did the pumpkin guts attack you in self-defense?" I ask.

He has an orange smear across one of his lenses, and an entire goopy, slimy string, complete with a seed, hangs from his cheek. "I could use a hand here when you're done chortling."

With a smile, I move closer, removing his glasses first and setting them on the counter. Then I wet a paper towel and wipe his face clean. I'm inches from Henry, definitely in the kissing zone, and there's that glint in his eyes again.

"Thank you, Franki." His voice is entirely too pleased.

No way. "Did you do that on purpose? You hate pumpkin guts."

He lowers his forehead to mine. "I hate you standing so far away more."

Dropping the paper towel to the counter, I shake my head against his. I don't want to fight this. Not right now. I'll think about it later.

When I kiss him this time, it's different from the first. Gentler and less wild, but no less wonderful. Because his gloved hands are covered in pumpkin, he holds them out away from both of us, almost in a gesture of surrender.

Henry stands completely still as I press my body against his warm, hard, lean strength. When he chases my tongue with his, I shiver in response. Then I place my palms on the crisp cotton covering the ridged surface of his abdomen and slide my hands up over his chest.

"Harder," he says against my mouth.

I freeze, and Henry says, "Don't stop touching me. Please. Just press harder."

I kiss him again, and I touch him using a firm, sweeping pressure until I've got my hands in his hair.

I can feel his erection, long and thick, as he presses against me. Still, those hands of his remain in the air in a posture similar to the one he'd held that night on the library balcony. With a very distinct difference.

I draw back so I can look into his eyes. "Henry."

I don't know why I say his name or even what I want or expect in response. For the first time in my life, I feel *powerful*. I know he wants me, but he's also content to stand there and coax me, allowing me to come to him.

The corner of his mouth lifts. "Franki."

His expression is so smug I want to laugh. "What?"

"You kissed me first. Twice."

Technically, I tried three times, but I don't remind him of that.

The creaking of the screen door alerts us a split second before Grandma re-enters the kitchen. When she sees me pulling my hands back and stepping away from Henry, she plants her fists on her hips. "You'll have to go home to your own kitchen for that kind of funny business. We're here for pie and soup, not making baby batter."

Henry snickers like a little kid, and nearly covers his mouth with the back of his hand before he remembers the pumpkin at the last second and uses his forearm, instead.

When he sees my embarrassed reaction, he sobers. "No funny business, Grandma. I had an accident with some pumpkin guts, and Franki was giving me a hand."

"More than one, looked like." Grandma winks at me, and, when Henry turns back to preparing the pumpkin to be pureed, she gives me a thumbs up.

Sixteen

Franki

Stargirl Interlude | The Weeknd, Lana Del Rey

From my position in the front passenger seat, I glance back at the two foil-wrapped pies that sit in a box on the backseat of Henry's SUV. "You're an expert pie transporter. I'm not sure I would have thought of strapping them in with a seatbelt."

For some strange reason, it made me think of what it would be like to watch him strap a child into a car seat. It was a weird, silly leap of logic, but Henry is *so good* at taking care of everything and everyone, and I still can't shake it.

"I don't want a quick stop to avoid hitting a deer to end with this car covered in pie," he says.

I turn to face him as we make our way down the long country road. "Blackwater is an entirely different life than one in a city. It's so peaceful and slow here. I wish we could stay forever."

His expression turns thoughtful, but he says nothing in response.

"Did you like the bisque enough to eat it again?" I ask.

He glances my way and reaches out briefly to squeeze my hand. "Pumpkin bisque is my new favorite."

"Are you fibbing?"

He shakes his head. "Not at all. If it were just soup, I'd say it was fine. But it's not just soup."

"What is it?"

Henry smiles, but the space between his eyebrows contracts in a frown, as if I asked him what letter comes after "C" in the alphabet. "It's a memory."

I lean back against the headrest. "It was fun."

"Next time, we should have a chef prep the pumpkin for us."

"Are you kidding me? That was the best part."

My work phone vibrates, and I reach in my coat pocket. "Hey, Bronwyn. What's up?"

"Are you with Henry?"

I look at my phone in consternation. How would she know? The man only kissed me this afternoon for the first time.

"I wouldn't say *with*...."

"His location tracker says he's only about ten minutes from the grocery store. And since you're not here, either, I assumed the two of you must have run out for errands together."

"Oh." I laugh weakly. She meant "with" literally. As in, sitting beside him right now.

Her whole family uses their own security app that keeps them dialed in to each other's location. She said they turn them off sometimes, but, for the most part, they're all up in each other's business all the time. I'm grateful it never occurred to my mother to use something like that.

The McRaes have a lot of security measures that might appear to be excessive to outsiders. Before we found our pumpkins, Henry had tossed a navy cardigan on like some kind of sexy Mr. Rogers, but beneath that cardigan he's wearing a holster with a handgun in it. If the SUV we're sitting in isn't armored, I'd be shocked.

"Yes. I'm with Henry. You're on speaker."

"Perfect. Henry?"

"Bronwyn," he drawls.

"If I text you a short list, can you stop by the store for me?"

"I'm certain you have staff for that."

"*Henry*," Bronwyn scolds.

The corner of his lip twitches. He is such a . . . *rascal*. It's a silly, old-fashioned word. Something his grandma would say, but, good heavens, he teases like crazy. He likes to get people all flustered and annoyed, and half the time the people around him don't even realize he's doing it on purpose.

He twists his lips to the side briefly, then says, "For once, I'm not trying to be an ass. Franki needs a break."

I look away in embarrassment. I never complained, but instead of feeling better with activity, my joint pain has gotten steadily worse today. I didn't think he noticed.

After a brief silence, Bronwyn says hurriedly, "Sorry. Ugh. I'm an idiot. It's no problem. I'll have one of the housekeepers run out."

"We'll do it," I say.

Henry looks my way, his brow furrowed.

He's right that I need to give my knees a rest, but I also want to go to the store. I hesitate for a moment because the biggest part of me wants to pretend that I can always do what most people my age do. I'm also terrified that after this shopping trip, Henry will stop flirting with me.

But this is me, and, honestly, what is the point in having him attracted to me if I have to hide huge parts of who I am? So, I say it. "Any normal-sized grocery store will have either an electric scooter or a wheelchair. As long as Henry doesn't mind if he has to give me a push."

He looks pleased with my solution and gives me a nod. "No problem. You know your own body and what you need."

If he weren't driving, I'd launch myself at him and kiss him all over his sweet face.

"Are you sure?" Bronwyn asks doubtfully. "I didn't think about how many hours you spent in the car and then whatever the two of you were already doing."

"Send me the list, Bronwyn. I mean it. I'll be very angry if you don't."

Bronwyn has a smile in her voice when she says, "You don't sound angry. You sound like a preschool teacher offering to feed me cupcakes."

Well, that's annoying. "I'll feed you something else. Something not a cupcake, and you won't like it."

Bronwyn snickers. "Are you threatening me with a knuckle sandwich?"

"I was thinking one of those disgusting protein shakes you said Dean drinks. I don't know what a knuckle sandwich is."

Henry presses his lips together, obviously fighting a smile. "She wanted to know if you were threatening to punch her in the mouth."

Reaching for my hand with one of his, he curls my fingers in, guiding my thumb to wrap around the outside. Henry lifts my fist to graze his lips with my knuckles.

I gasp and pull my hand back to my lap.

"Never thrown a punch?" he asks.

I tighten my hand and imagine what that would be like to plow my fist into another person's face. At the moment, Jonny's comes to mind. I ignored his voicemail earlier. I'm sure it's about Leo Kingston, and I don't want to hear it.

I can picture myself hurting the guys who harassed me in the street. My mother's boyfriend, David Vance, pulled the last one away from me, but I wish I'd been the one to deal with him.

"Does it hurt?" If I did punch someone, I'd probably injure myself more than I did the other person. My hands ache and burn often enough without impact. Even the thought of it makes me wince.

"Yeah, it hurts," Bronwyn says. "How much depends on where the punch lands, whether you were ready for it, and how much force is behind it. Sucker punches are the worst."

"She's not asking if it hurts to be on the receiving end," Henry corrects. "She wants to know if it hurts to be the one throwing the punch."

"Oh. Yeah. It does. If you do it wrong or hit a bony area, you can break your hand. When you're sparring, wrap your knuckles and remember to aim for soft places. Don't get distracted by your own pain in a fight," she says.

It takes a lot of pain to distract me. I'm used to it.

"But I don't think punching anything, even a bag, would be a good idea for you," she says. "Ask Henry to set you up with a firearm."

"I don't know . . ."

"Then a taser, at least. They only work about 50 percent of the time, but you know I think you should be carrying something after all the crap that's happened to you."

Henry's brows snap together in a fierce frown. "Send the shopping list. We'll see you when we're done." Jaw flexing, Henry reaches out and hits End Call on my phone.

I put the phone into my purse, then twist in my seat. I examine my hand, curling it back into that fist.

"Franki." Henry's voice is quiet, but there's anger there. And resolve. "Give me a name."

Startled, I glance his way. "What?"

He pulls the SUV off the road and onto the wide gravel berm, glancing in his rearview mirror with a lift of his hand. I frown, confused.

As Henry shifts his body toward me, his eyes have gone almost frighteningly flat. He folds my hand back into a fist and presses it gently into his palm. "You're sitting here imagining what it would be like to fight back. Give me a name. Tell me who you need me to hurt."

I sit, frozen, as I process his words. This is the first time he's ever said the quiet part out loud. I'm not a naive teenager anymore, and I spent too much time in the McRae home not to have figured some things out in retrospect. Those missions he goes on aren't government-sanctioned. That house has more than alarm systems and panic rooms. There isn't a room in the place that doesn't have a stash of weapons hidden inside the walls or secret drawer spaces accessed with a thumbprint. The security guards move like soldiers because they *are* soldiers. Henry doesn't carry a knife strapped to his calf for slicing apples.

"Tell me," he repeats.

I shake my head. "You're not going out on some vigilante revenge mission on my behalf. I don't need it."

"No one hurt you?"

"I've been assaulted a few times by people who thought I was my mother. Imagine if you hadn't been there in the hotel lobby to step in with those guys. It was that sort of thing. The last one tried to drag me into a car."

Something chases behind Henry's eyes, and I hurry to explain. "I wasn't hurt badly. It was only a few bruises."

It's not true that I was unaffected, especially the most recent time, but Henry looks like he needs someone to walk him off a ledge. The look on his face is like nothing I've ever seen. I shiver at the blank sort of hardness that falls over him.

"What happened to the men who hurt you?" he asks softly.

I shake my head helplessly. "Nothing. They ran away. I couldn't report it, so nobody even looked for them. The publicity would have been terrible for my mother."

"I see. You were more worried about making your mother uncomfortable than your own safety."

"That's not fair. Negative publicity affects her livelihood. They were random acts of violence. Reporting one of those guys wouldn't have stopped the next one." I quote my mother directly.

"You didn't consider that by not reporting it, you were leaving someone on the street who would go on to hurt another woman?"

"Yes, I considered it, but no one would have caught them. There was no point to making my mother's life more difficult when nothing would have come from it." I hate the way my voice shakes. I don't like to think about any of it.

He leans back, giving me space. "I shouldn't have said that. It's easy for someone standing on the outside to judge."

"You were primed to go after someone the moment you thought I was upset. I could have been picturing punching someone who cut me off in traffic."

He rubs his chin and dips his head. "There's such a thing as a proportional response. That's not something I usually forget. You're a much nicer person than I am."

I shake my head, and he scalds me with his heated gaze.

"I don't need anyone to blow smoke up my ass about who or what I am. Not even you. Remember what I said. You never need to worry about whether it hurts to throw a punch. I'll be your fist. All you need to do is say the word."

I take it for the vow it is. "Thank you."

He leans down to drop a lingering kiss on my mouth, then he puts the vehicle back into Drive. "I'm also hooking you up with at *least* a taser and training you on how to use it. I'll beat the shit out of anyone who comes at you, then you can shock the shit out of him."

His comment startles a laugh out of me. "Oh my gosh. *Henry.*"

His lips twitch. "It's always nice to have a plan."

Seventeen

Henry

Motion Sickness | Phoebe Bridgers

I'M RARELY A FAN of these rowdy family dinners, and tonight is no exception. When Franki and I returned from shopping, she took a nap, and I holed up to work in Bronwyn's office. Being away from New York isn't an excuse to take a break from the pressures there.

By the time I get to the dinner table, only one available chair remains. I'm now located four people away and on the opposite side of the table from Franki, who happens to be sitting next to Gabriel.

The flush on my brother's face and his glassy grin tell me he's already been drinking even before he lifts his glass of wine to his lips. I pick up my fork.

I don't believe Franki has any romantic interest in Gabriel, but I'm not sure my brother won't come on to her when he's drunk. She would turn him down, but there's a sick weight in my gut at the realization that I no longer trust my own brother. He's a different person when he's trashed.

Franki laughs, and I glance her way. Gabriel is not that funny, and half his jokes are of the dirty variety.

Dean scowls at me across the table, as if the weight of his glare means anything to me at all. "Henry."

My name isn't a greeting from my brother-in-law; it's a curse. I move my lips into a smile and pretend I don't know he's pissed that I invited that douche, Louis Larrabie, here for the weekend. Louis is a smarmy prick who's been carrying a torch for my sister for years and hangs out with her group of friends. He's an absolute dickhead, and I'm honestly not sure why Bronwyn lets him hang around at all.

Louis, with his overly coiffed blond hair and spray tan, shovels in a mouthful of lasagna, then alternates between gazing longingly at my goofy sister and shooting venomous glares at Dean.

I catch Louis's eye and nod, giving him my best "Buck up, little buddy" expression. His eyebrows lift in the middle and he nods back with a heavy sigh.

Bronwyn isn't paying any attention to him at all. The guy isn't a threat to Dean, but Dean is desperately in love with my sister, and, though he rarely lets on to Bronwyn, it's clear as glass to me that he's the jealous type.

Which is exactly why Larrabie was on my guest list. There's no way we'll find Dean sleeping on a sofa if Louis Larrabie is on the premises. Dean will be in bed with his wife or sleeping in front of her door on guard duty.

I might find myself doing the same thing with Franki tonight. So maybe Dean isn't as unhinged as I originally thought. Or maybe I'm becoming as obsessed with Franki as Dean is with my sister.

I spent the last hour reviewing Franki's files. I'd never noticed anything in them in the last five years that indicated any specific red flags, but we weren't exactly doing a deep dive. Her surveillance, if you can even call it that, was little more than a standard wellness check. I'd been attempting to respect her privacy, to the best of my ability.

Regret gnaws at me. She was assaulted, more than once, and because she didn't seek medical attention or report it to the police, I hadn't known. My sister kept it to herself because she didn't know I would care.

I don't feel numb when I think about what Franki experienced. That first rush of rage nearly took my ability to reason. I almost allowed what she went through to become about me, rather than what she needed from me. It was her distress that reminded me to get a fucking grip and think about what she was feeling, not what I was.

I pull out my phone and open the shopping app. Franki doesn't need an unhinged, angry man. She needs one who can think of ways to make her life better. What I'm doing isn't exactly romantic, but these will have to be things I picked up that are outside my plan.

The way she dives straight for the seat warmer every time we get in the car gave me some ideas. There are, to me, a surprising number of things I can get her that might help. Heated throw blankets, heated mattress pads, jackets with—

"Henry." I can guess from the irritated tone of my father's voice that he's probably been attempting to get my attention for some time.

I glance his way. My father is in his late fifties, but he's as formidable as he ever was, his blue eyes sharp beneath dark brows and a head of steel gray hair. "We don't use our phones at family dinners," he reminds me.

I click "Buy" on a blanket. "Acknowledged, but this is an emergency."

"What kind of emergency?" Bronwyn demands, not believing me for a second.

I purse my lips and say something that will both reassure her that it isn't a safety issue and put the attention squarely back on my sister and her husband, where it belongs. "Shopping. I need a black light. Immediately."

She squeals in affront that I dared to bring up the way she and her husband were caught in flagrante delicto on the family room sofa, of all places.

"You prissy diva." She fumes.

Order complete, I put my phone in my pocket and give her an arch look. "It's not prissy to be concerned about accidentally touching surfaces that have been contaminated by—"

At the last moment, I notice my nineteen-month-old niece watching me from her high chair with rapt attention, so I change my wording to something slightly more child friendly. I clear my throat. "*Shenanigans.*"

Franki smiles, amused by my antics.

Good. If she can laugh at Gabriel's tacky joke about Dean *"eating out,"* then she can laugh at my fussy act. Besides, it's completely true that I'd rather not think about my sister and Dean being intimate in any form. I'd especially prefer not to think of them doing *any of that* in a location where there is a risk that I'll need to apply bleach to my eyeballs. I want them to work out their issues. I do not want to know the private details of their *sex lives*.

I barely repress a shudder. Grandmother Rose, my father's mother and the very woman who started me on my quest for a wife, is seated directly across from me. She gives me a commiserating tilt of her head. After what she considers her own mistakes with Bronwyn, she's actively working not to say or do anything Bronwyn might take as criticism of her marriage.

Anytime there's a hint of anyone referring to Bronwyn and Dean and their inappropriate location for their *display of affection*, she flaps her napkin near her face or literally clutches her pearls. Grandmother is holding on to her benevolent tolerance of "crass behavior" by a thread.

Bronwyn cinches her lips up tight. "You're the one who told us we'd have privacy because you'd be in the office."

"To encourage you to *talk* to each other. Not to soil public surfaces."

"You make it sound like we were getting it on at a bus stop," Bronwyn fumes, voice rising. "This is our home. You brought everyone here for a surprise house party without warning us. When was there time or opportunity for Dean and me to do anything?"

"How do I know what you've been up to with The Stealth Husband?" I ask incredulously.

"Stop. Calling him. The Stealth Husband. And you probably know the same way you know everything else about him. Because you stick your nose everywhere, Henry. Just mind your own business for two whole minu–"

"Quiet," Dad says. "Bronwyn, you're getting loud."

Bronwyn backs off her rant, and I take a few automatic bites of my dinner and surreptitiously observe Franki. She's turned to give attention to one of Bronwyn's former college housemates, Sydney Walsh, essentially giving her back to Gabriel.

Good.

"Apologize." Dean's voice is quiet but deadly serious.

I heave a sigh and open my mouth to say the words *"I'm sorry"* to my sister. Teasing her was a dick move, and I took it too far.

Before I can speak, Dad says, "I beg your pardon?"

"You just shushed my wife like she was a barking dog. Apologize to her. Now."

Oh. Dean is talking to Dad. Truth be told, I hadn't even noticed that Dad shushed her.

He corrects all of us. Didn't he tell me to put my phone away like I was a teenager? Mom does it too. She scolded Gabriel for telling a dirty joke at the start of the meal.

Dad sits for a moment, shocked that someone would dare to tell him such a thing, but his expression changes when he looks back at Bronwyn, dawning awareness filtering in.

When I follow the direction of his gaze, real guilt hits me like a right hook to the jaw. Our father telling her to be quiet hurt her feelings.

I won't pretend I understand it, but I don't always need to understand these things. It's enough to know that it's true that people feel a certain way, even if I can't relate.

On the other hand, Dean standing up for her like this can only be a good thing, as far as I can see. I respect him for it.

Bronwyn leans into Dean and murmurs, "Please don't. The least I owe them is to try to remember to use my inside voice."

He says something in response that I can't hear and kisses her hand.

"It's not their fault. Believe me, they had their work cut out for them when they decided to try to turn *me* into a McRae," she says in a watery voice.

I suck in a breath and drop my fork to the tablecloth-covered surface. *Tried to turn her into a McRae.* As if this family is something she has to earn. As if, all these years after her adoption, she doesn't know she simply is a member of this family.

Bronwyn is our own little Tasmanian Devil and ray of sunshine rolled into one. I can't imagine the hole that would exist in our lives without her. When she'd nearly died, it was as though the fabric of our lives was being torn to shreds.

Who and what is this family without Charlotte and Bronwyn McRae?

"You are my child," Dad says roughly. "There's no 'turning you into' anything. There isn't a single thing on this earth that you could do or not do that would change that. I apologize if I ever made you feel like you needed to earn your place in this family. You're an amazing person, Bronwyn. You're wonderful exactly the way you are."

She looks doubtful, and Dad blinks his blue eyes hard a couple of times before he continues. "You've got a heart like the ocean, Bronwyn. You're awe-inspiring,"

Bronwyn answers with a watery laugh. "The roar of my surf gets a little loud, sometimes."

Dad smiles. "It does."

Bronwyn *is* like an ocean in many ways. She can certainly be overwhelming. Expecting her to act like less than herself would be a tragedy. "You can't expect the ocean to sound like a pond," I say, in what I hope is a reassuring tone. "Who would even want it to?"

Bronwyn makes eye contact and holds it. She dips her chin with a smile. "Thank you, Henry."

"I have something deep and meaningful to add too," Gabriel interjects.

When everyone looks in his direction, his eyes go wide. "I didn't mean right now. I'm not telling you how much I love you in front of all these people," he says, pouring himself a second glass of wine. "I'm shy."

All the tension that had been building from the moment we started this dinner drains away with the laughter that follows. He's good at that. What he said wasn't funny, but his timing was impeccable, the sentiment was sincere, and he created a break from the uncomfortable emotion that had us in a chokehold.

I envy him that ability. I'm good at escalation. At poking wounds and annoying people. I'm absolutely good at manipulating a situation to get what I want, but I'm not good at making other people smile and relax the way he is. Gabriel has a gift that I'm not sure he recognizes or appreciates.

The conversation moves on, and I zone out as I think about my next move with Franki. Until I catch the tail end of Grandma Miller making some comment about having caught my parents going at it in the family car. I scrape my fork through my lasagna and try to ignore what the rest of them seem to think is hilarious, and I think is private and not meant to be discussed at a family dinner.

"It sounded like some animal was trapped and dying," Grandad Miller says, sounding every bit as irritated as I am.

I've been told I think too literally and that other people don't really picture what they say when they say it. But *how* do you say something like that and not get an immediate, horrifying visual? Of my parents, no less.

I gag and shove my plate away.

Immediately, from her high chair, Phee bangs her baby spoon and imitates the sound.

I will not turn red over this. I refuse. If I blush in embarrassment like a teenager, Franki is going to think I'm an idiot. I can play this off as a joke.

Except, I can't . . . Because, *dammit, Grandad*, that was graphic and unnecessary.

"Aww, come on, Henry," Franki says.

When I look up and catch her eye, my neck heats. Her smile is so fucking kind. Even before she speaks, I know what she's really saying. *"I'm here, and I like you just the way you are."*

"I think it's cute when old people are still sweet on each other." The real words that end up leaving her lips are meant to pull the attention away from me and onto herself. In her own way, Franki is trying to protect me. It's not necessary, but she's so damn wonderful.

Dad puffs up and joins in her fun. "Hurtful words, young lady. Hurtful words."

"I hate to say it, but I think you've lost the moral high ground here." Gabriel grins at our mother.

Then he throws an arm around Franki and leans into her. I tense, ready to push my chair back and go straight at him. Rip that arm away from her. He can't touch her like that. He can't—

He whispers something in her ear, and she turns to him and smiles. Then she pats his hand where it rests on her shoulder.

Inside, I don't go cold; I burn hot with something I've never felt in my life. There's no logic in it at all. It's coming straight from my limbic cortex, the part of my brain that controls "Fight, Flight, Feed, and Fuck."

My reaction is unreasonable. It's unfair to Franki. She deserves better. *I need to be better.* I look down and shove my food around on my plate. If this is what jealousy feels like, maybe bringing Louis Larrabie here to encourage Dean wasn't my best idea.

Eighteen

Franki

Matilda | Harry Styles

"Wow. You have so much space," I say.

Two large tables with ergonomic seating anchor Bronwyn's craft room, and a cozy chair with an ottoman cuddles into a nook near a large window. Bronwyn has decorated the room with houseplants of various sizes, and a colorful painting holds pride-of-place above an antique sideboard she uses for storage. The effect is expansive, but warm and eclectic.

Bronwyn walks over to throw an arm around my waist. Meanwhile, Charlotte, Sydney, and Janessa are already seated on a comfortable-looking sofa and loveseat. Bronwyn's grandmother, Rose McRae, sits in the chair near the window with knitting needles already in hand, working on what appears to be a green blanket.

It always throws me off when I see Mrs. McRae doing something so normal. She's changed into a high-necked ruffled nightgown covered in an elegant silver brocade robe and fluffy slippers for the sleepover craft party. It had been so long since I last saw Mrs. McRae that her new fragility pulls at my heartstrings.

I remember her as an intimidating woman, one who hurt Bronwyn's feelings so often. Yet, she's the one who taught Bronwyn how to knit, and Bronwyn's ubiquitous pearl necklace was a gift from her Grandmother Rose. Even now, Mrs. McRae eyes Bronwyn with a combination of exasperation and love. "Bronwyn, don't bounce around like that. You need to sit down and rest. Act like a lady."

Bronwyn pulls a face, then turns back to her grandmother. "I took a nap earlier, Grandmother. But thank you for worrying about me."

Mrs. McRae purses her lips at Bronwyn's response, then shakes her head. "You should be convalescing, not entertaining. Don't overdo things. We almost lost you."

Bronwyn walks over to bend down and press her cheek to Mrs. McRae's. "I love you too, Grandmother."

Mrs. McRae huffs. "Goodness, child." But she holds Bronwyn's face to hers with a heavily veined hand for several seconds before she pats her and says, "Go sit down. I don't like to see you limping around like this."

For years, I've attempted to convince myself that my mother and father love me like Mrs. McRae loves her family. I told myself that they're simply not the kind of people who know how to show love, and deep down, where I can't see it, they feel it. But the truth is, I *can* see Mrs. McRae's love.

Bronwyn walks to one of the long tables and sits, motioning me closer. "Make yourself at home." She indicates the table, the shelf-lined walls, and the cabinetry that wraps around the space. "Pick a project. Any project."

A combination of overhead, ambient, and task lighting lend a cozy, but practical vibe to Bronwyn's craft room. Bronwyn likes to scrapbook sometimes, and she has a bookcase filled with those. Charlotte started some of them for her when we were just kids.

Charlotte might be an award-winning architect, but she also makes badass scrapbooks. Bronwyn's are cute and a little cheesy. Charlotte's look like every page is designed by an expensive New York ad agency.

Mostly, this room is loaded up with tons of different yarn.

"How does it feel to live my dream?" I tease.

Bronwyn smiles. "Advantages to living in a big house in the country." She indicates my pink pajamas. "I like the pj's."

I finger the soft, fleecy fabric covered in cartoon wiener dogs. I put my hair into a braid and took out my contact lenses too. "Henry bought them for me when we were shopping."

I'd seen them in the store and gushed about how cute they were. He immediately put them in the cart, but I stopped him. "My parents would kill me for wearing something like that."

He scowled. "What does anyone else have to say about what you do with your own body?" Then he distracted me and, apparently, bought them anyway. As far as the fact that I used an electric scooter to get around the store, he showed very little reaction at all. He definitely didn't appear to be embarrassed by me.

When I went up to change for our sleepover craft night, the pajamas lay folded on my pillow with a note that read: **"Dear Franki, If you want them, you should have them. The pajamas and your bedding have been laundered with the unscented detergent you prefer. Wear them or don't. It's your choice. Always Your Henry."**

Bronwyn narrows her eyes, but Charlotte has risen and moved to the center of the room to put an arm around my shoulders.

Charlotte's blonde hair, several shades darker than Bronwyn's, is tucked into a headband, and she's wearing blue and green plaid flannel. She's always been so down-to-earth. To me, this is what "normal" is supposed to be.

"Do you remember the pajamas I got for you when you were little and came for your first sleepover with Bronwyn?" she asks.

I nod. It was right before the divorce when I still lived with my parents. "I told you my father wouldn't let me keep them, so you saved them for me at your house."

These cute dachshund pj's feel like those ones did, not in fabric or design, but as though, by wearing them, I'm being rebellious, in the warmest, happiest way possible.

Charlotte scrunches her face up with a nose wrinkle. "You wore them until your ankles showed. I gave you bigger ones, but you didn't want to give up those ducky pajamas for the longest time."

I smile and lift one shoulder. "They made me feel like I was home."

Charlotte squeezes harder. "You're always home with us."

Emotion rises up inside me, fast and painful. The McRae's aren't my family, no matter how much I tried to pretend they were when I was a child.

I hug Charlotte back as Bronwyn says, "I'm sure it didn't occur to Henry how bad buying an unrelated woman sleepwear would look."

Charlotte laughs. "Bronwyn, Henry has always been thoughtful. They probably reminded him of Oliver. No one thinks your brother is attempting to seduce Franki with cartoon sausage dogs and fleece loungewear. They're friends."

Everyone laughs, including the elder Mrs. McRae. Charlotte has a point. If Henry's goal were seduction, I imagine something sexy would be the order of the day.

I attempt to shift her focus. "So, what have we got to work with?"

"Scrapbooking over here. Jewelry-making supplies on the table over there."

Bronwyn holds up a handful of photos. "I'm finally putting my wedding photos in an album."

I peer over her shoulder, and she spreads them out on the table. They're all what I assume are cellphone photos. Bronwyn and Dean look so happy. It gives me a pang because I know what happened next and how much they both went through. If I'd seen these, I'd never have doubted her relationship in a million years. "The way he looks at you with his heart in his eyes . . . I don't know how I didn't see it before."

"I felt so guilty that you guys weren't there."

"Don't waste time on regrets. We should organize a big anniversary party for you guys. Then we'll celebrate."

She wraps an arm around my waist. "That's a perfect idea."

"So, what did you wear under the dress?" I ask.

Janessa calls from the sofa, "If you say anything other than Agent Provacateur, I won't believe you."

"You don't need to know about my knickers," Bronwyn says.

"Aha! Then it was definitely AP," I say in triumph.

She laughs and shoves a box across the table to me. "If you don't want to scrapbook."

I open the box and grin as I pull the thread and beads out. "When was the last time we made friendship bracelets?"

"Too long. Remember when we used to FaceTime while we worked and mailed them to each other?"

"Of course, I remember."

"Yours were always the best," Bronwyn says.

"Seriously," Janessa agrees. "You made the rest of us look like kindergartners."

I shake my head, but I smile at the memory of how they wore my bracelets until they fell off. After which, they each texted me photos of their bare arms and begged me to send them new ones.

Carrying the box with me, I lower myself carefully onto the big floor pillow near the sofa, lifting the supplies first for Janessa, then Sydney, to choose their colors.

Bronwyn screws her face up, her tongue sticking out one side of her mouth, as she trims a photo with scissors. "Dean is leaning against a railing in this photo, and I'm gonna cut him out so he looks *sassy.*"

She's speaking really loudly, almost a shout, but she does that when she's excited. Charlotte laughs, then covers her mouth with the back of her hand.

Bronwyn looks up at us, her eyes innocently wide. "What? You think my big, muscle-y husband can't be sassy?"

Through the open doorway, and from a little way down the hall, Dean hollers in a deep, booming voice laced with humor, "Woman, behave yourself."

Phee giggles from the hall, and we all break into peals of laughter.

Bronwyn must have seen him walking past the door and decided to jerk his chain. Honestly, I don't know how she ever got the nerve up to tease that man.

Dean is scary looking. Or he was. I haven't figured out exactly what's changed. Dean looks the same, but there's a gentleness in his eyes that I'd never noticed before. He loves Bronwyn just the way she is, and he's not just patient with Phee, he adores her.

Henry and I could never have a life like this. Even if we were together, we'd be in an apartment in the city, and he would be busy all the time. That's not even taking into consideration that his marriage proposal all but spelled out that if I married him, I'd be on the back burner of his life. There for the sake of being conveniently available when *he* was available.

I concentrate on my bracelet, ignoring my achey and clumsy fingers as I weave. I want to do this.

Janessa reaches down and pokes me gently. "Hey, where's our sunny girl? You look upset."

"Nothing is wrong." I'm definitely not worked up over something stupid that I can't control like wondering how Henry feels about me. This thing with him feels like braiding this bracelet. A little clumsy on my part, and with the potential to turn painful. But, oh, it could be beautiful.

"Who is that one for?" Sydney asks, noting the bracelet I've started doesn't match any of the colors they selected for me to make for them.

"I thought I'd make one for Henry too. In thanks, for the pj's."

Bronwyn's smile is half-cringe. "That's sweet, but don't get your feelings hurt if he doesn't wear it. He's really picky about what he puts on his body, and he's not very sentimental. It's not personal."

"I know. My feelings won't be hurt." Honestly, I can't imagine him wearing it at all. It's meant as a gesture on my part, not a demand. "What he does with it is up to him. He can use it as a bookmark or shove it in a drawer."

I probably won't work up the nerve to give it to him at all. I hesitate. "You don't think we're too old for this? We aren't teenagers anymore."

"I don't give a flying f—" Bronwyn shoots a sidelong glance at her mother, then corrects herself. "Fig if anyone thinks we're juvenile. We're grown women. We should be able to enjoy what we enjoy without worrying about what other people think about it. As long as you're not hurting anyone, what you like to do to relax is your own business."

There's something comfortingly nostalgic in the repetitive motions involved, in the sentiment, and even the smell of the cotton embroidery floss. The world is a constant wild riot of change around us, and this one moment feels like an anchor to the best parts of my past. I swipe a tear from under my glasses. I don't know why emotion has chosen this evening to spill over, and I work to push it back down and keep a smile on my face.

Charlotte reaches down to hug my shoulders and hand me a Kleenex. "You okay, honey?" she whispers.

"I'm being silly. It's just so rare for us to be together like this anymore."

"Arden and I didn't even get to see you when you went to Europe with the girls two summers ago," she says.

I dab under my eyes with the tissue. "Yes. It's been too long."

And I've known such a dearth of real affection that experiencing it now is inexplicably painful. I've been out in the cold for so long my toes have gone numb. Now, I'm sinking into what should be a comfortable bath, but instead of gentle warmth, it's an open flame. I've become so desperately aware of how much I want. And want. And *want*.

If I sit in the dark, it's easy to imagine the room around me has everything I need, but Henry's attention, and the easy affection the entire McRae family shares . . . They're shining a light on my empty spaces and making it impossible to pretend that loneliness hasn't been the soundtrack to my days and nights.

I'm giving myself permission to see what happens with Henry. To remember to look on the bright side and anticipate the possibility of good things. I'll talk to him, and I'll take his answers at face value. If I can't trust Henry, I can't trust anyone at all.

Nineteen

Henry

Take Your Love | Olly Murs

The library is conveniently positioned next to the craft room, so I pull a random novel from Bronwyn's shelves and sit myself in a chair near the open doorway. I've chosen an urban fantasy romance novel. I should put it back, but the blurb catches my attention. The story sucks me in fast, not only because the plot is interesting, but because it offers valuable insight into what things a woman might find romantic or sexy. It's too soon to compile and test my romance theories. I'll need a larger sampling than this, but I make mental notes as I read.

When Franki emerges from the craft room more than an hour later, I meet her as she heads for the stairs. "Do you need a hand?"

She shakes her head, then stops. "You know what? Yes. Can you carry these?"

I reach for the small plastic box she's carrying, and she hands me her phone, as well. "It'll be easier. One hand holding my cane, one hand on the rail."

"Do you need help up the stairs or for your room to be moved downstairs? I should have thought of that."

Franki shakes her head. "If I need help, I'll speak up."

She turns her head toward me and smiles. "Thank you for offering, though, and thank you for carrying my stuff."

As we walk up the stairs, she's much slower than I would be, but I match her pace. "Of course."

She clears her throat. "I owe you an apology."

I stop, surprised, then continue on as she takes another step. "For?"

She cringes. "I ran into someone who wanted to go out with me, and I basically used you as a shield. I let him think we were together even before we'd gone on a date. I didn't think about how if you were looking for a wife, me confirming rumors about us might have made that more difficult for you. It was inconsiderate."

We've reached the top of the landing. "You and I should talk."

"We could go in my room."

I usher her into her room and close the door behind us. She sets her cane aside, takes the box from my hands and places it on her dresser, then tosses her phone onto the bed. She smooths her hands down the soft fabric of her pajamas. "I'm sorry. I shouldn't have done that."

"Don't apologize to me for this. You can use me as a shield anytime. And, since I *want* us to be together, I hardly see you telling people we are as a problem."

Her lips part on an indrawn breath.

"Do you think I'd be kissing you today and looking for someone else to sign on the dotted line tomorrow?"

"You said you need a wife."

Slowly, I crowd into her space. She backs up as I approach until her shoulder blades touch the wall, but the lift at the corner of her mouth and her narrowed eyes are pure sass.

I plant both my hands on the wall on either side of her head. It's not a posture I would assume with anyone else. It leaves me open and vulnerable, despite the fact that I'm the one looming over her. "What I need"—I lean closer—"is you."

She makes a huffy little sound. "Okay."

I lean back, slightly suspicious. I expected this to go quickly, but something here is off. I'm not certain we're talking about the same thing.

Her phone vibrates. She flinches, but makes no move to retrieve it.

"Why do you look afraid of your phone?"

She thunks her head back against the wall as the incessant vibration continues. "Because it's one of two people. If it's my mother, she's calling to yell at me because I'm not in California. If it's my father, he's calling to yell at me for refusing to go out with one of his business partners." She takes a deep breath. "I haven't answered his phone calls all day, but I have to face the music sooner or later."

"Do you?" I ask softly.

A new phone call comes through, and I glance over to see Jonny's name as the incoming call. He's trying again. I step back and tip my head to the phone. "By all means, Franki. Let's hear what Jonny Lennox has to say."

"Should I tell him we're together? You don't mind me doing that?"

I show her my teeth in a facsimile of a smile. "I'd accept nothing less."

She picks up her phone and puts it on speaker. "Hey, Jonny. How are you?" Her voice shakes, and I could kill him for that alone.

"You've upset Leo," Jonny barks.

Franki swallows hard. "He upset me. I guess we're even."

"I literally give you the clothes on your back, and you can't throw me one fucking bone."

"I said I wouldn't—"

"And *I said you would*. Is this because I didn't return your phone calls for a couple of weeks? Grow the hell up."

He takes an audible breath. "He made it clear that he's willing to accept you if you change your mind, even after you embarrassed him. He's giving you another chance. I reassured him that Henry McRae is just an old friend of the family. Leo is going to pull out of this deal if you don't cooperate. You will call that number he gave you and beg his forgiveness."

"I'm not apologizing—"

"You will do as you're told."

I curl my hand in a fist and shove it in my pocket to prevent myself from barging over and scaring the shit out of Franki.

Jonny's next words are more controlled as his voice becomes coaxing. "I'll find you somewhere to live. I'll pay for your health insurance, and I'll pay for your grad school. All I need is for you to play nice with the man."

I have a moment of pure self-loathing when I hear his words. No wonder she'd wanted to stab me with a fork. I sounded just like her piece-of-shit father when I proposed.

She shakes her head. "I don't need—"

"Say, 'Thank you, Jonny,'" he snaps.

I've heard enough.

When I reach over her shoulder to lift the phone from her hand, she barely startles. Eyes wide, she turns my way and watches.

I move my lips into a reassuring smile for her sake.

"Hello, Jonny," I say pleasantly. "How are you this evening?"

"Who is this?" Jonny sounds wary. Feeling out exactly whom he's speaking to before he lets the vitriol fly.

No one can say he's unintelligent, and it makes me hate him more. He's not an equal-opportunity asshole. No, he looks at Franki and abuses the power he believes he holds over her because he's done so from the time she was a vulnerable child. He's groomed her to accept his treatment of her as normal.

The same cold numbness that fills my veins when I snap on a pair of surgical gloves to torture someone for information, floods through me now.

"Franki didn't mention she was living with me? This is her fiancé." I affect a genial tone. Butter wouldn't melt in my mouth.

This, Franki reacts to. Gaze flying to mine, she drops to sit on the edge of her bed and chews on her lip.

I pause to let my words sink in and for Franki's father to realize what it means. Then I clear my throat. "Henry McRae," I say gently.

He's silent for a long, satisfying moment while he absorbs that information. He knows my reputation. The carefully cultivated rumors surrounding me aren't exaggerations. In fact, they're mild compared to what I'm actually capable of. He has to know that, at the very least, I would dismantle his business and his reputation without blinking if I view him as my enemy.

Finally, he says, voice strangled, "She didn't mention she was engaged."

I sigh dramatically. "Understandable when you won't take her calls. We would have preferred to share our happy news in person."

I glance at Franki and say, "Isn't that right, darling?"

I don't expect her to say anything in response, but a martial light enters her eyes, and she says, quite loudly, "We were planning a family dinner where we'd share the news. It was a surprise."

This time, my smile is slow, but real. I wink and mouth, "Good girl." Color blazes in her cheeks in response.

It takes Jonny a beat too long to recover from my announcement before he says suspiciously, "She hasn't been back in New York long enough for this."

I laugh. "Have you heard of airplanes? Telephones? It's amazing how two people who live on opposite sides of the country can manage to stay connected over the years."

Franki chews on the inside of her cheek, frowning in response to my comment, and I'm struck by an uncomfortable realization. I shouldn't have waited for her. I should have gotten on a plane and gone to her.

Instead of going through the motions and existing with a Franki-shaped hole in my life for years, reading and re-reading her reports every month, and wondering how she was . . . I should have picked up the phone and said, *"You're important to me. How are you?"*

Franki's father clears his throat. "Then, congratulations are in order. And of course I take her calls. She's so dramatic if I don't answer the phone immediately. Franki has been a little spoiled over the years. I hope you'll forgive me for that. She'll certainly have high expectations of you. You'll need to put your foot down, or she'll treat you like that little trained rat she calls a dog."

Franki makes a sound of outrage.

"I could only dream of being so lucky," I say.

He laughs, obviously taking my words as sarcasm. It's clear that Jonny doesn't realize he was on speaker earlier. Now he's scrambling to figure out how he can leverage an "in-law" connection with the McRae family. And he's definitely worried about what my *fiancée* might have shared with me.

"Franki's not nearly demanding enough. There's not a thing she could ask for that it won't be my pleasure to provide," I say.

He chuckles. "You say that now. But it's better to start as you mean to go on. You have to be firm with them."

I've got more than enough *firmness* going on behind my zipper when I'm near her.

It will make my revenge easier if he's confident that he's in control, so I play along. "I believe I'll do just that."

Franki marches over to me, expression calm, but mouth pressed tight, reaches out, finds my nipple through the cotton broadcloth of my shirt and *twists*.

Jonny's laugh covers my yelp as I cup my abused nipple and squirm away from her.

I mouth, "It was a joke."

She stomps away and searches through her suitcase for something I hope is not a handgun.

"We should definitely make time for that dinner," he says. I can hear the way the tension has slowly leached out of Jonny's voice under my pleasant demeanor.

Franki finds what she was looking for. A sketch pad and pencil. She writes me a note that contains two words: **"Not funny."**

I nod sharply in acknowledgment and mouth back, "Sorry."

She's right that it isn't funny. Even if I was thinking about something entirely different than what her father implied.

I'm in a confounding place at the moment. My mind is mapping out all the beautiful revenge scenarios I'll enact on this asshole. I'm cognizant that it's necessary to lull him into complacency for my plans to be most effective. I'm also unwilling to hurt Franki's feelings in the process because then what will be the point of any of it?

I'm strangely giddy because I've found the perfect segue into her life, but it's *also* enraging that it's because her father is garbage. My emotions, which I'm used to having closed off entirely, are not only emerging, but have *layers* I'm struggling to navigate. Only years of practice staying cool under fire allows me to maintain a bland, unassuming tone with Jonny. "Hmm."

"What did you say?" Jonny asks.

"Apologies. Your daughter distracted me for a moment." How far to go? I run my hand over Franki's hair and down her thick braid.

She shivers a little, leaning into my touch and peering at me with big, brown eyes wide behind her glasses. The Sexy Librarian in wiener dog pajamas. Who knew this is what would do it for me?

"One thing I need to make perfectly clear. Franki isn't going to be entertaining any of your business partners. I'm a possessive man. You understand."

This time, Franki grins and lifts her palm to hover in the air in front of me. At my puzzled expression, she lifts my hand for me and slaps it against her own.

She's turned me into an idiot.

But context is everything. High fives are friend and sibling behavior. They're *"awesome job making brown belt, little buddy."* Not hot woman in nightwear, standing in her bedroom, and close enough I catch a faint sweet scent that reminds me of the panties in my pocket.

I shake my head and glance at the ceiling. She holds on to the high five, threading her fingers through mine, and I give them a gentle squeeze.

When Jonny grumbles his agreement, we both glance at her phone, brought back to where we are and what we're doing.

"Francesca grew out of her ugly duckling stage. She's pretty enough to be a trophy wife now," Jonny says.

I'd believed myself as angry as I could be with Franki's father. A full cup of cold-blooded, icy rage. Any more of his transgressions would pour over the sides. I was wrong, because I've leveled the hell up. The ice cracks, and beneath it surges molten hot lava. This man is why she called herself an ugly duckling that night. The parents who should have told her she was amazing were the very ones constantly working to undermine her confidence.

"She was never an ugly *anything*," I bite out, losing the iron hold on my temper. "She's a funny, intelligent, creative, thoughtful, beautiful *person*. And she's nobody's *trophy,* you—"

Franki rips the phone out of my hand, presses End Call, and throws it onto the bed.

I watch her, startled and wary, wondering where I went wrong and if I should protect my nipples. Then she grabs my shirt in both her hands, yanks me to her, and crashes her mouth against mine.

Twenty

Franki

4 Minutes | Madonna, Justin Timberlake, Timbaland

I should have been smoother about this kiss. More patient. This is awkward and . . . *shoot*. Our glasses scrape together and squish against our faces.

But the things Henry said have me overwhelmed with feelings that need an outlet.

Henry was acting to shield me from my father, and I know I should have been stronger on my own. I shouldn't need help to handle the man. But having someone . . . Henry . . . here in my corner feels so damn good. I'm not alone. I don't have to do this myself.

At first, Henry was so cold with Jonny that I doubt most people would have even caught on to the anger riding him. Then white-hot fury had torn through his frigid calculation.

Henry said I was *"a person"* that night on the balcony too. He'd called me *"fine the way you are."* In my insecure, wounded heart, I'd found it dismissive, but that's not how he'd meant it.

Henry draws away from me, and I ease back, embarrassed by my enthusiasm. "Sorr—"

He doesn't let me get my apology out. He's too busy taking both of our glasses off, tossing them to the nightstand, then backing me toward the bed with his mouth on mine before I can finish the word.

He's filling my senses, completely taking over, his enthusiasm more than a match for mine. Henry searches my mouth, as if he's starving for me. It's the most carnal thing I've experienced in my life.

He doesn't act as if kissing me is a perfunctory task that must be performed in order to move on to the part where he tries to get me to take my clothes off. He kisses me as if he can't bear to take his mouth from mine. His body is strong and hard. His hands are everywhere. My back. Easing under my pajama top.

What would happen if I gave myself over to him? Let go and put myself in those hands? That's what I want. To stop the thinking and fighting and trying to protect my heart.

He's touching my waist now.

Now, he spans my rib cage, thumbs tracing the undersides of my breasts.

Now, his hands are on my hips, fingers digging into my butt. Though, for all the frantic energy between us and all the hard strength in him, he remains gentle.

When I feel the bed against my legs, I hold onto his shoulders and ease down until I'm lying on my back with Henry lowering himself on top of me. He groans when our entire bodies line up against each other. With a roll of his hips, his erection nudges into the cradle of my thighs. I *want* him to touch me. I'll die if he stops. My hands in his hair, I shift and slide against him, rubbing on him like a cat.

He moves to kiss my neck, and I angle my head to give him access. His lips there, his tongue. His breath. Goose bumps and a pleasurable shiver take me, my nipples pebbling as a lush, molten, heat floods my pelvis.

My pajama top is rucked up, my abdomen bare. I need his skin against mine, but as I slide my hands to his waist, determined to start by untucking his shirt, a woman's scream rents the air.

I freeze at the sound, but Henry explodes into action, rolling off me, grabbing his glasses, and heading toward the door in the space of a heartbeat. He spares me a glance. "Stay here."

He's gone before I even have time to close my mouth.

A virtual stampede is taking place in the hallway. Everyone is out there, talking and muttering about Louis Larrabie, and I'm not staying in this room just because Henry said, *"Stay here,"* the same way I'd tell Oliver to sit.

When I enter the hallway, I'm met by Sydney and Janessa, who are both fuming.

"What's happening?" I ask.

"Even I can't see what's going on," Janessa says, referring to her height. "The McRaes have formed a barricade in front of her door."

"It sounds like Louis tried something with Bronwyn, which would be incredibly stupid of him, but I don't know if he tried something. Or he *tried something*," Sydney says.

That sentence might sound nonsensical to a guy, but any woman understands the distinction. Given her scream, I think it was the latter. If he'd politely expressed feelings to her, she'd have asked him to leave, not screamed, *"Louis, no!"* loudly enough to bring the household running.

"Is she kicking the shit out of him in there? Is that why they're all just standing in the hall instead of helping her?" Janessa asks.

"How would we know?" Sydney asks in exasperation.

"I don't think she's well enough for that," I say.

"One of us has to get in there and make sure she's okay," Sydney says.

As a unit, they turn assessing eyes on me. I stare back warily. "What? Why are you looking at me like that?"

"You have to volunteer as tribute," Janessa says. "I'd have to try to shove my way in past three McRae men, and that's never going to work."

"But you want *me* to? You're tall," I say to Janessa. "Can't you just look over or through the cracks or something?"

"They still have a few inches on me, so, no, I can't."

Sydney plants her hands on her hips and says, "I barely know them. I can't force my way in there, but you're practically family. They treat you like you're their little sister. It won't be weird if you do it."

I almost choke. Henry's hand on my boob four minutes ago didn't feel very sisterly.

"Come on," Sydney's dark eyes bore into me. "Take one for the team."

"You were the soccer player, not me," I argue.

Just then, another muffled scream of outrage and the vague sound of male threats emanate from the room at the end of the hall.

"I'm going in. You better appreciate that I am about to attempt to breach a barricade made from 100 percent McRae," I say.

Janessa gives me a gentle nudge. "Go forth and conquer, then report back for your award ceremony."

I hesitate and Sydney starts humming a song from *Les Misérables*.

I wave her away. "Stop pressuring me. I'm thinking."

I start by trying to find a space to wedge my way into. Charlotte allows me through the first line of defense, probably because she's too startled to stand her ground, but then I reach Henry, Arden, and Gabriel. When I try to slip between Henry and Arden, neither budges. Arden gives me a pat on the shoulder, but otherwise ignores me. Henry scowls back at me. "I told you to stay in your room."

"Don't speak to me like I'm a dog, Henry," I snap.

Horror floods his face. "I didn't mean it like that. I was concerned for your safety."

"Is something dangerous happening?"

He glances into the room then back toward me, a glint of amusement entering his eyes. "Not for Bronwyn and Dean."

To hell with it. I crouch down onto all fours, ignoring my sore knees, and insert my hands between Henry's thighs. He looks down at me, and there's no question now that he's amused. He also probably feels guilty that he spoke to me in a way I found offensive.

"Let me in," I whisper.

"Will you stay with me until Louis isn't likely to accidentally catch you in the crossfire?"

What is the creep even doing in there that Henry's talking like that? "I'll stay with you," I promise.

Henry widens his stance, and I pop my head and shoulders between his knees, holding on to his calves, just in time to see Bronwyn poke Louis in the chest with a finger and hiss, "My husband saved me from you."

Dean puts his hands around Bronwyn's waist, and, with what looks like no effort whatsoever, picks her straight up and sets her on the bed before he turns back to Louis.

Bronwyn's husband is back to being "scary Dean." If that man ever looked at me the way he's looking at Louis, I'd definitely cry.

Louis spits out accusations about Dean. I know for a fact they aren't true because Bronwyn is the one who convinced Dean to marry her, not the other way around. Then Louis starts shit-talking Phee. Who bad-mouths a *baby*?

I'm not sure what Louis expects after the things he's doing and saying, but I'm not surprised when Bronwyn scrambles off the bed, slides in front of Dean, and pops Louis in the mouth.

Louis staggers back away from her, holding his bleeding lip, squealing, and saying the nastiest things. When he insults the baby again, I twist through Henry's legs to try to go to Bronwyn. I know the moment I do it that I shouldn't have.

My left hip makes a popping sound and burns like heck. It's not my hip per se, but actually my sacroiliac joint. Because of my shorter leg, it's been pushed out of alignment many times, so it happens way too easily now. Between my knees, which are already aching, and now my misaligned SI joint, I suck in a breath through my teeth at the pain.

Henry crouches down in concern, reaching for me. "You okay?" he asks quietly.

I give him my serene face. "Fine." I will be, anyway. This isn't anything worth fussing over.

He straightens, taking me at my word, both of us distracted by Louis's next words.

Oh my God. He did *not* just say that. I hold on to Henry's legs so hard I can't believe he doesn't push me away, but I need something to hold on to, or *I'll* punch Louis.

The guys continue to stand in the doorway, in perfect control. Dean looks terrifying, but he hasn't lost his temper either. These men are saints.

"Louis, get out of my house," Bronwyn says.

"I have witnesses." He points at us. "They all saw you and the hulk assault me."

Henry disagrees, "That's not what I saw. I heard my sister scream, 'Stop hurting yourself, Louis.' And when I got here, I saw Louis punch himself in the face and say he was going to frame Dean for it."

Gabriel straightens his cuffs. "That's exactly what I saw too."

"Me three," I collaborate because *screw Louis*.

Everything escalates fast from there, with Louis nearly knocking Bronwyn off her, admittedly still wobbly, feet.

Henry swears under his breath, tensing under my hands. Dean puts Louis in a painful-looking hold with his arms shoved behind his back, and Henry places a palm on my head, murmuring, "Be back soon. Just making sure Louis doesn't forget his luggage."

Somehow, I doubt luggage is the reason Louis has a four-man escort off the premises, but while Louis raves like a lunatic, not one of the men loses his cool.

I'm more concerned about Bronwyn, but when I try to stand and go to her, I can't. I need something to hold on to, so I crawl toward her as the guys rearrange themselves to make room for Dean to drag Louis out.

Crawling isn't particularly easy, either, because my knees are not happy with me. I'm more dragging my left leg than anything, but, luckily, I don't have far to go before I reach Bronwyn. Between her hand and the edge of the bed, I drag myself to stand and wrap my arms around her.

She isn't crying, but she is shaking. Charlotte joins us and assists Bronwyn to the bathroom to wash her hand and check to see if her knuckles need ice.

I lower myself to the edge of her bed as Sydney and Janessa join me, then lie back and grimace to Janessa, indicating my left leg. "Want to play footsie?"

It's a code word she understands. There are a few exercises and stretches I can do to work the joint back into place, and one of the easiest involves another person planting my foot against her chest and leaning toward me.

I concentrate on awareness of my body and pushing the pain from my conscious mind.

Mouth tight, Janessa lifts my heel, and I'm careful not to let my calm expression falter. *It's not that bad, only discomfort. Not that bad. Not that bad.* If I keep telling myself those words, I can convince myself of the truth of them.

Sydney looks confused. "Wait. Are you two together? Is this *another* secret relationship?"

Her question pulls me out of my meditative state, even as the joint works its way back into place with a barely audible *pop*.

Sydney's tan skin goes gray. "What was that? Did she just crack your hip like a walnut?"

"It's nothing. Never had a chiropractor crack your back?"

She looks doubtful. "Really?"

I distract her. "You think Janessa and I would make a good couple?"

Janessa laughs. Her long, dark hair slid forward when she worked on my leg, and she pushes it over her shoulder now. "We'd be the grumpy/sunshine trope. Franki needs a cinnamon roll hero."

"I think I could go for the sexy professor type," I venture, offering up a ginormous hint to feel out what they might think about me potentially hooking up with Henry.

They both look doubtful.

"Maybe," Sydney says, "if he's also got golden retriever energy."

"Definitely no grumps, alphas, or anyone with even a hint of morally gray."

Bronwyn emerges from her bathroom. "Who is morally gray?"

"No one. We're just discussing Franki's type."

Her expression clears. "That's easy. You need someone who will treat you like the queen you are. Likes to cuddle. Is emotionally intelligent. Recognizes how funny, capable, and talented you are. Worships the ground you walk on. Likes dogs. And has a huge d—"

"*Bronwyn*," her mother warns.

She winks at her mother. "I was going to say 'has a huge duck call collection.'"

Charlotte rolls her eyes.

I snort.

Janessa nods. "As long as he's sweet enough to give the rest of us a toothache. That's what you need. One of those himbo, sunshine boy types."

Twenty-One

Henry

Brother | Kodaline

I pull the visor down to look in the mirror. The blood splatter isn't that bad. At least there's no arterial spray. It's not as though I killed Louis. A little light torture, nothing more.

"That was a waste of time, but I can't say it wasn't fun," Gabriel says.

I frown at my brother. "Torture isn't fun. It's something you do when it's necessary."

"Are you seriously telling me it didn't feel good to hurt the man who hurt our sister?"

"That's not why we did it." Not that there turned out to be much more information to extract. The man had already confessed to several crimes before we even took him to the garden shed. The idiot was bragging.

"We should have let Dean have him," Gabriel says.

"Dean might have killed him. His emotions were too involved. It's never wise to do something like that because you *want* to vs. *need* to."

I don't pretend to myself that my soul isn't painted with tar, but I have lines I don't cross. That's one of them. I let my emotions get in the way earlier when

I considered murdering Jonny Lennox, but I don't need to physically harm the man to make him live a life of regret.

Gabriel reaches into the backseat of my SUV and pulls a duffel forward to rest in his lap. Unzipping the bag, he sorts through the items and hands me a couple of baby wipes. I lift a sardonic eyebrow.

"Yeah, yeah. Obviously, you need a shower, but you can't walk back in the house looking like that. What if one of Bronwyn's friends is downstairs looking for a glass of water or Phee needed a bottle or something? You'd scare the girls."

I don't think Phee still drinks from baby bottles. She uses cups with spouts on them, but his point still stands. I snatch the wipes from his hand and clean my face. I should have taken the time to find a splash guard and gloves, but this was impromptu information collection, not planned. "Did I get it all?"

He pulls out another wipe and rubs vigorously at a place near my ear that I couldn't see in the mirror. "Come here, little man. Let Mommy get you all cleaned up."

I huff a laugh. For a moment, it feels like my brother is here.

He sobered up after dinner, for starters, which is rare lately. He tried to flirt with Sydney Walsh, and she told him the smell of alcohol made her want to vomit. Several of us heard the exchange. She wasn't exactly subtle about it.

I don't remember my biological mother. I was only two when she died of a drug overdose when Gabriel was only a few months old, but Dad has occasionally spoken of the sense of helplessness associated with watching another person spiral. I'm beginning to understand that feeling.

When Gabriel has downtime, he's got a drink in his hand. Unfortunately, he has a *lot* of downtime. My brother is unraveling, and I can't fix this for him. No matter how much I wish I could.

Lately, I miss my brother even when we're in the same room. I don't know if Gabriel is an alcoholic or not, but if he isn't yet, he's on his way.

I work on getting the blood off my hands as Gabriel pulls a clean black T-shirt from the bag.

"The shirt has to go. Your pants are fine until you shower," he says.

I remove my bloodstained, white button-down, and he stuffs it, along with the wipes, into a plastic bag. I'll burn the whole thing later.

I catch him glaring at the old scar on my abdomen before he shakes his head with a jerk and looks back down at his hands, clearing his throat. "How are things going with Franki?"

I pull the shirt over my head. "We're getting married."

"Just like that?"

"It has to be fast. I don't have time for anything else." Now that I think about it, I'm not sure she did agree. She said *"okay,"* but even at the time I wasn't certain we were talking about the same thing. She enthusiastically backed me up with her father, but she may have thought I was lying to him to get him off her case.

He frowns. "I assumed you had feelings for her. If your real goal is to get your hands on MPD, then you need someone mercenary, not sweet. Choose someone prickly and capable of standing up to you, not someone who will roll over and give you everything you demand. It's not a fair exchange. There's no honor in it."

I eye Gabriel speculatively then take a shot in the dark to see what happens. "You may have a point. I understand Sydney Walsh has some financial problems. She'd probably agree to be my wife, and she's plenty prickly."

Gabriel turns on me in fury. "Don't touch Sydney. Don't even talk to Sydney. Stay the fuck away from her—"

He clamps his mouth shut, and I affect a surprised tone. "Is that how it is?"

"Whatever you're thinking, you're wrong."

"I'm thinking that in the future, if you put your arm around Franki and whisper in her ear again, I'll have to encourage the single guys on the team to take a look Sydney's way. I hear women are really fond of Ryan. Harris too. Sydney's cute, *if you go for the prickly type.* I'm certain if I let the guys know that dating her isn't a conflict of interest, they'll be lining up to whisper in her ear," I say silkily.

Gabriel's jaw flexes tightly, then he smiles. "I was acting brotherly with Franki. Your jealousy is unfounded."

"It wouldn't bother you to see a man holding Sydney and whispering in her ear?"

He looks away, his muscles tight.

"How about I stay out of your love life, and you stay out of mine?" I offer.

Gabriel huffs. "I don't have a love life, but even I know having a wife who can trust you is more important than whether you take control of one more damn company."

"What would you know about it? Your life is one party after the other."

He snorts. "You're the golden boy. I'm the fuck u—"

"How do you afford your lifestyle? Who funds our missions? Who pays for our security? Who keeps our employees working with fair wages? Do you think I like working a hundred hours a week? Do you think I want to be the only person in this family who gives a shit about logistics? I studied physics and astronomy. I never wanted any of this. You've got an MBA and can't be bothered to drag your ass out of bed until noon. Don't leave me hanging by a fucking noose, then tell me *you don't like the way I'm dying*."

Gabriel goes utterly still.

I suck in a breath through my nose.

He shakes his head stiffly. "I didn't know. I should have....I didn't want to step on your toes."

I scoff in disbelief, and he looks away.

"I didn't want to disappoint you," he says.

"I don't understand that statement."

"I'm the reason you were shot, Henry. You were protecting me from my own stupidity. I'm the fuck up, and you're the one who saves everyone. I didn't think you'd want my interference. You don't trust me, and why would you?"

I stare at him, trying to understand. "We were children. The only person at fault for shooting me was the woman who did it. If I don't trust you now, it's because you're rarely sober enough for me to rely on."

He leans back against the headrest and stares out the front windshield at the clear night sky. He's quiet for a long moment. Finally, he admits, "I fucked up. Sydney...knows things she shouldn't."

"You were drunk," I say flatly.

"Yep."

"Are we talking blackmail or is it worse than that?"

"Dad and I came up with a solution, but if she'd been a federal agent"—He closes his eyes—"I'm heading to rehab on Monday and getting my shit together."

I do my best to hide my doubts. "Sounds good."

"I'll get this figured out, Henry."

This time, my words are sincere. "You're acknowledging there's a problem. That's the first step. You call me when you need me. I'll be there," I say.

"I will. I won't let you down."

"Don't let yourself down."

He opens his door. "You do the same. Find an answer for MPD that doesn't involve screwing up the best thing that's ever happened to you."

I open my own door and speak over the hood of the car as he walks away. "I love her. Needing to marry her sooner, rather than later, doesn't change that. She'll understand."

He turns back and shakes his head slowly. "I don't know much about love, but I know a train wreck when I see it."

Twenty-Two

Henry

Legend | The Score

When I return to my bedroom, I move straight to the en suite bathroom to grab a shower. It's too early to feel relief that Gabriel is getting help, but some of Franki's attitude must be rubbing off on me because there's a new lightness inside me.

I'm also anxious to get back to Franki. We were in the middle of something important when the situation with Louis happened.

Gabriel's take on this is dead wrong. Our relationship has nothing to do with financial incentive. I would be asking her to marry me whether MPD was in the picture or not.

Hearing the way her father attempted to leverage money against her made me physically ill with the realization that I'd tried the same methods the night I proposed. This isn't about using her. It never was. I can make her happy and take care of my responsibilities. It doesn't have to be one or the other.

Given the time, I'm certain Franki is asleep, but if she hasn't locked the door between our rooms, I'll check on her before I go to bed. *Who am I kidding?* I'll check on her if she has locked it too.

As I step out of the shower and snag a towel, I hear it. *Tap. Tap.*

I almost slip and face-plant on the white and black vintage-style tiled flooring in my haste to get out there and see who is knocking on my door. The knock doesn't sound again, but a light shines beneath the door to Franki's room.

I rub the towel over my wet hair enough to take care of the dripping mess. Then I scramble for something to throw on, grabbing the first thing in my drawer and dragging the sweatpants up my damp thighs.

Confident I'm decent, I swing open our connecting door, but Franki isn't standing there waiting for me. She's in her bed, reaching to turn off the lamp, her hair a loose cloud of light brown and caramel-colored waves.

Franki pauses, arm stretched and eyes wide, as she takes in the sight of me, mapping my body, starting with the top of my head and trailing over my still damp and glistening torso.

Like my brother, her gaze catches on the gunshot scar on my abdomen located near where my left kidney should be. Startled, she makes a sound of distress. "What happened to you?"

She's never seen me like this, not even when we were children on the beach. I've always covered my scar. No woman besides medical professionals and my mother, Charlotte, has ever seen me with my shirt off. Until tonight.

I step farther into the room, gently kicking the door closed behind me as I go. "Ancient history. Gunshot and subsequent surgery. It happened when I was a kid before you and I ever met."

I thought my words would reassure her. Instead, she looks devastated.

"No one ever told me that."

"We don't talk about it."

"If you want to, I'll liste—"

"I don't."

Her gaze continues to drift over my body. Then her attention flies to my eyes, then back again, as though she can't help herself.

I glance down, and . . . I hadn't considered the damp fabric/no underwear effect. But the entire scope and breadth of my cock is visible through these sweatpants. The longer she stares, the more prominent it becomes.

"Duck call collection," she breathes.

I rub the back of my neck, a little embarrassed, but determined not to show it. With any luck, she'll eventually see a lot more of me than this. "What about duck calls?"

She shakes her head, eyes back on mine, but this time with a small smile on her face. "Bronwyn almost said 'dick' in front of your mom earlier but changed it to 'duck call collection' at the last minute."

Franki has always done this. Where someone else would have said, *"Nothing"* or *"private joke,"* she lets me in.

"I'd prefer if we don't refer to my genitalia as a duck call collection," I admit.

"It is a tad undignified. What would you prefer I call it?" she asks cheekily.

I narrow my eyes. "No need for any special word. Call it what it is."

Flushing pink, but eyes sparkling with mirth, she says, "I don't know. 'I want to suck your penis,' doesn't sound very sexy."

My now rock-hard penis disagrees.

I lunge at her, climbing across her bed, and looming over her in the span of less than two heartbeats.

She responds by lying back against her pillows with an exaggerated expression of innocence.

I hover there, my mouth inches from hers. "I've changed my mind. You can call it anything you like, as long as you say that first part with it."

She's under the covers, with layers of fabric between us, but she smiles and holds her palm to my jaw. "Hello, Henry."

I drink her in. "Hello, Franki."

Her dark eyes catch on mine, and she bites her lip. Neither of us is wearing glasses, and now that I'm closer, she's in sharper focus. Her skin is virtually luminescent in the low light from her lamp and as smooth as glass.

I run my fingers across her eyebrow and over the crest of her cheekbone. "You knocked on my door."

She nods.

"Did you need something?"

"A towel."

I raise an eyebrow, the corner of my mouth lifting entirely on its own. "Really? At two in the morning?"

She looks to the ceiling as if she's thinking. "I meant to say that my pillow was lumpy."

"How dare any pillow be less than a cloud for your precious head?"

"I thought you might have better ones on your bed."

I'm supposed to say something clever and act like this is no big deal. Gabriel would already have her clothes off. *It doesn't matter what Gabriel would do.*

When I don't say anything in response, she lifts her shoulder. "I'm cold?"

She says it with the lift at the end, as if it's a question. I'm making her nervous.

She's made herself vulnerable to me, and I'm hovering here, speechless, like the twenty-seven-year-old virgin I am.

I draw away far enough to pull her blankets back and slide under them with her. "Then I better warm you up."

I prop my head on one hand, elbow bent, and wrap my arm around her waist over the blankets.

Franki moves closer. "I'm cozier already."

She traces the divot in my chin far more firmly than the first time she touched me. "You told my father we were getting married. When he finds out we lied because he annoyed you, he's going to come down on me like a ton of bricks for humiliating him."

"I didn't lie. I am going to marry you."

She eases back, her expression hardening and her voice barely audible when she asks, "*Why do you want to marry me?*"

MPD may be why I have to get married, but Franki is why I *want* to get married. "Because you're my person."

"How do you know that so soon?"

"Franki," I scold gently. "I've always known. Our timing wasn't right back then. You were too young. Or I wasn't young enough, but you were always my favorite person."

I give a self-deprecating huff. "And then I was overwhelmed and acted like an ass. But tell me I'm wrong. Tell me you don't know, all the way down to your soul, that you and I were always meant to be."

She catches her breath. "I'm your favorite person?"

"Without a doubt."

"This is fast."

"It feels the opposite of fast to me. You asked me to wait for you. That's what I've been doing for a very long time."

"When I said that, I wasn't sure you understood the subtext, and I couldn't bear to clarify it and have you tell me I was wrong. The longer I was away from you, the more I convinced myself you couldn't possibly have wanted me."

"I tend to have very black and white thinking. The idea of a relationship with you when you were only eighteen fucked with my head. It wouldn't have worked for either of us, but don't ever doubt that I wanted you."

Her eyes shine with an emotion I recognize. I feel it too. It's one of the new ones inside me emerging from what I thought were the long-cold ashes of my soul: hope.

"We need time together to get used to this. To make sure it's real and is going to work," she whispers.

"I already know it's going to work."

She laughs, her hand on my face. "Henry!"

"Marry me, Franki."

She sobers. "No."

"What will it take for you to say you will?"

"Time. Trust."

I narrow my eyes and think. I have to get creative. "I'll buy you a house in the country and hire a farmer to grow you all the pumpkins you could ever want."

She shakes her head with a *pfft*.

"I'll buy you a diamond so big you could see it on Google Earth."

She rolls her eyes.

I purse my lips. "I'll cook you breakfast every single morning for the rest of your life."

She shakes her head, but her lips twitch.

I run my tongue across my bottom lip. "I'll hand knit you socks without seams."

She leans toward me, her eyes heavy with lust.

I've nearly got her. "I'll buy the most comfortable, ergonomically correct dog bed ever made and all those little ramps that dachshunds need so Oliver doesn't hurt his back. All over. Every single place we ever stay will look like Ramp City."

She tries, unsuccessfully, to hide her smile.

"I'll take you to see The Front Bottoms live, even though I tried listening to them myself, and I don't see the appeal."

She laughs and puts her hand over my mouth. "Stop."

She pulls her palm away. "I think you should kiss me now."

I do, and it feels like falling. I've lost my balance. There's no up or down. There's only the way she wraps both her hands in my damp hair and holds me to her so tightly.

I lower the blanket to get closer, and electricity shoots through me as I make contact with bare skin. I noticed she'd let her hair down and changed into a tiny T-shirt to sleep, but it's ridden up. As I slide my hand down her hip to explore, along with tantalizingly soft skin, I discover a texture that's become achingly familiar to me. She was planning to sleep in her panties.

She knocked on my door like this.

"I figured out why you were cold," I say against her mouth, as I slide my fingers under the stretchy material cupping her ass. "Your panties have holes in them."

She shivers, but gurgles with laughter. "They're lace. There are supposed to be holes."

"I need a closer look. So I can be sure I understand."

I slide down her body. And then I'm between her slender thighs, her black lace-covered slit close enough for me to kiss. And I'm going to. First, I trail a finger down her seam. The fabric is damp, and she squirms against me. "Harder?" I ask. "Softer? How do you like to be touched?"

"That was perfect."

"Tell me if I do something you don't like."

When she doesn't answer, I lift my gaze to hold hers. "I mean it. We can't learn each other if we aren't honest."

"I'm nervous. I've never actually done anything like this before."

Oh, my sweet darling. "Neither have I."

"You've never had oral sex?"

"I've never done anything at all. I"—I place a sucking, exploring kiss on that fabric, right where my earlier touch told me her little clit is hiding—"am a virgin."

"Ohh." The word is a breathy exclamation of pleasure. "Me too. I was afraid."

I lift my head, frowning. "Afraid of what?"

"To trust, I guess. It isn't always logical."

It may not be logical, but I understand.

"Did your doctor warn you that sex could be a problem or…?"

"No. It's just a knee-jerk reaction when anyone touches my hip. Especially my left."

"Is this hurting you?"

"No. I'm a little sore there, and my knees, but it's not bad."

"You tell me if I do anything that has you worried. We don't have to do anything at all, if you'd rather not."

She nods. "I'll tell you, but I want to. With you, I do."

She hesitates, then asks. "Why haven't you done this before?"

"I told you. I was waiting for you."

She searches my eyes. "You're telling the truth."

"Yes."

"Now neither one of us knows what we're doing," she says with a laugh.

"I've done some research." I gather the fabric of her panties and give it a little tug, teasing her with it before I slide it to the side and get my first look at paradise.

I've heard the phrase "the scent of a woman" but had no idea what that really meant. There's nothing to compare it to. My mouth waters for a taste of her. She's entirely bare down here. So smooth that she either waxes or has had laser treatments. Her outer labia are glistening and damp, the seam closed, even with her legs parted for me. Using my thumbs, I press her open.

Everything about her sex is delicate. More so than I expected.

She looks like a pretty pink flower, and though I fall within normal parameters in terms of my size, my cock looks and feels like a monstrous battering ram in comparison. Her vaginal opening is smaller than I thought it would be. The mental image of her body stretching to make room for my cock has me fighting not to come in my pants.

We have to fit. I will fucking *make* it fit, and I'll make sure it feels good when it does. If that means I have to give her fifteen orgasms and a perineal massage first, then that's what's going to happen.

Her clitoris peeks from beneath its hood, and I try to remember the techniques most likely to bring her to climax. No hurry. Women take longer to get there than men. These things take time, and we've got hours.

I draw a figure eight with my tongue. She moans and grinds up against me. I work her clit until my jaw needs a rest and she's panting, then I move further down and press my tongue into her opening.

She's slippery, her wetness coating my chin and cheeks. I'm dying of thirst, and she's my oasis. I can barely get my tongue in an inch, but that's fine. I set up a counterclockwise rhythm with my thumb on the outer edge of her clit and fuck her with just the tip of my tongue. I'm so turned on by the feel and taste of her that it's becoming impossible to concentrate on her and fight my own orgasm at the same time. Coming now would only help my stamina later when I'm inside her.

The thought of her pussy squeezing my cock the way she's squeezing my tongue sends me over the edge, just as Franki's body shakes and jerks against me. I keep going until she nudges my head. "No more."

I lift to look at her. "Was that an orgasm? Or are you not enjoying this?"

Breathless, she says, "Orgasm."

I glance at the clock on the bedside table. "That took eleven minutes. I expected closer to half an hour."

She slaps her hands over her face. "Way to turn this clinical, Henry."

"I'm covered in your pussy juice, and I ejaculated in my sweats." I slide up over her, pulling her hands away from her face, to take her mouth with mine. "Do I taste clinical to you?"

When I lift my head to evaluate her reaction, I'm gratified by the glazed expression in her eyes. She grinds against my thigh, her face and chest flushed with the proof of her pleasure.

"You finished in your pants?" she asks.

"I'm far from *finished*."

"Does that mean you were into it? You didn't mind doing that?"

I don't like the insecurity in her voice. She needs something from me, and I'm failing her. When I rub my thumb over her bottom lip, she sucks it into her mouth, and it feels like she's sucking my cock. That's the intensity of this moment. "I've never been more turned on by anything in my life."

She visibly relaxes, and a lightbulb turns on for me. She needs praise and reassurance. Needs to know how she's making me feel.

I never planned to be a "talker" in bed. Some women find it a turnoff, and it's a next-level skill that will take time and practice to develop.

If I do it wrong, it's more likely to make her cringe than arouse her. But I can tell her she's amazing. That I can *easily* do.

"You're the best thing I've ever tasted in my life, Franki. Can I keep going or are you ready to rest?"

She releases my thumb and gives me a slow smile. "You should definitely keep going."

Twenty-Three

Franki

You Are Enough | Sleeping At Last

If someone had told me two weeks ago that I'd be spending tonight in bed with Henry McRae after he tried to bribe me into marrying him, I'd have applauded their overactive imagination.

Henry rises onto his knees, indicating his sweatpants. "I'm taking these off now. Is that all right with you?"

Please take them off. I'll die if you don't. "Yes."

He pulls his sweats down, and as the elastic stretches over the length of him, his cock rebounds and slaps his abdomen. I shoot to a sitting position. I thought I knew what I was dealing with, but it got even bigger from when he was standing by the door.

I blink. "How do you walk with that thing?"

He uses the sweats to wipe away the evidence that he definitely did orgasm earlier. "I don't usually walk around with an erection," he says dryly.

Anxiety spikes through my system the longer I look at him. My SI joint and my knees already hurt. There's no getting around it. I took a prescription anti-inflammatory hours ago, but my hip is going to ache until it heals completely. It's not terrible, but it's still a distraction. I'd decided that it would be manageable. I'm used to ignoring it.

Until I saw his dick.

"Franki? What's wrong?"

I take a deep breath. Slow. Breathe slow. Finally, I say, "Nothing. This is just new to me."

He sits back on his heels, watching me warily.

"I'm making it awkward," I say.

Henry moves into my space carefully. Slowly.

"Be as awkward as you like." He speaks against my temple, one hand moving to gently circle my throat, the other in my hair, doing that thing again where he's taking my pulse. It makes me feel strangely safe, but only because it's him. I flick a glance down at his cock. The head is wide, blunt, and an almost purplish red. If a dick could look angry, his looks ready to flip some tables. But when I glance up at his face, *Henry* doesn't look angry at all.

"Do you want to stop? Or do you want to play? We don't have to use penetration. Or"—he raises an eyebrow—"I can use my fingers."

"I just destroyed this entire moment."

"You didn't." He takes my hand and places it against his chest, holding it tightly against him.

"I've seen things you wouldn't believe," he says quietly. "Things I pray you never will. And I'm steady as a rock. But with you? Do you feel how my heart races?"

I do, and the realization that I'm not alone in this settles something inside me. "Let's play and see what happens."

He smiles.

"There are condoms in the drawer. I saw them earlier."

He eases us both back against the pillows. "I know."

"You?"

I shiver when he kisses my neck. "Mmm. Yes. Me. There's another box in my bedroom and one in your bathroom . . ."

He lifts my T-shirt over my chest and swallows hard, seeming to forget what he was saying.

He holds two fingers to my mouth. "Suck these for me, darling."

My abdomen and pelvis clench so hard and fast at his words that I gasp before I draw his fingers into my mouth and swirl them with my tongue.

He groans, and lust pools inside me, as hot and relentlessly needy as it was before he gave me the first orgasm.

He trails his wet fingers over my nipples. "Look how your nipples pucker for me. They're begging to be kissed. Your breasts are perfect."

He truly believes that. I told myself that I hadn't let my mother's opinions sink in, but some small part of me must have been worried that he'd share her feelings, because his sincere admiration gives me a shot of pure confidence.

He sends me an apologetic glance. "I did this backward. I was supposed to kiss your breasts first."

He drops his head, and does just that, while he continues to pluck and tease the other with his fingers.

"There's no 'supposed to.' Right?" I ask breathlessly.

He doesn't answer, but his mouth is occupied, and I don't mind. I run my hands over his shoulders, into the damp strands of his hair, keeping my touch firm, the way he asked me to.

He curls his fingers in the waistband of my underwear and slides them down. I lift my butt to make it easier for him, and he makes eye contact as he drags them off completely. "Thank you, Franki. You keep this pussy so pretty."

My mouth falls open, as pure liquid warmth floods through me. "H-Henry?"

He slides up to lie beside me, his right hand cushioning my head. Then he kisses me as his left hand trails over my breasts, over my abdomen, and then his hand is there, sliding between my thighs. He's gentle, but firm as he explores.

"You are so precious," he murmurs.

A terrible, aching pressure builds in my chest and clogs my throat.

No one has ever said anything like that to me in my life.

No one has made me feel like what I want or need matters.

Growing up, Bronwyn was my best friend, but Clarissa was hers. I was my mother's caretaker, but she was never mine, no matter how desperately I needed it. All my life, I've been an inconvenience, a tool, or an afterthought.

Henry is shifting my world, changing everything in ways I never even imagined.

"You're my person." That's what he said. I was so caught up in attempting to decode what he *really* meant that I didn't let those words sink in. I didn't believe them. How could I? This is what he meant. I'm precious to him.

I kiss him back hard, rolling into and partially onto him, so that my right leg rests on his thigh, his erection hot and hard against me.

His hand rests briefly on my hip before he lifts it away to my back.

"No. You can touch me. *Touch me, Henry.*"

His hand moves back to my hip and his fingers splay across my butt cheek, his movements gentle and sweeping. His fingers dip into the crease and squeeze. Then he slides that hand down, down. He dips a finger inside, just the tip, then uses the wetness to circle my clit.

It feels amazing, but I've let him do everything while I just laid here and received his attention. I drag my hands down his chest, following with kisses. I stop at his nipples and kiss.

I look up to catch him watching me. "Do you like that?"

"I like anywhere you touch me, but my nipples don't appear to be any more sensitive than any other part of my body."

I slide down further and kiss his scar. He jerks, then says, "That tickles."

I take a very gentle bite out of his side, and he laughs and squirms away.

I sit up on my knees and eye him speculatively. Pressing hard on his leg so that it doesn't irritate or tickle him, I slide my hand up his inner thigh.

His cock flexes, and a dot of clear fluid forms at the tip.

I reach for his testicles, then draw back. I've heard this part of a man is sensitive and easily damaged, but he doesn't enjoy light touches. "Show me what you like."

He watches me, expression serious as he takes my hand. "Imagine your eye itches. You don't press hard on your eye, but enough to feel it."

He wraps my fingers around his sac and keeps his own on mine.

I understand his reference immediately. This part of him is weighted, the skin delicate.

"Would it tickle if I kissed you there?"

His blue eyes gleam in the lamp light. "There's only one way to find out."

I kiss him. Lick tentatively. Suck as I continue to fondle him.

He tangles a hand in my hair. "Holy shit," he groans.

Well, if he likes that . . .

He smiles at my expression. "What are you thinking?"

"I want you to show me how me how to touch you here."

He wraps my fingers around his cock. It reminds me of when he showed me how to make a real fist. Then, with his hand over mine, he squeezes and strokes. His skin is hot and smooth and incredibly soft, gliding over a core of iron.

He likes to be held more tightly than I ever would have imagined.

"Like this. God, Franki, your hand on me . . ."

He swipes his thumb over the head, so I try that as well. He drops back onto the pillow and closes his eyes. I lick across the tip, mimicking the way he used his thumb. His flavor is salty, but not unpleasant.

A harsh breath leaves him, and he releases me. "This part is as new to me as it is to you."

I don't have any technique to speak of, but he doesn't seem to mind at all.

Henry gathers my hair in both of his hands, holding it for me like a ponytail to keep it out of my face, but he never tries to control me with it or move my head.

The feel of him in my mouth, his obvious bliss . . . has me turned on so much that my thighs slip together with my movements. There are so many things I'm discovering tonight. There was an entire hidden part of myself that I didn't even know existed. She was waiting inside me to be let free.

One of those discoveries is how much arousal takes place entirely separately from touch, itself. Touch is amazing, but it's not all of it. The things he's saying to me. His own pleasure. His smell. His taste. Everything swirls together to make me feel almost drunk on Henry.

"You are fucking amazing. You are so sweet. I'm going to come if you keep doing that."

That sounds like encouragement to me, so I continue until he grates, "Stop."

He sounds pained, and I pull away immediately in concern. "Are you okay?"

He screws his eyes shut. "Yes."

The word sounds ripped from his chest as he reaches down and squeezes the base of his cock.

"Oh my gosh. Did I hurt you?"

He laughs, even as he remains exactly as he was, body tense, cock held tightly between his fingers and thumb, eyes shut. "You made me feel too good. I don't want to come in your mouth on our first night."

Slowly, he relaxes his grip and opens his eyes. "That was incredible. Thank you."

It feels strange that he's thanking me, but it also fills me with warmth. He's sincerely grateful I did something I wanted to do in the first place.

"Come back here," he says with a smile.

I move in for a kiss, and he wraps both of his arms around me in a bear hug, rolling me until we're on our sides facing each other. He kisses me and moves his hand back between my thighs, performing that circular movement again on my clit.

An orgasm builds so fast and hard, that I gasp at the spiraling tension inside me.

Then he stops.

My eyes fly open in confusion, but he smiles and cups his palm firmly against my entire pussy. Not pressing hard, but not a millimeter of space between my body and his hand.

"You're so wet and swollen on my fingers. Your body is opening up. Do you feel that?"

I need him to touch me the way I need water when I'm thirsty. Food when I'm hungry. Rest when I'm exhausted. A *pulse* throbs in my pelvis. "I feel it."

"It's your body trying to draw me in. Can I give you a finger, and we'll see how that feels?"

I nod.

His finger glides in effortlessly, and he pumps gently. It feels amazing, but it also feels like . . . not enough.

"I'm going to put a condom on now," he says. "It doesn't mean we have to have intercourse, but if you decide you want to, we won't have to stop what we're doing and lose momentum."

"Okay."

He places his palm back against my pussy, and that unbelievably erotic sensation doesn't abate in the slightest. A pulse inside me thrums against his hand. I'm on the verge of an orgasm but desperate for him to fill me up.

Never removing his palm, Henry stretches across to the nightstand, removes a condom, rips it open with his teeth, and puts it on one-handed.

My pussy flutters, and he smiles because he *feels* it. He eases a finger back inside me, his thumb lazy on my clit. I push back in response.

Reaching for my hand, he guides it down to where he's touching me. "I want you to feel this. I know you're nervous, but your body is a fucking wonderland."

He adjusts his grip so that he's got his hand wrapped around mine, his finger next to mine. Then he moves our two fingers to my entrance. This pulsing, soft woman doesn't feel like me. Our fingers enter easily, my body snug and clinging, but not tight. That heartbeat I've been feeling pulses again, and I feel it inside and out.

The corner of his mouth lifts as he draws our hands away. My expression has to be nothing short of awe.

He grins back. "I *know*. You're brilliant."

I squirm against him.

"Let me try another finger. That's it. You can take it."

He stretches me with his fingers, and I want more and more. "It feels so good."

"You don't have a hymen. Most women your age don't. So nothing we do should hurt, darling. If it does, tell me right away."

I laugh, even as I push myself against him. "Did you . . . go to med school . . . to learn how to have sex?"

He leans down and sucks on my nipple before searing me with a look. "Hush. I believe in thorough research."

I grind against his hand in a desperate rhythm. He's being too gentle. I need more. I'm so close to orgasm—

"More, Henry."

"Do you want my cock?"

"Yes. Please. Yes."

"This position makes penetration more shallow. We'll ease into it for your first time." He rolls me onto my side, facing away from him. But when I try to lift my leg, he holds it in place.

"This will be more comfortable for your hip. Keep your legs together. Stay relaxed. That's it. Perfect."

He presses tightly against my back in a classic spooning position. I'm still on the verge of an orgasm. I have been for what feels like forever.

He glides his cock between my thighs, bumping against my clit on each pass. Kissing my cheek, he nuzzles in, then murmurs close to my ear, "This is called a cuddle fuck."

He positions himself and slowly, slowly eases himself into my body. The feel of him is shocking. Delicious.

"You're taking me so well. I've never felt anything so fucking good."

If my eyes were open, they'd be rolled back into my head in pleasure.

He slides in deeper, and we both gasp.

For the first time, I'm not alone in my own body. Henry is inside me. I never dreamed the sensation would fly through my nerve endings until he became part of me. Like a full body shiver, but not cold. Not discomfort.

Henry. Everywhere.

It can't feel like this for everyone or there would be no such thing as "casual sex." It feels as though I'm handing him pieces of my soul.

Neither of us has been loud through any of this. Quiet gasps, panting breaths . . . nothing like I've read in books or seen in videos. As I continue to hover on the edge of orgasm, full of Henry, his warm, solid, strong weight behind and against me, a sobbing sound of utter need escapes me. I don't even realize I've done it until Henry responds.

Still and unmoving inside me, he brushes over my shoulder, down my arm and holds my hand against my abdomen. "I'm not hurting you?"

Reaching my other hand up, I hold onto his forearm and hug myself with Henry.

"It's so good. But I need you to move."

He drops his head to my shoulder with a shudder. Henry releases my hand, but I keep mine on his forearm as his fingers circle my clit, the muscles moving under my palm as he works my body.

I'll never forget this feeling, never look at his forearms again without remembering the way the lean, hard muscle flexes with his movements as he gives me the single greatest pleasure of my life.

He starts a gentle rhythmic pumping, pushing his body into mine. In and in and in and in.

Every sense of reality distorts. My awareness of anything except us . . . this . . . is gone.

I've been on the edge of orgasm for so long now. Over and over, he had me right there, then backed off. Now, I'm pretty sure even without his fingers on my clit, there would be no stopping this tsunami.

When it crashes over me, stars burst behind my eyelids as I jerk and shake and clench so hard that he has to hold on to keep himself inside. It goes on and on as my body flutters around his, trying to coax him into his own release. To give me his pleasure.

Henry jerks, his cock flexing inside me. We come in silence until a sound seems to tear out of him. Then we're still. Holding onto each other. Gasping.

He pulls me even closer against him. I try to move away and roll over to see him, but he holds me too tightly, refusing to allow me to move.

"Not yet." His voice is gruff; his temple pressed to mine.

"Henry."

"Wait." After a moment, he releases me. Then he separates from my body, careful of the condom, leaving me empty at the loss of him.

Turning to face him fully, I place my palm on his cheek, smiling through my tears.

"Oh, shit." He uses his thumbs to wipe my face as he searches my eyes. "It wasn't good?"

I shake my head. "It was overwhelmingly wonderful."

"Emotional and sensory overload. I lack the vocabulary to do it justice."

Smiling, I lean into him, my forehead resting on the hard plane of his chest, as he wraps me tightly against him once more.

"I like this. You. In my arms," he says.

"I do too."

We lay together for long minutes as Henry trails his fingers up and down my back. Neither of us falls asleep, despite the lateness of the hour.

"I'm not ready for today to be over," I say.

Henry pauses his motion. "There's a clear sky tonight. We'd have a good view from the roof."

Twenty-Four

Henry

The Night We Met | Lord Huron

"I'll be right back. Put on something warm and comfortable." I kiss her forehead.

She nods, and I slip from the bed, heading for our connecting door. The moment it shuts behind me, I jump and punch the air. "Yes! *Fucking yes!*" The words are a shout in the form of a whisper.

I collapse against the door, leaning my head back harder than I intended with an audible *thunk* and laugh in utter relief.

Two orgasms. Two. Fucking. Orgasms. *Each*.

When I'd imagined what making love would feel like, I'd assumed it would be similar to a soapy fist in the shower. I was so naive. The things I'd studied about giving a woman pleasure were just as lacking. It was the difference between looking at an architect's schematics and stepping into a home. I'll be more prepared for the sensory and emotional deluge next time, and we're only getting better together from here.

I try to imagine having that experience with anyone else, and my entire being rejects it. Who besides Franki would I allow to touch me like that? Only *ever* Franki.

A knock sounds from the other side of the door. "Is everything okay?"

I straighten and call back with a smile filling my entire body. "No problems. Just give me a minute, and I'll be right there."

I do a quick security check-in and find no issues. As expected, Louis won't be creating any problems. His injuries are being treated as the result of the car accident we concocted as cover. If he were stupid enough to talk, there's no evidence and a number of "witnesses" who will be happy to provide alibis. If it ever even got to that point.

We have, after all, provided any number of college scholarships for three generations of local law enforcement, built a pediatric annex for the hospital, and donate generously to the community. More significantly, we've avoided harm to innocents, and we have friends.

In other words, we've established goodwill—something Grandmother didn't understand when she controlled Bronwyn's trust fund.

I clean up so I can get back to Franki in record time, throw on flannel drawstring pants and a long-sleeved T-shirt, and gather a couple items for Franki. Leaving them on the end of my bed, I return to find Franki closing the buttons on her pink pajama top. I take over the small task for her, because even though we just finished touching each other, I want more. I want all the closeness we're capable of. When I've finished and covered her feet with a pair of fluffy socks, I lead her back to my room. "My windows are larger and easier for an adult to climb through."

When we get within reach of the items I left on my bed, I collect them for her. First, I open the lid and pass her a bottle of water. "Drink that. Your body needs it."

She accepts the water, taking a sip and smiling as I stretch a black beanie hat over her light brown and caramel hair.

"It's getting chilly," I explain.

After I drape a thick red blanket over her shoulders, I turn off the bedroom light and lead her to the window.

Once I've opened it, I duck through to the slight incline of the black asphalt-shingled porch roof. Smiling like I'm still a kid who thinks his parents don't have a clue he's sneaking onto porch roofs to look at the stars, I prop my hands on the sill and poke my head back into the room.

"Why does that smile make me feel like we're being naughty?" she asks.

"You can be as naughty with me as you like, my darling."

"I love that you call me that."

"Excellent. I considered several terms of endearment, but that one felt like you."

"You planned out what to call me?"

"Not exactly. I'll explain when we're outside." I reach in to pick her up in a bridal carry. "I'm lifting you through the window. Let me do the work."

She clutches the bottle and the blanket with a small gasping giggle. Then I'm standing on the roof with Franki in my arms, the night clear and bright.

I drop a quick kiss to her mouth. When I pull back, she continues to stare into my eyes, and I smile. "Look up, Franki."

She tips her head back, eyes widening, mouth opening slightly. She's silent for a long moment before she speaks in reverent tones. "I've never seen something like this in person. The internet, maybe."

"One day, if you like, we'll travel. There are places with much better visibility. The skies I'll show you . . . you'll struggle to believe they're real."

"This already doesn't feel real. It's completely endless, but, somehow, so close. If I stretch up just a little, I could flick Cassiopeia with my finger. The heavens are right here."

She is so damn beautiful. Brown eyes huge behind her glasses, hair that's gone staticky where it sticks out under the cap, pink lips damp and smiling.

"Incredible," I murmur.

Her nose is reddening, and her breath turns to vapor with every exhale as she glances at me. "You're not even looking."

"I'm looking."

I lower her to the roof and lie beside her with my bicep acting as her pillow and my other arm under my head. "Don't forget to drink your water."

At my reminder, she smiles at me with a look of adoration and takes a sip. "Thank you."

"You confuse me," I admit. "I offered you diamonds and houses, and you rejected them. I give you a bottle of water, and you behave as though I've given you the penultimate gift."

She cuddles into me and looks up at the night sky. "I know."

We lie there, on the roof, and look at the stars for long minutes, Franki snug against my side to stay warm.

She readjusts and pulls the blanket around so she can cover me with it too. "Now, explain why you call me darling."

"There's research to indicate that nicknames and terms of endearment may lead the person being addressed to experience a sense of belonging and feeling valued. It has to be specific to that person, to be most effective."

She leans against me harder. "That's the most romantic thing I've ever heard."

I sigh, certain she's using sarcasm. "You think I'm being too clinical again."

"No. I think you're Henry, and I love it. The fact that you decided to use a term of endearment on purpose because you hoped it would make me feel cared for," she chokes on her words before she finishes, "is wonderful. I shouldn't have joked about your attention to detail. I can be awkward sometimes, if you haven't noticed."

"I haven't."

She smiles and shakes her head. "You made my first time perfect when it could have been painful or a disappointment."

"There's a lot of advice on the internet telling women not to expect sex to be good the first time, but the more I studied, the more I questioned why that appears to be the case. Many experts agree that disappointing experiences are often the result of a lack of adequate arousal, relaxation, and preparation. I didn't know you were a virgin, but I had concerns you might have had a bad sexual encounter in the past . . ."

"You're trying to figure out why I never had relationships. I've dated here and there, but . . . I don't know how to explain it. As soon as someone tried to get close, I'd get claustrophobic. It felt stupid to force myself to be with someone just so I could check off some random list of 'things I was supposed to do by a certain age' to avoid people's judgment."

"I know that feeling well. For me, the thought of anyone but you felt like a cage."

She squeezes me tighter. "Then you understand. I was also leery because my parents' relationships were a god-awful example. I don't trust easily. There are a lot of *filannerers* in the world." There's a smile in her voice at the end.

The weight of her words sinks in slowly. It may be instinctual or memories of our past, but she trusted me when she's never trusted anyone else. I rub my chest, right over the inexplicable ache in my heart.

"Now tell me the nicknames you considered and rejected before you settled on 'darling,'" she says.

"'Honey.' You're sweet enough, but it felt generic. A grandmother might say it. Not sexual or romantic enough for you."

"Mmm. Not babe or baby?"

I cringe and shake my head. "I did consider 'sweetheart.' I have no idea why, but when I say it, it sounds patronizing."

She laughs.

"At any rate, I decided to wait and see if something came naturally in the moment. And it di—" I cock my head, listening. "Do you hear that?"

"Yes."

We both still.

"Someone is out here playing the guitar," she says.

"It has to be Dean." The fact that he's outside, presumably alone, instead of with my sister, isn't a good sign.

"It's nice background music."

We settle in and listen quietly, content to look at the stars and hold each other, as Dean works his way through several songs.

It's late, and it's been an eventful twenty-four hours. Despite the chilly night air, Franki is warm and comfortable against me, and, over the course of long minutes, I drift into a contented state of drowsiness.

My eyes snap open when a feminine wail cuts through the crisp October air, an absolute verbal assault. "Dean. *Fuck*, yes . . ."

What follows, I can only describe as the sound of my sister, somewhere in the distance, *caterwauling*.

I shoot straight up to sitting, virtually dragging Franki with me. She hunches over with laughter, her eyes gone wide and hands over her mouth.

"This is disturbing." I'm glad Bronwyn and Dean are together out there, but why is she so lou—

"Why is she so *loud*?" Franki gasps on a laugh.

Exactly.

Another cry lights up the night, and, completely without ceremony or discussion, I pick Franki up and head straight back inside.

Franki is still laughing as I set her down in my room and close the window with an unnecessarily firm *thwump*. Blessed silence descends as we stand in the dim room, lit only by the light from the bathroom where the door is cracked open.

"Bronwyn and De—"

"Tch." I place a finger over her lips.

When she lapses into silence, I cautiously withdraw.

"I was just going to say that Bron—"

I gently place my palm over her mouth. "I'm sorry. I can't hear you with your mouth covered like that."

She clutches my shirt and convulses with laughter.

"Blink once if I can trust you not to traumatize me."

She blinks.

I remove my hand, and she straightens with a smile, glancing at the connecting door before looking back at me.

An expression I can't interpret crosses her face. Fidgeting with her empty water bottle, she says, "Today was really nice."

Her words feel like a dismissal. "Nice?"

"You've been so kind to me ever since I came back to New York. I feel safe with you. My father isn't the best. He's not the worst either, but I think I probably have what would be described as 'daddy issues.' The fact that I can even admit that to you is crazy," she says with a small laugh.

I watch her, listening carefully. Suddenly, this conversation feels important.

"My parents play games. They've always known I craved their attention, and they used it against me my entire life. I was afraid, at first, that your flirting was more of the same, but I trust you not to use my feelings to manipulate me to get your hands on that company."

Bile churns in my gut. I thought Gabriel was full of shit when he didn't understand that I could want her and still find the company an added benefit, but that Franki would understand. What I'm doing isn't manipulation. It isn't fake simply because it's also tactical. This can be real with her, and I can still want those shares. They aren't mutually exclusive.

"I shouldn't have doubted you. I knew you were one of the good guys all along," she says.

"I'm not a *good guy*." I haven't lost sleep when I've had to kill someone in years. I feel zero guilt over exterminating cockroaches. I'm a man built of flaws cobbled together with a rigid code of honor.

At my almost vicious tone, she clears her throat and looks away. Color seems to fade from her face until she looks nearly ill. Shoving the water bottle at me, Franki rips off her beanie and tries to give me both the hat and blanket. I accept them, confused by her change in attitude.

She gives me a shaky smile. "I guess this is good night. I'll see you tomorrow. Technically, it's already today, but—" She stops talking abruptly. "Anyway, good night."

She turns to leave, and I place the items she's returned to me on the nearby side table. Before she's taken two steps, I wrap one arm around her chest and one around her waist to halt her progress. I'm gentle with her, but im-fucking-movable. "Where do you think you're going?"

She shivers at the low rumble of my voice in her ear. "I thought you wanted me to leave because I made it weird when I overshared about my father?"

"Henceforth and furthermore, if you are ever in doubt, always assume I don't want you to leave."

Eyes closed, she blows out a slow breath.

"Do you know why I despise the term 'daddy issues'?" I struggle to regulate the flatness of my tone for her sake, but my anger is riding me too hard to sound like the nice, kind, good guy she thinks I am.

She shakes her head.

"Any time you hear that phrase, it's being used as an indictment against the person who has been harmed, rather than the person who did the harm. It's an insidious form of victim blaming."

"I'm not a victim. My father wasn't abusive."

"There are many ways to abuse someone. They don't all show themselves on your skin. I want you to share your thoughts with me. When it comes to you and me, there's nothing you can't tell me."

"You stared at me, Henry. You weren't very encouraging."

"It wasn't my intention to make you feel anxious. Sometimes I do that when I'm thinking. If I take issue with something, I'll say so."

She relaxes against me.

"You and I," I say quietly as I turn her in my arms, "have a higher risk of miscommunication than average. You have to talk to me, not run away."

"There's something in that sentence that I should be arguing with, but it's four a.m. and I'm too tired to figure out what it is," she says on a yawn.

I lead her to my bed and pull back the covers. "We'll sleep. You can tell me why I'm wrong in the morning."

She climbs into the bed, and I turn off the bathroom light before joining her and drawing the comforter over both of us. Under the covers, I lift her pajama top until I feel warm, smooth skin, then wrap my arm around her waist.

Her hair smells like the outdoors. I breathe her in as the entire length of her body lies flush against mine.

The position is similar to the way I held her when we had sex, and my cock hardens in response.

"I've never slept in the same bed with another person," I murmur.

Her only answer is a quiet huff that isn't a snore but isn't *not* a snore.

I draw her more tightly against my body. I won't give her up simply because I acquired her affection through planning, rather than organic means. This thing between us is real, and it would have happened sooner or later, with or without those shares as an added benefit.

I may not be "good," but I am hers, and I will use any means at my disposal to make sure she knows it.

Twenty-Five

Henry

Where's My Love | SYML

"Unca Jerk!" *Rap, rap, rap!*

I wake to the sound of a toddler tyrant giggling, pounding on my door, and calling my "name."

Phee heard Bronwyn call me a jerk yesterday and has found immense delight in repeating it. The more I react to it, the harder she giggles, so I've made a point to always react.

Franki stirs in my arms, and I untangle her hair out of my morning scruff with a smile. After brushing my lips across her forehead, I slip from the bed, put on my glasses, and pad to the door.

I'm usually the first one awake in any household, but given that Franki and I fell asleep near the time I'm normally rising from my bed, it makes sense that I slept in.

I slip out into the hallway and close the door behind me so that I can crouch next to Phee. Dean leans against the far wall with his arms crossed, looking stoic as always. Phee, wearing yellow footie pajamas, her hair a tangled blonde halo, and her cheeks full and pink, reaches for me.

"Good morning, Ophelia," I murmur.

She throws her arms around my neck and hangs on, smacking a sloppy kiss against my bristled cheek.

I pat her head. "You behave surprisingly affectionately for someone who calls her wonderful uncle a jerk."

"Wunnerful Unca," she parrots.

I lift her as I stand, her little diapered butt resting on my forearm. "Why did you pound on Wonderful Uncle Henry's door at this uncharitable hour?"

"Daddy said, 'Time fo bekdrift.'"

"Bekdrift?"

"She wants you to eat breakfast. She's afraid you're hungry"—Dean pauses for effect—"because your muscles are puny."

I'm not puny, but I'm not built like Phee's father and have never had a desire to be. Gagging down protein shakes isn't my idea of a good time. Besides, no amount of jerking my chain is going to put a dent in my fantastic mood this morning. "We both know, regardless of your muscle mass, that I'm faster and fight dirtier."

He grunts in the affirmative. "You and your sister, both."

I turn my attention back to Phee. "Thank you for your concern, Ophelia. I'll get ready and come down for breakfast."

"Yay!"

I kiss her forehead and pass her to Dean.

As he heads for the stairs, Phee stretches in his arms toward Franki's bedroom door. "Fankeee!"

Dean shakes his head. "We'll let Franki sleep. Only Uncle Henry is lucky enough to get your wake-up call."

My bed is empty when I return to the bedroom. In Franki's place, a folded piece of paper with something colorful sitting on top of it rests on her pillow.

When I get closer, I see that Franki has torn the paper from her sketch pad. She's written me a note. Instead of my name, the folded paper has a quick sketch of the two of us in cartoon form. We're lying on the porch roof together, with my hand raised to point out a constellation, and she's looking at me instead of the stars.

Smiling, I lift the short length of braided string first. It's maybe an inch wide and a combination of blues and browns.

I set it back down and pick up the note.

"Dear Henry,

I made this friendship bracelet for you, then I never gave it to you because I was worried about what your reaction would be.

I know this isn't the wedding ring you wanted, but I hope you'll accept this piece of sentimentality commemorating our years of friendship.

Always, Franki"

I stare at the note for a long time, reading and rereading. Trying to understand the layers of subtext in it. Friendship instead of a wedding ring. She was worried about how I'd react to her note.

I didn't mistake her last night. I couldn't have. But she's changed her mind.

She told me she gets claustrophobic.

Dad warned me. *"Don't smother her."*

I should have said I lied to her father and dropped the actual wedding until we were further along. I shouldn't have stopped her from leaving when she said goodnight. *I admitted that I waited for her.*

I'll give her time and try again slower. I spooked her. I should have known it by her reaction last night when she tried to go back to her own room.

This is why I went numb, because emotions suck. They rip you up and make you bleed on the inside. I shower, shave, and dress on autopilot as I go over the events of last night in my mind on repeat, attempting to find the place where I went so completely wrong. By the time I knock on Franki's door, she's already gone downstairs without me.

The kitchen, when I enter, is in full swing, but Franki is nowhere in sight. The thought of food revolts me, so I search through the tea drawer. *Who the hell doesn't keep Earl Grey in the house?*

I ignore the fact that my sister has been ill. *Someone* was responsible for keeping this place stocked, and whatever staff member that was has not been doing an adequate job. Resentfully, I pour myself a cup of coffee and sit at the table, scowling into the bitter black liquid.

Franki and Dad enter from the porch door, laughing about something. She's not using her cane, and I assume from how smoothly she's moving that her RA isn't bothering her too much this morning. It comes and goes in flares.

Dad has an arm around her shoulders, and she appears happy and relaxed. No doubt an expression of relief after cutting me loose. Dad and Franki must have stepped outside for only a moment because neither are wearing a jacket, and they each have a cup of coffee in hand.

She catches me looking at her and smiles, giving me a little finger wave. I'm not ready to smile back. I will. Later. For now, I pretend to be distracted by Phee in her high chair saying, "Banananana"—big breath—"nananana." Even though there's not a banana in sight.

There are too many people in this room. Clattering dishes, bacon sizzling on the griddle, talking, food smells. It's way too bright in here, the sunshine pouring through the windows. My sister's laugh reminds me of the porn audio from last night, and my mood sours further.

"The next time I sleep here, I'm bringing noise cancelling headphones," I snarl.

Bronwyn whirls my way, then waves a spatula at me, precariously close to actually hitting me with it. "You will respect my husband, or you will leave," she snaps.

Her reaction is over the top and completely inappropriate to the situation. "This has nothing to do with your husband. He's not the one who makes me want to wash my eardrums with bleach," I say acidly.

Then, to make sure she understands exactly what I'm saying, I clarify further, "My bedroom faces west. My windows were *open*."

The spatula clatters to the floor. When she picks it up and limps to the sink, she sputters, "Why would you have your windows open in October?"

I glance at Franki, who looks as calm and content as ever.

"I was overheated," I mutter.

Franki puts her arm around Bronwyn and tries to soothe ruffled feathers. "He was fine. He closed his window, and we went right to sleep."

Silence descends. Does she not understand what she just did? How many explanations this could end up requiring? *We're just friends who fucked?* In front of my mother, who freaks out if one of us says the word "dick" in her presence?

Mom looks at me with an avaricious smile I've never seen before. More than once she's asked if I was interested in finding someone. She adores Franki. She would assume if we slept together, we'd be serious because she knows I don't do casual. She's already imagining the grandchildren we'll give her. I can see it on her face.

"Are you seeing each other?" She turns to Dad where he's refilling his coffee. "Arden, did you know this?"

I stand abruptly and attempt damage control. "We are not in a relationship. No." I force a laugh. "That would be absurd."

Then I leave because I can't stand another second in this room. I glance at my watch. I'll walk off some of this tension and give myself until ten a.m., then come back ready to be as *friendly* as Franki needs me to be.

I toss on a blue wool cardigan after pulling it from a wooden locker in the mudroom and take off for the tree line where the hiking path starts, nodding to security as I go.

This place is now even better fortified than my parents' homes and my own.

The air is comfortably crisp this morning, but not cold. Bright morning sun slices through the remaining low-lying fog, making the dew sparkle on grass and fallen leaves. The air is redolent with the scent of autumn in Pennsylvania and reminds me of the pumpkin patch and our kiss in Grandma's kitchen. Gravel crunches beneath my heels.

"Henry!" Franki calls my name.

I stop, adjust my glasses, and shove my hands in my pockets. *Flick, flick, flick.* When I've managed to wipe the scowl from my face, I turn. "Hello, Fran—"

"You can take your 'hello Franki' and shove it up your asinine ego."

Her expression has the air seizing in my chest.

"You didn't have to pretend I meant something special to you to convince me to sleep with you. I'd already decided to do it. You're the one who made me think it was more than a one-night stand. You didn't have to play these stupid, cruel games."

She laughs bitterly. "Was this your revenge because I said no to your proposal? Your ego is really that fragile?"

I stare at her for way too long before I manage to say, "You said you'd always be my friend."

She glares. "I'm sorry. Should I have clarified 'as long as you don't treat me like straight-up trash'?"

"You left me a note." Yeah, I sound accusatory and pissed, but, "What the fuck, Franki?"

"What does that have to do with you lying about me being 'your person' then freaking ghosting me the next morning in front of everyone?"

The import of her words soaks in, and a jolt of realization lights me up. I glance around. We're on the path that winds into the woods, but given the security protocols here, we're in full view of two different guards and on camera.

I wrap my hand around hers. "Come with me."

She trips along behind me for a few steps before planting her heels and yanking against my grip. "We'll talk here."

"You want to make up in front of an audience?"

"What audien— Oh, crap."

It's not just security guards and cameras now. Up the rolling hill, Gabriel, Mom, and Janessa are gathered at the end of the porch and virtually hanging over the railing watching us.

"This"—I indicate the two of us—"is a misunderstanding. I need privacy to beg your forgiveness." I swoop in front of her and haul her over my shoulder.

"What are you doing?" She kicks her legs.

I pat her ass gently as I stride in the direction of the driveway. "I'm taking you somewhere quiet to woo you."

"*Woo me?* Who says that?" She squirms, and I tighten my grip so she doesn't fall.

"I do."

"Put me down."

"In a minute, darling." I take a bracing breath of fresh, autumn air. "It's a beautiful morning, you should relax and enjoy the view."

My ass cheek twinges. "What is *with* you and the pinching?"

"Your ass *is* my view. I was enjoying it. You're the one who said to fight dirty."

"If you want to fight dirty, use your elbow and go for a solid strike to the kidney. I only have the one, so I'm extra attached to it. Another option: my sidearm is within easy reach for you. Steal it and shoot me. Or hold on tightly to the waistband of my pants, then buck your body up and toward the ground headfirst. When I adjust my hold for even a second, vault yourself forward and use your grip on my waistband to assist your flip so you land feet first."

She goes quiet and still for a moment, then says, "I think that last one would take practice. I could take a bobby pin out of my hair and stab you somewhere extra-sensitive."

"Good thinking."

"I could give you an atomic wedgie."

"You're in a prime location for that. I'd drop you like a hot potato. I cannot abide anything in my ass crack." I shudder. "The horror."

Franki swats my butt.

"Joke's on you, darling. I think I liked that," I say.

She lets out an inadvertent snicker before she swats me once more. This time it feels more like a grope than anything.

There it is again. She is 100 percent feeling me up.

We're close enough to the house now that our audience can hear us, as well as see us, so I call out in stentorian tones, "I want all of you to know that Franki and I are most definitely in a relationship. You may ignore my earlier remarks."

She freezes. "They're watching us?"

"Are you okay, Frank?" Gabriel hollers.

I roll my eyes.

"I'm fine. Thank you," she wheezes back.

"Yes, they're watching us," I drawl.

When I continue around the house to the circular driveway where my car is parked, she fidgets once more. "I thought we were going in the house."

"I'm absconding with you. This place is crawling with people. If we stay here, they'll continue to watch every single thing we say and do. If I take you upstairs to our rooms, we'll have people knocking on our doors and constant interruptions."

I tip my head to a nearby guard as I open the passenger door of my car. "Good morning, Ryan."

"Mornin', Henry."

"Ryan, Henry says he's kidnapping me," Franki says sweetly.

"I am, indeed, kidnapping her, but if anyone plans on taking her from me, you'll need more than reinforcements. I'd recommend an army. And a missile launcher."

Ryan runs a hand over his military-cut, dark-blond, bristled hair and peers around my back to get a look at her face, then straightens with a grin and a shake of his head. "Have fun, I guess."

"*Ryan*," she scolds with a laugh in her voice, even though I guarantee she's never met the man in her life before this moment. "Shame on you. What happened to your duty to serve and protect?"

Gently, I settle her in the passenger seat as Ryan says, "Ma'am, you know I'm not a cop, right? I'm loyal to The McRae."

"I'm loyal to The McRae," she mimics.

My lips twitch at her snark as I close the door, then jog around the vehicle to slide into the driver's seat. I'm unsure if she's going to cooperate or attempt to get out of the car, but she never makes a move to open her door.

When I hit the ignition, she folds her arms across her chest. "Should I call you 'Laird'?"

I reach for her seatbelt, drawing it across her body. She drops her crossed arms long enough for me to snap the belt in place, then resumes her former position.

I put the car in Drive and maneuver through the security checkpoints on my way to the main road. "*The McRae* refers to this family, not to me. However, if you're into role-play, I'm happy to accommodate you. Bridnapping is a well-loved trope in Highlander romance novels, according to my research."

A snort of laughter escapes her before she cinches her mouth tight. "I'm not playing *Maiden Stolen by the Highlander*."

"Unfortunate. I'd look great in a kilt."

"Where are you taking me?"

"A cabin about a two-hour drive from here. I'll have someone bring your luggage. Is there anything else you need?"

"You're not actually kidnapping me," she says in disbelief.

"Just for tonight." I bounce my head back and forth. "Maybe a week. It depends on how long it takes me to grovel effectively."

"Stealing me away is the opposite of groveling."

"I'm going to be honest, I know a lot more about kidnapping than I do apologizing. I'm following my instincts."

She scowls and pokes a finger into my thigh. "You're the most frustrating man I have ever known."

"I hear that a lot," I say.

She pulls out her phone, and with a contemplative expression, taps the side of it for a moment. "You're not a very good kidnapper. You didn't even take my phone. I could call the police right now. Or your sister."

The word "sister" has a distinctly sinister bent to it. I know a threat when I hear one.

I glance at her out of the corner of my eye and hide my smile. "You're a special case. I'm usually less friendly about my abductions. Of course, they're terrible people, as a rule."

I reach into the backseat and pull a green and blue plaid blanket from the back. "This is for you. It's heated. I figured if the seat warmer feels good on your joints, this might work too. It'll warm up your knees."

She spreads the blanket over her lap, and I hand her the attached thermostat controller.

"Thank you." She leans back and turns only her head toward me with an expression I can't read. "Make sure when someone brings my suitcase that they don't forget my meds. They're in a blue case on the top shelf of the linen closet in my bathroom. I didn't want to leave them anywhere the baby might find them. I'm due for my injection tonight."

"You give yourself a shot?"

"Only once a week. It's not a big deal." Her words are in direct contrast to the tense set of her shoulders and tightness in her voice.

"It bothers you, though."

She shrugs. "It's hard to do it myself. My hands . . ." She flexes her left hand then shakes her head. "My insurance wouldn't cover an auto-injector."

"Did your mother give you the shot when you lived with her?"

She laughs, but the sound subsides quickly, and her expression becomes the bland, placid one I know hides something else. It's her *"Sometimes dads don't want to be dad"* face. The one she's used since early childhood when she's trying to convince herself that the things that hurt her don't.

"Caretaking isn't exactly in her wheelhouse," she says at last.

She watches the scenery pass, and I make a phone call to make arrangements for Garrett to meet us at the cabin with her things.

When I hang up, I glance her way. "I'm sorry for rejecting you at breakfast."

Her mouth tightens. "Why did you do it?"

"I misunderstood your note. I was trying to give you the space I thought you were asking for. You said relationships make you claustrophobic, then you offered me friendship instead of a wedding ring. In the note, you said you were afraid to tell me. I thought what you said in the kitchen was you slipping up."

"I'm not an idiot, Henry."

I scowl. "I know that, but social subtext does not always . . . come easily to me, particularly when my emotions are engaged. I don't have much recent experience allowing myself to *feel* things. My brain, apparently, goes offline around you far too often."

Her chin wobbles. I shouldn't have done this while we were driving. I want to hold her, and there's nowhere safe to pull off the road at the moment. I lift her hand to my mouth and kiss her knuckles, instead. "Please forgive me."

She squeezes back. "I wasn't asking for space. The bracelet was meant to show you I cared. I was hesitant to give it to you because it was something my friends and I used to do as teenagers. I worried you'd think I was strange. People think I am. If I act like myself, anyway. My friends don't. But . . . other people."

"You're not strange. You're wonderful."

Her frown dissolves, and her lips curve. "That's a nice thing to say."

I'm not trying to be *nice*.

"This whole thing was my fault. I should have made an excuse to Charlotte and waited for you to get out of the shower instead of going downstairs without you," she says.

"The likelihood of the two of us having a problem that is your fault, rather than mine, is virtually nil. Let's establish that as a baseline," I say.

"I can't tell if you're being facetious or ridiculous."

"Darling, I'm a pain in the ass. I'd like to say I'll stop, but—"

"Don't."

"Don't be a pain in the ass?"

"No." Her lips twitch in a repressed smile. "*Don't stop.*"

Twenty-Six

Franki

You Say | Lauren Daigle

I spend the next half hour in silence wrestling with the conflicting emotions inside me. I went with Henry willingly because I want to believe we're going to work out. I want all of it. Frightened was the last thing I felt when he picked me up over his shoulder.

Exhilaration and hope are at war with distrust and fear. Henry wants something more than just me. I knew that from his very first proposal. When he said he needed *me*, I thought he'd made a choice.

Then he asked me to marry him again last night, and the longer I've had for that proposal to sink in, the more it makes me question his motives. Especially after this morning. At the time, it was couched so sweetly and framed with sentiments that made me feel special. Made me feel loved. Who's to say that when I shot down a business arrangement, he didn't decide stupid, gullible Franki will do it if I convince her I care about her?

I don't want to believe that. This past week has been the best one of my life. I feel good, not just about Henry, but about myself. Then he told his family that a relationship with me would be absurd, and it's made me question everything that's come before.

He says his rejection was a misunderstanding. Maybe it's true, but I've lived through similar scenarios with my parents too many times to simply trust that there isn't some level of manipulation happening.

This is how love bombing works. Time. Attention. Affection. Take it away, then give it back, but not quite as much as you had before. Lather, rinse, repeat. Until the object of your manipulation spends every moment striving to earn back what they think they've lost. My mother, swooping in periodically for mother-daughter bonding. Hugging me, telling me she loved me, then turning on me. Over and over. Wanting me to need her, but never willing to satisfy the need she deliberately fostered.

My father, smiling and indulgent when he saw me once a year or so, but harsh and dismissive if I wanted to speak to him outside of his own schedule.

My personal phone vibrates in my jacket pocket. I want to throw the thing straight out the window. *What phone? I don't have a phone.* Instead, I fish it out of my pocket to see which of my parents wants to talk to me.

With a silent sigh, I accept the call. "Hey, Mom, how are you?"

"You can't have heard what your asshole father has done, or you would not be saying, 'Hey, Mom' to me right now." Her voice blares over the speaker.

"Whatever it is, it's not worth letting it affect your peace."

"It's going to affect your peace too. You're the one he's lying about on social media. Henry McRae is going to go ballistic. How have you avoided the press?"

My stomach drops. "I'm not in New York at the moment."

"Are you on a business trip?"

"No. I'm visiting a friend."

"Without Henry, right? You didn't take your boss on a weekend getaway with a friend. This is good. You need to put some distance between you."

I scroll through Jonny's social media accounts, nausea rising when I see the things he's posted. "I'm with Henry. We're visiting his sister."

Mom moans. "When that gets out, it's going to make things worse. There's enough truth about being friends of the family to make it believable to people who don't know you."

I drop my head back against the headrest. Jonny has announced our "engagement" to the world and reposted photos of Henry and me from Finn's wedding. He's also added one of Henry and me when I was around twelve and Henry was sixteen. I don't know how my father got his hands on the picture. I suppose Charlotte could have sent my parents photos I knew nothing about when I stayed with them.

The two of us aren't touching in that picture. It was taken in the McRae kitchen over my spring break from school. Henry has a pencil in his hand, my algebra textbook laid out on the counter, and he's explaining an equation. Henry is focused on the page before him. I, of course, am looking at Henry.

The fact that I was convinced he was the most wonderful person I'd ever known is written all over my face. If it were the photo, alone, I could forgive it, but there's a caption: **How could he have known one day this sweet girl would grow into a beautiful woman and win his heart?**

It's a deliberate dig, and it's perfectly executed because no one else will see the insult behind it. I don't know if his point is to punish me for ruining his plans or to attempt to wriggle his way back into Henry's seemingly good graces by showing him that Jonny wasn't wrong to call me an ugly duckling. Either way, I want to sink into the upholstery and never come back out.

I like seeing photos of Henry and me together from our past, but seeing it from this perspective makes me look exactly like the pathetic fool my mother called me. A dumb girl fantasizing over a man so far out of her league that other people saw it and laughed at her.

I don't even consider clicking on the comments. There's no way the internet isn't having a field day making fun of me in this photo. I know Henry never saw me as ugly. I truly believe that he isn't acting any differently with me now than if I'd never had surgery. To him, my smile is the same. He wasn't lying, so why does this photo and caption hurt so damn much?

I breathe in deeply through my nose to try to work past it. This isn't important. I have a great job that I love. I have friends. I have Henry who cares about me, and a precious dog who thinks I hung the moon.

I click out to the main part of the post. Jonny has strongly implied that Henry is working on a "very special partnership" with Jonny Lennox decor, something I know Henry would never do. He despises my father.

I close the app, then I check Jonny's other accounts. He's done the same with his others, but one post is different. In this one, he's written a deep, supposedly heartfelt post with a photo of the two of us with his arm draped around my waist. It was taken fourteen months ago, which was the last time I saw him in person. **You don't have social media, so I can't tag you, but I had to take a moment to express my feelings . . . .I couldn't be prouder of the amazing young woman you've grown into . . . .Overcoming your physical challenges . . . .I'll always be here for you.** There's no need for me to read the rest, so I don't.

"Franki? Franki, are you still there? Did you hear me?"

"I'm here."

"I know you hate being in the public eye, but you're going to have to make a statement renouncing that stupidity or you're going to end up in the middle of the slander lawsuit Henry McRae brings against your father. You probably still will."

I make a sound, neither confirmation nor denial.

"How does Jonny plan to explain the fact that you and Henry aren't even dating, let alone engaged? What does he think will come out of this prank? You'll have to resign your position. You can't work for him under these circumstances."

I freeze, unsure of what to say. Henry taps my thigh and when I glance at him, he winks and mouths, "Own it."

He turns back, his eyes on the road, and I look at him. His beautiful, beloved face. Those scarred, elegant hands. The scattered freckles on his muscular forearms. I have been in love with this man since before I even knew what love was. I've pined for him and missed him and yearned for him all of my adult life. This time we've spent together has been better than any fantasy I'd ever had.

Henry started this rumor to get my father to back off. I shouldn't have gone along with it then. I shouldn't do it now. He wants me to confirm it with my mother, and telling my parents two different versions of things will only blow up in my face.

Most of all, though, I don't want to say it isn't true. I can't *bear* to do it. "Henry and I are getting married."

After a brief shocked silence, Mom wails loudly enough that I turn the volume down on the phone. "No, no, no. You did not do this. That's the stupidest thing I've ever heard. Tell me this is a joke."

I stiffen my spine and try to sound cheerful. "Not a joke. Incredible, right?"

"Do you know how bad this looks for me? I've already made a statement saying it isn't true. You haven't been back on the East Coast long enough for this to happen." She's bordering on hysterical, pausing her cries of grief just long enough to deliver her lines with devastating clarity "You break up with that man right now."

We're on a country road, but Henry pulls over and puts the SUV in Park as I huff in frustration. "I'm not breaking up with Henry. I'm sure you can find a way to spin this that won't look bad for you. Ask your publicity people for help. You should be happy for me. You're the one who said I couldn't pull a man like Henry."

Henry scowls at me, and I shrug sheepishly. I shouldn't have said it. It's the last thing that will calm her down, but some part of me couldn't resist.

She howls, and I try to talk over her. "Mom, you're going to make yourself sick. Please stop crying."

"He ignored you. He let you leave with me. He never cared about you while you made a fool of yourself waiting around for him to notice you existed. You can have anyone now, Franki. I'll help you. Instead, you go to New York and pick the coldest"—hiccuping sob—"most dangerous man in New York to marry? I didn't fix you so you could leave me."

A shocked laugh punches out of me. "I wasn't broken. You didn't fix me, and Henry has never been anything but kind to me."

"How can you be with someone who fantasizes about your mother while he's with you? He didn't want you before, but he does now? It's not a coincidence."

Beside me, Henry makes a low sound of disgust, and I finally force myself to look his way. He's facing forward with the flattest expression I've ever seen. His eyes appear almost shark-like.

People refer to Guinevere Jones as the most beautiful woman in the world. Five years ago, a band won a Grammy for a song with her name in it as a metaphor for unattainable female perfection, but Henry saw straight through her. She's ugly where it matters.

"You need to book a flight to Los Angeles now. Tomorrow morning. I thought you were in danger before from random fans, but this is different. There are rumors about him," she says desperately.

I shake my head. "Absolutely not. Henry would never hurt me."

"Yes," she screams. "He will, and you're so pathetic that you're handing yourself over on a silver platter."

For the second time in my life, Henry lifts the phone from my lax grip and speaks to my parent. "This is Henry McRae. The man Franki is going to marry, and you will shut the *fuck* up right the *fuck* now."

I stare at him in shock. My mother must be similarly affected because she doesn't make a single sound.

Henry's next words are deceptively soft, yet sharp enough to draw blood. "Speak to her like that ever again, and there will be consequences. Do you understand what I'm saying, Guinevere?"

"Sh-she'd never forgive you," Mom says in a shaking voice.

"I'd never forgive myself if I didn't."

I put my hand out for my phone.

Henry looks like a stranger as he holds it out of my reach and disconnects the call. "I wouldn't let someone talk to a dog the way she was talking to you."

"I was handling her, myself. I told her 'no.'"

He lifts an eyebrow, then shakes his head in apparent disbelief, muttering something under his breath.

"What?" I demand.

"Why didn't you tell that woman to fuck right the hell off?" he demands back.

"That woman is my *family*."

"Your parents are abusive garbage. I'll be your family."

My mind reels at both his accusation and his offer. He's right that my parents are awful. It took watching Henry react to the way they speak to me for me to acknowledge to myself just *how* bad they are. If anyone treated Henry the way my parents treat me, I'd be livid. They've gaslit me into thinking the way they behave is normal, and I'm the crazy one to take offense at it. Because I was subjected to their toxicity from an early age, and I was the one being manipulated, I didn't recognize what was happening.

It doesn't mean he's right to take over for me without asking first. "When you did this with my father, I accepted it because I had already asked to use you as a shield. You may offer your help, and I may choose to accept it. What you don't get to do is take the power to make that decision out of my hands."

He fills both cheeks with air, then blows out in a frustrated gust. "*Shit*."

He runs a hand through his hair, squeezes his head, then passes me my phone.

I accept its return. "I like that you want to take care of me."

He shoots me an alert glance.

"I've never had that. The way you take charge of things feels secure and safe to me. I appreciate the way you make decisions and plans. I don't like to always be the one keeping everyone else on the rails. I was forced into that role because of my mother, and to find someone who allows me to relax because I can trust that you have things handled, is . . . I can't even explain what it's like to imagine not carrying every burden in life by myself."

He reaches out and squeezes my hand.

I look down at where we're connected. His shirt cuff is folded back neatly, but I ignore the bolt of lust that shoots through me so I can say what I need to. "Protecting me is not the same thing as controlling me, though. Do you know the difference?"

He swallows hard. "I do."

"You mean that?"

"Yes."

I trace my fingers over the black case covered in raised silver stars. "And the part about being my family? Did you mean that too?"

He searches my eyes. "Yes."

"For how long?"

He reaches out to grasp my head in both hands. In typical Henry fashion it's not some delicate, romantic thing you'd see in the movies. It's him grabbing me and peering into my soul. "For the rest of our lives."

"Oh." I try to nod, but he's holding me too tightly.

"I want to kiss you now," he mutters.

"Yes."

His eyes flare with heat, then he shakes his head, glancing out the back window. "I can't do that here. Pulling over was already stupid and dangerous."

He kisses me, anyway. Hard and fast. When he draws away, he swipes his thumb over my lip. "Worth it."

Henry settles back in his seat, checks his mirrors, and pulls out onto the road.

My phone rests in my hand. So innocuous looking. Nothing more than a shiny piece of technology.

I should cut her out of my life for good right now, then block her, and be done with it. I try to think through the words I'll say and hype myself up to press her contact. *Get it over with, then it'll be over.*

I can't make myself do it. I'm not ready for that final confrontation. Instead, I power the phone off. It's a cop-out, but I'm giving myself a deadline. When I turn it back on, my relationship with my mother will be over.

In the meantime, I don't have to look at the thing like it's a snake waiting to bite me. I'm tired of tensing up every time my phone vibrates with an incoming call or text.

Twenty-Seven

Franki

Eyes Don't Lie | Isabel La Rosa

Henry gets on the interstate, and, as the minutes pass, I absorb the worst of my inner turmoil. It settles into my brain and lungs and gut and bones. Diffused, nearly unnoticed. Simply part of me.

I've been primed from early childhood to exist in a state of heightened anxiety, so this stress, in many ways, feels familiar. Zoning out is my favorite coping mechanism when it comes to my mother. One I employ way too often, if I'm honest with myself.

So I push her out of my mind and focus instead on the spectacular view. Tree-covered rolling hills dressed in their fall finery hulk in the distance. We cross a bridge high above a sparkling river.

Henry rubs his thumb over my knuckles, and, with a sigh, I turn my hand over and squeeze. We haven't resolved all of our issues yet, but while we drive, I allow myself to enjoy the moment.

Three minutes later, I'm watching Henry, not the road, when his expression grows intent as he checks his rearview mirror. I'm about to ask if there's a problem when Henry's arm shoots out to hold me against the seat as he veers sharply left, then right.

I startle, gasping, and turn in my seat to see what's happening. Henry's palm lands on the back of my head and he pushes me over. "*Get down. Under the windows. Now, Franki.*"

I shift lower, sliding out of the chest strap of my seat belt, and cover my head with my arms two seconds before I hear the crack of gunfire. "Is someone *shooting* at us?!"

"We have bullet-resistant glass. They'd need armor-piercing rounds or to hit the exact same spot over and over to get through. We're fine," he says calmly.

Two more shots. "*This doesn't feel fine, Henry!*"

"Can we discuss this later, darling?" Henry slams on the brakes, our tires screaming in protest, as he spins the SUV in a tight circle and fires his own weapon at the person who shot at us. "I'm a little busy."

Head below the window height, I see nothing except the flash of blue sky and fluffy clouds overhead. Then Henry straightens out the vehicle and we careen in the wrong direction. Horns blare at us as Henry swerves in and out of the oncoming traffic.

The heavy SUV isn't built for rapid acceleration, but from my vantage point nearly on the floor, I can see Henry's foot pressing the gas pedal down as far as it will go.

"I need you to take the wheel for a minute."

It takes too long for his words to make sense, then I creep up enough to see the road. We are absolutely driving the wrong direction on the highway. I wrap my fingers around the wheel.

"That's it. Keep your head down as low as you can and still see. Use my body as a shield. Breathe, darling."

I suck in a deep breath.

Henry slides his window down about halfway, turns around, and sticks his arm out the window.

Our assailant fires two more shots, and I shriek and shake so hard I'm surprised I don't crash us immediately. The cars we pass honk their horns, but the noise barely penetrates. *Keep us on the road. Don't hit anyone.*

Henry fires three shots in succession, and I narrowly manage not to run us into a guardrail as oncoming traffic fills both lanes and barrels toward us. The left lane has a semitruck and the right a minivan. *It's probably full of kids or somebody's dad.* I'm not screaming or crying because I have no time. No time, only split-second decisions and decisions and decisions.

Our SUV grinds against the guardrail on the passenger side and narrowly misses the semitruck on the driver's side. If Henry wanted to, he could reach out and touch it.

Then Henry is facing forward, gun moved to his left hand and taking control of the SUV once more. "You can let go. Well done."

I release the wheel and turn to see a smoking lump of dark gray SUV behind us. The person or people shooting at us crashed through the same guardrail I'd nearly hit myself.

I sink back into my seat and start to hyperventilate. First, I'd forgotten to breathe. Now, I can't stop sucking in air. Spots bounce in my vision.

"Stay below the windows a little longer for me, please."

I crouch back down and reach my hand over to hold on to his thigh. "They're gone, aren't they? They wrecked their car."

"There were two, initially. We lost the second when we turned around. But we're going to exercise caution."

"If the glass in this vehicle is bullet resistant, why am I hiding?"

"Because I don't know if they know you're with me or assume I'm alone. If they don't know, I'd rather not provide the information to them."

A hysterical giggle rises up inside me before I squelch it. We're driving the wrong way down a one-way highway, and he's talking about exercising caution.

"Did you kill them?"

Henry shakes his head. "I didn't aim to kill the driver. If I had, he'd have swerved into traffic and taken innocent bystanders with him. I aimed for damage to the radiator and intimidation."

I don't even have a word for the sound that comes out of me. It's something between a laugh and a keening wail.

"You're a natural, Franki. Maybe for your birthday, I'll buy you one of those Formula 1 racing experience packages."

I squeeze my eyes closed, and he says, "Darling, deep breath in and hold it. Slow. Hold it. I'm counting for you. One . . . two . . . three. Excellent. Slow breath out."

We bump across what must be the highway divider, though I can't see much of anything. Then we're back on the interstate headed in the same direction as traffic. Henry takes the first exit off the interstate, checking his mirrors.

"Grab my phone for me, will you?"

When I sit up, he steers with his knees and puts his hand back on my head. "Stay down. Just for a few more minutes, love."

He sounds so bizarrely cool and collected that I'm almost questioning my sanity. *He called me "love."* He said he chose to call me "darling" by what came naturally. Is he saying he loves me or is this a result of stress? He doesn't look stressed. He looks completely calm. "What?"

"My phone. Pick it up."

It's in the center console, and I snatch it into my sweating grip. "You need me to call 911?"

"Not at the moment, no. Just hold on to it for me." He tells me his code. "Can you remember that?"

"Yes."

"Excellent. Put it in your pocket. If we're separated at any point, you're going to call the first number in my contacts. You'll tell them what's happening. They'll ask you for a code word. It's 'Cassiopeia.' Can you remember that?"

"Yes."

"Thank you." Through his car, he initiates a call to his security team who'd been shadowing us for this trip. I hadn't known they even existed. "Status?"

The voice coming through his speakers is so fast and uses so many code phrases that I have no clue what's happening beyond the fact that they are apparently alive.

Henry responds with a flurry of his own words, then a "Roger that" and continues to check his mirrors and the sky as he drives. Eventually, he pulls down a country lane and to a stop in front of a tiny gas station. "You can sit up now."

He gets out, and I sit in the car as he speaks to someone who must be a member of his security team, then he's opening my door and ushering me into a different vehicle.

He reaches past me for the blanket. "Don't forget your knee warmer."

The new SUV looks similar to the last one, but is white, rather than gray. Then Henry and I get back on a twisting country road until we reach a gravel lane flanked by forest on both sides, and Henry drives us deep into the shady woods.

I shift stiffly and wince. He reaches to click the seat warmer. "Is your blanket turned on?"

I glance down at the floor. "I forgot to plug it in. I was distracted by the fact that someone was shooting at us." If my voice sounds a wee bit hysterical, I believe I may be excused.

"Everything is under control. You handled that well, Franki."

"If it's under control, why do you still have your gun in your hand?"

"That's what I'm using to keep it under control," he quips. "Go ahead and put the blanket on. It will help if you're experiencing symptoms of shock."

I pull the blanket onto my lap. "You're lucky I'm not peeing my pants."

"You've never struck me as a submissive pee-er. If you can manage not to soil the leather, that would be ideal."

"Ha. Ha."

"You're doing great. You're going to hold on for me just a little longer, love."

I take a shuddering breath as Henry continues to drive down the bumpy road. He doesn't hesitate to turn at what, to me, looks like a nearly invisible one-lane muddy path.

No longer gravel, it's more of a long weed-choked driveway that slowly works its way up a mountainside in a winding trail.

This is way more "country" than I'm used to. It feels as though we're in the middle of a horror movie set, with tree trunks crowding the road. There are no houses. No sign of anyone else at all. Sometimes the trees give way on one side because the road is cut into a hillside with a ravine looming feet from my car door. If another vehicle approached us head-on, we'd both be in trouble. One of us would be backing up for miles before there was any place for traffic to cross.

Henry knows exactly where he's going. He anticipates potholes and ruts even when they're hidden by a curve in the road. At one point, we come to a standstill to wait for two deer to meander their way out of our path.

Henry pops an earpiece into his ear, and I can no longer hear anything but his side of a conversation that involves phrases like "how they made us" and "bogeys." Henry's also talking about an asset, which sounds hopeful and encouraging, until I realize he's talking about a person and calling him "the asset" not "an asset." I don't know what the difference is, but I have a feeling it's important.

The vehicle in pursuit managed to run our backup off the road before shooting at us. When Henry's people arrived at the scene, the car Henry shot at was already abandoned, its occupants long gone. A search on the plates revealed it had been stolen two days earlier.

We've driven miles and miles without any sign of habitation beyond the rutted mess that Henry seems to think is a road. Finally, we emerge into a clearing. The ruts smooth out. I make out a hulking metal building in the near distance and what I think may be an airstrip. We pass a helicopter pad. Then an open field.

Finally, we pull up in front of an adorable wooden cabin with a cute porch and swing. Henry slides the shifter into Park as a man wearing a flannel shirt, his bearded face shadowed by the brim of a ball cap, emerges through the front door with a shotgun resting on his shoulder.

"Stay here." Henry pops open the glove box, retrieves a Glock, racks it, and places it on the dashboard. "Do you remember how to use one of these from when Dad took you and Bronwyn to the range when you were kids?"

"Vaguely."

"I'm leaving it on the dashboard for you. I'm 99 percent sure we lost our tail, but, if you need it, don't hesitate to use it. Remember the glass is bulletproof. Don't try to shoot through it from the inside."

"Got it. Won't try to shoot through the glass." I nod. Over and over and over.

"When I get out, move into the driver's seat, then keep down. You have the keys if you need to drive. Doors stay locked. Open them for no one but me or someone with the code word."

"Where are you going?"

"Making arrangements."

Then he's gone.

I sit and listen to my own wheezing breaths and the wind rustling through the creepy woods that less than an hour ago I would have said were peaceful and beautiful. He returns what feels like hours later but is probably only a few minutes. When he knocks on the window, I shriek and do almost pee my pants, but Henry's gun is back in its holster.

I open the car door, and he gives me his hand to assist me from the car, as if we're at some red-carpet event. All of me is stiff and aching. My knees barely keep me upright, and I gratefully accept his support.

He eyes me warily, his posture formal. "Garrett flew in and beat us here with your things. One kidnapping vacation coming up."

"Henry?"

"Yes?" He takes a step away from me and lifts his hands. "I would never hurt you."

Incredulous, I wail, "I know that. I need you to hold me."

He blows out a breath and blinks rapidly. Then he yanks me against him, one arm around my back, the other hand clutching my head to his chest as he rocks me gently. "You were amazing, but you can lose your shit now. I've got you, love."

So I do.

Twenty-Eight

Henry

In My Room | Chance Pena

Franki curls up on one of the comfortably worn leather armchairs tucked into a corner and looks around the rustic cabin with curious eyes. She's no longer crying or shaking, but she's biting her lip and isn't quite herself either.

I crouch before her, cupping her hands and blowing on them as I attempt to transfer some of my heat to her. I lit the wood burning stove as soon as she was ready to sit down, but it will take some time for the chill to dissipate from the cabin entirely. "Are you okay?"

She nods. "Yes. Of course. Are you?"

I blink, startled by her question.

"Are you okay?" she repeats.

"Ah." I glance down at her hands. "I'm a great number of things. Grateful you're unharmed. Also seething that someone shot at us and impatient to learn who hired them. I'm also concerned for your emotional and physical well-being. And we missed lunch. So I'm feeling peckish."

She lifts my hands to her face and leans into them with a smile before straightening. "Do you know who did this?"

I shake my head. "Not yet. This was a hired job. Were they poorly prepared to take on an armored vehicle, not realizing we wouldn't be an easy mark, or was this meant to act as a warning? How did they know where we were? And who has motive and opportunity?"

"You have enemies?"

"None that I hadn't believed to be neutralized."

Her eyebrows lift slowly, then she purses her lips and gives a small nod.

"You're safe here, Franki."

She glances around. "This place isn't what I expected. I thought your country retreat would be some luxury lodge."

This place is a bunker that's been made to look like a cabin in the woods. The walls are lined with steel. The windows are bulletproof, and beneath us is a panic room equipped for a siege and a tunnel that leads to the airplane hangar.

The cabin appears to be well-maintained but has little in the way of anything I'd consider decorative or extraneous. It's also small, rustic, and the furthest thing from elegant. I enjoy the wood beams that cross the open kitchen and living room space, but I'd never call it a great room because the entire space is less than twenty-four-feet wide total. It's a single floor, though a loft contains a modest open space filled with books and a comfortable chair overlooking the living room. A door leads from the living room to the only bedroom, which adjoins the single bathroom in the cabin.

The visible walls and flooring are made of natural knotty pine boards, though two area rugs in shades of blue and green anchor the living and dining spaces. The hearth and wall behind the wood burner are constructed of stacked river rock and visually ground the wall facing the kitchen.

I hoped she'd like it, but I suppose her tastes have changed. "I can buy you a lodge. Someplace huge with massive windows. Do you want one in the Sierra Nevada mountains? Vail?"

When she shakes her head, I ask, "Switzerland?"

She heaves one of those sighs that means *"You're being ridiculous,"* but she says, "Your cabin is perfect. I love it. I'm surprised that it's something you like. That's all."

I stand to my full height. "Good. You said you wanted one of these."

She gives me a bemused smile. "Did I?"

"You wanted to run away from home into a forest and live off the land. You were reading a book at the time."

"*My Side of the Mountain.* I wanted the adventure, but not the suffering." She laughs. "I was ten years old and told you to come with me and help me build a cabin because I didn't want to live in a hollowed-out tree. You said if I was patient, you'd build one for me when we were adults. I can't believe you remembered that."

"I don't forget when I make a promise. I built this place for you. In case you came back."

Her brows draw together and her chin drops.

I indicate the bedroom. "Your luggage is stacked on the dresser, along with your purse, and the case with your meds."

She nods. "Okay." She steps away, then turns. "You know this is nuts, right?"

"I'm pretty sure that's just us."

She swallows hard, and the corner of my mouth lifts. "You're safe with me. There are perimeter alarms surrounding the property. No one followed us or has any way of tracking us. This property is hidden behind a shell corporation and doesn't appear in any way connected to me, and"—I lift the corner of the area rug at my feet to expose a hatch—"if anyone makes their way up here, you climb down the ladder. You'll have two choices when you get down there. Left door is a panic room. You can survive there for more than a month, if necessary, though it would never take that long for reinforcements to arrive. Right door leads to a tunnel that brings us out to the planes."

"This place looks lived in."

"I come here when I need to hit the reset button. Listen."

She cocks her head. "I don't hear anything."

"Sublime, isn't it?"

Her lips curve upward in response.

"Trouble hasn't come to this mountain. Whoever our pursuers are, they don't know where we've gone. We have a plane. A helicopter. A fully stocked kitchen, and, most importantly, time together."

"I can't believe you built this place for me." Her words match her expression. She doesn't trust easily.

"I would do anything to see you smile. I'll give you anything you ask for." I huff. "I'll even carry your friendship bracelet, if you want me to."

She squints. "You don't have to carry it, but what is the big deal? It's a piece of cotton."

I reach in my pocket and remove her panties. I hold them aloft and give them a shake. I'm trying to avoid any more misunderstandings, and I can't live my life hiding the fact that I stole them. I may as well face the music now. "I don't need your *friendship* in my pocket. I already have your panties."

She props her hands on her hips, her eyebrows crawling to her hairline. "You've been carrying around my underwear?"

"What did you think I was doing with them?" I drawl.

Color floods her cheeks, and her brown eyes sparkle as she makes a grab for the lacy fabric and presses the front of her body flush against mine. As distractions go, it almost works. My eyes glaze with lust before I snap back to attention and stretch my arm out of her reach.

"Give me back my underwear," she says in an exasperated tone.

"I'd rather not."

She circles me and I move with her, until my back is against the bedroom door. She presses against me. Rubs, really. Like a cat seeking affection, but I'm the one who wants to purr. I slide her panties back into my pocket, then widen my stance slightly to bring my height closer to hers.

She drops a kiss on the center of my chin. "Why would you want to carry something like that around?"

Her body is warm and pliant against me, and she's wearing her sweet, sexy smile. The one where I see it in her eyes more than anywhere else. It isn't a fair fight, and I give a jerk of my head in a failed attempt to shake off the trance she's put me under. "1) They remind me of you, and 2) The fabric has a distinctive stretch to it that I find to be a satisfying tactile experience."

I halt her hand as it slides down my abdomen in the general direction of my pocket and guide it gently behind her back. "I'll buy you new lingerie."

She squirms her lower body against mine, seeking friction. "This isn't a negotiation."

Her nipples are hard as diamonds under her blouse, and I'm damned confident it has nothing to do with the chill in the air. I slide my thigh between hers. "Everything is a negotiation."

She shivers and bites her lip, her pupils dilating as she watches me take off my glasses. *Good to know.* I'll be taking off my glasses in the most inconvenient places for her now, just to see if it gets her hot.

I place them on the nearby table and give her clit a nudge with my thigh.

She's forgotten her desire to steal back her panties, her left hand sliding up my chest, even as I continue to restrain her right. She kisses me, a soft press of lips that, when I open in welcome, becomes a slick meeting of tongues. When I release her arm, it's only so I can slide my hands up to cup her lovely face. She squirms against me with a moan of frustration. I turn us once more, and the door rattles on its hinges as I press her against it and slide my thigh more firmly between hers, giving her the friction we both need.

Her pussy is hot and damp against me. I groan as she yanks my shirt from my pants. This feeling is beyond the desire for sex. It's unadulterated need. I spare one last thought to remind myself that this location is secure, then let Franki fill every one of my senses. I trail hot, sucking kisses along her neck, her skin salty on my tongue, a result of clean sweat from her earlier fear.

Wanting to fuck is a well-known reaction to a near miss like the one we faced. It's one of the ways people remind themselves that they're still here, and it provides a physical release for the adrenaline thrumming in their veins.

I've never responded to danger like this before in my life. Never even considered it. Now, I'm not certain I'd survive this life without her to come home to.

She thinks I wasn't affected because I kept my cool. She's wrong. If I'd been alone, my nonchalance would have been real, but someone put her in the crossfire, and I'd had to clamp down hard on the fear and rage that threatened to turn me into someone who would terrify her as much as the person shooting at us did.

Now, we're here, and I *need* to feel her skin against mine. I crave her taste in my mouth. The scent of her filling my lungs. I want to fill her up and drown myself in Franki. It's more than arousal. It's a feral demand for satisfaction.

I force myself to unbutton her blouse and divest Franki of her remaining clothing gently, rather than tear the fabric off her. She wasn't wearing a bra. That's why I could see her nipples so clearly. I swallow hard and skim my thumb over one turgid nipple. "You're going to give me a heart attack."

Pulling her into my body, I open the door behind her and back her through it. It's four steps until we reach the bed, then I lower her to the soft, duvet-covered down comforter. She falls into it, and it lofts around her like a cloud. She's a work of art, lying there in navy blue panties and thick cotton socks.

She uses her arms to cover her breasts and her stomach. "Are you going to stand there and stare or take your clothes off too?"

She has no idea the effort it takes for me not to pounce on her. I'm practicing self-restraint for both our sakes, but I forgot she's sometimes insecure about her body. To me, she's the most perfect woman in existence. I'll convince her of that, someday. "Let me look, love. The sight of you is a privilege I'll never deserve. But I'm asking for it, anyway."

She swallows hard and drops her arms.

"You are so damn beautiful."

Her gaze follows me as I remove every piece of clothing from my body. Then I join her, my knees digging into the mattress, my hands tracing the shape of her. I run a knuckle over the seam of her sex, right on top of the blue fabric that hides her pretty pussy from my searching gaze.

I lift my head. "Your panties are wet. That can't be comfortable. I'll make you a trade. You can have the other ones back if you give me these."

The flash of humor in her eyes is so obvious to me. I might love to be a "pain in the ass," but she's more than happy to play along.

"Henry McRae, you're a pervert."

"Apparently, I am. I had no idea." Moving up beside her, I slide her panties down her thighs, kissing her long and slow before I work my way down. I'm deliberately gentle *because I don't want to be*, exploring her body with fingers and lips and tongue. Then I'm at the apex of her thighs, kissing, tasting, watching, always watching, her every reaction. Adjusting to drive her up further until she crests a wave of bliss and shakes under me, her thighs clamping tight around my ears.

I recognize her signals, now, and back off before she pushes me away. Then she's got her hands and mouth on me. My cock leaks pre-cum, and I groan in pleasure. She rolls us both so that she's on top, and I slide against her clit. The urge to pull her down onto me clouds my every thought. There's supposed to be something I'm worried about. Something I should think of.

When I do, my gaze jerks to hers. "I have to find a condom."

"I'm on the pill to help with my periods, but it means we could skip the condoms. If you wanted to."

I frown. "You mean you're okay if we—"

"Yes." She nods eagerly.

"Do it. Take me inside."

Franki slides down on my cock, enveloping me in her snug, wet heat. I blow out a slow breath through my mouth, caught unaware once more. This is different. Blissful. Even harder to maintain control. I feel *everything*.

She rocks against me, and I slide my right hand up to circle her throat, fingers stroking her pulse gently. "That's it. Look how well you take me."

She works herself on my cock, and I push my thumb between her lips. "Get me wet for you."

She swirls her tongue over me, then I'm giving her clit the attention it deserves.

"Eyes on me, love."

Her lids lift. Her brows furrow, her bottom lip twists, and white teeth clamp down on the side. Her dark amber eyes look back at me with something infinitely more tender than sexual need alone.

"Can you come one more time, love?"

Her eyelashes flutter, then she's throwing her head back with her palms planted behind her on my thighs. She rides me as I work her clit. When her orgasm comes, she jerks hard in achingly tight convulsions that latch onto my spine and drag me under in a quaking release of my own.

She collapses over me, and I take her mouth with mine, rolling her beneath me.

One at a time, I collect her hands and draw them over her head. Transferring them to one of mine, I lift my head. "What are you doing to me?" My voice is hoarse.

Her brows come together. "What do you mean?"

I release her hands and roll off her, tucking her against me. I don't know why I asked her that question. I only know that I'm drowning in a deluge of feeling. I have no intention of fighting it either. I'd sooner cut out my own heart.

She rubs her thumb between my eyebrows. "What upset you?"

Kissing her forehead, I drag the blanket over both of us and soak in the almost overwhelming comfort of holding her in my arms. I carry secrets far beyond her panties in my pocket. In the car, I told her I understood the difference between protecting her and controlling her, but hiding the darkest parts of myself wasn't about protecting Franki. It was an attempt to protect myself. "I have some things I need to tell you."

Twenty-Nine

Franki

Safe & Sound | Kurt Hugo Schneider

Henry sinks into the tub behind me, pulling me back to recline against him.

The hot water soothes, and his body anchors me. Henry's muscular thighs extend to either side of mine, and his arms wrap around my torso, so that I'm effectively surrounded by the man I love.

Henry's tension is palpable, and I try to lighten the mood. "I'm ready. Is it worse than carrying my underwear around like a weirdo?"

"Yes." One firm word. No equivocation or teasing reply.

My heart lurches with a burst of anxiety.

"You're aware I'm involved in certain activities that are outside of normal legal channels." He runs a wet hand up my arm. "Would it surprise you to know that we investigated Dean?"

I sit forward, then turn to face him, resting on my knees. "Why? Is he . . . did Dean do something?"

Henry lifts a sardonic eyebrow. "We rarely know anyone is a criminal for certain until we start looking at evidence. But no. Dean is squeaky clean. We investigate anyone with direct access to our family. Anyone who could potentially be bought, coerced, or manipulated."

It takes a moment for me to understand. When I do, betrayal hits me like a slap to the face. "You're going to investigate me?"

"I already have."

The words sink in with claws and teeth. "You said you trusted me."

What once sounded like praise so faint as to be an insult has taken on greater weight. Trust is hard-earned for Henry.

"I trust *you*." He runs a hand over my hair. "But my family has enemies who could use you."

"You mean criminals who know the type of work you do."

"Possibly. Yes."

"When did you investigate me?" I don't know why this bothers me so much. It's not like there was anything terrible for them to find, but it feels like a violation.

He rubs the back of his neck and looks away. "You started coming to our home when you were eight."

I don't even realize my mouth has fallen open until I have to shut it to speak. "You investigated a child?"

"I didn't. I was a child then too. But yes, we did. We investigated your parents and you. And since you remained close to Bronwyn, we've always kept eyes on you."

"Kept eyes on me. Literally? You had people *watching* me?"

"There was no one following you. We kept an ear out for rumors, changes in spending habits, unexplained absences. Financial or medical upheaval. New people entering your sphere."

"This is sick. I'm not a criminal. I have a right to privacy."

Henry's jaw flexes, and his brows furrow as he trains his blue gaze on mine.

"You're not even sorry. You'd do it again," I say in disbelief.

Never breaking eye contact, he reaches for my hand and presses it under the water to the scar on his abdomen, his skin hot under my touch. "A child was responsible for this. My brother had no idea what was happening until it was too late. They manipulated him. It doesn't mean we couldn't trust him. It meant he was vulnerable, and we have a responsibility to protect our vulnerable," he says gently.

Stricken, I look down at the place where he's holding my hand against him.

"My biggest regret is that I didn't ask you not to go with your mother in the first place. My second biggest regret is that I didn't tell you to call me to bring you home the moment you realized you were unhappy with her. The one thing I'm *not* sorry for is checking on you. I wish I'd been more thorough about it. You were hurt and afraid, physically and emotionally, and *I didn't know*. That's my regret."

I lean forward and rest my forehead on his shoulder.

His wet hand moves up to splay wide across the center of my back. "I don't like ripping off your rose-colored glasses. I'm not a hero and I never have been. I'm not going to lie to you about this and pretend I give a fuck about laws written in books. I care about your feelings, but I care about keeping you and my family safe more."

"Your parents did everything they could to give you normal lives, including friends." It's a denial, not because I don't believe him, but because I wish I didn't.

"I've never had a normal life, but they gave us what they knew how to. Within reason."

"You could have been raised like Clarissa." Clarissa's childhood and teenage years were spent as a virtual prisoner. Even inside the classroom, a private bodyguard hovered in the background.

"The only reason Clarissa Harcourt's father permitted her the small freedoms he did was because we claimed her as ours. Most of the time, our reputation acts as a deterrent to harm. Few come after us when they know annihilation will be the result. We aren't under constant guard unless we have reason to believe there's an active threat. But it only works if we're diligent enough to root out problems early. We can't get sloppy."

He avoids my eyes and plays with my fingers. "Do you understand what I do, Franki?"

"You investigate criminals. Organized crime bosses. Sex traffickers. People running guns. Pedophiles and murderers."

"I do more than investigate."

I press his hand to my heart. "I know there are people with so much power that charges never stick, no matter how much evidence you find. I know there are monsters who need someone like you to stop them."

"I've killed. Many times. I need you to know that I would end myself before I ever hurt you."

"Do you like to kill people?" I know the answer, but I want to give him the opportunity to say it.

"Does it matter?" He asks in evident exasperation.

"It matters."

"No. I don't like it. I kill when it's necessary to save lives or stop atrocities. I've never killed anyone because I *wanted* to."

"Then you're still one of the good guys."

He closes his eyes. "You need that from me. For me to be a hero."

It wasn't a question, but I answer anyway. "No. I don't need you to be perfect, and I sure don't want you living your life for everyone but yourself. As long as you're trying to do the right thing, that's all I care about."

"Are you afraid of me now?"

"No." I try to smile, but my heart hurts for him. "I already knew."

I guide his hand to my throat. "Feel. I'm not afraid."

Henry's thumb skates over my steady pulse. His fingers tighten just enough that I know he's holding me on his own now. Then he leans forward and presses his lips to mine, before pulling back and searching my eyes. "I'll always try."

Henry releases me, then makes room for me once more, so I sit with my back to his front.

I lift the sponge from beside the tub and make bubbles with the body wash. He huffs in laughter when I plop two white globs of suds on his upraised knees, then he gives a full-body shiver and rinses them off.

No more bubbles on Henry. Got it. "You know, I can't help but wonder how, if you investigated all of us, you could let a jerk like Louis hang around Bronwyn."

"Obviously, it's an imperfect system. We're making some adjustments."

I hold the sponge high and squeeze, letting bubbles trail down my arm before they slide onto my thighs. "The life I had before I returned to New York is over," I say in satisfaction. No matter what. My mother is my past. She has no part in my future.

"My sister and mother lead mostly normal lives. You can, too, when the current threat is under control." His voice is cold and flat, but his hand flexes on my hip. "After that, whether you're with me or not, the primary difference will be that now you know you're being watched."

I turn my head to take in his expression.

He's still worried I'll leave him. He thinks his revelations haven't sunk in for me yet. That I'll think about it later and want to run away.

Anyone else would think Henry looked and sounded like an arrogant dick right now, but I know better than to take that heavy-lidded expression and drawling coldness at face value. Henry is the last thing from bored or arrogant. His knuckles are white where he grips the edge of the tub, and a pulse thrums like hummingbird wings in his throat.

He's coped with this stress since childhood, and he'll continue to live with at least some version of it for the rest of his life. He invited me in because he knows I can handle it, and because he respects my right to know more than he fears losing me. But he does fear losing me. Desperately.

"I'm happy that my life has changed, and I always want the truth. Will you tell me what happened the night you were shot?"

His expression remains flat; his tone bored. "I was twelve. Gabriel was ten. Our father was the hero who'd cleaned up New York City. Mobsters were afraid to even dip their toes in the Hudson as far as Gabriel and I could see."

Oh no.

"Our parents' rules were stupid and unfair. What twelve-year-old isn't allowed to surf the internet? We didn't need bodyguards. We could take care of ourselves.

That's what we thought. My training started at five years old. Gabriel was three. It was . . . relentless. Martial arts. Weapons. I was stabbing watermelons at six and fully articulated human dummies by seven. We studied languages like our lives would depend on them. Anatomy and physiology. Criminal psychology. It was a game to me. I know you saw some of the training. We let you practice with Bronwyn."

"Firearm training was the only one I did with her," I say.

He tips his head back to look at the ceiling. "We were convinced we were invincible. Gabriel started sneaking out past the guards to meet a friend. I caught him doing it, but instead of raising the alarm, I followed him. All the way into an ambush in an underground fight club owned by a Russian syndicate."

He runs damp fingers up my arm. Down. "There were three men torturing my brother. They didn't know I'd followed him. To get him out, I killed them all. Before that night, I thought I'd never be able to do it. The sight of blood made me gag. But all the training and repetition kicked in."

I straddle him, so we're face-to-face, and he pulls me against his chest.

"You were shot in the fight?" I ask.

He shakes his head and gives a huff of sardonic laughter. "Part of our training was distinguishing threats from innocent bystanders. You can't lose your cool and hurt random people in the crossfire. In our practice sessions, I had a near 100 percent success rate. When a woman came into the room, my guard went down. She acted sympathetic. Asked if we were okay and if she could call our parents for help. I thought we were going to be okay. I lowered my weapon."

His lips twist. "And she shot me through the pocket of her cardigan sweater."

I clutch him tighter, as if his wound is fresh, and I'm losing him to it now.

He sighs without sound and runs his fingers up my spine. "Then Gabriel shot her. I had to threaten to shoot *him* to leave me and get help. I thought I was going to die and didn't want someone to catch him while he tried to carry a corpse out of the building."

"I'm sorry."

"Don't be sorry. You saved me." The flatness has left his voice.

He guides me to sit up, and I look at him in confusion.

Henry smooths my hair behind my ear. "I met you two months after that night. I was shutting down. The doctors couldn't help. The therapist wasn't making a dent because I didn't want him to. I wanted to punish myself. Everything that happened was my fault because I didn't stop my brother when I should have. I followed him to see what he was doing. I was *jealous* of his adventures."

"You were a child."

He swallows hard and shakes his head. "I know. But I was using a child's logic. When I closed my eyes, all I could see was blood. All I heard was gunfire and screams. And then there you were. You didn't look at me like I was a monster or a victim. You thought I had all the answers. You showed me that the person I used to be was still alive inside me."

He holds my head between both hands. "You reminded me that there was strength in gentleness and resilience. I felt like myself again when I was with you. For you, I was just your friend's brother. For me? You were my salvation."

Thirty

Henry

Angry Too | Lola Blanc

"No rest for the wicked," I say.

Franki, wearing glasses and the same pink tank top she slept in last night, sits in the armchair catty-corner from me with a blanket covering her lap. Setting her cup of tea on the table beside her, she lifts her head from the book she's reading. "You're the wicked one. I'm the nice person who knows how to relax."

She nods at the kitchen table, where she's left the small handgun I gave her. "I've already run your safety and self-defense drills this morning."

She doesn't like to wear it all the time, and I don't press the point. Something like that has to be her own decision, not something I coerce her into. Spencer doesn't like to carry either. I wasn't given a choice as a child. I'll never take away her right to decide how she wants to handle this.

I recline against the sofa back and adjust the laptop on my knees. "Are you calling off work today? Because you're on shaky ground there. Sick days? Yes. Personal days? You have to work for a month first. Take it up with your HR department," I say blandly.

She snaps her paperback closed and leans toward me with a glint of humor in her eyes. "I'm certain that being kidnapped and/or abducted to a remote cabin qualifies me for an excused absence."

"Ah. Well. I see your point. Then, I suppose you're not interested in seeing the files that came through this morning from France regarding—"

I make space for her as she abandons her book and lurches across the arm of the couch, tapping at the file on my laptop screen to pull it up.

"Ms. Lennox," I murmur, "I commend your enthusiasm, but some comportment is in order. I am your *employer*."

"Sir, you do know you're not my actual boss, and you're the one with your hand on my butt?"

"Hmm. So I am." I give her a squeeze, and she fights a smile.

"There. Perfect. I'll get my laptop and complete the translation this morning," she says.

Most of the translations I request from her involve her speaking into an audio file and speech-to-text. It limits her need to type due to her joint pain. As I can multitask when I access those files later, it's also useful for me. I'm not ashamed to admit the sound of her voice is an added benefit.

"Monsieur Mercier must like you. He's three days early with these files," I say.

She shakes her head. "First, never say '*Mon-sewer*' or '*Mercy-er*' again. I'm begging you."

I pronounce it incorrectly on purpose because her reaction every time I mangle French is funny. *Sue me.*

"Second, none of these people even know me. I'm the translator for what you say. They're responding to you, not me." She shuffles back onto her chair, then rises and walks across the room to open her laptop at the kitchen table.

"And the part where you throw in all the nice words I didn't say?" I safely eject a thumb drive after I've saved the files for her and walk across the room to hand it to her.

She settles into the kitchen chair and inserts the USB drive into her own computer. "Making sure you don't blunder into accidentally giving offense by not understanding their culture is part of my job description."

"May we never forget the American Theme Park in France Debacle of our forefathers," I intone.

She hums in agreement and slides her phone and handgun behind the laptop so she doesn't have to see either one while she's working.

I've utilized a number of different translators over the years for many different languages, and she's the best I've ever had. When we're meeting with business associates, her persona is impeccable. She's competent, professional, friendly, and respectful without being a pushover. She speaks both French and German like a native, has briefly lived in both of those countries, and she's had years of an exemplary education that included study on etiquette and social expectations, as well as the academic studies she was passionate about.

When we're behind closed doors, it's her very lack of standing on ceremony that makes her easy to work with. She doesn't waste my time hedging around me while she tries to guide me out of making a blunder. She looks me in the eyes and says, *"We're not saying that unless you want to tick them off."*

When an alert vibrates on my phone, I rap my knuckles on the table. "I forgot to mention we'll be having visitors in approximately two minutes."

She scrambles to stand and close her laptop. "What? Who?"

"It's the asset Dante has been guarding. He'll be staying with us."

Her eyes go wide. "Here? This is a one-bedroom cabin. Where is he sleeping?"

My gaze trails over her upper body. *Oh, hell no.*

Removing my button-down, I mutter, "As long as he stays out of our bed, I don't care where he sleeps."

Her brows lift. "You're way too nonchalant about this. You don't care that some guy will be walking through our bedroom to get to the bathroom? That's not weird to you?"

"You look cold, love." I draw her arms through the sleeves of my shirt and close the buttons all the way up to her chin.

Franki's lips twitch. "I would have run into the bedroom and put on a bra before they got here."

"I like you in my shirt. It provides a piquant hint of debauchery." I wink, and her smile breaks through.

Now shirtless, I walk to the front door and open it a crack, peering outside just as a black SUV pulls up in front of the cabin. When the engine shuts off, Dante and Spencer close the doors on their vehicle, and Dante physically assists our reluctant asset from the backseat.

I speak over my shoulder to Franki. "Fair warning. Apparently, he's in a mood today. He doesn't appreciate being managed. Brace yourself."

She nudges in to try to peer around me, but I stay where I am.

Dante huffs under his breath as he's forced to physically carry the asset when he balks at the base of the stairs. "Dude. It does not have to be this difficult."

When the asset hits the porch and his footfalls become a familiar *pitter-patter-pitter* across the wood, Franki shouts, "Oliver!"

With a grin, I move out of his way as he barrels toward the sound of her voice. "Surprise."

She crouches and holds him as he wiggles and licks her and dances in her arms.

"Ah. True love," I say.

Dante smiles. "He missed you, Franki."

"Thank you for bringing him. Thank you." Franki rises and puts her arms around Dante, wrapping him in a bear hug.

My left eye twitches as he pats her back. Bringing the dog here was my idea. Where's my hug?

When I give Dante the sign for "I'm watching you," he eases away from her with a wary glance my way.

Spencer evaluates my shirtless state with the air of a racehorse at the starting gate. He's responsible for wardrobe management when I'm in New York or traveling for business, and he treats my closet like a dog resource guarding a toy.

"Spencer!" Franki hugs him too. "Thank you for bringing Oliver."

Spencer's round cheeks nearly match his hair in color by the time she's done squeezing him. When she steps back, he straightens his bow tie and speaks stiffly. "I'm merely doing my job, Ms. Lennox. Henry asked me to bring him."

Apparently uncomfortable with Franki's show of gratitude, Spencer turns to face me and eagerly indicates the bedroom door. "Allow me to find you something appropriate to wear."

"Love, will it bother you if Spencer goes in our bedroom closet to find me a shirt?"

Spencer's eyes widen as it becomes clear he hadn't considered that he was asking to enter my future wife's private space. His lips flatten, and he pivots toward Franki to await her response.

Franki nods. "That's fine, but could you stay out of my dresser?"

After years of her mother overstepping, I know how she values her privacy.

He gives Franki a shallow bow, which equates to little more than a dip of his head. "Certainly, Miss Lennox."

Spencer retreats behind the closed bedroom door, where he will, no doubt reorganize the entire closet after neatly pressing a shirt that only Franki and Oliver will see me wear after he's gone.

Dante clears his throat, eyes Franki and Oliver, then gives a jerk of his chin toward the front door.

"If whatever you're trying to tell me has anything to do with Franki, then speak," I say.

Addressing both of us, Dante says, "Jonny Lennox came to your penthouse and demanded to speak to with his daughter. He was denied access. I was returning from taking Oliver for a walk at the time, and when Mr. Lennox saw him in the lobby of the building, he insisted he was taking the dog home with him."

Franki lifts Oliver into her arms and clutches him to her. "He did *what*?"

Dante runs a hand through his dark hair. "First, he claimed that if you weren't home, you would want him to keep Oliver for you while you were away. When the guard on duty refused to confirm or deny that you weren't staying at the penthouse, he moved on to claiming that Oliver was his property because he bought him."

Crimson color floods up her neck into her face, and her eyes narrow in fury as she holds Oliver protectively to her chest. "He's a *liar*. I found Oliver at a shelter, and Henry got him for me."

"It wouldn't matter where he came from. He's your dog." I attempt to soothe her.

Dante nods. "Henry is right. None of us would let him near Oliver. Jonny made threats of legal action, and when that got him nowhere, he attempted, badly, to break into the property. He had an armed escort back to his car."

Where his driver, then, no doubt, took him to a hospital to have his broken bones set.

Franki is one of the most even-tempered people I've ever known. She rarely gets angry, and when she does, she doesn't lose her temper or hold onto grudges. Franki gives people the benefit of the doubt, even when she shouldn't. But no one comes after her dog.

She sets Oliver on the floor. "I could *kill* him."

"Relatable," I say dryly.

She whirls on me. "Are you making a joke out of this?" she asks incredulously.

Oliver, picking up on her mood, growls a warning.

Shit. "*No.* I was trying, clearly ineffectually, to help you calm down."

Face red with rage, she balls her hands into fists. "I am calm. I'm *always* calm. I'm a ray of fucking *sunshine*." She starts out in a normal, if angry, tone and volume, but each successive word gets louder until she ends on a scream of rage.

I raise my hands in surrender. "Okay, fair enough, sunshine-y girl. Do you want to take a walk or—"

"You're not going to interfere this time. I'm not asking for your help." She lunges for her phone.

The next seconds happen in a blur. Dante pushes himself between us as he reaches for his sidearm. Before his hand makes full contact with his gun, I yank him away and shove his arm behind his back, spinning in a violent arc to slam him face-first into the kitchen wall.

Behind me, Franki shushes Oliver as he growls and snaps in our direction.

I tighten my grip on Dante, pushing his arm further up his back until I know exactly the level of burn he feels and lean nearer to the man I consider as close as a brother. "If you ever pull a weapon on her for any reason, know that I will kill you without hesitation or regret."

Dante grunts but doesn't struggle. "She was going for a gun, you lunatic."

"Franki's safety is your priority. If she wants a gun, you *give her a fucking gun*."

Dante tries to turn his head in Franki's direction.

I don't budge an inch. "Am. I. Clear?"

Dante swallows hard. "Affirmative."

When I release him, he steps away, scraping a hand over his head.

Spencer stands in the bedroom doorway with a hand pressed to his mouth.

Franki watches Dante warily, then scowls at me. "I was reaching for my phone, not my gun, and you know it."

Dante clears his throat. "I apologize, Franki."

She nods stiffly.

The tension in this cabin is in the stratosphere. Soothing tempers has never been in my wheelhouse. But distraction? That, I can do. I lean toward her and murmur, "It turned you on a little when I did the whole *give her a fucking gun thing*, though, didn't it?"

Her eyes narrow, and she huffs. "No."

Almost there. I lift an eyebrow. "Are you sure? Because you look hot and bothered. I didn't realize you'd be into the dominatrix thing. Naughty minx."

She channels a little bit of me when she lets her eyelids drop to half-mast and gives me a flat look that says, *"I know what you're doing"* as plainly as if she'd spoken the words out loud.

"Would it be possible for the two of you to table this conversation until Dante and I leave? I'm endeavoring not to hear something that is clearly none of my business, because, and *I cannot emphasize this enough*, I do not want to know," Spencer says.

"Speak for yourself. I want to hear about the weird-ass kinky games they play. It's the quiet ones you'd never expect it from. Know what I mean?" Dante says.

"You're very disrespectful employees," I say, keeping my tone mild.

Franki has never seen me engage in real violence before today, despite the fact that she knows I do. The shoot-out in the car was different. Less personal.

Dante is trying to come across as less intimidating after his show of aggression, and I'm giving her the opportunity to see that I don't respond with violence out of a loss of temper or something as simple as being challenged or disrespected.

Maybe she already knows that, but I can't stand the wariness lurking behind her eyes.

Never mind that I *was* furious that he would go for his sidearm near her.

The fact is, if Dante believed she was an imminent danger to me, he would have fired on her without hesitation. He'd have taken her out and asked questions of the corpse, and though I'd explained that she was the one whose safety was our primary concern, he hadn't understood. She's more important than I am. She's more important than anything or anyone else. She's our priority.

Now, he knows.

I heave a sigh, wrap my arm around her waist, and lean in confidingly. "It's impossible to find good help these days."

Some of the tension in her muscles relaxes, and she blows out a slow breath.

Spencer hands me a shirt. I shrug into it and jerk my head toward the front door. "You two get some air."

When Spencer and Dante have gone outside, Franki carries Oliver to the sofa and sits, looking lost. "Why would he try to take my dog? He doesn't even like him."

Crouching in front of her, I rub her back and give Oliver a scratch behind his silky ear. "His brand is floundering. He now needs a large investment of capital to bail him out, and he's getting desperate. His last conversation with you didn't go as planned. So, he attempted damage control with his social media posts."

"He tried to control you through me," she says.

"He failed. This morning, my PR team issued a statement indicating the two new companies that I'm 'excited' to be working with. Your father's name was conspicuously absent. At the same time, several of his investors withdrew their financial support, and others demanded payment for outstanding debts. I'd say he's panicking. His goal was to speak to you. Taking Oliver would have been a crime of opportunity. He could use him as leverage."

"Did you do that? Wreck his businesses?"

"Ahh . . . yes. And no. He was already in financial trouble. He made some very poor decisions. I did, shall we say, bring the situation to a head sooner, rather than later."

"Good." Her fury is banked, not fully abated.

She leans back and looks at the ceiling, then sits up and squares her shoulders. "Will you pass me my phone, please?"

I don't want to do it. I want to protect her from him, but if she needs this, I won't rob her of her power. I'll keep my hands to myself if I have to sit on them. I cross to the kitchen table and return with her work phone in my hand. "Do you want me to stay here, or do you want privacy?"

"Stay here. Please. But don't say a word."

"You do like to test me." I pass her the phone.

Thirty-One

Franki

Skyscraper | Demi Lovato

I hit the FaceTime button. I want to see Jonny's face. More than that, I want him to see mine. My call is automatically forwarded to Jonny's assistant. I'm not at all surprised. The only part that surprises me is that when I say, "Put him on the phone *now*," he does.

Jonny's face comes into view. His normally perfectly styled white hair is disheveled and a bruise shadows his jaw. He smiles. "Francesca. I've been trying to reach you."

"I heard."

His brows come together before he visibly forces his face to relax. "Sweetheart, I've been concerned. You didn't answer your phone. Your mother called me with a crazy story about you being abducted. She went to the police, and they brushed her off. Henry McRae isn't a situation like your old nanny where she can throw around accusations like that and make them stick. He's too powerful. She doesn't understand that he isn't like other people. She's not the one in control here, but I thought he'd want to know what she's doing. So he could prepare a defense, and so you don't fall for her tricks."

I watch him, but don't say anything at all.

He clears his throat. "I thought he'd appreciate a heads up. I can help you. I scratch your back. You scratch mine."

"He is powerful," I say.

He nods and gives me a hopeful smile. "You're a good girl, Francesca. You've always been a good girl. When you were little, no one ever had to yell at you to get you to behave. All anyone ever had to do was give you a look."

I don't react at all. Just watch and let him talk.

"Honey, I need your help. This is important. I'm in trouble. I should have told you that when I asked you to go out with Leo in the first place. I'll admit it. I didn't ask you to date him because I thought you'd like him. I'm losing it all, honey. If you can't be with Leo, I understand. No one betrays a McRae, but I *need* you to intervene with Henry. Be a good girl. Tell him to bail me out, Francesca. He can do it with a snap of his fingers. He seems like he cares about you. He'll do it for you. Tell him it's a wedding present."

"Mom had my nanny arrested?" My question is flat. Unemotional.

He frowns in confusion. "Yes. That was years ago. Will you speak to Henry for me?"

"Did you speak up for her?"

"What?"

"What did you do when Mom went off the rails because she was jealous of a nanny?"

He shakes his head. "It was a long time ago."

"You did nothing. You didn't get involved," I say.

"She was just a nanny. It wasn't worth the publicity. She didn't end up in prison. There wasn't enough evidence to even go to trial. It was best to just forget about it."

"When I begged to stay with you so I didn't have to go to boarding school? What did you do then?"

He shakes his head, his expression turning desperate. "I wasn't equipped to take care of a child on my own. You were better off there with professionals."

"When I left voicemails begging you not to let Mom move me every time I settled in and gave the slightest indication of being happy?"

"Your schooling wasn't something I knew anything about. I assumed she had good reasons for changing your schools."

"When I begged you to move me from the last one where I was bullied relentlessly, and she decided to leave me at that one for years?" I ask curiously.

"If you've got some laundry list of my parenting failures, I don't know what to tell you. I did my best. I loved you. That's what matters."

"Did you?"

He stiffens with affront. "Of course I did. I paid for you. Even more than what the child support agreement included. Didn't you see my post online? You should read it. I told you how proud I am of you. You turned out to be beautiful."

At my expression of disgust, he narrows his eyes. "I couldn't have been that bad of a father. I still have the 'World's Best Dad' mugs you sent me for Father's Day."

Henry's hand rests on my back. No pressure. Just there.

My breaths come hard, though my face remains blank.

At my continued silence, Jonny's attitude cracks fully and unrestrained anger pours through. "You selfish bitch! Not everything is about you."

"This is."

He frowns and shakes his head.

"You tried to sell me to a business associate for money. You're trying to use my relationship with Henry. You tried to steal my dog." I bite out my last words.

"It wasn't like that."

"It was exactly like that. Say, 'I'm sorry, Franki.'"

He shakes with fury, his face vermillion against the white of his hair as he chokes on his words. "I'm sorry, Franki."

I dip my head. "I accept your apology."

"Will you help me?" he grinds out. "Please. I'm begging you."

I shake my head. "I'm swamped. You know how it is. You'll figure it out on your own. I'm blocking your number. If you mail me anything at all, it will be returned to you. If we're on the same street, I will look right past you. If you speak to me, a bodyguard will remove you from my presence."

"You can't do this." He has the nerve to look like I've hurt his feelings.

I press End Call.

I sit like that, leaning forward on the edge of the sofa, phone held loose in my hands between my knees. I stare at the screen, but my vision blurs too much for me to read the numbers in my contacts. A fat teardrop lands on the glass screen. Then another. Another. Hands shaking, I pass the phone to Henry. I choke on my words, but he still manages to understand me through my ragged breaths. "Will you block . . . his number . . . for me? I can't . . . see what I'm doing right now."

He presses his lips to my temple. "Anything you need."

Henry blocks my father for me, then sets the phone on the coffee table and lifts me onto his lap. Oliver whines at his knee. Henry lifts him onto my lap. I wrap my arms around Oliver, and Henry curls his around us both. He holds me, arms tight, rocking gently, a hand on my back and one holding my head to his shoulder as I grieve the loss of the father I never had.

Thirty-Two

FRANKI

One Week Later

Princesses Don't Cry | CARYS

Henry throws on a pair of gray sweatpants and a black T-shirt, while I dig through my dresser for clean clothes. When my stomach growls, he nuzzles my neck. "I meant to feed us two hours ago."

"We were distracted." I lift the back of my hand to my forehead. "But now I may faint from hunger."

He turns me to face him, his worried expression clearing when he sees that I'm teasing him. "I hate to be the bearer of bad news, love, but you'll have to trek through the forest and hunt down your dinner first. That was your childhood dream, if I recall."

"I didn't want to hunt; I wanted to fish and forage for nuts and berries. At the moment, I'd rather eat a peanut butter sandwich."

"I'll teach you to fish another time if you want. I think you'd like it. For now, I can do better than a sandwich. Any requests?"

I smile and stretch up to kiss the divot on his chin. "Surprise me."

He runs his knuckles lightly over my cheekbone and searches my eyes. "I l—"

I frown in confusion. "You?"

He huffs. "I . . . left Oliver . . . in the kitchen. I'd better get him his dinner."

Henry drops a kiss to my lips, then he's gone. I sink to the edge of the bed with a smile and pull on loose cotton pants and a black cable-knit sweater. I've got one foot in a thick sock and am reaching for the other when the jacket I was wearing earlier chimes a text tone where it lays on the dresser.

My personal phone is on the shelf in the closet, and I never turned it back on, anyway. My business phone is on the coffee table in the living room.

I lift the jacket to find I'd covered Henry's phone with it when we returned from our earlier walk. I pick it up, intending to take it to Henry in the kitchen. Instead, I stand, arrested, as my name flashes on the screen.

Spencer: I'm attaching the updated file we discussed regarding methods to secure Ms. Lennox's cooperation. I would be remiss if I didn't . . .

I can't see the rest without entering Henry's passcode. I do it without a second thought.

Spencer: . . .caution you against allowing her to delay much longer. Her father's public announcement of your engagement has gone some way toward mollifying your grandmother. Well done. I must admit, initially, I felt your decision to convince her to fall in love was misplaced. I hadn't fully taken her preexisting feelings for you into consideration. If you haven't managed to secure her as your wife by the end of the week, we have a report indicating your sister's former housemate, Sydney Walsh, is experiencing financial difficulties and may welcome a business relationship that better suits your needs. Your time is nearly up.

A stab of agony arrows through me, as every bit of heat exits my body. Then rage pours over me like kerosene tossed on a grill, a conflagration obliterating everything in its path.

I scroll up through previous texts.

Spencer: Your cousin Lawrence reportedly threw a public tantrum when Mr. Lennox posted the engagement announcement. Your grandmother won't be happy with him when she hears of it. You may be able to

leverage his lack of control to your advantage. The photo of you and Ms. Lennox from your teenage years was a brilliant touch.

I sink to the bed and open a file with my name on it that Spencer sent Henry two weeks ago. It's a list of suggestions ranging from cooking my favorite meals to "sharing a vulnerable moment from our shared past" to taking me to an isolated location where we can "bond" without outside influences. There's an asterisk with a note indicating the location should have "only one bed," and it should be no larger than a full-size mattress.

Everything in this cabin is well-used. The leather on the living room furniture is comfortably worn in. I'd been surprised by that fact. I'd also been surprised by the size of the bed because it was smaller than I would have imagined Henry would use.

I rip the comforter back, then drag off the sheets and electric heated mattress pad. Further down, I find the mattress. The bed frame and headboard show no wear, whatsoever, and don't appear to match any of the other furniture in the cabin. The mattress looks brand new.

I have no way of knowing for certain. Like a crazy person, I shove my face into the mattress to see if it smells new, but it's impossible to tell. We've been here for a week already.

The list is insane, ranging from telling Henry exactly how many seconds to hold eye contact with me, to when and how long to hold my hand. Henry told me he'd chosen his terms of endearment deliberately, and I'd thought it was *sweet*. But this puts things in an entirely different light. This was manipulation.

I thought I knew what a master at work looked like. I thought I was someone who couldn't be tricked by love bombing and gaslighting ever again. I thought Henry wasn't the kind of person who would do something like that.

I press my palm to my mouth hard, holding in the sob that wants to break free.

I should march out there and tell him to kiss my ass and that I want to leave. I should be nice and tell him he can forget marrying me, and he'd better scurry off and ask Sydney to be his wife so he doesn't miss his deadline for gaining control of his precious company.

I don't feel like being nice. I feel like ruining all his fucking plans.

I tap out of his phone and put it back under my jacket on the dresser. Then I go in the bathroom to wash my face and figure out what comes next. I'm in here for only a few seconds when Henry taps on the door. "Love? Have you seen my phone? I have some things I need to deal with."

I turn off the water and take a fortifying breath. "Yep. It's on the dresser under my jacket."

"Thanks. My watch is blowing up with texts from my PA."

A nasty suspicion niggles at me, but surely he wouldn't contrive a dangerous situation to make me feel like I needed his protection. There were other innocent people on the road who could have been hurt. He wouldn't.

But not a single bullet from our attackers hit our car.

"What's going on with the bed?" he calls.

"I was trying to figure out how to use the mattress pad."

"I think the instructions are in the drawer next to it. I ordered it for you, so I haven't used it either. I thought it might help if your joints were bothering you."

I huff silently. "That's very sweet of you."

"Dinner is chicken piccata. I have the moscato you like too."

"My favorite," I say flatly. "I'm not drinking tonight, though. I can't have alcohol in the twenty-four hours before or after my injection."

"All right. Love, are you okay? You sound upset."

I scrub my hands over my face.

"Franki?" When I don't respond, he rattles the doorknob.

I know what my mother would do. She'd string him along until it was too late, and he was out of time. Then when he'd lost the stupid shares that mean so much to him, she'd laugh in his face in revenge.

But I wasn't made for lies and manipulation, no matter how many years I lived with it. I'm not my mother, and I never want to be. I'm done playing other people's games.

I rip open the door and stand there, panting and staring him down. His brows furrow in concern, as he places his beautiful hands on my biceps. "You were crying?"

When he starts to pull me close, I resist. "Stop."

He steps back and drops his hands. "Tell me what's happening."

"I read your texts. And your list."

He frowns. "I see. If you'll forgive me, *I* haven't read them fully yet. Would you like to tell me what the problem is, and why you're angry?"

I laugh bitterly. "Classic. Gaslighting 101. Up your game and throw in an accusation about me invading your privacy. You're still in amateur territory."

A muscle flexes in his jaw. "I gave you my passcode. I can hardly complain when you use it."

"I know you're enacting some master plan to trick me into marrying you so you can get those shares. I know none of it was real."

He steps closer, crowding me. "It wasn't real?"

He props both of his hands flat against the wall on either side of my head and leans closer. "All of it was real."

"Stop. Lying," I scream and shove him away. Oliver runs in the room and stands at my feet. "Everything. The way you held my hand. The eye contact. The compliments, and pretending I was important." My voice cracks, and I shove the hurt down. He doesn't get to see me break down over this. "Cooking my favorite food. Our date to the pumpkin farm wasn't some fun whim. You didn't introduce me to your grandparents as a coincidence."

"You are important. You're *everything*. Just because I felt more comfortable with a game plan in place doesn't mean what I was doing wasn't real. It sure as fuck wasn't all planned. I've gone off-script with you so often that the script is pointless. I didn't count how long I maintained eye contact with you because I wouldn't have been able to remember to do it. I was too busy being distracted by your eyes."

"I'm not marrying you. Go find Sydney and ask her. She's way more practical than I am. You won't have to work so hard. She'll take your money in a heartbeat."

His chest rises and falls, as he glares back at me with fury to match my own. "I don't want anyone but you."

"You can't have me."

He shakes his head. "It's you or no one."

A crack forms in my rage, and I work to shore it back up. When my anger is gone, the only thing left will be pain. "Then I guess it's no one."

He wraps his hands around the back of his neck and paces. "What do you need from me that I'm not giving you? Tell me, and I'll do it."

"I need you to tell your grandmother you don't want those shares. And I need you to sit there like a good boy when she gives them to your cousin."

He stops walking and faces me with a frustrated frown. "You have no idea what you're asking for. MPD is my grandfather's legacy. This family can't afford to walk away from that company. Even if we could, Lawrence likes to buy up properties he doesn't even have plans to use. He'll artificially inflate the market until people who have lived in communities for generations will no longer be able to afford even the taxes on their own homes. I've seen his track record. He buys up every small, independently-owned hotel he can in a community. Then he shuts them down and sells them off for parts to eliminate the competition."

His words arrest me, and I frown, blinking rapidly. Because . . . surely not. *It's a coincidence.* It has to be. And yet, it makes perfect sense.

I cover my lower face with my hands before I drop them. "Lawrence owns hotels?"

Henry shakes his head slightly. "Yes."

"What's your cousin's last name? What does he look like?"

He tilts his head slightly to the side in confusion. "Lawrence Kingston. He's thirty-four. Blond."

I drop my head into my hands briefly, then lift it, and search the room for Henry's iPad. Finding it on the bedside table, I do a Google search, typing "Leo Kingston" into the search bar.

Henry looks over my shoulder at the screen.

No one who looks anything like the man I met shows up in the results. So I type "Lawrence Kingston." And there he is, smiling back at me in a publicity photo taken in the lobby of one of his hotels. I could read the articles about him and his hotels, but I don't need or want to.

"I didn't know his last name. I assumed the man your father wanted you to date was older and someone in the fashion industry," Henry says.

A bitter laugh punches out of me. "Your cousin saw our photos online, realized you were closing in on your goal, and tried to insert himself between us."

"He's a prick," Henry says.

I nod. "He absolutely is. Only a prick would pretend to want to date me so he could get his hands on a company. What kind of asshole would do something like that?" Sarcasm drips from my tone.

Henry narrows his eyes. "I didn't pretend anything. If all I'd wanted was the company, I'd have left your hotel room, gone back to the wedding reception, and found one of the other fifteen names on Spencer's list that I refused to even consider *because they weren't you*. Don't pretend I'm anything like him."

His answer doesn't soothe me. It infuriates me. "When I wouldn't date Lawrence, he offered me a job. Did I tell you that?"

Henry shakes his head, but never loses eye contact with me.

"It's interesting, isn't it? The way when he failed to get me away from you one way, he turned to a job he coincidentally needed someone like me for. Even at the time, it sounded ludicrous."

Henry's eyes flare.

"It makes me wonder," I say.

Henry shakes his head slowly. "Don't."

I toss the iPad to the bed. "The job you offered me felt out of nowhere too. You have other departments, but somehow I'm miraculously working from your penthouse and your office?"

He looks away.

I pull my own hair in frustration. "You created a job to keep me close. Nothing has been real."

"Have you been working? Have you assisted me in expanding my businesses into new markets? The answer is 'yes.' So, your job is real. What difference does it make what inspired me to tackle those markets?"

"I'm such an idiot. I thought I was proving my mother wrong. That I didn't need her help or anyone else's. I let you step right into her shoes. Now, it's not my mother who controls my health insurance and finances. It's you."

He scowls. "If I'd wanted to do that, I have far more effective ways at my disposal. I've never held your employment over your head in any way, and I never would. If you stop working for me, your company will send you out on another job somewhere else. I wasn't controlling you. I was giving you the tools to become independent, not holding you back. I gave you a ladder, not a cage."

"This is you acting the part of savior? It's not about what you can get from it, at all?" I ask sarcastically.

He runs his hands through his hair and squeezes his temples. "I didn't lie to you," he snaps. "My cards were on the table on the very first night. A person can want more than one thing at the same time."

"Did you put Jonny up to making the engagement announcement to buy yourself time with your grandmother or pressure me?"

"No." One clear, concise, furious syllable.

"Where did Jonny get the picture of us?"

His eyebrows lift. "I don't know. Not from me. If I had to guess, he called my mother sometime after breakfast that morning and made her year when he told her we were getting married."

He looks so sincere.

"Did you orchestrate having someone shoot at us to manipulate me?"

He stares at me for five long, cold seconds as every ounce of emotion and warmth bleeds out of his expression, until the man who stands before me looks like an utter stranger. This is the face his enemies see.

His eyelids drop to half-mast, and he rakes his gaze from the top of my head to my feet, and back up again. "This is what you think of me? Who you think I am?"

I look away, inexplicable shame flooding through me, as if I'm the one who's hurting him. "I want you to take me—" I falter. I'd almost said "home." But I don't have one of those and never have. "Back to New York. I'll go to a hotel."

He straightens. "A hotel isn't an option. If you have an alternate solution that doesn't put your life at risk, I'm open to discussion."

My mother. It's what I've done every other time I got into trouble in the past five years. She's on the other side of the country and has plenty of security, but I won't go back there. Never again. "Whoever shot at us wasn't after me. They were after you. You can stay here and have someone pick me up. No one will follow or remember me."

"You don't know that."

I narrow my eyes. "Of the two of us, which one is most likely to inspire someone to commit murder?"

"You're associated with me now. They'd consider you a pinch point, even if I were the target."

"I won't marry you, and your deadline is almost up. You're wasting time with me."

His coldness hasn't lifted an iota. "Not a single moment with you is wasted time."

Thirty-Three

Franki

Already Gone | Sleeping At Last

Dinner passes with only the occasional sound of cutlery clattering, ice clinking in our water glasses, and my "Thank you for cooking," and his "You're welcome."

When he finishes his meal, he rises from the table. "I'll take care of the kitchen when I come back inside. I'm going to deal with the firewood while we still have daylight."

"I'll wash the dishes."

Henry barely nods in acknowledgment as he heads for the bedroom, then emerges minutes later wearing well-worn jeans, a pair of boots in his hand. At the back door, he stuffs his feet into the boots, tugging the laces into place and tying them with brisk efficiency.

When I turn back to the table, the door snicks closed behind me as Henry escapes the breath-stealing tension between us.

I wish I could do the same. I hate everything about the way we're acting with each other, but I don't know the answer to fix it either. Every tender moment we've shared is now something I feel the need to put under a microscope and examine to determine his motives.

I believe him about his cousin and that creates a layer of guilt for me, as if by refusing to marry him, I'm about to be personally responsible for thousands of people losing their jobs and homes. Ridiculous. He could find someone else in a day.

Someone who will marry him for his money, who doesn't understand his humor. Someone who doesn't appreciate his intelligence and quiet, bossy, interfering kindness. Or understand that his feelings can be hurt because he hides his pain by pretending he has no feelings at all.

My face crumples, and I scrape my palms across my eyes to wipe away my tears. There's no mascara to make a mess because I've never scrambled to put on my mask with him. He doesn't treat me any differently whether I'm in a silk gown or pink pajamas. Or if I'm having good days and able to get around on my own or driving around a grocery store on an electric scooter.

He manipulated me because he wanted to use me, and I promised myself I'd never be that person again. I practiced saying "no" over and over. I can't give him what he wants.

I've earned every ounce of my self-respect. I dragged it back when bullies at school wanted me to feel like garbage for being different than they were. In elementary school, I sent Jonny those humiliating Father's Day gifts in some twisted belief that if I loved him hard enough, he'd love me back. Then I stopped. And I clawed my way to a place where I could let go.

My mother, with all her tantrums and control issues. I'd tried to extricate myself from her so many times. I'd known within six months of going to live with her that I'd made a mistake, but she pulled me back every time I tried to leave, convincing me that I needed her. Until this last time, when I took my self-respect, wrapped it around me like a fucking cloak, and walked away.

It was one more attempt that neither of us was convinced would stick, but I'm not the same person I was.

"I gave you a ladder, not a cage."

He did. Not just that Henry gave me a job, but that he put me in positions where I could prove to myself that I was capable of handling things on my own. I have lots of useful skills. I'm educated and intelligent, and the voice I heard telling me I couldn't survive was never mine. It was my mother's.

Fear kept me from cutting those last ties with my parents. I thought I couldn't do it unless I had a safety net. If I had Henry, I wouldn't be alone.

What I did with my parents was every bit as half-assed as what I'm doing now when I sit here and debate whether letting Henry use me is something I can live with if only he keeps looking at me like I matter.

I rise from the table, walk to the bedroom, and open the closet door. My personal phone sits there on the shelf, a silent accusation of my cowardice. *"You thought you could hide me in a closet and pretend?"*

It's been in here since the first day. I've used Henry's iPad and the work phone he provided me to talk to my friends while I left my personal phone powered off and stuck on a shelf in the closet. Never once did he pressure me to do anything else.

I was playing a game with myself. As if pretending mine didn't exist would mean that I didn't have to deal with any of it. I could stay here on the mountain, exactly the way ten-year-old me imagined. All the adventure, but none of the suffering or work. I could hide from my life and not have to deal with it or make a choice.

I power the phone on. The moment I do, the screen fills with notification after notification from both of my parents. A pop-up warns me I have less than 5 percent battery life, and I carry it to the charger on my nightstand, plugging it in and sitting on the edge of the bed. I dismiss and delete every notification, every voicemail and text from my parents without bothering to read or listen to them. I block my father's number. Then I call Guinevere Jones.

She picks up on the first ring. "Oh my God, Franki. Are you okay?"

"I'm great."

"I don't think that's true. I'm worried sick about you," she cries.

"I'm not yours to worry about anymore."

Shocked silence descends before she regroups. "You can't tell a mother to stop worrying about her own child. I don't know what that man is telling you, but you're not safe there. You can't trust a man who tries to keep you away from your own family."

"Mom, I'm giving you the courtesy of a phone call to tell you this because I know if I didn't, you'd find some way to convince yourself that any text or email I sent didn't come from me. This is me telling you that our relationship is over. You're not good for me. I'm better, stronger, and so much happier without you in my life."

She gasps. "He's brainwashed you. You need help."

"When you took me to live with you in the UK, it was because I made the critical error of telling you I was happy."

"It was Christmas. I was there for the holiday to see you. I didn't want to tell you this. I knew it would hurt you, but . . . I ran into Henry on that trip. He came on to me. I told him I wasn't interested because you were in love with him, and he laughed at you. He was cruel. I knew I had to take you with me, then. I had to get you away from him before he broke your heart."

I breathe in deeply. I'm not even angry at her. I'm tired. "Do you know when you're lying? Or do you convince yourself your made-up version of events is the truth?"

"It is the truth. Don't punish me because you don't like to hear it," she screams.

"I'm not punishing you. I'm done. I don't want to hear from you again. I won't take your calls. I hope you find something that satisfies you and makes you happy. Goodbye."

I hang up and block her number. Maybe I'm numb. Maybe the confrontation first with Penelope Stanton, then my father, paved the way. Maybe I waited so long to do this and hashed it out in my mind so many times that when I finally did it, it was anticlimactic.

Maybe my heart is so broken by Henry's betrayal that I don't have room to feel devastation over my mother. Instead, I feel nothing but relief.

A steady *thunk . . . thunk . . . thunk* starts up behind the cabin. I walk back to the kitchen to clear the table and clean up our dinner. Somehow, Henry found my favorite chicken piccata recipe, or at least a very close version of it. A glance at his plate reveals he picked off every caper from his own chicken. The man made me something he hates, just to please me.

No. To manipulate me. *How could I forget it so quickly?*

There aren't many dishes to wash, but I have a feeling it's going to take me a long time to clean up a couple plates and a few pots and pans. Because above the sink, a window offers a hint of Henry hard at work at the corner edge of the yard.

I resist the urge to get a better look for all of five seconds, but the steady sound of metal splitting wood has me more curious than I can stand. Before I even decide to do it, I've moved into the small utility room off the kitchen. Cautiously, I crack open the back door. *Please don't let him catch me watching him.*

Henry tosses two pieces of wood onto an already chest-high stack, then resumes his wood splitting, going at the logs like they've personally attacked him.

Henry ignored his jacket when he left, but his skin glistens with sweat, regardless of the forty-degree temperature. Bits of bark cling to his black T-shirt, neck, and arms as he swings.

I know nothing about splitting wood, but he must, because every strike is practiced and efficient. His biceps and forearms flex with corded muscle, and the early evening sun brings out auburn highlights in his hair. Under his shirt, Henry's pecs twitch with every swing. A familiar grunt of exertion leaves him as the axe makes contact, and heat pools in my pelvis. The last time I heard him make that sound was this afternoon when he was inside my body.

He sets his axe aside, tears the remainder of the log into two pieces with his bare hands, and tosses them onto his growing pile of firewood. When the wood has left his hands, Henry takes off his glasses and drags the hem of his shirt up to wipe the sweat off his face revealing the ridges of his toned abdomen and the defined V of an Adonis belt.

Then, breathing heavily, he sits on the huge log he'd been using to brace the wood and drops his head to his hands. He stays like that for long moments, staring at nothing. Finally, he stands, returning his glasses to his face and glancing toward the cabin.

His gaze catches on mine through the crack in the door, his eyebrows lifting in surprise.

I close the door with a snap and lean against it, my heart thundering in my chest.

The sound of metal tearing through wood begins again.

Thirty-Four

Henry

Run | Snow Patrol

I CLEAN AND PREP the blade on the maul, then hang it with the other tools in the shed, lingering longer than necessary with the scents of fresh-cut oak and blade oil. I want to keep going and wear myself out, but that would be stupid when I have work to do and an unknown threat lingering around us like a bad smell.

I kick the shed door shut behind me with unnecessary violence as I head back to the woodpile. Lawrence has gone to extraordinary lengths to attempt to come between Franki and me. It's not a stretch to suspect him as our unsub. He was already on my list of suspects, but now he's flown straight to the top. Normally, I'd be the one heading the investigation and leave our asset with someone else to guard, but Franki isn't an asset. She's the love of my life. I don't trust her protection to anyone else.

I rub my chest and breathe through the ache. She can barely stand to look at me. She thinks I betrayed her with divided loyalties to her and MPD. She should know that she'll always come first for me.

I load my arms with firewood to haul inside and try to work past the regret to make a plan to fix this. Why *wouldn't* she believe my loyalties are divided? When I saw her again for the first time, I'd imagined her on a *list* of priorities, as if she wouldn't be right there at the top, every single time. She doesn't realize that I've changed. If I could go back to the night of the reception, I'd handle everything differently.

As I reach for one last piece of wood to add to my already large armload, a splinter lodges itself deep in my thumb, and I hiss at the annoyance of it.

I have things to do and standing here ruminating over my regret changes nothing.

I carry the wood into the cabin, stacking it next to the hearth, then move to the kitchen sink. The splinter is large enough that I should be able to remove it without tweezers, but my fingers slip off the wood when I try, so I use my teeth and yank the fucker out. Blood gushes from my thumb as I spit the splinter into the sink. I turn on the faucet, letting the small wound bleed for a few seconds under the stream of water, then I wrap it in a paper towel to stop the crimson flow.

This is what Franki expects me to do with MPD. She wants me to rip it out of our lives entirely to prove that she's my priority.

I turn back to face the living room. She's closed the door to the bedroom against me.

I try to access the numbness I've lived with for the last several years, but Franki burned it away, and now every raw, aching nerve inside me is nothing but feeling. I'm filled with layer after layer of emotions. Hurt and regret and, more than any of it, tenderness and love for her, even though she's infuriating. Strangely enough, there's relief in the realization. Going back to being that man would mean respite from the pain, but it would also be a return to the hollow void of my life without her.

I tap on her door with a knuckle.

"What do you want?" Her voice is muffled.

"I need a shower. The only bathroom is on the other side of this door," I say testily. I suppose she'll tell me to bathe in the sink or the panic room. It's her cabin, after all. She can tell me to sleep on the porch, and I'll do it.

"The door's not locked."

When I try the knob, it turns easily under my hand. Franki is lying in bed with her hair piled in a sloppy bun and glasses perched on her nose, a book in her lap. She refuses to look up at me as she waves her hand toward the bathroom door. "Go ahead, before you stink the place up with man sweat."

I prowl through the bedroom on my way to the bathroom and try to pretend my heart doesn't feel as though it's been stabbed, then set on fire. I shower, washing away the grime and *man sweat*, and work through a different plan. Controlling MPD is no longer my goal. I no longer even want it. It's nothing but a reminder of how I've hurt Franki.

I return to the bedroom, a towel wrapped around my waist to find Franki standing at the dresser and sorting through one of her cases. I join her, opening a drawer and removing a pair of boxer briefs, pajama bottoms, a T-shirt, and a cardigan sweater. It's sheer habit to strap on my ankle holster. I won't remove it until I'm ready to climb into bed for the night.

Franki is silent beside me as she pulls out a tiny cardboard box with a prescription label on it, a Band-Aid, two alcohol wipes, and a syringe shrink-wrapped in plastic. She lays the items out on the bedside stand, then goes into the bathroom to wash her hands. When she returns, I've dressed and torn open the box and syringe packaging. She freezes at the sight of me, then shakes her head. "I can do it."

"I know you can. You've been doing it for months by yourself, but you don't have to because you have me now." I hadn't realized she'd done it last week until it was over. She never even considered asking for my help.

She shakes her head in one brief jerk, then appears to reconsider and gives a stiff nod. "I'm not cutting off my nose to spite my face. Tonight would have been rough. Go wash your hands, please."

I do, despite the fact that I've recently showered. I use a clean hand towel from the linen closet to dry off and return to find her reclining on the left side of the bed.

After I read the prescription, I confirm the number of cc's with her. She tells me, then starts to give me directions, but stops when she sees me swipe the alcohol wipe over the top of the bottle unbidden and begin the process.

"How do you know how to do this?"

"Training."

"You've given injections before?"

She has no idea. "Yes. Usually under far more harrowing circumstances than this. You're not even bleeding, love, and you're entirely conscious. You'll have to start screaming and frothing at the mouth if you want to rattle me. At the very least, we need a good explosion or two going off around us."

Her eyes go wide, then they narrow. "I'll skip the screaming, thanks. Maybe next time we can arrange for some fireworks."

She doesn't seem to realize what she said. *"Next time."* As in, we'll be doing this again. She's not leaving me, whether she's ready to admit it yet or not.

She shimmies her fleece pants down her legs. "It's the left thigh this week."

I swab the area with another alcohol wipe and wait for it to dry, sneaking a look up at her as I do. Her knuckles are red and swollen tonight, so I'm not surprised the injections are a challenge for her. The plunger in the syringe is tight and requires a steady pressure to both fill and depress it.

I squeeze her thigh when the alcohol is dry and gently slide in the needle. Franki doesn't react to the poke at all, but a few seconds after I've withdrawn and applied the bandage, she breathes out through her teeth. "Ouch."

"It hurts?"

"Not the jab, but the medication, itself, feels like a wasp sting. It'll settle down in a few minutes." Franki pulls up her pants and indicates a sharps container she's set on the dresser.

By the time I turn back after discarding the syringe and cleaning up, she's sitting cross-legged on top of the covers, watching me with a serious expression.

"I'll marry you," she says.

I blink, thrown by her unexpected offer, hope lifting me like a kite on a breeze. "You will?"

She crosses her arms defensively. "So your cousin doesn't throw a bunch of old people and babies out into the street. Yes, I will. But no more flirting with me. I'll give you your business deal."

And now my kite is in the trees.

"Really?" I ask silkily, lifting one eyebrow and covering my hurt and anger with snark.

"That's what I said," she snarls.

I draw the corners of my mouth into a smile. "I'm afraid I have to decline."

She drops her arms and gapes. "What? This was your idea. You said you needed me to marry you. It's what you've been working for all this time."

"I was wrong. I'm not interested in a business arrangement." It's a direct quote of the words she said to me.

She sputters, and I lean closer, using my finger to tip her mouth closed.

"I find I need all the traditional trappings. Romance and emotional investment. You understand," I say.

Straightening, I head for the living room. When I close the door behind me, something, probably a pillow, thuds against it. Seconds later, an incoherent scream of rage filters through the door.

I snap it open and poke my head inside. "You're all right in here, love?"

She shows me her teeth. "I'm fine. Thanks for asking."

"I'm going to leave this door open after all"—I shoot her a finger gun—"so you don't get cold."

"Great."

"If you need me"—I use my thumb to point awkwardly behind me—"I'll be getting a little work done out here."

"I won't. I'm taking a bath, then going to bed."

I nod.

"Good night, Henry," she says.

I stand in the doorway and watch her get off the bed and head for the bathroom. Before Franki woke me up, I'd have convinced myself this ache in my chest was a heart attack. "Good night, love."

When the bathroom door closes behind her, and the sound of running water begins, I return to the kitchen and set up my laptop, determined to focus on work for a while.

Oliver stands up from his little bed in the corner, gives himself a shake, then trots for the front door. I run a hand through my hair. "Little man, Franki took you out to do your business half an hour ago."

He whines and scratches at the door, so after a quick check of the alarm system, I shove my feet into a pair of shoes and let him outside. Dachshunds aren't supposed to climb stairs because of the potential for back injuries. So, like the well-trained pup he is, he stands on the wooden porch in the wash of the outdoor floodlights, waiting for me to carry him down the six steps from the porch to the pea gravel walkway.

With the side of my foot, I complete our usual routine of nudging the metal doorstop shaped like a turtle into place and leave the front door propped open a few inches. If it were winter, I'd bother with grabbing the keys and arming the cabin, but this should take no more than a minute or two. Oliver watches me patiently until I carefully lift him into my arms. He doesn't wag his tail or snuggle into me the way he usually does. Instead, he puts his nose in the air and turns his face away in rejection. In fact, I'd call the way he's been behaving since Franki read my texts from Spencer as "pissy." He may not know why she's upset with me, but he knows she is, and that's enough for him to take sides.

I carry him down the steps. "Listen, I'm not the one being unreasonable here. She's mad because I loved her on purpose? That doesn't even make sense. I wasn't choosing the company over her, and she'll realize I'm telling the truth eventually when I don't marry anyone else or take MPD for myself."

He makes a sound in his chest in response, a blatant disagreement with my assessment. Dachshunds look like small dogs, but Oliver's growls and barks always sound deep chested, like they come from a much larger canine.

I set him down on the section of lawn illuminated by the lights from the cabin. "Hurry up and do your thing. The temperature is dropping, and I shouldn't have left the door open. The cabin's going to get too cold for Franki."

Oliver takes off like a shot, but instead of heading around the side of the cabin or anywhere on the lawn, he heads straight back up the porch steps.

I lunge after him. "Don't you dare climb those sta—"

Too late. He's inside the cabin before my feet have hit the porch, then the little Machiavelli shoves the doorstop aside and pushes the door shut behind him just as my fingertips graze the wood. I blink in consternation.

I've been locked out. By the dog.

Thirty-Five

Henry

Brother | NEEDTOBREATHE

"Do you think I don't know you did this on purpose?" I rattle the knob. "Oliver, this is petty as fuck. You're a bigger dog than this."

He doesn't bark when I rattle the door. Proof, in my estimation, of his perfidy. Normally, he'd be barking his head off that someone was on the porch, let alone making noise. Then, Franki would come investigate and let me in. Not tonight. No. Tonight he doesn't make a sound.

The sun set half an hour ago, and a frigid November wind cuts through my white T-shirt and navy cardigan with vicious glee.

Inside, Oliver sticks his nose through the opening in the curtains, smudging the window glass as he sits on the back of the sofa, inside the warm, cozy cabin and watches me shiver on the porch.

I point a finger at him. "You're not allowed to climb on the furniture without a ramp or Franki or me lifting you up. Bad dog."

He jumps off the back of the sofa, and I flinch. I should have let him stay there until I got back inside and lifted him down. Pressing my face to the window, I prop my hands over my eyes and peer through the space in the curtains to see if he hurt himself, just in time to watch him trot his little ass across the living room, into the bedroom, and nudge that door shut behind him too.

I run both my hands through my hair and move back to the front door. This cabin is built to provide maximum security, and the doors lock automatically as a safety precaution.

I knock and call out, "Franki?!"

I'm not surprised when there's no response. She's in the one room in the place that doesn't have a window to the exterior, and there are two solidly built closed doors between us. It's quiet inside the cabin because it's built to be a fortress. Franki probably also has the water running, and she likes to turn on music when she takes a bath.

There's no doorbell. It's a one-bedroom cabin in the woods. Getting into the place through the usual means a person might use to break in, is out. It's fortified against that. It doesn't mean I can't get in, but that it will be a pain in my ass. It's already dark outside, and the temperatures have dropped until my breath fogs the air. At least I have on shoes.

I walk around back to the bedroom window. It'll get me closer to where Franki is, and if I'm loud enough, she may hear me and come let me in. I drag over a log, prop it under the window, and climb on top of it to get a look inside. The bedside lamp is on. The bathroom door is shut. Oliver is lying on his back on my side of the bed *on my pillow*. I don't knock on the glass because that would set off the alarms, and I don't want to scare Franki. So, I stand here like an idiot and shout.

Oliver gives me side-eye, and I don't care what people say, dogs can smile, because he is absolutely laughing at me.

I call again. "Franki?!"

Normally, someone shouting outside of a window would send Oliver into a barking fit. A squirrel scurried across the front porch yesterday, and he barked at the door for ten solid minutes. Not tonight. Tonight, he watches me with petty satisfaction and doesn't make a sound.

Approximately five minutes of hollering yields no results. I could stay here for an hour until she's done with her bath, but it's getting cold enough that my nose is running, and my fingers are going numb.

Both of Franki's phones sit on the nightstand. They're always on vibrate, or I could call her.

Dad has told us all over and over *"Never get comfortable."* This is what he meant. Franki and I could be separated from each other. She needs a way to communicate besides the built-in systems in the cabin that send alerts to my father and brother. What if Franki were the one who was locked out? I'm putting in new systems tomorrow.

I know a number of ways to get into this cabin, but only one of them won't involve potentially traumatizing Franki by having her think the cabin is under attack. I jump off the log, put it back where it belongs near the shed, and set out through the field on the half-mile trek to the airplane hangar.

I already spoke to Spencer before I came in from the woodpile. I'd like to put some blame on him, but, aside from a case of overly enthusiastic-itis and not understanding that when I said, *"no other names"* I'd meant *"no matter what,"* he hasn't done anything wrong. The wording he used was the wording *I* used when I decided to go through with finding a wife. I never explicitly told Spencer that Franki was different or that my feelings for her were real. I've barely seen or spoken to him, in fact, since any of this started. The pain I've caused Franki is my own fault.

I need advice on how to proceed, and I may as well use this time as I walk to the hangar to get it. I can't call Gabriel. He's still in rehab. Dante and Spencer are both married to their jobs. I'm 47.3 percent convinced they're each fighting a thing for the other, but for once I'm minding my own business. At least until such time as I am 90 percent certain. Either way, neither of them is a relationship guru.

If I call Dad, he'll already be in bed with Mom. He'll answer my call. They'll both get on speakerphone, and Mom will give me a well-earned tongue lashing when she finds out what I did. I deserve it, but I don't have time to submit myself for flagellation. Not from anyone but Franki, anyway.

My cousin Jack is probably working at his bar. My cousin Marie will react every bit as badly as Mom. Bronwyn is still recovering and needs her rest.

I pinch my temples between my fingers and my thumb. Desperate times call for desperate measures. I hit Call.

The phone rings, then a gruff voice with a light Virginia accent says, "Henry."

I make my way through the dark woods, using the flashlight from my phone to illuminate the path ahead. "Dean. I have need of your assistance."

"Why do you talk like that? Just say 'I need your help.'"

"Because the first sounds like a reasonable and measured request. The second sounds—Jesus. *I need your help.*"

"You in trouble?" I hear the scrape of chair legs and a scratch, as though Dean is dragging his hand over his scruff.

"Not the kind you mean. I have questions of a personal nature."

"Your mic is picking up a lot of wind. Do I hear coyotes?"

"Yes. Nothing to be concerned about. They're half a mile away." I hope. Besides, I'm armed if it becomes necessary to defend myself. "I apologize for sound quality. I already have my hand cupped around the mic to be heard. This is the best I can do. I'm taking a walk."

"At night in the wilderness?"

I breathe loudly and nearly cough when the frigid air hits my lungs. "Ahh. Refreshing. Nothing like it."

"You're in the doghouse with Franki." I can hear the satisfaction in his voice.

"You can bask in the pleasure of my suffering later. Right now, I need to know exactly what you did to fix things with my sister."

"The hell you do."

"I meant 'what did you say?'" I step over a large rut in the uneven ground and start a light jog.

"I told her I loved her the way *you* told me to."

"I already do that. Probably twenty times a day."

"You look Franki in the eyes and say 'I love you' twenty times a day? Maybe you're doing it *too* much."

"I . . . call her 'love.' I haven't made a word for word confession. It was my understanding I was supposed to wait at least three months for a full love declaration."

"It seems to me you shouldn't be worried about following a timeline. I'm learning honesty trumps strategy when it comes to relationships."

"How did you get Bronwyn to forgive you?"

"Henry, I don't know. I said I was sorry, and that I couldn't live without her. Your sister is an angel."

I snort. "Bronwyn is no angel."

Dean huffs. "Have you tried the standing in the doorway thing yet?"

"You mean hovering there like a psycho while she sleeps? Yes. It's pointless." Not that it stops me.

Dean barks out a laugh. "No. The next time you talk to her when she's in another room, untuck your shirt first and prop your hands on top of the doorframe so you flash her your abs."

He pauses, then asks, "You do have abs, don't you? I don't think the technique works if your gut is flabby or you look like the underside of a toad."

"I'm not using any more techniques on her."

Dean is quiet for a moment, then blows out a breath. "Then I think all you got left is groveling."

"How do you grovel?"

"I'm not a relationship expert, so, take what I'm about to say for what it is: a shot in the dark, but you have to prove you learned your lesson. Some things are unforgivable, but if you made an honest mistake, I guess you gotta be sincere and vulnerable? If she's an angel like Bronwyn, she won't stomp you into the dirt when you're already on your knees."

I reach the hangar without having to shoot at any coyotes and go to the far-left main door, using the emergency key hidden in an electronically coded box under a hinged faux panel on the building.

I set off the countdown on the alarm when I enter with the manual lock, but I have the security codes and move immediately to tap in the override and fit my eye to the retinal scan. I make it with five seconds to spare, so Franki won't hear anything of concern in the cabin.

After I've locked the place back down, I jog to the walled-off office in the back corner. Another entry. Another alarm turned off. Then I lock the office door behind me and step to the large wall of metal shelves that hold everything from emergency supplies to a fake potted fern that my sister thought would be a funny birthday gift. A hidden keypad under the bottom shelf slides the metal shelving to the right, revealing a hatch much like the one that opens up under the rug in the cabin living room. Down the ladder I go, then I hit the coordinating button to move the shelving back into place and make the much more quiet jog back to the cabin.

When I've entered the cabin through the living room hatch and returned the rug to its former position, I bank the woodstove for the night and glance toward the closed bedroom door. I don't know exactly what I'll find on the other side. Franki and Oliver asleep? Franki still in the bath? Or Franki awake and ready to throw another pillow my way?

When I reach the door, I open it to find her a quiet mound under the comforter. In the darkness, I remove my clothing, and, when I'm dressed in nothing but my underwear, I approach our bed. As I pull back the duvet, Franki's stomach growls.

I sit on the edge of the bed, and the growl sounds again. Louder.

I snap on the bedside lamp to find, just as I suspected, Oliver cuddled in Franki's arms.

Franki doesn't stir, but he does, watching me with glittering, possessive intelligence.

"There's a reason I didn't put a ramp on this bed, Oliver," I whisper.

He huffs and snuggles harder into Franki.

"You"—I point imperiously—"have your own bed in the kitchen. Go."

He lifts his head and looks at the door before he smirks and drops back to cuddle under her chin.

I reach to lift him off the bed, and he whines. Loudly.

I put my finger to my lips. "Shhh."

Franki doesn't wake, clearly exhausted, but she tightens her arms around him and pats him like he's her baby.

"I, too, would like Franki to pat me, Oliver. It's my turn," I whisper. Not that patting is likely whether Oliver is here or not. In fact, when she realizes she forgot to tell me to sleep somewhere else, she might make me to move to the couch.

Oliver closes his eyes and nuzzles her with his head.

I'm on my knees on the bed now, glaring. "Move it. Right. Now," I whisper.

Oliver does no such thing.

Stomping to the kitchen, I dig around in his treat jar and return with one of his sweet potato and chicken snacks. Then I waggle it by the edge of the bed as I attempt to coax him in a cheerful, friendly-sounding whisper. "Come on, you little woman-hogging jerk. That's it. Good boy. Come get your disgusting snack."

He rolls his eyes and doesn't budge.

With a huff, I set the treat on my nightstand and climb in under the covers, moving over to put my arm around Franki, determined to ignore the fact that Oliver is between us.

He puts out one stubby front leg and shoves my face away from both of them.

I jerk back in outrage. "Why do your paws smell like Fritos? Did you eat corn chips where I sleep?"

He bats at me again, and I retreat to lie cold and alone on the edge of my own damn bed.

"You haven't won. I want you to know that. This is a temporary ceasefire because I appreciate the fact that you're offering her comfort when she's upset, and because I don't want to wake her up. But this is *my bed* and Franki is *my woman*, and *You. Are. A. Dog.*"

He gives a slow blink, smug triumph written in every long line of his body.

"Good. Night. Sir," I hiss and click off the lamp.

He rolls in Franki's arms until he gives me his back. Then a prolonged squeaking sound emanates from his direction.

Seconds later, I gag at the smell.

"You are such a dick," I mutter.

Oliver doesn't answer. He's too busy snoring.

Thirty-Six

Henry

How Long Will I Love You | Ellie Goulding

THE GRAY LIGHT OF a cool November morning filters into the living room. It's a new day. A fresh start. I know what I have to do, starting with telling my grandmother I don't want MPD. After which, Franki will, hopefully, believe me that she's my priority and find it in her heart to forgive me, but a man has his limits, and I've reached mine.

"I have always treated you well." My voice verges on feral. "I give you affection. Attention. Respect. I make the disgusting food you like that, if I'm going to be honest . . . *and I am* . . . I personally find revolting. But I'm done with your *judgmental bullshit*."

The bedroom door whips open and Franki stands there, eyes squinted without glasses or contacts. Her hair is a sexy, disheveled mess, and she's wearing a blue T shirt with no bra and striped loose pajama pants. She props her hands on her hips. "What in the world is going on out here?"

I point an accusatory finger at Oliver as he sits at my feet, wagging his tail and giving a happy yip. "That. Right there. He's trying to mess with my head."

She blinks in confusion. "Henry, do you feel okay? Your hair looks like you stuck your finger in a light socket."

My hair is the least of it. I'd dressed in my normal clothing this morning. Black trousers, white shirt. My feet, however, are in a pair of steel-toed boots because my normal shoes are currently outside. Where I threw them. "He *shit*"—I force back my visceral reaction, then manfully continue—"in my shoe."

She turns wide eyes on Oliver. "You didn't."

When Oliver runs to her and does his majestic wiener dog pose, she lifts him into her arms. He whines and nuzzles into her, and she rubs his back in comfort. "It was an accident. Dachshunds don't like to go outside in the cold. He's very sorry."

Oliver turns his head toward me and sneers.

I point at him again. "He's not sorry. He's taunting me," I say in a malevolent near whisper.

She shakes her head in disbelief.

"Last night, he locked me out of the cabin while you were in the bathroom. He stole my spot in bed . . . You know what? No. I'm not listing his transgressions." I lean toward Oliver, my voice low and accusing. "He knows what he did."

She turns away protectively. "Don't speak to him like that. He's a dog. You're acting like a lunatic."

"That's where you're wrong. He's more than a dog. He's an evil genius."

"Well, I guess it takes an evil genius to know an evil genius," she snaps.

"So it does," I agree.

She stares at me. I stare back. Then her face crumples, and she starts to shake. I step closer, concerned, and she wails, "I'm angry at you, *dammit*."

"I know. I'm sorry."

Her last vestige of control over her face cracks, and a laugh pushes its way past her closed lips in a helpless sputter. *"Oliver shit in your shoe."*

I blink. She's not crying. She's been trying not to laugh. My own mouth twitches in response. "It's not funny."

"It's a little bit funny." She struggles to even speak the words.

Unable to remain standing upright, she leans into me as she loses her last shred of self-control, laughing so hard tears streak down her face. "Not Oliver, but you . . . you . . . I thought there was a . . . person. I thought . . . but . . . you . . . and Oliver . . ."

I drop my forehead onto her shoulder and struggle to speak through my own laughter. "He's so pissed at me. He . . . is . . . so petty."

"You talk to him . . . like he understands you," she wheezes.

"*He does*," I say through my own laughter.

She cracks up even harder. Oliver wiggles in her arms and stretches over to lick my face. I put a hand up to gently push him back and wipe his kiss onto my sleeve-covered bicep. Something about that dog kiss strikes me as even funnier. He knows I hate his spit on my face.

She sets Oliver on the floor and drops down onto her butt, leaning back against the coffee table, rocking with laughter.

I join her on the rug, leaning against her and trying to catch my breath. When I wrap my arm around her shoulders, Oliver, tail wagging in delight, climbs onto my lap, one paw dangerously close to unmanning me. I shift him slightly and stroke his back as he cuddles against me. "Does this mean he forgives me?"

Her giggles turn to sobs, and I want to rip my heart out of my chest and give it to her, so she understands she is everything. I would do anything for her. I move Oliver to the floor and pull her tighter against me, rubbing her back and rocking us both.

"I love you." My voice sounds like gravel in a rock tumbler.

Breath catching, she lifts her head, but I can't look into her eyes and see her rejection of my words.

I tighten my hold. "I'm in love with you. Wholly. Entirely. There's no end to it, and there never will be. I know I'm not technically supposed to say it yet, but it's true." I clear my throat. "Sorry about that."

"You're sorry?"

"Not sorry that I love you. I'm sorry I haven't done it right, so that no part of you ever has any reason to doubt who you are to me. There's nothing I'll ever put ahead of you. Not my own life. Not my family. And certainly not some damn company."

She doesn't move or say anything. It barely feels as though she's breathing, and I rush forward before she shuts down again and pushes me away. "I wanted to give you everything you ever needed. I wasn't trying to trick you. The first night we made love, I held you afterward, and I had to force myself not to tell you I loved you because I thought I'd smother you or you wouldn't believe me."

She shifts subtly closer.

"Do you remember the first night I proposed to you?" I ask.

Brows knitted, she nods, and I continue, "I'd lost faith that there was anything worth the pain of allowing myself to feel. Every moment of my life was filled with acquisition and working hundred-hour weeks. I was busy enough that I didn't have time to think about how empty my life was."

I lean away slightly and take her hand, running my thumb over my favorite freckle on her pinkie. I don't lift my head. "I hadn't seen you in four years, nine months, and twelve days. And every minute of it had hollowed me out a piece at a time. I'd numbed myself so effectively that when you woke me up, I didn't even know what was happening to me. I tried to talk to you in your hotel room, and I was freaking the fuck out. My heart was racing. I couldn't think straight. I thought there was something wrong with me. I was so closed off from my emotions that I didn't even recognize them."

"Henry," she says quietly.

I shake my head. "You're the reason I see a future that means anything at all. I can't go back. Franki, I can't live without you again. I'll turn into the biggest asshole on the planet. I'll be some lonely old cartoonish villain hoarding money and never giving Spencer a vacation in his life—"

"Look at me." She turns her hand over and squeezes.

I meet her gaze at last.

With a watery smile, she presses her hand against my jaw. I layer my own over hers, holding her to me.

I swallow hard. "When you wanted me to call my grandmother and tell her to give Lawrence those shares, I should have dialed her number right then and there. I'm doing it today. I don't want any part of anything that hurts you."

Her brows knit. "You said you were worried about the people your cousin would hurt."

"I am, but I'm not weighing what you need against anything or anyone else and having you come up short. Not ever. I'm not a hero. I've told you that before and you persist in believing I'm a better person than I am. If you were thirsty, I would step over three people who were on fire to give you a glass of water."

She shakes her head with a smile and lifts my other hand to kiss my scarred knuckles.

"That's terrible," she says gently.

I nod. "I know."

She burrows against me, and I haul her onto my lap.

"I love you too," she says.

I speak against her hair. "That's because you're the kindest, most forgiving, wonderful woman on the planet. I'm going to treat you like the queen you are, every day of your life."

"I'm sorry I made us both wallow in misery last night."

"I deserved it. There's nothing like a good, hard wallow to put things into perspective. When you offered me a business arrangement, it hurt like hell."

She rests her forehead against mine. "I kept telling myself that you were like my parents."

How could she not? It's what she knows, and I tried to bribe her into matrimony.

"Those texts felt like confirmation of my biggest fear. My parents have both made productions out of how much they 'love' me, but they've never done anything real that made me feel loved. You never said it, but you *showed* me. Even when you were furious, you did things *to love* me. You served me dinner while you were pissed. You took care of me and gave me my injection, while you were angry."

She sniffs. "I thought about it all night. Your stupid list I thought proved you didn't care wasn't stupid at all. It was you *doing* the loving. You could have come at me a hundred ways to convince me to marry you. You *know* me. You could have played on my sympathy by telling me people would lose their homes. It would have worked if I thought you had no other option. You could have found some way to blackmail me with some awful thing my parents have done."

I scowl. "What would be the point if you weren't happy?"

"If you hadn't cared, the point would have been those shares."

Leaning over Franki, I guide her until her back is flat to the thick rug. "I love you, Franki. How many times a day do you think is too many for me to say it?"

"I love you too. Why don't you say it when you want to and try not to worry about keeping track?"

I slide my hand under her pajama top, her skin warm and soft and so damned beautiful.

Something hot and sexual demands that I make this right. I need this connection to her.

When I remove my glasses, she gives me a secret smile. I take her mouth, licking into her and loving the electric shock of pleasure that jolts through me at the touch of her sweet tongue against mine. Every one of her kisses does this to me. I'm lit up and flung into orbit.

The hard ball of tension inside me unspools into nearly painful arousal. "You're staying with me."

It's not a question, but she answers. "Yes."

Franki nuzzles into my neck, then drops kisses along the sensitive skin there until she's reached my ear. I shudder as the vibration of her voice against me sets my nerve endings alight. I can't decide if I like it or if it's too much sensation.

"If we go to Vegas tonight, your cousin won't be a problem."

I've decided. I like it. I like it a lot. She's using the edge of her teeth. Not too gentle, but not too rough. My cock is hard as steel, nudging against her outer thigh.

Her words register on a delay. "No. I'll find another way to deal with him. I'm not having our wedding tainted by the stench of *eau de Lawrence*."

She sucks my earlobe between her teeth, then speaks into my ear again. "You're so sexy when you mangle French."

My palm and fingers span her ribcage. Mine. And I'm hers. All of me. Everything I have to give. I tug gently on her bottom lip with my teeth, and she sighs and shivers. When she reaches for my zipper, I still her hand.

"We're moving to the bedroom and shutting the door." I tip my head toward Oliver, where he's curled in his bed, snoring in whistling huffs. "If your attack wiener wakes up and decides I'm hurting you, I'll end up with stitches in my ass." *As it should be.*

She laughs, and I rise, giving her a boost until she's standing before me.

When we enter the bedroom, I close the door then walk to the bedside stand and remove my firearm from its ankle holster, placing it in a custom drawer in the nightstand. I remove my suspenders and undo the buttons on my shirt as she stands near the end of the bed and chews her lip. When I yank the shirttails from my waistband, she makes the cutest sound. I finish taking it off and shake it out, folding it and placing it on the dresser.

"What would it take for you to really go nuts?" she asks.

I trail my fingers across Franki's collarbone before I wrap her hair around my hand. "How crazy are we talking?"

Her breath skates across my lips when she whispers, "Throw your clothes on the floor."

I whip her shirt over her head and toss it over my shoulder with a grin. I don't even look to see where it lands because I'm too busy thumbing, then kissing, her nipples and swallowing back a groan.

When she frees my cock and shoves my trousers and boxer briefs down my thighs, I kick them and my boots off and leave them where they land.

She wrinkles her nose in delight. "Now, you're out of control."

Franki clasps me in a firm grip and strokes.

"If anyone could make me forget what I'm doing, it's you," I say.

When she begins to drop to her knees, I lift her into my arms, instead.

She huffs out a surprised laugh. "What are you doing?"

I carry her to the bed and lay her out with her hair spread in a light brown and caramel swirl on the pillow. "I'm taking care of you."

I let my gaze trail down her body, over the shape of her, the limbs that give the impression of length despite her average height. Over the mounds of her breasts and little brown nipples. I continue my perusal over the gentle slope of her abdomen and navel. Hooking my hands into her waistband, I drag the pajama bottoms and panties off her body. "I want you to lie back and relax"—I kiss her knee—"and allow me the great honor of servicing you."

Her eyes go wide, then she shakes her head. "I can't do that."

I trail kisses up her leg toward her center, shifting my body until I'm between her thighs. "Why not?"

"Because it's selfish . . ." I think she intended to sound outraged, but I give my first sucking kiss of her clitoris halfway through her sentence, and she trails off on a blissful sigh.

"It's not selfish to give me what I want." I lift my head to make eye contact. "Let me take care of you."

"But I should—"

"You should lie there and tell me what feels good." I swirl my thumb across her clit and ease a finger inside her silky heat.

"Ohhhh."

"If you'd rather I hold you instead of sex, you'll tell me. If I do something that hurts you, you'll tell me. If I make you feel good . . . You. Will. Tell me."

"Will I?" she breathes.

I give her my sternest scowl. "You will."

"You—" She gasps in pleasure, as I kiss her clit once more and ease another finger inside. "Really like control."

"I don't like control, love. I need it."

"That feels . . . I can't . . . talk when you . . . Oh."

Sliding my palm up her thigh in a long, sweeping motion, I come to rest on her hip, my grip firm, but not rough, bracing her as I work her pussy with my mouth.

"That feels amazing. So . . ."

I take my time pushing her up until she tips over that edge. When she orgasms, she cries out, her thighs clamping against my ears.

Franki is delicious. Warm, and wet, and ready. I kiss her shoulder and brace myself over her, fitting myself between her thighs. Then I shackle both of her wrists in one of my hands. Not tightly. She can be hurt too easily for that. Just enough for her to feel me holding her in place.

She gasps as my cock bumps and glides through her wetness, grazing her clit. I dip my head to tongue one tight nipple.

"Ohh."

I speak quietly near her ear. "Do you want it hard and fast? Or do you want it sweet and slow?"

She squirms and thrusts up against me, attempting to catch me and draw me inside, as she makes a sound somewhere between a gasp and an incoherent sob.

I smile against her skin. "Use your words."

"I want whatever you want."

I want her out of her head with pleasure, whatever it takes to get her there.

"Then I'll give you both." Brushing a kiss over her eyelids, I ease inside. Her snug heat envelops my cock, squeezing and flexing. We both groan in pleasure.

Slowly, I slide nearly all the way out, then just as gently, push inside. I bottom out and watch her face and body language. All I read from Franki is bliss. I'm gentle. Slow. Pacing us. Occasionally, kissing her. More often, watching her. I'll pick up the pace later. Regardless, I have to stay cognizant of her reactions. Always careful I won't exacerbate her RA or cause her pain. Her SI joint dislocates easily, so I'm measured in my responses.

I can't hold her wrists, keep the majority of my weight off her, and stimulate her clit at the same time this way. I need to consider changing positions slightly so I can reach her, but also maintain her comfort. I should—

She attempts to pull her hands from my grip, so I release her.

Franki cups my face. "Henry," she gasps. Quietly. Teasingly.

I swallow, even as I continue my slow, gentle, relentless ride. "Yes?"

"I love you."

I search her eyes, tenderness flooding my system. "I love you too."

"Close your eyes."

I can't see her reactions if I do, but I'll never deny her, so I acquiesce.

Then a black cloak hides her from my sight, one of my senses cut off entirely, even as I can't stop myself from seeking her behind my eyelids.

She kisses me, hands still on my face. "Time for you to stop thinking and fuck me."

Her words break something free inside me. I don't let go entirely, still aware of her body language, but I'm doing it through feel now. Through the sensations I'm absorbing. Through instinct and the taste of her. The delicate feminine scent.

I'm intensely aware of the searing pleasure and desire in my own body. *I want to fuck her.*

In this moment, with her untrammeled encouragement and enthusiasm, hidden in the dark and unable to keep my thoughts coherent, the urge to rut on her is impossible to resist. I draw out, then slam back into her, my balls slapping against her ass when I sheathe myself to the hilt.

"Yes. Yes, Henry," she says.

I try to keep my head one last time. "I need to know you'll stop me if I hurt you." The words are a grating demand, forced through vocal cords that have forgotten how to function.

"I promise."

I trust her to be my partner and to know what she wants. I fuck her. Harder than I ever have. Over and over. I pound my way into her body. She feels like heaven. The way she squeezes me. Her damp skin against the entire length of me as I forget to hold myself away from her and make full body contact. Her breasts soft against the hard planes of my chest, nipples tight little peaks.

She wraps her legs around my back, locking her ankles, and meeting every one of my thrusts with her own.

Open-mouthed kisses. Hers. Mine. The scratch and claw of her fingernails on my back. Her breathy little gasps of pleasure. The relentless beat in my body and heart. Love her. *Love* her.

She nudges my shoulder. "Roll over."

I let her take me with her until she's on top, and I open my eyes to look into hers. She bites the side of her bottom lip and takes me back inside. My hips punch up; my hands a vise grip on her ass driving her down.

She gasps, and we work together, pushing each other closer and closer to orgasm.

I can't come yet. Not yet. Not. Yet.

She rolls again, and I stay inside her, leaning back on my knees and reaching for a pillow. Finding one and, lifting her, sliding it under her ass.

There. *There.*

I brace myself with one hand on the headboard and loom over her. "Touch your clit. I want to feel you come on my cock."

She does. The rapid movement of her circling fingers brushing and bumping into me as I piston into her.

"So good. You feel so good inside me," she gasps.

Her encouragement drives me. My spine buzzes, sending radio static into my brain and groin. Incoherent pleasure. Love. Lust. Franki tightens on me, her walls squeezing and fluttering. Jerking beneath me. Around me.

I lose my last fingertip hold on control, as release tears through me. My mind sheets white, and nothing has ever felt so good.

Thirty-Seven

Franki

Paint It Black | Hidden Citizens, Ranya

I stand on the small front lawn of the cabin, wearing comfortable pants and shoes, with Henry's black fleece jacket over my own long-sleeved T-shirt. It'd be a nice day to be inside with a good book and a cup of tea. We've been out here for forty-five minutes already, and my knees, hips, and knuckles ache with the cold.

"Again." Henry grabs my ponytail and pulls me backward.

I turn rapidly in a quick circle, twisting under his arm. He keeps his fist in my hair, resulting in him yanking his own arm behind his back. When he bends to relieve the pressure on his shoulder, I fake a knee to his nose.

Releasing my hair, Henry straightens. "Good."

He's wearing contact lenses, as he often does when we practice, though he'll take them out the moment we're back inside because he can't stand them. He looks naked to me when he takes his glasses off, and Henry naked is hot as hell. The glasses are also a turn on for me. Who am I kidding? I never find him *not sexy*.

Henry lifts my hands and pulls them to his mouth, blowing on my swollen knuckles to warm them up.

"Am I ready to kick somebody's butt?" I wink.

He doesn't smile. "Not even close, but that doesn't mean you're helpless. You have tools to escape."

Henry would protect me with his last breath, but we both need to know that if he's not with me, I won't be a sitting duck.

"You don't think the danger is over now that Lawrence has been arrested?" Henry's people dug around and found evidence of Lawrence having been into some shady business. According to reports, he was taken into police custody last night.

"It may end up enough for Grandmother to remove him as a prospect for MPD, but we haven't found any link yet between him and our attack. The crimes he was arrested for are unrelated. More importantly, there are a lot of strings someone can pull from behind bars. So, no. It's not time to relax." Henry comes at me, and I evade his grasp.

"Your grandmother will be that upset over his arrest? It's not like she doesn't at least have a vague idea that you're not always on the straight and narrow, yourself."

He circles me, and I move in response.

"She won't like it, but it's not what he's done or even the drugs or evidence of his violence and temper tantrums. It's the embarrassment and scandal. Right now, I guarantee she's grateful he doesn't share our last name."

He lunges at me again, and though I don't manage to avoid his side headlock, I have enough time to lift my shoulders at the last second to improve my chance of keeping my airway unrestricted. I turn my head toward him to make breathing easier and graze him with a fake punch to the groin.

He bends over and loosens his hold slightly but doesn't release me. "Good. What if I'm a woman?"

I've never had a woman come at me physically. But his point is, if the dick punch doesn't work, keep going. So I slide my arm closest to him behind his back, and reach over to grab his face, yanking his head backward on his neck. The body follows the head, and he bends backward and loses his grip. He twists and changes his hold, yanking me into a different position. I respond.

I take his lessons seriously. I've had too many incidents in my own life not to understand the value of being able to defend myself.

When I break away from him, I straighten and shake out my arms.

"Keep going," I say.

He comes at me again. And again. Different grabs. Different responses from me.

A half-hour later, I'm bent over wheezing. "That's enough for now. I need a break."

He runs his hand over the top of my head. "You did well."

As the distinct reverb of a helicopter in flight slowly reaches my ears, I turn toward the airfield and landing pad to observe Dante and Spencer's arrival.

Henry checks his watch. "Right on time. I'll head over to give them a hand."

"Do you need help?"

"No." When I shiver, he rubs my biceps in an attempt to warm me up. "You get inside. You could put the kettle on for some tea?"

"If you cut yourself, do you have blood left in you, or do you leak Earl Grey?"

"Let's not find out." He drops a kiss to my nose, then indicates the landing pad. "This should only take about twenty minutes."

Eight minutes after he's gone, the perimeter security system sends an alert to the new watch Henry got me. Since I expected the alert with their arrival from the airfield, I dismiss the notification. If the guys decided to drive the supplies over in the truck he keeps in the hangar, it would account for the time difference.

As I reach to fill the kettle, Oliver barks at the front door. Every chipmunk or squirrel that catches his attention gets an announcement from him. "Quiet."

When he responds to my command by subsiding, but remains alert and distrustful by the door, I bend to give him some attention. "Good boy. It's just Henry and the guys."

His tail thumps once, and I return to the kitchen. When Oliver doesn't follow me, I point to his corner. "Bed."

I don't want him accidentally underfoot if the men enter with armloads of groceries. Oliver trots to his bed, head bopping side to side as he goes, then settles himself down, but he keeps his attention firmly on the entrance to the cabin.

Less than a minute later, a knock sounds, and I frown. Oliver barks, and I reissue the quiet command in a low voice, as I eye the door with suspicion. Henry can't have locked himself out again. He made changes, so he and I both can override the manual locks with a combination of a keypad at the door and a coded digital "key" we can access from our watches.

He has his own company with a Research and Development Department that works exclusively on creating tech and what I call "nifty spy gadgets" for his family's personal use.

According to Henry, it's a perk of the "billionaire vigilante lifestyle." I'd told him he was "super badass" then handed him the toilet bowl cleaner and reminded him he was on bathroom duty today.

The knock sounds again and then a familiar voice. "Ms. Lennox?"

I peer out the window to see Spencer standing on the porch. When he sees me peek through the window, he lifts a vase full of yellow roses to show me.

I open the door. "Spencer. Hi. Where are Henry and Dante? I thought they'd be with you."

"They're only a few minutes behind me. They're bringing the . . . what do you call it? It looks like a miniature open truck?"

"The Gator?"

"Yes. It only seats two, and since Henry knows I wanted a moment alone with you, he sent me ahead."

"You wanted to be alone with me?"

He shivers. "Brrr. It's quite frigid today."

I step back to allow him to enter. When he does, I close the door behind us. Spencer extends the flowers to me, and I accept them with a small smile of confusion. As Spencer removes his overcoat and leather gloves, I place the vase on the kitchen table.

"I owe you an apology, Ms. Lennox. I didn't fully comprehend Henry's commitment to you. I consider him to be a friend, as much as an employer. I've known him for a long time, and I'd never seen him express any interest in a romantic relationship.

"I believed his desire to find a spouse and request for information on courtship to be a practical consideration. I based my assumptions on years' worth of his previous behavior, but, obviously, I was very wrong."

He wrings his hands together, his expression sincerely distraught.

"It's all right, Spencer. Henry and I have worked out our misunderstanding. I know you weren't trying to sabotage us. Neither of us blames you."

He straightens. "You're too kind, Ms. Lennox."

"Please call me Franki."

At the small shake of his head, I plow on before he can protest. "Please. I call you by your first name."

His brows lift.

"Spencer is your last name?" I ask in realization.

He dips his head with a smile. "My given name is Noah. I'd be honored if you used it."

"Franki?"

We both startle at the sound of a strident woman's voice, then a series of hard knocks at the door. Oliver barks in a frenzy and leaves his bed to stand between me and the door.

"I know my daughter is here. Open this door!"

My heart lurches into a drumbeat in my chest and pounds in my ears. I knew I'd end up speaking to her one way or another again. I had the last word when I hung up on her.

I step toward the door, and Spencer places a hand on my forearm. "Ms. Len—Franki, I don't think it's wise to let her in. At least not until Henry and Dante get here."

"I'm calling the police if someone doesn't open this door!" Mom shouts.

I shake my head. "I have to get this over with. She'll have the cops up here trying to arrest Henry if I don't talk to her."

"At least make certain she's alone."

An iPad sits on the counter, and I tap on the exterior cameras. She's not alone, but I'd have been shocked if she were. A driver sits, partially obscured, inside a black SUV with tinted windows, and one of her regular bodyguards, a humorless man named Nick, stands beside her.

"It's fine."

I open the door and slide through to stand on the porch, shutting Oliver and Spencer inside. Mom stands there, a look of shocked joy on her face. She lifts a hand to my cheek. "I was so afraid. Your boyfriend made those threats, then you disappeared. Your friends wouldn't tell me where you were. I thought he'd killed you."

"I told you he'd never hurt me, and I told you I didn't want to see you again. How did you find me?"

She throws herself against me, holding me and sobbing. "I'm here now. I have you."

I try to step back, but she clings like Saran Wrap. "Stop it."

She shakes her head and sobs. "You have Stockholm syndrome. I'm getting you out of here."

For as much as Henry and I have made light of my "abduction," we both know it was never that. He'd never force me to do anything.

The security guard at Bronwyn's house would have tried to stop him if I hadn't winked at him when he'd peeked around Henry. Gabriel would have stepped in. "Remain loyal" doesn't mean blind faith to a person, even a family member. It means loyalty to what the McRae family stands for. "I'm not a prisoner. I'm here because I want to be. How did you find me?"

"I used the location services on your phone before he made you block me."

"Henry didn't make me do anything." I don't even know what she believes is true and what is deliberate manipulation.

"Why didn't you call me when you knew you were in danger? I'd have taken care of you. I'm the only place you have to go that's safe."

She tries to guide me off the porch, but I balk and refuse to budge an inch. "Stop. I said I'm fine. I'm not in danger. I'm happy here."

"Where is he? Is he standing behind you telling you to get rid of me? Is that it?"

I scoff. "He's not even here right now. This is me, telling you, for the fiftieth time, I'm not coming back with you. I'm not going to remain in contact with you. I blocked you for a reason. Get back in your car and leave."

She stares at me, her sobs miraculously drying as she narrows her eyes. "You need me."

I shake my head. "I don't."

Her expression turns pitying. "Are you going to leech off your friends and Henry McRae indefinitely?"

"I'm not leeching—"

"They'll get frustrated eventually. They let you hang on to them because they pity you. Is that what you want? To be a burden to these people?"

I shake my head. "It won't work."

"It's the truth."

"None of what you said is the truth. You're not even consistent. Henry wants me because he wants you? You disgust him. He wants me out of pity, but he's also holding me prisoner? I have a job, and I'm good at it. I'm capable of taking care of myself. Henry loves me. He doesn't care that the shape of my face or body is different. He doesn't even care that I may change over time. He won't love me less because of it."

She gives me a pitying look, her big gray eyes limpid and filled with tears. "I know you believe that, and I wish it were true."

"I've been the one taking care of you," I snap. "If I'm so incapable, how is it I managed your life? Your schedule? How was I able to go to school and still be there to cater to you? Why is it so damned important to you that I feel unlovable?"

She steps back with a wounded expression. "I never said you're unlovable. You're putting words in my mouth. He poisoned you against me."

I take a deep breath in through my nose. There's no point in continuing this conversation. "Leave."

"Even if I believed you that he wouldn't hurt you, just being near that man puts you in danger," she says desperately. "When I heard someone shot at you, and you were in a car chase on the highway, I've never been so afraid in my life. Every time you try to go off without me, something horrible happens to you. How are you not terrified? Because I *am*. You're my child. I'm trying to protect you."

The world goes still around me. I no longer hear the wind in the trees or Oliver's frantic barking behind the door as I look at my beautiful, manipulative, awful mother. "How did you know I was in a car chase or that someone shot at me?"

She blinks in bewilderment. "What?"

"How did you know?" I repeat slowly.

"One of your friends told me."

I shake my head. "Try again."

"I don't know. I must have seen the car chase on a news report."

"You pretended you had no idea where I was, but you were using location services on my phone. You're here now because I turned the phone back on long enough to block you last night. You knew before I answered your call that I was in Pennsylvania. It was you."

She shakes her head, her face contorted in pain. "How can you believe that?" she whispers.

"Were you responsible for every time someone came after me or assaulted me? Or was the first one a happy accident that gave you the idea to keep going?"

"You're insane."

"What did you give Oliver to make him sick so I wouldn't leave?"

"You're mentally unwell," she says.

"I was assaulted by your unhinged fans three times, nearly four if you count the one in the hotel lobby, but always managed to escape by pure, dumb luck without any real injuries. You convinced me every time not to contact the police. Not a single bullet made contact with our car. It didn't make sense. He drove like a professional, but couldn't hit his target even once? Credit where it's due, at least you weren't actually trying to kill me. Though you're clearly escalating. You could have killed someone in that car chase. It probably wouldn't even have been me. Henry and I were in an armored vehicle. Do you have any idea how close we came to hitting a minivan with a bunch of kids in it?"

Her eyes flare briefly before her lips tighten. "You need help. You've completely lost your grip on reality," she says.

"So, if I go to the police, and a judge subpoenas you and and your boyfriend's phone records, or your plane tickets to Pennsylvania, they aren't going to show any evidence that you and David Vance—"

"Nick, take her."

I have less than a second for my mother's words to penetrate before her bodyguard gets his beefy arms around me and lifts me over his shoulder as I kick and scream. I try the evasive maneuvers I practiced with Henry, but I can't think through my panic, and when I do try, he compensates too quickly.

"I'm doing this for your own good, Franki. You'll see that when I get you home," she says. "This is an intervention."

Nick has me down the steps before I've even oriented myself.

"Remove your hands from her this instant." The words are shouted in a crisp British accent, as Oliver barrels down the steps and straight for us.

The driver, whom I can make out in my peripheral vision, has exited the car and drawn his weapon. "Call him off, or I'm shooting the dog," he says in a hard voice.

"Stay!" I scream.

Oliver skids to a stop and snarls at Nick, his growl malevolent.

Nick turns to face the cabin, and in his distraction, I hit him in the kidney with my elbow, then reach up and grab the back of his hair, yanking his head back as fast and hard as I can. The body follows the head, and he fights to stay on his feet as I drag him into a back bend.

Nick loses his grip, scrabbling to keep hold of me. I slip from his hands when my momentum drags us both backward and, rather than lose his own balance, he lets go. I land hard on my right hand and arm, then my face and shoulder, before crashing onto my back.

Pain radiates from my right wrist and up my arm. My left leg sprawls at an angle briefly before I scramble away from Nick. My cheekbone throbs and my hip burns like fire as I hang onto the car handle and drag myself to stand, whirling to face the others.

Nick doesn't look back at me, his attention on Spencer as Henry's PA advances toward us. I reach beneath the oversized fleece jacket I'm still wearing and manage to unsnap my holster. With stiff fingers, I attempt to wrap my hand around the butt of the Sig Sauer P365 Henry gave me, but I don't draw it. I'm not certain I can even lift it. My wrist is sprained or broken. Either way, gripping the gun, even one that is smaller and lighter weight, isn't something I want to try yet. I can barely feel my fingers making contact with the weapon and have no idea if I can maintain my grip on it to pull it from the holster. Even if I weren't afraid it would fall from my nerveless fingers the moment it cleared the holster, I need to de-escalate this scene, and drawing another weapon, especially one I may not be able to control, could make things worse.

"Give me the gun," Mom says.

Heart in my throat, I turn my head her way, but her attention isn't on me. It's on her boyfriend David, the stuntman who conveniently "saved" me from the supposedly obsessed fan who tried to kidnap me.

He passes his weapon into her waiting hand.

"Get in the car, Franki." She's not pointing the gun anywhere in particular. Instead, she waves it around like it's one of her movie props.

I shake my head slowly. "Just go, and we'll forget this happened. It's not too late for you to leave without getting hurt."

"David, go get the dog. If we have him, Franki will cooperate."

David shoots her a look that couldn't more clearly express *"Do I have to?"*

Her lips tighten. "Do it."

"Don't touch him," I say. "Oliver, run."

Chaos ensues as Oliver attempts to get to me, David attempts to catch Oliver, and Spencer bravely inserts himself between Oliver and his attempted captor.

"Get out of my way," David says.

Spencer shakes his head and swallows hard. "I will not. You're not taking Franki or her dog."

"How are you going to stop me? Butler me into submission?"

Spencer lifts his fists in a boxer's stance. David laughs, then throws a punch, but Spencer dodges it and nails him with a right hook.

David's next strike makes contact in a glancing blow to Spencer's jaw, but Spencer counters with an uppercut that sends David reeling and punch-drunk into the gravel.

Then Spencer draws a taser from beneath his suit jacket, directs it at David, and lifts his chin. "I'm not a butler. I'm Henry McRae's personal assistant."

David scrambles back toward me, and Spencer shocks the shit out of him. When the charge is complete, he says, "Stay away from her."

For the first time, Nick speaks. "You said this was a rescue mission. I didn't sign on to be an accessory to kidnapping."

Mom lifts her hand to her chest. "It *is* a rescue mission. She's confused. Franki, I know you want to come with me. Remember when you were little, and I had to leave, and you cried like your heart was broken? All the cards you'd send me. All the pictures."

Spencer speaks again, his steps crunching on the pea gravel as he moves closer and closer. "Ms. Jones, you have no idea what a mistake you're making. If you take her, he *will kill* you."

"Oh," Henry says coldly from somewhere to my right, "he absolutely will."

Thirty-Eight

Henry

Fire on Fire | Sam Smith

Franki leans against the SUV, her right hand hidden under black fleece, but on her gun. A goose egg has risen on her temple, and her cheekbone is swollen. The lurid pink will eventually blossom into a purple bruise and a spectacular black eye.

She turns her head toward me when I speak and nearly collapses against the SUV, relief flaring in her eyes.

I have my Glock trained on Guinevere. Dante came around the other side at an angle and has his weapon trained on the bodyguard. I trust Spencer to handle the unarmed man he's got a taser directed at.

I'd nearly squeezed the trigger and dropped all three of them before they'd realized Dante and I were here.

I hesitated because of the trauma it would cause Franki. Then the guard had spoken, and, reluctantly, I decided to give them the opportunity to redeem themselves.

A month ago, the question of whether I simply killed Guinevere, the guard, and the driver wouldn't have been an issue. I'd have evaluated the situation dispassionately and made a choice.

Now, my emotions are front and center. And they're exactly the problem I knew they'd be. If I open fire so close to Franki, let alone on people she knows, she'll never recover completely from the trauma.

I'll do whatever it takes to keep her alive, no matter what that is, but if there's a possibility of getting this situation under control without further violence, I have to try. I promised her I'd be that man.

Franki's heart is in her eyes as she looks at me. She won't blame me. She'll believe anything I do is because it's necessary, not because rage pumps through my veins demanding I destroy anyone who has ever hurt her. She believes I'm a hero.

Other men make choices based on whether they can stand to look in the mirror afterward. I've never cared what I see in the mirror. I've spent most of my life making choices based on whether I could look Franki in the eyes and deserve her trust.

Emotions right now are the worst kind of liability. I reach for the numbness. I need to do nothing but think in this moment, not feel. Emotional novocaine serves a purpose. Where there used to be ice, molten lava flows in my veins.

The war inside me rages on, but I give no hint of it on the outside. My hand is steady as a rock, my voice frigid. "Guinevere, gun on the ground. All of you put your hands behind your heads. Now. You're surrounded."

Guinevere drops the gun, and she and the two men lift their hands.

"Franki, come over here." I'm not certain she can walk, given that she hasn't stopped leaning against the car, but she'll tell me if she can't.

As Franki straightens and steps forward, Guinevere dives at her and grabs Franki by the right arm, attempting to drag her into the car. Franki cries out, but she doesn't hesitate. Just as we practiced, she twists until Guinevere's arm is behind her back, and the actress is bent forward at the waist.

Immediately, she grasps her mother by the back of her head with her left hand and slams the woman's face downward as she brings her knee up, nailing her in the nose.

Guinevere screams and falls to her ass on the gravel, both of her hands covering the damage as blood gushes through her fingers. "My *face*."

Franki runs in an awkward limping jog toward me. Oliver fights his way out of Spencer's arms in an attempt to get to Franki as Dante descends on Guinevere, flex-cuffs at the ready.

"I'll deal with her. You take the men," I say.

As I pull Guinevere's arms behind her back and apply a set of restraints, one of the men yells something.

At first, his words don't make sense. I keep hearing the word "bank" until finally he strings his thoughts together in coherent sentences.

"Listen to me . . ." The man Spencer is securing with his own set of cuffs speaks desperately. Attempting to explain. " . . . It wasn't supposed to go like this. It's loaded with blanks. We wouldn't have shot anyone. It was a threat. To scare her. That's all. No bullets. Only blanks."

When the meaning of his words penetrates, I glance back at the man talking. "You have no idea how close you came to getting all of you killed."

He blanches.

Franki rests on the grass and clutches Oliver against her chest with her left arm while Guinevere shrieks at her.

"My face will never look the same. *How could you be so horrible?*"

Franki ignores her, and the lack of response enrages Guinevere further. "Look at me when I'm talking to you!"

I secure the flex-cuffs on the woman's wrists. "You're right that a cosmetic surgeon will never manage a perfect match for your old nose, but you can stop worrying about your career. You're going to a federal penitentiary. Your nose wouldn't have lasted past your first fight over a bar of soap, anyway." I use an obnoxiously reassuring tone.

"No one will convict me of anything. They'll put me on the stand, and I'll tell them it was all David." Her expression softens. "We were trying to save her from her toxic boyfriend. I was protecting her. I didn't have a clue how far he'd go."

"I'm the reason we didn't bring bullets, and this isn't going to be an attempted murder charge," David says bitterly. "You're the one who made me keep going on the interstate when a couple of shots fired would have gotten the point across. I'm not taking the fall for this myself."

I secure her from her upper arms to her ankles, and connect the cuffs behind her back, speaking too quietly for the mics on the cameras to pick up and presenting my back. "Part of me likes the idea of murdering you, but an even bigger part is going to enjoy every moment of what's about to happen to you next. When you're taken to trial, and the world watches and listens to the video feed from the cameras recording every second of this scene, and when the evidence of every crime you've committed against your daughter is presented in court, you're going to rot in prison for a very long time. Franki and I are going to have a beautiful life. On the rare occasions we do think of you, it'll be with pity and disgust. You're about to become the one thing worse than dead for someone like you."

I move my mouth into a close-lipped smile. "You'll be irrelevant."

I lean closer. "But you should know. If you and your accomplices aren't suffering adequately, I'll make certain to rectify that. There's nowhere I can't get to you. You'll beg me to kill you."

I leave Guinevere behind and walk to crouch beside Franki as she cradles Oliver to her.

Oliver whines, leaning toward me, and I lift him against me, where he lays his head on my shoulder. I rub his back, one arm tight around Franki's waist as she hides her face in my chest, the other holding him against me.

"Good dog, Oliver," I say. "Good fucking dog."

With Guinevere's accomplices secure, Dante stomps over to Spencer.

"What the hell were you thinking? You knew we were almost here," he says, voice hoarse.

"I couldn't let them take Franki or the dog."

"You didn't know there weren't bullets in that gun. She could have shot you. He *hit* you."

Spencer lifts a hand to his swollen jaw. "You would have done the same."

Dante leans into Spencer, his forehead resting against the other man's. "You scared the shit out of me."

Spencer closes his eyes and admits, "I was quite terrified myself."

Dante mutters, "What am I going to do with you?"

"You're going to kiss me," Spencer says.

Dante huffs. "Finally."

With my arm around Franki, I lift her to stand and lead her toward the cabin. I'm a nosy bastard, but even I can appreciate that the two of them deserve some privacy. "Let's get some ice on that cheek of yours and let me get a look at you."

Franki pulls away from me, and I tighten my grip briefly, before releasing her and setting Oliver on the ground. If she needs space, I'll give her sp—

She staggers two wobbly steps and loses the contents of her stomach. I rush to catch her, my gaze raking over her. I haven't assessed her injuries, yet. I knew she was limping and had the bruise on her face, but she hasn't said anything.

I resist the temptation to sweep her into my arms as she lists against me. Instead, I assist her to lie on a clear section of grass. Franki's skin is pale and waxy, her normally tan complexion ashy. Perspiration beads on her forehead, and she appears to be having trouble focusing her eyes.

All the dire things that could be happening inside her flood through me in near panic. What happened before I arrived? Is she bleeding internally? Fractured skull? Shock? *Has she been dying as she stood beside me and didn't say a word?*

"How's the air situation? Any trouble breathing?" Her pulse is rapid and thready beneath my fingertips.

"No."

"Excellent. Follow my finger with your eyes. There you go," I say gently.

Her tracking isn't good, and her pupils are uneven. "Not trying to be a buzzkill, gentlemen. But I could use a hand," I snap, some of my panic breaking past the calm demeanor I'm presenting for Franki's sake.

Franki whimpers as I prod her head, seeking injuries beyond what I find on her face.

"Can you tell me where it hurts?"

She seems to shore up her energy before she speaks. "Everywhere. But I'm pretty sure I broke my arm."

Spencer arrives and stands at my left. "Dante is bringing the first aid kit."

"Take Oliver inside and put him in our bedroom. Stay with him a few minutes. Give him his treats. Confirm an ETA on our backup. We're not waiting on them to get Franki to medical care."

Spencer goes, taking one anxious wiener dog with him.

Dante drops a first aid kit on the grass beside me, opens it, and gets to work cleaning the scrapes on her face.

I reach for the scissors to cut back the sleeve on her right arm. The one I'd have noticed she's been favoring if I'd been thinking clearly.

As I cut, Franki fights back a scream through gritted teeth, though I do my best not to jostle her. When I reveal her forearm and wrist, I look up to meet Dante's eyes, then back down at the swollen, discolored, misshapen mess of her arm. Her hand hangs at an odd angle. A buzzing turmoil inside me threatens to crack my self-control, but I speak dispassionately. "Concussion. Likely fractured cheekbone, fractured distal radius and ulna."

This was the same arm her mother had yanked on. The pain would have put most men on their knees, but she'd fought through it and kept going.

"Who knew you were such a badass, Franki?" Dante cleans the cut on her cheek and presses an ice pack to her face.

"Henry did," she says.

She's right that I'm not surprised by her strength. "Any other broken bones we need to look at? Or are you keeping all the good stuff to yourself?" I ask, deliberately casual.

She speaks through her teeth, her face contorted in pain. "Might have a dislocated shoulder. Sacroiliac joint is out of place."

Only the fact that Franki needs me prevents me from returning to the people currently in restraints and enacting torture. They should suffer as she suffers.

I'm no stranger to delivering pain, but the knowledge that I'm going to have to hurt Franki to help her has nausea rising. I could hustle her straight to the helipad, but if I don't stabilize her first, everything will be worse in the long run.

"I need to splint these fractures now. Then we'll get you in the air."

She gives a tight nod.

"I'm resetting the bones. It's going to hurt. Feel free to call me terrible names."

"Gaah!" An incoherent cry rips out of her as I realign the bones in her arm, then secure a splint.

When it's done, she pants, and I press my cheek to her uninjured one. "I'm sorry."

Her breathing slows. "I'm okay."

I tug her sacroiliac joint back into alignment, then straighten and watch her face carefully. "The longer we wait to realign your shoulder, the worse the swelling becomes, but if you'd prefer to wait for a more controlled environment, it's your call."

"Do it now."

I knew she'd say that. She's not avoiding my eyes or looking around her in fear. I haven't broken her trust. She screams when I complete the process, then closes her eyes, tears squeezing beneath her lids. I ease her against me. "Shhh. Breathe, love. It's over. I promise. It's over."

"Thank you."

I press my mouth against her temple, holding her to me. "I really want to kill them."

"But you won't. And that's what matters."

"Acting like the 'good guy' is unspeakably tedious. I don't like it."

The sound she makes is weak and quiet, but, somehow, she manages to laugh. "I love you."

"I love you too."

Thirty-Nine

Henry

Three Days Later

The Man Who Can't Be Moved | The Script

I pass Grandmother Rose a cup of tea, then lower myself into an armchair.

"And how is the girl?" Grandmother refers to Franki as "the girl" because she's having trouble remembering names, though she'll never admit to it.

"Franki is going to take some time to heal."

"I'm sorry to hear that." Positioned diagonally from me, Grandmother sits stiffly in her chair in my Park Avenue penthouse and lifts the delicate porcelain cup to her lips.

"Franki is resilient. She'll make a full recovery," I say.

Grandmother glances toward the bedroom hallway then back at me with a disapproving pinch of her lips. She's not a fan of *cohabitation*, as she refers to it.

My furniture is slightly too large for Grandmother, but she poses elegantly, nonetheless: knees together, ankles crossed, weight on one hip as she leans against the arm of the chair.

"Would you like an ottoman so you can rest more comfortably?"

She shakes her head. "I'm not interested in comfort. I came here for a reason. I've decided to reconsider my plans for MPD."

When I say nothing, she continues. "I want to give those shares to you, Henry."

I lift my eyebrows, not fooled for a moment. "And you have a new requirement for me to be worthy of them." *Despite the fact that I already informed her that I don't want them.* I take a sip of tea before setting my cup on the table.

She frowns, her blue eyes sharp. "My sister's grandson is a disgrace. The scandal surrounding him is intolerable. But the girl you decided on isn't much better. I offered you those shares if you found an *appropriate* wife. A relationship with that one is out of the question. Her father is all over the news due to bankruptcy and a fraud investigation, and her mother . . ." Grandmother shudders. "She's a sweet girl, and she has my sympathy, but you have to do what's right for yourself."

I smile. "You're absolutely correct."

She nods. "You've always been a practical boy. I don't expect you to find someone else to replace her. I'm not unreasonable."

A shadow in the hallway to our bedroom moves in my peripheral vision, and I stand, stepping closer so I'm certain Franki hears every word I say. "Grandmother, you misunderstand. I'm never walking away from Franki. There's not a thing on earth that could make me. I'm walking away from MPD."

She blinks in confusion. "What?"

"I don't want your shares."

"Of course you do. I suppose, if you keep your relationship private and don't marry her, we could work around it on a probationary period. You'll need to distance yourself during the trial."

"*Grandmother.*" I shake my head. "I'm marrying Franki. If you give me those shares, regardless, I'm immediately passing them on to Gabriel. I suggest you skip the middleman. I'm off the table."

Her eyes narrow as she looks behind me. "There's a dog under your chair."

I glance back. Oliver is flat on his stomach splayed with his legs behind him in what I call his "Superman pose." He's hiding from our visitor, with only his lower half visible.

"Oliver is shy." It didn't used to be true, but he's recovering from the traumatic events of three days ago too.

He wags his tail at the sound of his name, and I smile.

Grandmother's lips quirk. "You're happy."

That's an oversimplification. And an understatement. What I am is *whole*. But for brevity's sake, sure. "I'm happy."

She places her cup on its saucer and rises from the chair. I offer Grandmother my arm and walk her to the door where her guard waits to assist her home.

When I help her into her coat, she reaches up and pats my cheek. "Your father was entirely unmanageable. Your sister insists on living life how she pleases. I thought you'd be the sensible one."

"There's still Gabriel."

Her eyes glint. "He's too charming for his own good. That boy is a directionless hussy."

I fight back my smile. "I'm not so sure about that, but I suppose he'd be a lot for someone like you to handle."

"Someone like me?" she asks, offense snapping in her words.

"Someone in her elder years. Surely, you're tired of worrying over all of us by now. You should find a new hobby. Take more naps," I suggest helpfully.

She shakes her head, her lips lifting in a partially repressed smile. "Insolent boy."

Grandmother removes her black leather gloves from her pockets and tugs them on. "I'll accept your marriage."

"You'll also be kind and gracious to my wife."

"Don't insult me. Of course I will." She looks out across the open plan of the penthouse to the lit skyline beyond. From here, the heavens are nothing but an artificially bright wash of violet blue. The bright points that glimmer are man-made and far too close to earth. There's not a real star in sight.

"Can Gabriel do it?" she asks.

"I suppose we'll find out."

New Year's Eve

Soulmate | Chanin

My mouth goes dry, and my heart rate picks up speed as Franki brushes her hair over her shoulder and walks farther into our dimly lit hotel suite. Intrigue lights her eyes, and she sends a curious glance my way. With every step she takes, her silver evening gown flows over her curves like living mercury.

I indicate the attached bedroom. "I packed an overnight bag for you. Spencer and Dante are pet sitting for the night."

She smiles in confusion. "Why did you get a suite? We're not that far from home."

"Not that far is still *too* far." I run my knuckles over the velvet softness of her right cheek and kiss the warm skin beneath her left ear, reveling in the feel of her. Drawing her scent into my lungs. I'm continually stunned that she's given me the privilege to be so close. I doubt I'll ever fully get used to it.

"The last time we were in this hotel was Finn's wedding reception. We ditched the party early that night too," she says.

"I thought you'd prefer dinner up here, rather than downstairs at one of those communal event tables with people we don't know."

We share a look and shudder in tandem. Franki and I are capable of that type of socializing. It doesn't mean we *like* sitting with six other guests at a round table and pretending to have fun.

Franki has barely recovered from her ordeal, and both of us have depleted our social batteries dealing with the fallout from her mother and David Vance, but Franki wouldn't miss a party thrown by her cousin if she could help it. Finn and his mother are the only living blood relatives she considers family.

She glances around and, for the first time, notices the table, dressed in white, adorned with peonies, and glowing with flickering ambient light. Our plates hide beneath silver domes, and a bottle of champagne on ice awaits. The entire scene reflects in the floor to ceiling windows. Though I'm behind her, I read her reaction in the glass. The lift of her hand. The softening of her eyes.

I drop to one knee beside her and wait for her to see me. To realize I'm here when she's ready.

Four years. Nine months. Twelve Days. Without her.

Never again.

She turns, and emotion chases across her beautiful face when she finds me at her feet. Momentary confusion. Love. Hope. Her dark amber eyes glint with unshed tears.

I lift the ring I chose for her myself. "I believe the two of us could reach an amicable agreement mutually beneficial for both parties—"

She sniffs a watery laugh.

"—I'd offer you my heart, but it's already in your possession. And possession is nine-tenths of the law. I can't give you something that's already yours."

Her breath hiccups.

"I'm asking for permission to be your husband. I promise I will make our marriage my life's work."

I frown. "That doesn't sound romantic. I don't mean that it will be difficult. I mean it the way someone with a calling speaks of their mission in life. You're my magnum opus. You're the discovery of the edge of the cosmos, and don't cite the Kuiper Belt, because you know I think that theory is ridiculous."

Franki nods.

"You will have my dedication, my passion, my time. I'll invest in us every day. You, and the family we build together, will always be my first priority. I will always take your side. I will always support you. There has never been another woman for me. And there never will be. Not if I have to wait a hundred lifetimes for you to come back to me again."

She presses her hand to my cheek.

I turn my head to kiss her palm. "I know I'm intractable. Often arrogant. I'm obnoxiously tidy. One of those annoying morning people. And I take unholy pleasure in pushing people's buttons. But if it's true that you are what you love, then I'm one hell of a catch. Because there's not a cell in my body that doesn't love you."

She lowers herself to the floor, kneeling with me. I use my thumbs to wipe the tears from her cheeks. Franki's mascara streaks into a black mess beneath her eyes. She sniffles as her nose runs, and her eyes are rimmed in red. She's so incredibly lovely.

She kisses me, then leans back and cups my face. "Yes."

I freeze, then confirm. "You're saying you will—"

"Yes! Yes, Henry. I'll marry you."

I slide the platinum band on her finger and smile so hard it turns into a shout of laughter. Then I kiss her again before speaking. "The first time I proposed, I assumed you'd be happier with something you chose yourself. I thought the ring was just a ring, but it's actually a metaphor for how I feel about you. So, I told the jeweler I wanted the best quality, ethically sourced, and in the largest size possible to still wear comfortably on your finger."

She holds her hand out to admire it and bites her lip. "It's absolutely . . . huge."

My lips curl at the corners, and I prepare to push her buttons because I love when she scolds me. "As I said. It's a symbol. You should know, this ring cost a lot more than Bronwyn or Clarissa's. Because I love you better."

"Oh my God. *Henry*. It's not a competition."

I frown, pretending to be puzzled. "How can it be a competition when our relationship is so quantifiably superior?"

She shakes her head and visibly fights a laugh. "You're not supposed to say it out loud."

I stand and help her to her feet. "Prepare yourself."

Her brows come together in confusion. I take off my glasses and toss them onto the nearby side table.

She bites her lip and eyes me like I'm dinner.

"I love the way your bosom heaves every time I take my glasses off." I stare blatantly in appreciation at her beautiful breasts as they lift and fall beneath the silver gown. Her nipples stand at attention, awaiting their kiss. "It's extremely gratifying."

"That's because you look naked to me without them. Also, never call my breasts a 'bosom' again. It's almost as unsexy as 'duck call collection.'"

"Noted."

I find her zipper easily. It was only a few hours ago that I slid it up in the first place. I pause. "I did this all backward. We were supposed to eat dinner. Then I'd propose. Then I'd give you a minimum of three orgasms."

She moves against me and kisses my neck. "Dinner can wait."

Forty

Franki

June

I'm Gonna Be | Sleeping At Last

"I still can't believe you renovated your cottage for our wedding." I lean on my mahogany cane. I'm flaring today, of all days, but not only is it not going to stop me from making my wedding vows, it's not going to keep me from enjoying every second of it.

Bronwyn had the florist decorate my cane with vines and tiny flowers. It's pretty and gives a bit of a fairy-in-the-wood vibe. It matches this cottage.

Bronwyn looks around the bedroom, with its cream-colored walls and romantic canopy. "This cottage was ugly, and it held really bad memories for Dean and me since this is where he found me. Now, it's pretty and has new, wonderful memories. Plus, it's nice because if they want it, our guests have their own cozy little love nest when they come to visit. You and Henry will be the first to stay here."

"It feels magical now." Clarissa, wearing a sage-green, polka-dot dress, smooths the quilt under her hand as she sits under the canopy of the white-painted four-poster bed.

The renovation was transformative. Aesthetically, the cottage no longer resembles the original structure that's been here since the 1950s. Bronwyn had the roofline changed, adding multiple gables. Tall, mullioned windows, their frames painted a deep green, overlook overflowing window boxes. The ones in this first-floor bedroom are thrown open to catch a warm breeze that caresses my skin and sets the sheer pale-green curtains dancing. The light of early evening washes the room in a golden glow. The sun will set soon. Phee took an extra nap this afternoon just so she could stay awake for the party tonight.

Charlotte, wearing a rose-colored tea-length dress, places her hands on my shoulders and turns me to face the cheval mirror. Standing behind me, she leans forward to look at me in the mirror, her soft cheek against mine. The faint scent of Lancome's La Vie est Belle feels familiar and comforting as she holds me close. "You're stunning. You belong in an enchanted forest today."

I meet her pale blue eyes in the mirror. "I feel pretty."

"Pretty? Good lord, you're gorgeous," Bronwyn shouts across the room.

I laugh and turn to face my family. Or most of the female members of my family, anyway. The guys are off doing whatever men do before weddings.

Clarissa nods, a huge smile lighting her piquant face. Auburn curls are piled on top of her head, and her freckles give the impression she's been sprinkled by a mischievous fairy. "It's true. You're utterly lovely."

Janessa, in scarlet pants and a matching corset-style top, rises from the chair in the corner. I didn't make a dress code for my bridesmaids. I told them I wanted them to wear something they felt beautiful in. It was my only requirement.

"The dress suits you to perfection," Janessa says.

I smooth the ivory fabric over my thighs. I decided against a corset to give me a fake hourglass figure, and, instead, had the dress altered to actually fit my body, apple shape and all. The bateau neckline shows off my collarbones, and my hair is in a loose mass on top of my head, exposing my neck. Henry really likes my neck. *Henry really likes all of me.*

I worried the long sleeves would be too hot, but they're made of soft, sheer lace, and I'm not overheated. Sparkly crystals encrust my custom tennis shoes.

Phee, a small tiara nestled in her mass of blonde ringlets and wearing a toddler version of my dress, runs to me and tries to pass me my bouquet with two hands. "Penis!"

Sydney's brown eyes go wide, her eyebrows shooting up, and she leans at the waist to look at Phee.

Bronwyn's lips twitch as she looks at her officially adopted daughter. "I beg your *finest* pardon, miss?"

Phee holds up the bouquet to her mother. "Pretty Pe-Nis. Pink penis. Penis. *Penis.*"

"It doesn't even sound like a real word, anymore," Janessa says in wonder.

"Yes, Phee Bee. Aunt Franki has *peonies*. So do you," Charlotte says.

Bronwyn straightens and lifts her fingers to her mouth. "That was a poor choice of phrasing."

Charlotte gives her a confused look. "What do you mean? I was helping her to say the word correctly."

"AUNT FANKEE HAB PENIS. MOMWYN HAB PENIS. I HAB PENIS." Phee sings.

Charlotte blinks. "I may have made an error in judgment."

I pray aloud. "Dear God, please allow me to be present when she tells her father Momwyn has a penis."

Bronwyn mock scowls. "My brother's sense of humor is rubbing off on you. You're supposed to be a calming influence on him, not the other way around."

"Henry is hilarious. The last thing I want to do is calm him down," I say.

Everyone, even Charlotte, snorts in laughter.

Sydney nods. "That right there is proof that there's someone for everyone, because when I tell you—"

Janessa nudges her elbow into Sydney's side.

"—how utterly perfect you two are for each other is what I was *going to say.*" Sydney gives a huge, cheesy smile.

"Good thing you fixed that sentence. I don't tolerate Henry slander." Someday, I'll tell her that Spencer thought she'd make a good wife for Henry. I haven't managed to find that funny, yet.

I put my hand out, and Phee gives me the bouquet. "Thank you for my *flowers*. Where are your *flowers*?"

"My fowers are by the window." She runs to her basket and lifts it carefully.

"Thank you," Bronwyn mouths, and I wink in response.

A knock sounds at the door, and I turn to see Henry's grandmother, Rose, standing in a peacock-blue gown. I've attended family functions with her many times in the last seven months, and she's always been gracious to me. Still, I can't help but remember the conversation I heard that night in Henry's penthouse. She thinks I'm a liability. It doesn't matter how polite she is to me; it's something I'll always be aware of.

I swallow and glance around. No one else has tensed the way I have, though Bronwyn sends me a commiserating glance. She knows how it feels to be on the receiving end of Rose McRae's disapproval, though she has the advantage of also being loved.

Mrs. McRae comes closer, and I step forward, meeting her in the middle. We're of a similar height, so she looks me straight in the eyes. I fight the urge to look away or down at my feet and keep my spine straight.

My mother was toxic, and a relationship with her was not good for me. I do, however, know how to carry myself to look confident and graceful in nearly any situation because of her. I can be grateful for the good parts, while still acknowledging that I owe her nothing. She's currently in prison, but someday she'll get out. Probably as soon as she's eligible for parole. I've asked Henry to leave her alone.

As long as she and David stay away from me, we'll get on with our lives as though she doesn't exist. It's hard for Henry, but he does it for me. I don't want anything about her tainting our future.

"Mrs. McRae, you look lovely," I say.

She waves a hand. "Thank you, dear. You make a beautiful bride."

She runs her eyes over me, and I force myself to hold my smile. "Thank you."

She lifts her chin. "I won't apologize."

Okay. So we're going there.

"I haven't asked you to. You're entitled to your opinion," I say.

"There are challenges to marrying someone in the public eye. Even when that person is put there through no fault of her own. You're blameless, but it doesn't make those challenges less significant."

I don't smile in response. I simply watch her and wait.

Charlotte clears her throat and steps forward. Mrs. McRae lifts her hand to wave her off. Everyone is aware, now, that this may not be a "friendly chat." Even Phee is quiet, clinging to the blue silk of Bronwyn's vintage dress and watching her great grandmother with wide hazel eyes.

"Henry needed to be resolute. There could be no wishy-washy nonsense. He doesn't like to be told what to do, but I would only be the first voice. I'd have been disappointed in him if he'd agreed with me." Her mouth works before she gives a small smile. "You gave him a reason to want a real life, but it takes fortitude to go beyond the wanting to the doing. I was giving him the opportunity to stand up and be a man who deserved to be your husband."

My own mouth opens slightly before I close it. My eyelashes flutter as I try to make sense of what she's saying. It's so similar to something Henry would do. A little manipulative, but, maybe, well-intentioned. I'm not sure if I believe her. Either she's messing with me now, or she was messing with Henry then.

I can't wait to ask him which he thinks it truly is.

"I brought you a gift. You don't have to wear them today if you'd rather not, but I wanted you to have them," she says.

She lifts a small jeweler's box. When my hands are too stiff and painful to flip the lid myself, Charlotte reaches over and does it for me.

My breath catches at what I find. Diamond pendant earrings, each with at least a combined total weight of three carats, in a vintage white-gold filigree setting.

Mrs. McRae looks down at the diamond earrings fondly. "They're your 'something old.' They were a gift from my parents to me on my wedding day."

I take a shuddering breath, and Bronwyn shouts, "No. Don't cry, yet. Your makeup."

I laugh. "The makeup artist used waterproof, just in case."

Bronwyn's words successfully break the chokehold my emotions have on me, though, and I smile at Henry's grandmother. "Thank you, Mrs. McRae. I'll treasure them. Maybe one day we'll be able to pass these down to one of your great-grandchildren."

She nods. "Call me Grandmother now, girl."

"I will." I give her a cheeky grin. "You can call me Franki."

"I'll try to remember," she says. "Feel free to remind me."

Oh. "I will."

I look at the earrings and contemplate how I'll get them on my ears. "Bronwyn, could you . . . ?"

She removes the pearl earrings I'd been wearing, then replaces them with the ones from Grandmother. I look in the mirror.

"Pwitty," Phee breathes.

Another knock, and we all look to the door. Arden stands, holding his arm out to me. "Your golf carts await."

The sun has set.

I take his arm, my flowers in the same hand, and my cane in the other. We troop outside to the row of golf carts. The guards are our drivers, and when Arden settles me on the seat with a kiss on my cheek, Ryan smiles at me from behind the steering wheel. "Nice to see you right-side-up today, Franki."

I grin, and we set off, headlights illuminating our way, as I brace myself, my veil flying in the wind. A short drive on the winding paved road, surrounded by mostly mature oaks, lightning bugs flickering in the darkness, then Ryan pulls up at the side of the house with the terraced flagstone patios.

Ryan assists me to stand. It takes more help than I like, but I push worries about the pain aside. I have more important things to focus on.

Janessa flicks my fingertip veil into place in the back, and Bronwyn fluffs out my small train. A combination of pillar candles in large glass vases on the path and strings of fairy lights overhead glow in the darkness. The wedding planner set up an elaborate trellis on the stone walkway that leads up to where Henry stands at the top, but a row of guards dressed in suits form a phalanx in front of me and my bridesmaids while we get settled in the darkness.

Our approximately forty guests, not counting the bridal party, sit on white wooden chairs near Henry and his groomsmen. Henry and I know every person here. Most of them are his aunts, uncles, and cousins. Clarissa's husband James is here. Grandma and Grandad Miller sit in the front row next to Nanny Lisa, who is simply Lisa to me now.

I decided to walk myself down the aisle, but as I step onto the stone pathway, I immediately realize my mistake. I was fine last night for the rehearsal, but my knees are rougher today than I expected them to be.

Clarissa leans in. "Are you all right?"

"I can't do this alone. I'm going to fall on my face."

"Will you let us walk you up the aisle?" Clarissa asks.

We won't all fit together through the trellis, but we'll be fine once we get past it, at least until I get to the chairs. "Yes, please."

Ryan informs the musicians of the change in plan. Then we line up at the trellis with Sydney and Janessa slightly behind. The string quartet transitions to the song we chose.

Bronwyn crouches next to Phee. "Time to walk and sprinkle your flowers until you get to Daddy."

Phee bounces. "Ready!"

Bronwyn comes back, and I slide my arm through hers. My left arm hooks through Clarissa's. Janessa, who carries my cane for me, and Sydney, who holds my flowers, fan out to either side.

The guards separate, and we step forward.

Our guests rise with an audible shuffle, though I only notice in my peripheral vision. Phee makes a meandering path as she tosses handfuls of flower petals on her way to the men at the front. Oliver, wearing his bow tie, sits politely on the flagstones between Henry and Gabriel. Dean, Noah, and Dante make up the rest of the groomsmen.

I don't have eyes for anyone but Henry. He got a haircut sometime today, and he stands with his hands clasped in front of him. When he sees me, his palm flies to press against his heart, and his smile fights with tears.

Joy so profound that it almost hurts bursts through me.

Bronwyn and Clarissa keep me steady as I go, though I lean into Clarissa harder each time I have to take one of the steps that occur approximately every ten feet.

Henry lifts his glasses to wipe under his eyes.

I'm halfway up the aisle when Henry takes a step forward, then another, and another, until he's jogging toward me.

I laugh when he meets in the middle of the path, and I lean toward him, whispering conspiratorially, "Did you forget you were supposed to wait at the end?"

He never breaks eye contact as he smiles back. "I'm done waiting."

He speaks to my bridesmaids, though he never looks away from me. "Thank you, ladies. We'll see you up there."

They pile onto me in a two-second group hug. Sydney passes me my bouquet, and when Henry has his arm around me, they file around Henry and me to walk to the front.

Henry lifts me into his arms. "I'm not supposed to kiss you yet either."

I lean in to press my lips to his lean cheek. He turns his head at the last second and catches my mouth, instead. Our guests chuckle.

Then he carries me to the bower on the patio.

Epilogue

Ten Years Later

Henry

A Sky Full of Stars | Coldplay

I CONTEMPLATE THE MAN in the chair before me. I need answers. I know he has them. He's lacking only the right . . . encouragement. "You may consult your notes."

The young man nods with a look of relief, floppy blond hair falling in his eyes, and scrolls through the laptop located on his desk until he finds what he needs. He clears his throat. "The majority of the universe is composed of dark matter and dark energy. We can't directly observe them, but their presence can be inferred by their gravitational effects on visible matter and the expansion of the universe."

"You are correct. You'll be expected to provide several specific examples of those effects on Tuesday."

A dark-haired twenty-year-old raises her hand behind him.

"Yes, Ms. Porter," I say.

"Will we be allowed to use our notes for the exam?" she asks.

I nod. "You will. There are certain circumstances where memorization is critical for success. This is not one of those times. It's far more important for me to see that you're capable of compiling information, locating that data, and utilizing it. This means the more thorough your preparation, the better your chance of success."

I perform my regular scan of the auditorium at Blackwater State University and smile at the gorgeous woman seated in the back row. She's wearing a black T-shirt-style dress, an oatmeal-colored cardigan, and white tennis shoes. She smiles back and gives me a finger wave, one hand resting on her adorable round belly. She glances at her watch, then says something to the four-year-old boy who stands beside her.

He bounces and waves, calling, "Dad, it's eight o'clock."

I grin and check my watch. "That's it for tonight, guys. I'll see you Tuesday. Study hard."

I gather my things and head for the doors as the classroom empties in a flurry of closing laptops and backpack zippers. Feet thud. Clothing shuffles.

Franki rises and moves toward me as I head her way.

Though Franki and Ian aren't near the door any longer, students send a constant stream of "good nights" their way.

"Good night, Dr. McRae."

"Lookin' good, Dr. McRae."

"Hey, Ian."

"How soon till the new little professor gets here?"

That's what happens when your wife teaches several Gen Ed history classes and a language. Even a lot of the math and science majors know her and love her.

She answers in her gentle voice, and then I'm there, leaning in to kiss her and take her bag from her shoulder. "How was your evening?"

She smiles. "It was good. This schedule works for now. How was yours?"

"I'm hopeful for this year's crop of students. They're showing promise."

I crouch down beside Ian and ruffle his hair. "And how was your evening?"

He pushes his glasses up his nose. "Nanny Lisa taught me how to make chocolate chip cookies while you and Mom were working. They're in a plastic container in the car because it's not healthy to eat them all at once, and they're meant for sharing. It's tedious to be patient."

"I agree, but some things are worth the wait."

"I liked your lecture. Dark matter is fascinating. Also, Mom says we're kidnapping you," he says.

"Is that right? Is this a short-term kidnapping for the evening or a full-on abduction?"

Franki pats my forearm. "Abduction for the entire long weekend. Resistance is futile."

The three of us troop our way out of the auditorium and head for the parking lot. Next semester, Franki and I will both be on parental leave. She's due to give birth the first week of January. We're both also taking the summer following spring semester to stay at home with our children.

After that, we'll see. Franki hasn't decided whether she'll want to return to work full-time, part-time, or stay at home until Ian and Baby Cassie are both in school. Nanny Lisa is technically retired, with a comfortable nest egg we provided, but she visits often and sometimes babysits.

We're lucky enough to have flexibility. I don't need to work, financially speaking. Gabriel is far more efficient in the corporate world than I ever was. He even manages to have a life while he's at it. I've changed direction in my *other* work now, as well. I act as a consultant and work behind the scenes, but it's been years since I pulled out a pair of surgical gloves for anything but cutting the cord when Ian was born and carving pumpkins.

I nod my thanks and "good night" to Ryan when we reach the car. Then I open Franki's door for her and assist her into the passenger seat. When I've closed her door, Ian and I walk around to the driver's side. I open the door to the backseat and give him a boost. He climbs into his car seat in the back, and I watch to be sure he straps himself in correctly.

"Spencer and Dante already have Oliver there, right?" he asks.

"That's right," Franki reassures him.

I kiss Ian's forehead, then I move to my seat. When I'm settled, I reach across and put a hand on Franki's belly, bending over to speak directly to our baby. "Are you cooperating with your mother tonight?"

She laughs when Cassie kicks out a foot and bumps my mouth. "She loves your voice."

I lift an eyebrow. "That remains to be seen. She could simply be so irritated by me that she's trying to shove me away."

She rolls her eyes. "Not possible."

"Are you sure you're up for this?" I ask.

"Absolutely. I feel great," she says.

Once she made it past the exhaustion of her first trimester, her energy has been off the charts. Her RA went into remission with both of her pregnancies, which isn't uncommon. She never had any significant morning sickness or serious aches or pains either.

"It occurs to me that maybe we should strive for a constant state of pregnancy for you. I'm willing to put in the effort that requires. For medicinal purposes," I say.

She laughs. "No thank you. Perpetual pregnancy is unreasonable."

I shrug. "The offer is on the table. By the way, you're not very good at this kidnapping thing. You didn't steal my phone or my car keys first."

"How would you drive if you didn't have your keys?" Ian asks reasonably.

"Good point." I put the car into gear. "One kidnapping cabin vacation coming up."

Ian drops off to sleep in the back, while Franki and I talk quietly for the two-hour drive. Then we're pulling up to our cabin.

Dante steps out onto the porch with Oliver, who sits beside him and thumps his tail with joy when we get out of the vehicle. The cabin has been through some renovations, expanding it to fit a family. We also added a second story observation deck, a fire pit, and a swing set in the back. But it's still our cabin.

Oliver is getting old, with gray peppering his chin. A dachshund's life span can be up to around eighteen, and Oliver is nearly sixteen. We'll pamper him and love him for every year we get. I lean down to pet him. "Hey, little man. You ready for some rest and relaxation?"

He sits up in his majestic wiener dog pose, and I pass him the treat he knew I had in my pocket.

I turn back to see Franki at the back door of the SUV, adjusting Ian as she plans to pick up our sleeping boy and carry him to his bedroom. With my hands on her hips, I guide her away from the backseat. "How about you don't do that?"

She huffs. "He's not that heavy, but it's getting awkward with the belly in the middle."

"He's too heavy right now. Let me. You could put on some tea?"

She drops a kiss onto the center of my chin. "Good idea. I'll meet you on the upper deck."

I pass Dante as I step onto the porch. "You guys settled in at your place?"

"All settled. Give us a call or send an alert if you need us." Dante gives a salute and heads for his car.

We built a guest cabin on the other side of the airfield. Dante and Spencer's place isn't visible from ours, but it's close enough that I can have security easily accessible for my family should we need it. It's worked out well. Bronwyn and Dean bring their kids up sometimes, as do Gabriel and his wife.

I settle Ian onto his bed. He barely stirs as I take off his shoes and street clothes, then dress him in his flannel pajamas. I tuck him under his blanket and gently lift Oliver where he waits on the floor by my feet. Oliver cuddles into the curve of Ian's arms and, instinctively, Ian pats his back. I kiss them both on the forehead.

Ian doesn't open his eyes, but he mumbles, "Love you, Dad."

"I love you, Ian. Happy dreams."

Then I head off in search of my wife. I find her on the rooftop observation deck, wrapped in a warm blanket and holding a cup of herbal tea in her hand. I lower myself to sit beside her and accept the mug of Earl Grey she passes me.

We sit quietly and soak in the night sky, and the sounds and scents of Pennsylvania in autumn. When I finish my tea, and she's finished hers, I lean us back on the cushions. My bicep curls under her head, and her blanket covers us both.

She places her hand on my cheek and kisses me. I slide my hand under the blanket, then under her dress. She's smooth. Warm. Luscious. It's a clear October night. The stars sparkle overhead. We have the telescopes and camera equipment in a room nearby, but we haven't bothered with those. Tonight, it's just us with a sky full of stars and a life full of love.

Thank You

Reviews are incredibly important for getting the word out so the right readers can find us. If you're inclined to leave a review or share your reading experience on social media or with friends, I would be so very grateful! If you'd like to keep up with what's next and be the first to receive bonus content, please visit my website at evangelinewilliams.com and sign up for my newsletter. When you do, please add evangeline@evangelinewilliams.com to your "safe" list to avoid my newsletters landing in your spam folder.

Also By

Evangeline Williams

Other Books

Trust & Tequila
(INTERCONNECTED STANDALONES)

I Almost Do

I Always Did

Say You Will

Acknowledgements

It really does take an entire team to bring a novel to life, and I am eternally grateful for everyone who had a hand in the creation of *Say You Will*. I absolutely could not have done it without each and every one of you:

To all of you in our little Romance, Spice, and Laughs Writer's Group! Thank you! You (arguably) kept me sane throughout the process. Ivy Fairbanks, PHW Love, Caroline Edmonston, Amber West and more! Alpha readers, Megan and Kurt. Thank you for your endless patience and feedback as I bounced ideas off of you. Thank you to my spectacular editor, Kaitlin Slowik and to my professional sensitivity reader, Hannah G. A special thank you to my autistic beta readers for your invaluable feedback. Thank you to Staci Hart at Quirky Bird Covers for a beautiful cover. And to my beta readers: Kaitlin Slowik, Amber West, William C., Trish Alexander, Kimberly Rose, PHW Love, CeeCee (Caroline) Edmonston, Jen, and Annie S.—Thank you. This book is better because of your contributions and support.

Printed in Great Britain
by Amazon